DeltaBlade Chronicles

Arkangel

Brandon Schultz

www.DeltaBladeBooks.com

Copyright © 2022 Brandon Schultz

All rights reserved.

ISBN: 9798814725882

DEDICATION

To my friends and family who always believed in me, and my greatest inspiration of all, my daughter Elena.

CONTENTS

Acknowledgments	i
Chapter 1 - Who Am I	1
Chapter 2 - The Elven Arker	16
Chapter 3 - Martis the Savior	35
Chapter 4 - A Leader Awakens	55
Chapter 5 - Misguided Archer	83
Chapter 6 - Beginning of a Bond	111
Chapter 7 - Secrets Below the Streets	136
Chapter 8 - The Journey North	160
Chapter 9 - Righting a Wrong	191
Chapter 10 - Betrayal	210
Chapter 11 - The Spark Ignites	229
Chapter 12 - An Old Friend	261
Chapter 13 - Darkness is Upon Us	284
Chapter 14 - The Arkangel	297
Chapter 15 - Fortify the Gates	308
Chapter 16 - Answers Lead to Questions	322
Chapter 17 - The Siege of Sanctuary	344
Chapter 18 - Victory in Defeat	371
Chapter 19 - The 1st Paladin	377

AILTERRA

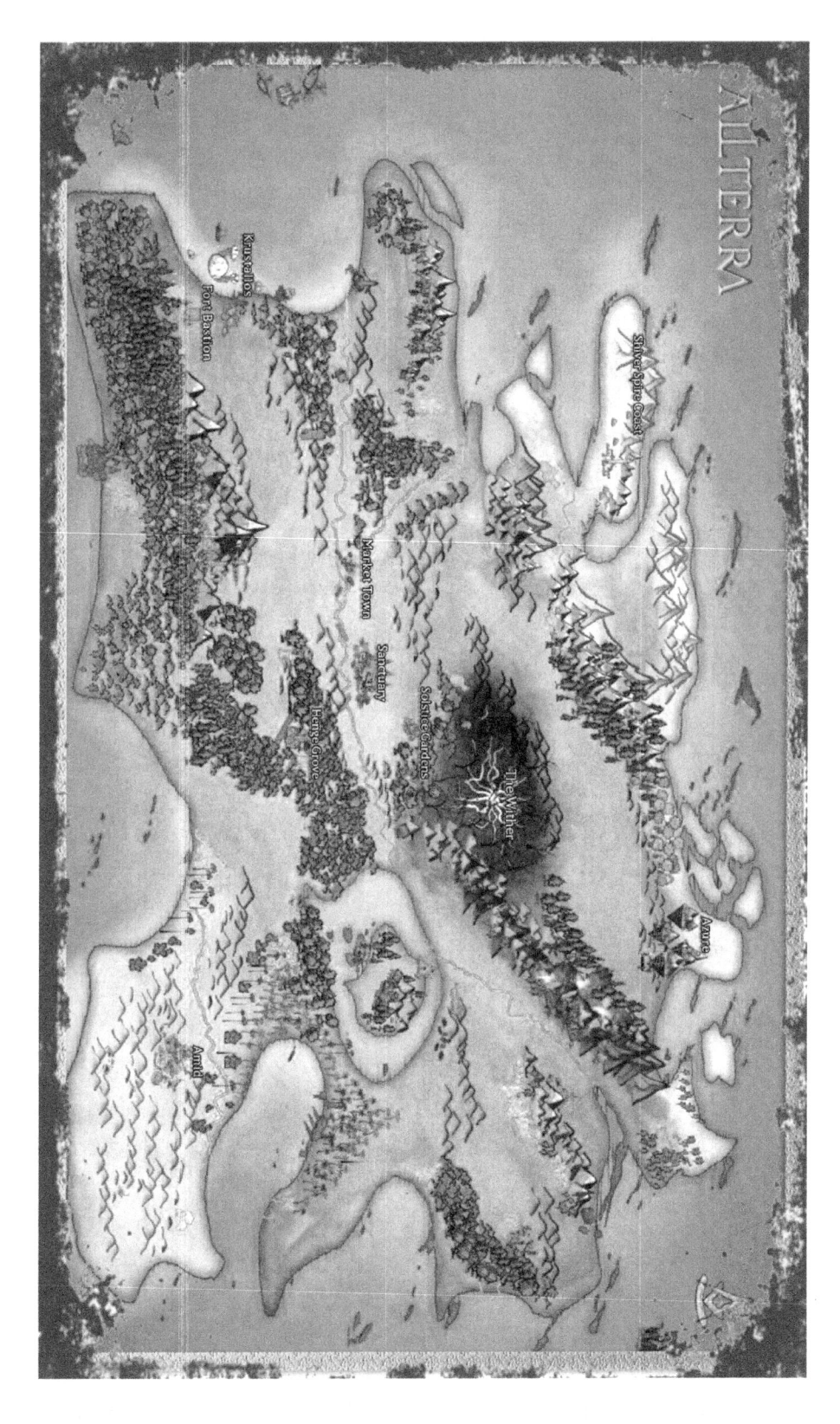

- Kraustallos
- Port Bastion
- Silver Spire Coast
- Market Town
- Sanctuary
- Henge Grove
- Solstice Gardens
- The Wither
- Azure
- Amid

CHAPTER I

"WHO AM I?"

Kaiden's eyes opened, and his vision was blurred by a blinding light. He noticed a ringing noise in his head that only got worse as he struggled to move his body. Then a piercing pain shot through him like lightning, traveling up and down his spine.

"Is you one of dem?" a loud, monstrous voice echoed through the pain. Kaiden's head bobbed left and right trying to make sense of what was happening. He found himself deep in the woods and in the middle of a battle. "Yous infected?" The voice boomed louder. A giant foot covering half his body slammed down on top of his chest, knocking the air from his lungs and pinning him firmly to the ground.

"What?" Kaiden managed in panic while watching an enormous crossbow sweep across to point down at him. A large spear tip hovered inches from his face. "I don't know what is happening!" he pleaded, struggling to get free from the weight of the massive figure. The giant leaned over him, his huge head looming into view. Kaiden could see a scarred flap of skin pulled and stapled over where his left eye would be, while the other was surrounded by several wars worth of scars.

The stout ogre had clearly been in many battles and, by the look of him, he had won almost all of them. His great, broad shoulders blocked out the sun, all but the glint of his dangling chainmail sleeves. Then out of the corner of his eye, a black lizard-like creature burst into sight, crashing hard into the ogre and knocking him off his chest. Razor sharp fingers slashed and stabbed in his direction, clawing and swiping in a frenzy. The creature looked almost human except its skin draped loosely off a body that glistened with sleek black and dark green scales. He could hear popping and snapping sounds come from its insides as it contorted and twisted violently, continuing its relentless clawing at the ogre, who was now on his back, swinging wildly with one fist while holding the creature back with another.

Kaiden stood in shock, looking at the battle taking place right before him. After a short time, he ventured his gaze around to see piles of skins stacked several feet high, without bones, as if the flesh had been torn off like a package wrapper. His heart pounded harder in his chest as the shock wore off. Another one of the lizard creatures shot out of the woods beside him, bellowing an ear-splitting shriek as its sickly yellow eyes narrowed and locked in on him. It hunched over and screamed, with long and sharp quills lifting out of its back and shredding off the skin of its human form. It raised its talons and charged.

Its speed was inhuman as it tore across the long field in mere seconds. Kaiden turned to sprint away as fast as he could but was no match for the creature's speed. He passed the ogre, whose massive hand had the first lizard pinned while he jabbed his spear repeatedly into its chest until it had stopped struggling. He raised his left arm as Kaiden ran past and a large, steel bolt shot out of his vambrace, tearing through the second lizard creature's head. A thick, green liquid oozed out, covering its face as its body lifelessly crashed to the ground. Kaiden paused and looked the ogre straight in the eye; the ogre's whole body heaved in exhaustion from the fight. He dared to let out a brief smile for saving his life.

"Name's Gorman, kid," the ogre said in a deep, scruffy voice.

Kaiden didn't respond right away as he looked around at all the carnage. He was in a small clearing surrounded by tall trees with his feet sinking into the long blades of blood-soaked grass. A small band of men armed with woodcutting axes and small, wooden shields walked around, inspecting the dead and the soon to be.

"What happened here?" Kaiden asked, wide-eyed as he watched several men slam their axes deep into the skulls of the creatures' lizard-like bodies. "What are those things?" he added, a quiver of panic still racing through him.

"You been unda a rock, kid?" Gorman snickered at him. "Those be da quillbacks from da plague. Dem humans be turnin' into da lizards an' killin' everyone," he added, wondering what the young man had been doing in the woods.

"You mean those are humans?" Kaiden managed to ask, his voice weakening.

"Da were, all of a sudden humans be turnin' left an' right, no reason. Me be sittin' in da dinin' hall one evenin' when da first one turned dat I seen. Killed three men before me could take it down." Gorman recounted, walking to retrieve the hefty bolt he had shot into the rampaging, lizard creature. "Den da turned to quills an I's killed dem, too."

Kaiden's eyes went wide, so confused about what was going on. "I'm Kaiden, by the way," he offered.

"Yous with dis lot?" Gorman asked, gesturing to the piles of blood drenched skins strewn about along with the carcasses of the dead lizards.

Kaiden paused in thought. "I don't know, actually," he stated, head tilting in wonderment as he realized he couldn't remember a thing before Gorman woke him up.

"I's knows dem hard to recognize, what you doin' before attack? Who's you wit?" Gorman asked, motioning for the men around him to gather up. Kaiden wondered if Gorman was the leader of these men. Furthermore, who they were and where they came from?

"That's the thing, I just don't know, I only know my name," he said, gazing down into the blood-soaked soil. "But that's it... nothing else." His heart pounded in frustration and panic, not understanding what was happening or where he was.

ARKANGEL

Gorman let out a hefty chuckle. "Dem musta scared da wits right out of ya, kid." He gestured to a few piles of logs that had been neatly stripped and stacked alongside the dirt road, then toward the men around them. "Com' on, men, dat be enough for da day, der will be more choppin' to do tomorrow," he said as several of the lumberjacks fell in line and lifted the logs up onto their shoulders.

Gorman looked down at Kaiden, who was wreathed in panic and fear. "Yous should come wit' us until yer head be right, kid," Gorman stated in concern. Kaiden could feel the way Gorman looked at him: a kid who clearly had no idea which way was up or down, too weak to survive out on his own.

"We lost William and Gerald," one of the men said, holding a torn leather piece of armor that had been serrated off its wearer.

Gorman shook his head in disappointment. "You take care of 'em?" he asked in a grim tone.

"Yes, Sir, they won't be turning into no quillback anytime soon," he said in a solemn voice, looking out into the vast forest, as if trying to erase the images of what he'd had to do.

Gorman turned to Kaiden as they walked down the long and winding dirt road. "Des men be fine lumberjacks and be forced to defend Hengegrove to keep up wit' dere lumber trade. Though demand is down dese guys ain't soldiers and won't be able to keep up wit' it fer long. Wes be needin' troops from Sanctuary to help defend." His tone spoke of the frustration of potentially losing more innocent lives. "But who knows, anyone of dem could be changin' any second now anyways, maybe dere is no Sanctuary left?"

"What is causing them to change?" Kaiden asked.

"Dats da thing, kid, no one knows, and it be only humans dat I've seen. Me's thought yous be turnin' for sure when I found ya there, just flounderin' about," Gorman said with a half-cocked smirk.

Kaiden didn't know how he felt about that smile; it made him feel uneasy. Though his feelings quickly gave way to thinking about how he still couldn't remember anything, what he was even doing there, or what had happened. He held his head with both hands. "Why can't I remember?" he whispered in frustration.

"What you say, runt?" Gorman grunted while lifting a bundle of tree-length logs up onto his shoulder.

The other men were strong, but not as strong as the ogre, barely able to lift small logs in pairs onto their shoulders before heading down the trail back home. Kaiden just shook his head in response to Gorman, lost in thought and realizing he didn't even know where he was going or how long it would take.

They walked late into the afternoon. To his surprise, nobody took a break; they were like ants just marching down the trail. Everyone was quiet. Given the circumstances, he guessed everyone was sad and not really in a chatty mood. The forest was thick with tall trees, the ground dense with ferns and other foliage. The trail they walked was wide and he could tell it was traversed often by how nicely compact the ground was and the remnants of grass that had given way to dirt. As they walked, Kaiden noticed all sounds of nature had stopped, except for their footsteps and Gorman's heavy breathing. The men suddenly halted and threw off their logs to the sides of the trial, each moving to a different side as Gorman stepped up into the middle and grabbed one of the massive spears from his back. He raised it up high, readying to throw it, when a frantic voice called for help.

Gorman lowered his arm and called out, "Who's dere?"

The voice became clearer as a woman called out for Gorman. "Gorman, help please, please come quickly," she pleaded, sobbing with tears and barely keeping herself together.

"Liz?" one of the lumberjacks said, running up to comfort the blood-soaked woman. "It's OK, calm down, what has happened?"

"Hengegrove… It's horrible," she sobbed.

"What is it? What happened?" he asked, holding her shoulders and rubbing her back in comfort.

ARKANGEL

"It's those things, they're killing everyone," she pleaded. Standing up, she went and frantically pulled on Gorman's arm. "We must leave now!"

All the men fell in line behind Gorman as they ran through the forest. Kaiden had a hard time keeping up with them, but he stayed back with the woman for support. Several minutes later they broke through the thick forest into a large, grassy clearing with a huge wooden wall surrounding a village. Pillars of smoke rose out from all over as screams and cries could be heard from several hundred yards away. Gorman pulled a spear from his back and rushed in, his giant crossbow loaded in the other hand as the men followed behind. Kaiden followed the woman close behind but wasn't sure what use he could be without a weapon. They rounded the side of the wall to find the gate had almost been torn straight off its hinges. The men froze in place, stunned at the sight of men, women, and children alike running helplessly around as the lizard creatures hunted and killed them one by one.

The beautiful grass and wildflowers now soaked in the villager's blood. Empty sacks of loose skin lay in piles scattered around the courtyard. A pair of quillbacks took down another large man with ease, their large claws tearing through his flesh and rending it clear off his bones. *This is a massacre,* Kaiden thought, his stomach turning in pain at the sight.

The creatures stopped and slowly looked up to see their new prey, their bright yellow eyes narrowing in on them. The lumberjacks took a step back, gauging if they should run, but Gorman stepped forward and fired his crossbow, hitting one square in the chest and pinning it against the wall of a small building. It howled in pain as it clawed frantically at the spear lodged within its chest. Kaiden looked to see the poor man the creatures had just taken down rose slowly to his feet. He looked at Kaiden, his face giving way to unrelenting pain as he cried. Then, suddenly, the man opened his mouth, shouting from the top of his lungs as his jaw tore off and the beak of a lizard burst through. The man's body somehow stretched taller and wider as his skin began to tear off, revealing a shiny, black-scaled skin beneath it. The creature then hunched over, letting out a shrill screech that rang throughout the whole village. The rest of the skin fell off as its quills lifted from its back, tearing through what was left of its human shell. The noise of terrifying shrieks was deafening as countless other creatures came forth, crawling over rooftops, bursting through windows, and sprinting down dirt walkways. Liz, the woman beside Kaiden, almost laughed as she started to convulse, kneeling as small, thin quills began to protrude from her back.

"Warden!" one of the men cried out, swinging his axe into her back and chopping several times before kicking the body over to the side. Gorman quickly glanced over while loading his crossbow with another spear. "Come at me, yous cowads!" he shouted.

The lizard pack started to move in, and with inhuman speed they were on them in a matter of seconds. Gorman, whirling his spear in a huge arc, sliced at anything that got close to him, shouting taunts at them as they drew near. He used a big knife attached to the bottom of his crossbow to stab at any that got past his spear and then quickly shooting at the ones flanking his friends. Kaiden watched as the ogre cut down creature after creature until one got through his defenses, tackling him to the ground.

The lumberjacks weren't as formidable but were able to take some of the creatures down before falling victim to the waves of claws and teeth. Before Kaiden could process all the death around him, he came to the realization he was the only one left standing. Gorman wrestled for his life with one of the lizards with several more in route to help finish him off. Kaiden realized there was no one left to protect him. He was struck with paralyzing fear, trying to turn and flee until he noticed the searing pain of claws wrapping around one of his legs. The force lifted him into the air as he came face to face with a quillback as another grasped tightly around his arm and began to tear. Suddenly he was slammed hard into the ground with such force his eyes rolled back, and he began to slip into darkness.

A shockwave erupted with enough force to fling off the two lizards who had been clawing at him, splattering their broken bodies against a nearby wall. Gorman had the creatures on top of him blown off as he

ARKANGEL

looked to see Kaiden's body hovering in midair. A golden glow began to emanate from his body, swirling and flowing around him as some sort of armor, dark grey and black, unfolded and encased his body. The dark, organic shell looked like interlocking scales, wrapping around his body and head to take on the appearance of some sort of armored creature. The armor landed on the ground and slowly looked up, its eyes flicking open to emit a bright, white light. Gorman stood up in shock, completely dumbfounded by what he was seeing.

The boy's body had been completely encased in an armor that he had never seen anything like before. In all his years fighting in the High Paladin's army, he had never seen anything like it, not even the great armor of the Paladins. Blades shot forth from its forearms as it turned its head to survey the battlefield. Its face had morphed into a broader, armored lizard with large scale plates molded to a transformed humanoid frame. Gorman was too transfixed to notice the nearby Quillbacks had recovered and were closing in fast. He tossed his crossbow and reached back, pulling two spears from his back ready to end the fight. Before his spear could make contact with the beast, Kaiden had spun through the air like a tornado of blades and sliced through the lizards, cleaving them into pieces with a mist of green blood showering the ground.

It moved at an incredible speed, from one creature to the next, as they attempted to fight back only to be struck down. Their long, spiny tails whipped around, which Kaiden's armored form quickly dodged as it stuck its forearm blade deep into their back, carving right up their spine. Kaiden's strength had increased so much that his punches hit with enough force that Gorman could hear the cracking of their bones under their thickly scaled hides. The last of the lizards grouped up to attack together and leaped through the air, snapping their jaws and desperately slashing their claws. Kaiden's armor quickly stepped to the side out of their way and came up behind them. It grasped onto their tails as they passed with a leap into the air, using its momentum to swing their bodies hard into the ground. Now behind the others, it lunged forward into the air and crashed knee first into the back of one while holding its arm blades out to the sides, slicing the other two almost completely in half. Gorman just watched as Kaiden stood up in the pile of death, green steam hissing off his armor. The mysterious armor wheeled around to face Gorman and locked eyes.

The glowing white eyes billowed out a white steam high into the air, and then closed. He fell forward to the ground, and, with a flash of golden light, the armor retracted, revealing an unconscious Kaiden underneath. He lay there for several seconds before letting out a loud groan and coming to. He slowly came to his feet, seeing all the dead creatures, and looked at the gaping-mouthed ogre in confusion.

"What happened?" Kaiden asked deliriously as he coughed. His thin muscular arms moving to stabilize him while fighting to stay upward and awake.

"What happened? WHAT HAPPENED?" Gorman shouted. He paced back and forth in frustration, looking at the blank-faced boy. He raised his crossbow at him ready to fire, then lowered it again as he continued to pace.

"What is you? What happened, kid, I's need answers. I's never seen nothin' like it before in all me years of trainin'."

Kaiden quickly shook his head with a shrug. "I don't know, I was attacked by those things," he said in fear and confusion, pointing at the still bodies at his feet. "They slammed me down and then my mind went blank, seconds later I woke up and here we are. Did you save me? Did you kill them all?" he asked, searching himself for wounds.

Gorman was visibly getting more frustrated, the normally confident and assertive half-ogre reduced to a confused fit of panic and anger.

"I think I may have answers," an excited, gurgling voice said through a shattered window of a small building. "Well sort of, but not really in the traditional sense, more questions really, but possibly some answers mingled in the middle somewhere." The cracked door swung open as a tall Aquarian stepped out, ducking under the doorway. He stepped down, easily clearing the several steps of the small wooden deck, eagerly approaching Kaiden.

Gorman raised his eyebrow in confusion. "An who be you, fish?" he demanded, not liking that his fit had been interrupted. His brow lowered with frustration. He had seen the aquatic race before through his travels but had not seen one this far south in many years. As far as he knew they were primarily a scholarly folk, with only a select few who ventured out to seek knowledge of the world and its inhabitants.

"Oh, I apologize for my rudeness. I am Finn, but not a fish, in fact I am an Aquarian, an awfully old one to be exact, although who really knows how long I have roamed Allterra. I am a half breed as well, like you Ogre, but my mother was a…"

"OK, we's get it, fish, where is these answers we be promised?" Gorman demanded.

Finn came uncomfortably close to Kaiden and looked straight into his bright blue eyes, clearly having no respect for personal space, and began to examine him like he was an ancient artifact. He eyed him up and down, inspecting all his limbs and pushing his long, scaly blue fingers into his skin. He even blew down into his short brown disheveled hair.

"Please stop," Kaiden managed as he took a step back, deflecting a poke to the ribs.

The Aquarian towered over him but wasn't quite as tall as Gorman and nowhere near as wide. His skin was a shiny light blue with thick-armored grey and white carapace attached to his vital areas. He wore nothing at all, which made Kaiden feel uncomfortable; he noticed long, thin slits along his protruded rib cage where his gills were. His big, solid black eyes blinked rapidly from angled lids as he attempted to continue his examination. His face looked less like a fish and more like a blue and white bug with small mandibles attached to his jaw that bounced when he was in deep thought.

Gorman stepped in, grabbing the Aquarian's arm, forcing him to snap out of his pondering. "Now tell mes what you know, fish, or be gone," he said, staring down slightly into his eyes in an attempt to intimidate him.

"Oh yes yes, let us talk, talk about this fascinating young man here but not now, not here, not with people around who may hear what I have to say," he said, glancing around at all the townspeople who had made their way out of their hiding places, now searching for fallen loved ones. Murmurs of dread and cries of fear could be heard between the closely built cabins.

Gorman looked around with grief and frustration, not knowing exactly what he could do to help out his fellow townsmen. "Me house be dis way," he pointed, leading them deeper into the town.

Kaiden was still unsure what was going on, or why Gorman was acting the way he was, but reluctantly decided to follow, not wanting to run into any more of the quillbacks outside if another outbreak broke loose. His home was surprisingly small for the giant, thinking he would be more comfortable in a more accommodating house. They entered the cabin and Kaiden sat in the first available chair next to the door, quickly dozing off from exhaustion.

Gorman took a seat next to a table, gesturing Finn to sit across from him. "Well to start this off I must say that you have a lovely home," Finn said with a big smile on his face. Gorman grunted, his expression warning of immediate danger if he didn't speak up now.

Finn nodded. "There is a very, very old prophecy that has been speculated and logged into our history books from when I was young, well I should say a fraction of a prophecy, a piece. There are a lot of ways to interpret its meaning as we have translated it but the most popular seems to revolve around the fall of an infant race and being overtaken by a destructive force that will plague Allterra with war and destruction but that there is hope of a savior who can unite the new races against this evil and possibly turn the tide though with all the different interpretations some have felt that they have made a profound discovery through dream or direct contact with the creator, and made changes including one who can Ark the elements but I believe that this is him, he can Ark, the only human that has ever had this ability, he would have been dead years ago, his body torn apart by the raw energy required to harness that type of power yet here he is, it must be him," Finn said in one excitable breath.

Gorman was put off by Finn's enthusiasm but decided to recount the day he had spent with the young man, and how he had found him in the middle of the woods with no memory. Finn cocked his head in puzzlement over the odd circumstances.

"Hmmm... a hero with no memory of who he is or what he is supposed to do, it is curious indeed, an adventure to be had for sure," Finn said, his eyes blinking rapidly as they darted back and forth in excitement. "We need to take him to Sanctuary, someone there surely must know about this and the plague that has been getting more and more dangerous, who knows who we might meet or what we might find, by the way it is the biggest human settlement to date you know?"

Gorman let out a tired sigh. "So many words from yer mouth, fish, I be familiar wit it," he said, looking over at Kaiden passed out in the oversized chair. "I's grab us some supplies, fer de long journey."

Finn held up a finger. "You know it's interesting you say that Gorman, you know Aquarians have gills in their chest so they are able to breathe and talk at the same time, so I never need to pause to take a breath of air. It is an ability my race has over many others," he said in a ramble as Gorman turned to sit away from him.

The night came swiftly, and the town was almost silent. After the attacks, everyone was with their families mourning their losses or crying to anyone who would listen. Gorman almost wished he was among the fallen, with Finn in nonstop chatter mode like he hadn't had anyone to talk to in months. Finn sat in the bathtub in the corner of the room and slowly poured buckets of water all over himself, making Gorman feel very uncomfortable with the situation. Gorman purposefully positioned himself so the half of his face with the missing eye was facing him. Finn chatted away about his life and studies and family and his journey, and and and. Gorman was just about to get to the point where he could tune him out and possibly get past the awkwardness of the large male fish man bathing himself in his tub only a few feet away when Finn blurted out awkwardly.

"I don't have any genitals," he said, eyeing the ogre with a smile.

Gorman let out a sudden cough, beating on his chest as he tried to catch his breath.

"You see, Aquarians don't mate the same way most humanoids do, so we pick a mate and if both are interested the female will expose the eggs between her abdomen scales and the male dances like this coating her with layer after layer of..."

"Enough! I hear enough!" Gorman shouted, standing out of his chair, unable to look Finn in the eyes. "I's need some fresh air, and doin' my rounds," Gorman grabbed a few spears from a rack on the wall and strapped them to his back. He then opened and rummaged through a small chest on the table, attaching several barbed bolts and a small harpoon to his belt. Being Warden of Hengegrove, it was his duty to keep the town safe as best he could, a burden that had weighed heavy on his heart that night.

Finn cocked his head sideways blinking rapidly, pondering what had just happened. "I will join you; I need to dry off as well and the cool weather feels revitalizing on my scales which dry out if not rehydrated often you know, some Aquarians stay out of water so long that they lose their scales and become what we call sleek skins."

Gorman just walked out of the door, slowly shaking his head from side to side. "May da plague take us all," he said under his breath as he shut the door.

He had his nightly route and liked to stick with it. He walked to his right down the long side of the wall of town, which passed by their small barracks and scout tower. He thought he should check in to see how many of his men were left in his town guard and help lift their spirits. He arrived in an empty room full of sturdy weapons, shields, and armor pieces scattered about. It seemed like the attack had happened so fast that nobody had time to get ready. He checked their armory rack and noticed a few swords hadn't been claimed; mainly his young friend Gavin's, who was a fine young soldier and would surely be missed. Gorman took his sword and strapped it to his back to take home in his memory. His heart weighed heavy as he left to continue his walk around the perimeter. He found it hard to keep his composure with the glimpses of dead bodies lit by flickering torchlight as he walked.

ARKANGEL

He knew that the next few days would be hard for the townspeople. He had been in so many wars, seen so many deaths, he didn't think it would affect him so much. But the thought of so many innocents being lost to an army that couldn't even be seen coming or fought fairly on the open battlefield... He felt his frustrations start to burn inside him, which quickly led his thoughts to Finn. That fish drove him crazy, and the talk of going to Sanctuary weighed heavily on his heart as well. He hadn't been there since his father's death over ten years ago. His father had led a small force against the town that had been overrun by ember elves. The elves took pride in burning down settlements and their inhabitants, expanding their empire over the other races. Gorman winced at the memory. After the battle, seeing his father, the most powerful warrior in his eyes, savagely taken down by an inexperienced orange elf. His world shattered that day and there was nothing he could do to save him. Barely escaping with his own life and losing an eye in the process. He never returned home and couldn't face seeing his mother. A tear rolled down his scarred face as he lightly touched where his eye had been, now folded under a flap of flesh.

His sorrow was interrupted by a shrill shrieking sound off in the distance. It was too dark to see what made the sound, but he rushed towards it. While sprinting he realized he was running straight towards his home and his pace quickened. In the flickering torch light, he could see Finn standing on his porch swinging his fist at some sort of flying creature, which had his other arm locked within its talons. Several of the town guard met him there with spears in hand, throwing them at the creature, whose powerful flapping wings easily knocked them away. Gorman saw Finn struggling to stay grounded as he started lifting off the porch, curling his legs around the guard rail.

Gorman pulled out a small harpoon from his belt and inserted it securely in his vambrace. He then pumped at the small, dwarven-made contraption until it began to hiss. He took aim and fired the harpoon, which pulled quickly at the reel of rope and sunk deeply into the wing of the creature. He planted his feet firmly on the ground and pulled. His men realized what he was doing and came in to help their warden. The creature's attention was drawn away from Finn and started to snap its alligator-like beak at the rope to get free. Finn took the opportunity to jump up and wrap his arm around the creature's neck, now that his arm was freed from the creature's grasp. He pulled himself up onto the creature's black, hairy back and, with one arm around its neck, kicked with all his might at his harpooned wing. Gorman used this to his advantage and yanked it down flat to the ground, where it landed with a loud thud. The soldiers surrounded the creature and severed its neck, ending the struggle, but not before it shrieked a terrifying laugh. Gorman briefly looked out into the dark woods and thought that he saw a pair of red eyes gazing back at them.

"My, thank you, good sir," Finn offered to Gorman as he jumped down from its back.

"What is it?" Gorman asked. He had been in these woods for ten years and had never seen a creature like that before. The men all offered up shrugs of confusion as well. Finn went into action, poking and prodding the large creature to learn more about it. Gorman wondered what this creature wanted, and why of all days it came today? He remembered Kaiden was still inside and ran in to see him still passed out in his chair. "Dat creature be after yous?" he said softly to himself. He began to think that maybe there was some truth to a prophecy, things just seemed to be spiraling out of control so fast. The thought of his mother and father briefly passed through his mind and decided that this was going to have to be the way things were, he would have to get this boy to Sanctuary and face his fears. If he failed, he worried that Allterra would be faced with an evil they were not prepared to fight.

CHAPTER 2

"THE ELVEN ARKER"

"That's excellent, Nirayus, do it again," Nimia coached.

Nirayus lifted her hand slowly off the large, jagged boulder in front of her. A small arc of blue energy danced between her hand and the rock.

"Ouch!" Nirayus whipped her hand away and rubbed it against her leg.

"You know for only twelve you are a real natural!" Nimia said, lightly running her fingers through her daughter's bright blue hair.

"Why does it hurt sometimes?" Nirayus whimpered.

Nimia held her arms out in front of herself and took a step back. She closed her eyes and started pulling long shards of green energy out of thin air. She swirled her hands around the amassing green light and slapped it into a ball, beginning to take a liquid-like form. She opened her eyes, then quickly ran her hands around the orb as if coaxing it to stay together in one solid mass. The liquid energy swirled into a hazy black as the ball started to spin in place. Nimia then put one hand under the orb and walked it over to another large stone. She gently laid it on top and let it go. A loud hiss filled the air with greenish mist filling the air. Nirayus watched in awe as the green liquid completely dissolved the boulder over ten times its size. Then with one smooth motion Nimia gestured the acidic liquid away and it was gone.

"It takes years of practice, little one, and you have just started. But we will practice every day until you have mastered your Ark."

"Why is yours green and mine blue?" Nirayus asked, confused. "What color is father's?"

Nimia chuckled. "Your father can't ark, dear, and if he could it would be black for how serious he is all the time." A warm smile spread wide on her delicate face.

"Why can't he? We could teach him." Nirayus' eyes lit up at the thought.

Nimia's chuckle turned into a laugh. "Oh, if he only had the patience," she managed, trying to catch her breath. She sat Nirayus down on a boulder along the small stream and gestured to the water, rocks, and the lush forest around them.

"Not all things can ark energy, it is a gift, unique to very few. I can manipulate forms of nature, poisons, and acidic matter. I can feel them, become one with these substances and in turn control and manipulate their essences. You will start to feel it in everything you do." She sat down on a larger stone with a smile.

"Not everyone has these gifts; for instance, humans, they hate and fear it because they can't understand it. Their frail bodies can't take the stress of manipulating elements, having the energies ripple through their being and projecting out at command. It would kill them because they have not been blessed with what it takes to wield the gift." She lightly moved her hand over the rock, drawing a green glow upon it and causing a thin moss to grow.

"There are many forms of arking which you will learn with more practice and training. It is very rare, but I have heard through the centuries some have been able to master multiple forms of energy where many can barely control one."

Nirayus jumped up, raising her hands in the air, and yelled, "I'm going to learn them all and be the most powerful arker father has ever seen!"

Nimia's grin spread wide across her face in pride; she knew she had a very special daughter. Her mouth contorted and her eyes blinked in confusion as she winced in pain.

"Mother, what's wrong?" Nirayus asked, reaching out her arm.

Before she could answer another arrow shot through her back, bursting through her thin, cloth shirt, the beautifully embroidered patterns quickly saturating with her blood. Her eyes rolled back into her head as she began to choke, gasping for air. She leaned forward to touch her daughter's hand one last time but came up short, collapsing hard into the wet ground below.

Horrified, Nirayus burst into tears and shouted for her to get up, barely noticing the three men stepping out from the bushes across the stream.

"Got one!" One of the men shouted triumphantly.

Another crossed the stream and lifted her lifeless body up by her light blue and white hair. "Nice shot," he said before throwing her back down into the shallow stream, the current beginning to pull at her almost weightless body.

The third man held out a large dagger and pointed it towards Nirayus. "What about the little one?" he grumbled.

"Is it inflicted, you think?" another man asked, crossing the stream. He slowly pulled an arrow from his quiver and knocked it, pulling it back to fire. Nirayus's heart raced, the shock of seeing her mother murdered right in front of her jerking her heart and crippling her. She stumbled back, tears flowing down her face as she struggled to stay standing.

"No use taking the chance, just kill it," came orders from one of the men. Nirayus's eyes darted back and forth between the men creeping closer to her.

"Stop, please don't," she pleaded, gasping for air in between the pounding within her chest.

"We got orders, sweetheart, all the way up from Paladin Malik, you'll have to take it up with him," the man said in an evil, uncaring chuckle. He looked to his friend opposite Nirayus with a nod.

The man lunged towards her with his dagger, Nirayus's frightened stare locked into his murderous gaze. Time slowed to a halt and only moved forward by the quick beats of her heart. Her head went back, and her eyelids clenched together tightly as she raised her small arms high to offer what little defense she could. A thunderous boom rang out with whips of electrical energy wrapping around his body and throwing him back several yards. His body hit with such force that his back instantly shattered against the trunk of a tree, wrapping his body around it before crashing to the ground. The concussive force staggered the other two men as they struggled to get their weapons up.

Nirayus's head lowered, and she angrily stared at the man with the bow, her eyes shifting into a golden color. The man released an arrow towards her face, and as it sailed through the air, she clawed at it, releasing lighting tendrils from her fingertips that vaporized the arrow as it flew. She whipped her other hand across as the whip-like tendrils lashed out at the man, wrapping his body in the ropes of blue cackling energy. The water beneath his feet began to quickly boil as he stood there, electrocuting, until he collapsed to the wet rocky ground.

The dust from the arrow splattered against her chest as her wild and frenzied gaze narrowed on her final target. He lost his footing in panic and fell to his knee, clasping his hands in front of him, pleading for his life.

"Please don't kill me!" he begged with beads of tears rolling down his face.

With all the rage pent up inside her, she surged her arms forward, flames began to flicker and dance around her hands. She waved them around, and with a lifting motion brought up rapid torrents of flame, like pillars of fire, that arose around him. He shouted and screamed for mercy, but they fell on deaf ears as the twisting pillars engulfed him. His hands went for his throat as he struggled to breath, his knee giving out from the heat, forcing him down to the burning hot rocks and boiling water. His clothes ignited as his shrill screams filled the air around her. The pillars momentarily rose higher into the air and then collapsed back down onto themselves, scorching everything they touched and leaving nothing but a pile of ash.

Nirayus's hands went to her face, covering her eyes in fear as she fell to her knees. Her body convulsing from the adrenaline pumping through her body, she fought to breathe in past her misery as she wept. The day turned to night and the cold night back into day. She lay there, exhausted, numb, and unable to get herself up. She realized she didn't even know where she was or how to get back home. Fear started to outweigh her sorrow and soon her hunger would even outweigh her fear and drive her mad. She lay on her back in the damp, rocky ground next to the stream, watching as the tall trees swayed in the breeze and the leaves shook.

She jolted up alert, the birds having stopped chirping and the critters of the forest gone to hiding. In the distance she could hear horses breathing and grunting, most likely pulling some sort of wagon. Her eyes widened as her heart sank. "Humans," she whispered. They were the only race who used horses to pull such contraptions that she could think of. She ran over towards the sound and came across an old road, hiding behind some thick foliage. She dared to peek over, hoping to find some evidence of some food. She saw that one of the carts was filled with items she didn't recognize and figured it must be some sort of traveling merchant of goods. Humans were so strange in their need to own so many items, she thought.

On the last cart that wheeled closer she saw a line of strung up game dangling over the edge. The intricate carvings and design of the wagon surely meant it belonged to a wealthy merchant of some type. She lurched forward slightly but halted when an armored man sitting atop a horse rode past her towards the front of the caravan. This was her chance! She rolled out from the heavy shrubs and leapt up, snatching the body of a fluffy white panjam. The line held fast, and she slammed against the side of the wagon with a loud thump.

From up ahead she heard the man call out, "All slow to a stop."

She panicked and grasped at the line again but this time a flash of fire lashed out from her fingers, burning straight through the line and scorching the side of the wagon. She fell to the dirt and rolled, coming to a hard stop against a large boulder at the side of the road. She panted, trying to catch her breath as her heart pumped faster and faster. She didn't want to see the humans and feared what they would do if they saw her. Her long, thin, elven ears lifted slightly at the sound of thumping horse steps coming up along the other side of the wagons. She jumped into the forest foliage just in time as the rider made his way around the back side of the last wagon.

Out of the corner of her eye she noticed the man's attention drawn to the long, black burn on the side of the wooden wagon. He turned his head slowly as he inspected the deep forest to find the cause of the burn. She retreated a few paces deeper into the woods and crouched behind a large formation of rocks. The smell of the burned panjam brought pain to her stomach, reminding her of her dire need for its meat and the essential blood that ran through its veins. She had wasted so much energy arking that it wouldn't be long until her body went into shock, and she lost her mind, giving into a lust for blood. The dried panjam was small with most of its body consisting of its furry shell that ran along its narrow back. She feared that it alone wouldn't be enough to sustain her until she could find her way home. She braced her back against the rock, her mind racing in fear, thinking of what to do next.

"Hello? Are you ok?" came a small voice.

Nirayus jumped in place, defensively raising her arms towards a young boy standing several feet away.

"It's ok, I won't hurt you, what is your name?" the young boy asked with a wide grin. He stood almost eye level with her since she was considered short even for a Moon Elf.

Nirayus blinked wide eyed and alert, wiping the dirt from her face. He was a lot younger than her, and she figured he couldn't be too much of a threat. "I am Nirayus," she said timidly, gauging if she should turn to flee.

The boy raised his hand to her, holding a large wedge of bread. "Are you hungry?" he asked, intrigued by her dirty blue hair tucked behind her long ears.

The little boy looked to be about six years old from what she could tell. The pale look in his face and yellowing in his eyes made him look sickly. His skinny frame was almost as slender as hers, which was small for a human boy, as elves were known for their petite figures. She knew he wouldn't be left alone long in the woods.

"Thank you," she said, quickly snatching at the bread and pulling it close.

A long grin spread across the boy's face. "I like your ears, they are pointy," he said with a giggle.

Nirayus suddenly felt self-conscious; she didn't know why the human boy was so interested in her or why he was out here away from his people. "I am a Moon Elf," she said, her ears lowering, not knowing how to take his compliment. "I am lost," she offered, finding herself less alert and wanting to change the subject from her ears.

The boy only seemed to get more excited. "You can come with us, my mother says we are traveling to the mountains, it would be so much fun if you came," he said, bouncing in excitement.

She smiled. "I can't, I need to find my father, I need to go home." Then she realized he was probably too young to understand.

Suddenly a loud voice called out from the direction of the road. "Where are you at, boy? Get back here!"

Nirayus quickly put her finger to her lips. "Shhh, don't tell anyone I am here, ok?" she whispered.

A playful smile came to his face. "Are you hiding?" he asked.

"No," she whispered back, "I just need to go home right away."

She turned from him to leave and paused. "Go back to your family, I have to leave now." Her eyes scanned through the trees, afraid of being seen by the humans. She took several paces away, waiting for the boy to do the same.

"Here," the boy said shyly, pulling something from his coat pocket.

"My Father gave me this for if I ever got lost, he said it would show me the way home one day." He pulled a fine gold chain, attached to a compass, out of the pocket. He lifted it up to her with a smile on his face, proud to be able to offer help to his new, elven friend.

She was taken back by his kindness and her heart filled with hope that she may find her way home at last. He stepped closer and rose up on his tiptoes to put it up over her head.

"There, now you can find your home." He gleamed, looking into her big blue eyes.

The thought of getting home after all she had been through drew tears to her eyes. She reached down and grabbed a slick, round river stone and held it firmly in her hands. She looked back at him, meeting his gaze, and her vision blurred slightly as her eyes turned to a vibrant golden color. Green light emanated from her clenched hands as they pulsated brighter and brighter. She released her power, holding her hand out to him with the smooth, round stone now glossed over with a glass-like sheen and a pattern etched around its edges. There was a smooth hole punched through the center; she placed her finger through it, marveling at what she had just created.

"Here," she offered. "So, you will never forget me."

His eyes went wide. "How did you do that?" he asked in excitement.

"I am learning how to ark."

A loud voice called out again. "Boy, where are you? Get over here now!"

He looked back, startled out of his excitement. "That's my dad, I don't want to get in trouble so I should go," he said sadly, turning around to leave. He looked back at her one last time, peering into her big blue doe eyes and returning her smile. He looked down to the special rock she had given him, and when he looked up, she was gone.

Nirayus ran for her life, stopping momentarily to feed, fearing she wouldn't make it home in time before her wild instincts took over. Now that she knew what direction to run in, she clenched tightly onto her small golden compass and effortlessly sprinted through the forest.

Nirayus opened her eyes and realized she had been gripping her golden compass all night long. Her fingers resisted to open up and the intricate carvings in the gold were pressed into her soft, pale skin. She wondered why she still had the same nightmare every night for so many years. Though now that she was older it had turned from nightmare to dream, for she had accepted her mother's death, and with a constant threat of ark hunters it served as a reminder of her hatred towards humans. Despite all her hate, though, she had a special place in her heart for the young boy who had saved her life that day. She hoped she would one day be able to find him and tell him how special he was to her, and also to return his compass. She didn't view herself as a romantic type, but for some reason she was unable to shake the thoughts of the boy even 15 years later. Since then, she had turned her attention away from teaching like her mother and had instead joined her father's hunting party. Her abilities weren't polished, but she knew enough to be a great asset to their team.

She pushed the door from her bed chamber open and stepped out into the light, feeling the chill of the grey stone marble on her feet as she stretched her arms high. She wasn't one for waking up early to get a jump on the day, especially without visiting the training halls and getting a hearty meal, but today was special. She suddenly remembered what day it was, and her excitement washed the sleepiness from her eyes and hastened her steps. She turned from the balcony where she had been overlooking the grassy fields at the foot of the castle walls and ran towards her closet. She sometimes wondered why her ancestors had picked the inside of a cave network as a good place for their family castle. The rough edges of rock had worn down over time and the constant cool breeze coming from its dark depths helped the Moon Elves with their intolerance to heat. Other than that, it was damp and ugly, aside from the bright marble colors they constructed the castle walls from that they had mined from within.

She swept through her room, swooping up pieces of her favorite hunting gear as she went. She stopped at her mirror and threw off her thin, teal blue nightwear in favor for her favorite dress her father had gotten her for special occasions like today. It started off as a deep royal blue up by her shoulders and faded to black towards the bottom. Silvery constellations had been woven into the fabric in beautiful patterns. Her shoulders were protected by thin, metal shoulder guards trimmed in gold with straps that pulled matching leather fabric across her chest and back for protection. Leather straps crossed her tiny waist to attach her daggers, along with pouches for supplies. Thin strips of fabric fell down her back off her shoulders like decorative strands of a cape that could be wrapped around her exposed arms if she needed protection from the elements. She looked into the mirror, eyeing herself as she thought the colors really went well with her big, icy blue eyes and her bright vibrant blue hair she kept up in a tight tail and draped over her shoulder. She threw her daggers around her waist and strapped on her high leather boots and flew out the door in a hurry to find her father.

"You're late, Rayus," her father, Valryn, said sternly with a matching expression. His long, thin, raven-colored hair flew over his shoulder as he turned to finish prepping his men.

She looked at the ground, clutching her necklace in one hand and reached for her horse with her other. "I know, I know."

"Are you prepared to be gone for three days, Rayus?" A slight curl of a smile betrayed his excitement. He was overjoyed to be out in the forest and away from the castle for a few days on their biggest hunt of the year.

"I am always ready, Father," she quickly replied, eager to confirm her previous requests. Then she added with a smile, "But we can still stop by the stream, can't we?"

"Yes, as I promised we will ride south through the forest there and up the path. Packs of short haired dryad are known to gather there and drink throughout the heated months." Valryn jumped onto his horse in a single leap and ran a check on his gear to make sure his short, curved bow was present, along with an abundance of long sleek arrows.

"Thank you, Father!" she said in excitement, pressing her heels into her horse's side to get it moving. "Come on, let's go," she shouted eagerly to get the other hunters' attention.

Every summer, when they went out on the first hunt of the season, she always wanted to go back to her favorite stream; unknowing to her father, it was where she had met the young boy so many years ago. She had hoped one day to run into him or catch sight of his caravan again; it may be a fruitless effort, but one she looked forward to every year. She guessed he would probably be in his twenties by now and feared he may not even remember her.

Valryn waved his hand, motioning for the hunters to move out in line behind him, followed by a small squad of soldiers. Their shiny chain and light plate armor glinted brightly in the morning sun. Nirayus rode up ahead, looking back for her father and letting out a wondrous breath, seeing the castle from a distance. The beautifully carved white and grey stone with golden etchings patterned into the walls really gave the castle a look of royalty. Walls and towers jutted out from within the massive cave encircling the castle completely inside, with a waterfall falling from above and splashing into a natural moat that ran along the inside of the courtyard and out along the main wall. The grounds were flourishing with beautiful flowers and plants that Nirayus always made time to wander through.

The sound of her horse's hooves pounded hard against the wooden bridge brought her attention back to the thoughts of their adventure. She slowed to wait for the rest of the men, antsy to see the countryside beyond the walls. They rode for many hours until dusk, the elves' pure white skin glowing in the moonlight, their eyes adapting to the night by changing to a vibrant, golden color to absorb the lower levels of light. They could almost see better at night than they could during the day, only sacrificing the ability to see their enhanced pallet of colors.

During the night their pace quickened, riding through the open countryside and scattered patches of trees. Elves could cover enormously large amounts of land on horseback with their mounts suffering very little burden from carrying their elven riders. One of the flank rider scouts galloped up to talk to Valryn as Nirayus tilted her head slightly to pick up their conversation.

"King Valryn, we have spotted a pack of horned gorgans to the south. I recommend we ride further to the north to skirt around them, Sir."

She winced; going further north would mean missing her detour to the stream, at best delaying her a day. She slowed her pace and angled in towards her father and the soldier.

"That will be all, soldier," she called, her eyes betraying her frustration. She looked down to see her hands were beginning to glow brightly in frustration as she clenched the reins tightly.

"Yes, Princess," he said with a nod, riding south to meet up with his scouting party.

"Father, you really can't be thinking of changing course from this far south because of some gorgans, that would delay us at least a day," she stated, hoping he wouldn't see through her intentions.

"Nirayus, I'm not putting our men at risk for you to visit that stream of yours. You will have to wait until our return trip if there is time or wait until next hunt." He did not even look in her direction.

Valryn raised an arm and gestured to all the men to change course and follow his lead north. Small bolts of electricity arced off Nirayus's hands as she scowled.

She slowed her pace so the king wouldn't see her sorrow, watching him as he galloped further ahead with the hunters. They had several mounts strapped together full of various packs and baskets for holding all the meat and hides for the return journey; they made up the rear of their hunting party. Her mind raced trying to figure out a solution so they could go the way she had wanted, the way her father had promised. Maybe if she went by herself and rode harder, she could get down and meet them on the other side of the forest, before they even knew she was missing. What if he was there, or his caravan was traveling close by, and she missed her chance to find him because her father feared some mindless beasts? She couldn't come up with a decent plan and didn't want to suffer her father's wrath, but she had to know.

She took several long, deep breaths to strengthen her resolve and to stop her hands from glowing. She couldn't afford being caught before she left their pack. As the scouts rode closer to report ahead, she turned wide around a formation of rocks and changed her direction south like she was just another scout. She hoped the guards riding close to the King wouldn't think anything different of her alteration to formation since they were new to the hunt this season.

She raced out from behind the cover of the rock formation, checking over her shoulder, just waiting to be caught. She let out a gasp as a smile spread wide across her face; she was free. She spotted the pack of gorgans as they entered the forest looking for prey. "No problem," she thought, knowing she could sneak in a little further south than she had planned and move herself north from the inside of the forest. She reached the forest edge and, without hesitation, had her horse leap over a downed tree and into the thick ferns and plant life. There was an old road that wound through the forest she needed to reach first, the very same one she had encountered the boy's caravan on when she was younger. She was getting close, and she knew it.

Before reaching the road, her eyes picked up faint flickers of firelight off in the distance. She stopped and leaped from her horse, looping its reigns around a few branches. She crept slowly, angling her ears in the direction of the light in hopes to pick up any sounds or voices. She could hear three to four distinct voices talking and laughing as she got closer, making sure to stay out of sight. The trees were tall and wide, heavily covered in moss with long vines hanging like spider webs from the high branches. She could also hear the flowing of the stream further up ahead, her mother's stream. She slowed her pace but breathed heavily in excitement at the possibility of this being his caravan. What if he was coming to find her? Her heart leapt from the thought.

Nirayus, lost in her thoughts, failed to stay cautious as she approached. She came to the edge of the fire light and scanned the men sitting and lying near their campfire. She looked at all the people and took notice of their crude weapons and tattered armor. She let out a gasp, choked in fear. She had lost herself in hope and these men were clearly not merchants. Her ears flicked back alert as she heard a twig gently snap behind her and a sharp pain pressed into her lower back.

"What do we have here?" A woman's voice asked in intrigue.

Nirayus gulped. "I am lost and hoping someone here can help me get back to the road?" she said, her voice wavering in fear.

"Awww, poor thing, you're lost? Isn't that a shame? You mean you're not the one that we saw leave the elven hunting party?" the woman said mockingly.

Nirayus's heart pounded hard in her chest. Why had they been watching her, she wondered? She shouldn't have come alone and felt ashamed of her choices.

"Hey, boys, look what we have here, she is inflicted," the woman said in lustful excitement as several men jumped to their feet, grabbing their weapons.

Nirayus's mind raced. Inflicted? She wondered what they had meant until she realized the smoke rising from her glowing, orange, clenched fists. She flinched trying to hide them but was too late as everyone circled around her with their weapons drawn.

"Don't' get any ideas, arker, I can pull the release of this crossbow and sink it in your spine faster than you can ark." She slid the razor-sharp point up her back to rest at the base of her exposed neck.

"What are you really doing here, elfy?" she asked with a hint of playfulness.

Nirayus was getting too frightened to speak, her body trembling as she could feel a bead of warm blood run down her neck. Why hadn't she just listened to father, she screamed inside her mind.

"You're really making this difficult on yourself, aren't you, sweetie?" the woman chuckled to herself. "My name is Vixis, and this is my merry band of fellow Arkhunters. You walked yourself into the wrong camp tonight, haven't you?" she whispered, her mouth getting close to her ear. "Too bad... you're kind of cute." She playfully traced the long tip of Nirayus's ear with her tongue. Nirayus squirmed violently, flames bursting up her arms.

"Ah ah, not so fast," Vixis said, jabbing the crossbow bolt harder into her neck.

Nirayus let out a cry of pain as she felt the tip of the bolt slowly tear into her flesh.

"Now tell me, how many Inflicted are there in your group? Should we even waste our time with them or will gutting you be enough to add to our pile here?" she asked in an innocent tone.

"I am the only gifted one, please, leave my father alone."

"Oh, your father, huh?" Vixis said with a little gasp. "If I'm not mistaken, those men looked of royalty to me... well of a sort. So, does this make you daddy's little princess?" She let out a giggle, clearly taking pleasure in toying with her.

"What do you think, boys? Add another to the pile or should we sell her back to daddy?" she asked, gesturing to an uncovered wagon with blood-soaked limbs of every race and size slipping through the separated side boards.

Taking a chance while Vixis was distracted, Nirayus darted to her left, spinning to the side of the tree, barely dodging the barbed point of the bolt as it sunk deep into the bark. She kicked at Vixis to put some distance between them and shouted at the top of her lungs, "Get off me!" She raised her glowing, orange hands across her chest as sparks lurched from her body and long tendrils of fire whipped into the night sky. Her adrenaline surged through her as she quickly uncrossed her arms, releasing a terrifying geyser of flame from her fists. She screamed in anger as her vibrant, blue hair flailed wildly behind her and her eyes narrowed in on her targets. The jet of flame slashed and cleaved through the air, engulfing one of the mercenaries in fire. He fell to the ground, frantically calling for help as he rolled around to put out the flames.

One of the other men charged in, mace held high in the air. She raised her right fist to meet him as an arked dagger of flame cut straight through his chest, instantly cauterizing his insides from where his heart used to be. Another lunged in from her other side, catching her off guard and sending her slamming into the side of a tree. She gasped for air and struck diagonally with her arm, sending a searing blade of flame straight through his torso and shoulder. The momentum of his attack separated his upper body, sending it tumbling through the campsite.

Her eyes flared with an intense, golden glow as she screamed, unearthing her hatred and fear from within for the human hunters. These humans were all the same to her, the very same ones who killed her mother, and all of them deserved to die by her hand for what they had taken from her. She exploded forth a shower of razor-sharp needles of flame in all directions as her anger bellowed from deep within. When the blast subsided, smoke arose from the charred ground and bodies that lay strewn across the ground in front of her.

Nirayus gasped when she saw Vixis standing there, right in front of where she had arked. Vixis shook her head at her, flicking her long, dark brown hair behind her shoulder. She wore a shiny, etched, dark bronze breastplate and leather corset that hugged her curves tightly. She was tall and slender with long muscular legs only covered by tight leather pants with laced sides and black knee-high boots. She wore a seductive smirk on her almost unnaturally beautiful face as she eyed Nirayus from head to toe, her hand gently fingering a glowing, golden amulet dangling low around her neck.

"Aww... poor princess, is that the best you can do?" she chuckled, swinging her fist unbelievably fast and hitting Nirayus square in the stomach. Nirayus's tiny figure lifted completely off the ground, sailing back and slamming into the tree right behind her. The branches of the tree shook so violently from the impact that a downpour of leaves rained down around her.

Nirayus let out a cry, gasping for air as she clambered to regain her bearings. Moon elves were more durable than most humans, but Vixis's strength was far more than human. "Who are you?" she asked, choking and clenching her stomach tightly.

"Oh, doll… wouldn't you just love to know?" she said with a long thin smile spread across her pursed lips.

From the dark forest came a man's desperate cry of, "Master!... Master, help!" Nirayus could hear his heavy footsteps getting closer as he ran. She glanced into the dense trees, seeing massive hulks thrashing through the forest after one of the hunters. Vixis, too, investigated the darkness, but was unable to see the creatures as the sound of snapping trees filled the air.

"MASTER!" he called out again, followed by a scream of pain and terror as the creatures caught up with him. His body crushed under the weight of the horned gorgans as they ran towards them, trampling everything in their path. Nirayus cringed at the noise of his bones being shattered under their tremendous weight, then turned to hide behind the sturdy tree beside her. Vixis stood her ground, drawing a long, ornate sword and shooting bolts at the beast. One of the bolts thudded hard into the beast's shoulder, causing it to briefly slow and grunt in pain. They continued their charge, unaware of Nirayus's presence behind the tree.

Vixis effortlessly dodged to the left of the first gorgan, running her blade deep into the side of the beast as it tried to tackle her with its long, burly arms. Its massive, curled horns lifted high into the air as it shouted out in pain, blood pouring freely from the open wound. It rested its brutish body against a tree, grasping at its side with its enormous hand, breathing heavily. They stood about eighteen feet tall when on their back legs but were easy to hit when they were running on all four legs, losing maneuverability and relying on brute strength. A second one swung its fist right over Vixis's head, barely missing as she ducked and rolled to the side. Her blade swung high, tearing the beast's knee open and causing it to lose control of its charge, crashing hard into the cart of dead bodies the hunters were collecting. As its body tumbled, dirt was tossed high into the air and rained down onto the small patches of fire, extinguishing all light in the dark woods. Nirayus blinked, her eyes turning to a bright, golden color, giving her an extreme advantage with her night vision.

She gasped from shock as the third gorgan lowered its horned head and viciously trampled into Vixis, throwing her violently through the air and into one of the other wounded beasts. The gorgan let out a ferocious call of victory as it followed suit to devour its prey. She had heard this call before, knowing it meant the creature was about to feed on its hard-earned meal. She could see the dark, thickly furred creatures rake their long-clawed fingers through the dirt to uncover the dead bodies from the night's fight.

Nirayus knew this was her chance, silently slipping away in the opposite direction, back towards the field. She was caught by surprise again as she was scooped up by a dark figure running undetectable in the thinning woods. She huffed when she was thrown onto the back of an already galloping horse right behind her father. She thrust her arms around his waist, holding him close in relief and embarrassment.

"Thank you, father," she managed in a quiet, guilty voice. His silence said a thousand words to her, and she could almost feel his anger boiling within him. She closed her eyes in shame but was relieved to be back with her party, safe from the horribly twisted humans. She looked to see them branch off separate from the group and wondered where the other hunters were going. She wondered how he even known where she was, thinking he must have noticed her missing and had been following her the whole time.

She looked up to see the first hints of morning glowing red and orange against the tall trees. The horse continued to run effortlessly through the countryside to a familiar road leading to Market Town. This was the place they went to sell the furs and precious stones that had been mined from their castle cave. She wanted nothing but to rest in the cozy beds at the inn, and for her father to finally speak to her again.

"You are going to lay low in Market Town until we know for sure the Arkhunter has lost your trail. You hear me, Rayus? Do you hear me?" he called back to her, raising his voice. She knew he was just worried for her.

"We will leave the horse and let it return home on its own and run the rest of the way" he said, leaping from the back of the horse and landing in a steady run. "Hopefully it will throw her off our tracks. Stick to the grasses and streams if possible."

"I know, father," she said, following suit, her skirt slightly hindering her speed. "They are all dead, I killed most of the men and the woman was about to be eaten by the gorgans." She'd hoped this would ease his anger.

A disappointed scowl grew on Valryn's face. "Nirayus, it will take a lot more than three gorgans to stop that woman," he said, trailing off in thought as they approached the gates of town.

They entered to see tall buildings, of both wooden and stone, lining the inside of the walls and separated by dirt roadways and paths. They walked towards the center of town, catching view of the exotic garden and trees in the center. Nirayus remembered the artistic fountains and statues that decorated the expertly kept garden trails and hoped to get a chance to explore them. She smiled at the sight of the merchant tents lining the streets and the shacks with the sounds of voices calling into the air, bartering prices or erupting into song. The town was a neutral melting pot for all the races of Allterra to conduct trade and contracts; she was always fascinated by the unique characters she found.

Nirayus followed close to Valryn as they walked through the crowd, making his way to their favorite inn, The Rested Wanderer. She loved the hustle and bustle of the town, and that it was a place everyone could come and visit no matter what race they were or who they happened to be, trading and learning from one another. Though, this time most seemed to be in a rush, sticking to their own with the talk of plague on everyone's lips

CHAPTER 3

"MARTIS THE SAVIOR"

Martis walked down the market street, in the Sanctuary merchant district, observing all the people and their well-being. He noticed a fruit merchant who had a small lot of goods available, which was highly unusual for this early in the morning.

"Slow crop, my good man?" Martis asked, analyzing his clothes, hygiene, and stock. He was clearly having a rough year.

"Yes, it's been, M'lord," the merchant said with a slight bow.

"No need for such formalities, my friend, I am just taking a morning stroll." Martis watched the merchant's mannerisms, judging his aptitude and schooling, if he'd had any. He could tell the man had been working exhaustive hours and somehow produced so little fruits, meaning a loss of a possible worker or, more likely, a son. The long days wore heavily on the man and the increased exposure of sun, and dirt stained his skin a dirty brown color.

Difficult to clean, he thought.

"Jed, M'lord, the name is Jed," the man said, looking at the tall and finely dressed Martis uneasily, uncomfortable with his intensions. "It's just with all them mander attacks, sir, the fields are dangerous and hard to keep good workers around these days. My son was wounded in an attack and has been ill for days, I fear he has the plague." Jed looked into Martis's piercing blue eyes; his cheek-to-cheek smile made Jed feel more at ease.

"Oh sorry, M'lord, to be takin your time away, please help yourself to my fruits. Free of charge, of course." Jed gestured to the best of his apples.

Martis took a step closer, pulling several coins from his satchel and placing them firmly in the man's hand.

"My dearest Jed, keep your fruit," he said with a smile. "Here are some coins to get you through the coming months. Hire some additional workers and bring your family to Solstice Gardens just north here of Sanctuary." He gestured through the northern gate. "Just follow the road north until you are west of Devil's Gorge. We have healers who can quicken your son's recovery, no charge."

Jed's eyes widened in disbelief, clenching the coins tightly. "Oh, thank you, M'lord, thank you!" Gratefully falling to a knee before Martis. "Praise be to you, kind sir, praise to you."

Martis gazed upon Jed, his back stiffening and his legs feeling weak as his breathing quickened. He placed his hand down for Jed to kiss. "All praise goes to our creator Baladar," Martis said, barely able to contain his smile of hubris.

Jed paused blinking in thought, looking up to Martis in confusion.

"I must be on my way if I am to make it to the council meeting, my friend. I hope to see you in Solstice soon."

He quickened his pace as he turned and walked away but took time to wave at youngsters or smile at passing women who swooned over him. Martis was irregularly muscular and well built; his rugged and chiseled appearance had people gazing at him constantly. He had found that with the right amount of persuasion, no man or woman could tell him no if he desired something enough. He walked the streets of Sanctuary frequently helping everyone he could. His estate was home to hundreds of people and was on its way to becoming its own town. Many people came to visit and stayed to be a part of its beauty and hospitality.

He rounded the street and went up into the staircase that spiraled up to the main walkway, then a bridge stretching over the garden district and leading to the base of Paladin's Tower. The large rings of walls that encircled the city divided it into different districts and housing, ranging from the very wealthy to the multiple guilds of the middle class. The poor were often shuffled outside the city walls to the outlaying farms and queries. Sanctuary had been built to defend against an army of giants, if they so happened to attack again; no human alive today could remember the horrors of their last attack. The giants had been forced back to their island, where they had stayed silent for over a hundred years. Not many dared to venture there for any reason.

Three white, grand towers extended over twice as tall as the walls, housing the bulk of the nobility with bridges and aqueducts tying them together. In the center sat a huge palace suspended between the massive towers, Paladin's Keep, housing the entire government of Sanctuary along with the Paladins, generals, and any other higher-up nobility. Martis had a palace suite there, in addition to his estate, and would stay in the palace during long business ventures. However, he usually let his advisors and operatives occupy the place in his stead. He walked the giant bridge over to the lifting platform that slowly raised him up into the bottom of Paladin's Keep. He eyed the elaborate craftsmanship of the dwarves who had been commissioned to craft such a complicated lift, then he stepped off the round lift before it slowly lowered back down into the main plaza.

A woman was waiting for him, long red-orange hair draped over her shoulder, covering almost more skin than her tight, red and black leather corset. "Welcome, Sir," she said to him as he approached the main hallways. Martis eyed her head to toe; she was the most alluring woman he had ever met, completely unreadable to him, and it drove him mad. She was a breathtaking beauty with big, beautiful orange eyes almost matching her fiery hair. She pursed her lips at him and locked her arm around his, drawing him close. As she walked, the thin chainmail skirt around her waist jangled with the swift sway of her hips.

Martis's heart lurched into his throat to feel her skin against his arm. He could have almost any woman he wanted, and this untamed beauty had him by the collar; he struggled to come to terms with it. He demanded such greatness of himself and his plans that he felt his affections for her were almost a breaking weakness, one he had lost control over.

He walked beside her as they approached the court where they were all to meet. Martis found his gaze drawn to Feora as she lightly caressed her small, golden neckless held delicately in her fingers, eying him from the corner of her vision.

"Shall I escort you to your chair, Sir?" she asked in her seductive tone. "Or shall I take my seat?"

He hated letting her arm go but knew it would look poor on his appearance to display their intimate affiliation with each other in front of everyone. Anything more than a casual walk might spark talks behind his back, and with his plans for Solstice Gardens unveiling soon, he couldn't risk it be tainted with the name of an Arkhunter. Some alliances were best left for the bedroom, he thought with a grin.

"Take your seat, I will meet up with you after. We have certain business to attend to before we get back to Solstice." They approached the guards and Martis waved them to the sides of the door.

"Welcome, Priest Martis," the guards said in unison, pulling their long ornate glaives away from the open door.

Martis's brows lowered in seriousness. "That is Minister Martis," he commanded.

"Ladies first," Martis said, gesturing for the alluring Feora to take lead, watching and examining her as she walked.

The council room was a big circle with several rows of seats, all wrapping around a big opening in the floor with a breathtaking view of the gardens below. One thing Sanctuary never lacked was its beautiful floral life. Across from the entrance was a raised portion where the Paladins sat, higher than everyone else to show their position of power.

Martis's attention went to his seat, not the one he would sit in today but the one he rightfully deserved, the First Paladin's throne.

Its carved, white, granite structure with intricate engravings and solid gold trim would do just fine for him, he thought. He decided when he took it that he would have it raised up another foot or so above the rest, for the thought of everyone looking up to him made his heartbeat quicken.

He gave First Paladin Lanthor, who had noticed his long gaze upon the throne, a smile and a nod. The proud Lanthor's head suddenly cocked as he coughed repeatedly before he continued to take his seat as he wiped beads of sweat from his forehead. Their encounters together had improved as of late, since Martis had been showing him what a loyal and trusted noble he was, as well as his grand visions for the future. *His* future.

Martis walked over to the landing where the supporting nobles sat to the right of the Paladins. He realized everyone's desire for power but decided he had more class, making him a far superior choice. He was kind and generous to his fellow nobles, especially those in positions he could use for his own gain. He was a healer and priest by trade, but sometimes his experiments required some finesse to be authorized, so being on everyone's good side was imperative.

He took his seat next to the beautiful Ravin, the fragrance from her long, curly, brown hair exciting him. She was the receiver to the Master Purser and would be of great use to him in his personal endeavors. He gave her a seductive smile as he sat close by and could almost hear her heart began to beat harder for him.

"How do you do, Martis?" Ravin asked, unable to take her eyes off him. He looked so handsome in his long, white robes with golden embroidery. His black belt that ran around his waist held various pouches, along with folded cloth running almost to the floor with the Solstice Gardens seal expertly sewn into the center.

"Well now, I am doing just fine," he said softly, capturing her gaze in his own, locking into her sight. "We really need to catch up, don't we?

It's been far too long." He drew out his hand, making sure to brush against her as he firmly pressed his palms against the arm rests. He searched the details of her attire while breathing in the intoxicating aromas of her perfume. Her outfit relied heavily on brown leather and dark purple, which he made sure he had previously mentioned were his favorite color combinations, and now knew he had her in his pocket.

"Martis, I would absolutely love to. I have heard you spend most your time up in Solstice now. Can I come visit you there?" Her cheeks blushed.

He leaned in closer, whispering, "No need to travel all that way, I will come for you when I am free and take you out for a ride. I have a lot of horses that need some exercise."

"Oh certainly, I am free whenever you call on me, Martis." She chuckled softly, shifting her position on her seat to get closer to him. She sat there patiently, waiting for his attention to return as he greeted the other nobles around him.

Paladin Lanthor pounded his heavy metal gauntlet on his chair arm to call attention to the council and its spectators. "We have called this meeting to discuss the threat we have been faced with over the passing months," he announced, standing stoically in front of the council, his gaze slowly taking in the entirety of the crowd.

"We have yet to determine the cause of this deadly and mysterious plague but please rest assured that we have our best healers on the job of tracking down its cause and a cure." He shifted the massive weight of his Paladin armor on his shoulders. "We have all been victims and have lost loved ones from the plague, but we will not stop or give up fighting until we solve this plight." Several beads of sweat rolled down his forehead.

Martis noticed him wavering and stood up without missing a beat. "I have been on the frontlines of this pandemic and risked my own life for yours," he said to the council. The people threw up their hands and cheered, shouting their gratitude, the sound echoing loudly through the chamber. "I have been working tirelessly to find a cure and I vow that I will not stop until I have found one." Martis looked up to Lanthor and nodded, then took his seat again.

"You are our savior," Ravin whispered, her hand going to her chest as if breathless.

Lanthor managed a smile. "Thank you, Martis." He pounded his fist to bring back order. "The mander Infection has unfortunately spread far and wide, affecting other settlements as well. We are forced in these desperate times to shut our gates to travelers until we have found a suitable cure. The more we quarantine ourselves away from the many the fewer casualties we will have."

He paused, bracing himself for the protests.

Citizens shouted in rage to the idea of the gates closing, it was their only source of trade income and travel. It was only being closed off to keep the rich safe while the farmers worked feverishly outside the city gates to feed them. 1st Paladin Rhyker looked across Lanthor to meet eyes with Scarlett, the 3rd paladin. A look of confusion spread across their faces.

"I have been told this will help control the spread of the plague and aid us in finding a cure faster," Lanthor called out, landing on deaf ears as the people argued amongst each other. Lanthor's appearance worsened as he looked over to Martis; he was only following the healers request and doing what he was told.

Martis arose to his feet, tall and unflinching to the masses. "Calm yourselves!" he shouted with authority as everyone paused. He gave the crowd a warm smile and spread his arms, open wide in offering. "As you heard, Lanthor will be closing the gates to the main city." He paused briefly. "For the good of the city, I am sure." He looked back to Lanthor with a defiant smirk. "But, friends, fear not, for there is still hope for all who seek it. I am opening my doors at Solstice Gardens for any and all who need it. We will get through this time together, noble or poor, and all are welcome. The Creator, Baladar will provide and keep us safe."

Rhyker and Scarlett shared a worried look. "Who is Baladar?" Rhyker whispered. No one had talked to them about these plans, and they felt unprepared.

ARKANGEL

Scarlett only shook her head in confusion as a worried look formed along her brows. "Shouldn't he mean Galigus?"

"It is there that we will defeat this evil together and rise up strong in the creator's name," Martis shouted with such passion and energy that he brought many to tears. The fits of rage and anger quickly turned to praise again as they cheered Martis's name in calling him their savior.

Martis's knees felt weak as he heard his name called out. *As it rightfully should be*, he thought. His heart pounded hard in his chest and his breathing became heavy. Ravin clapped hard and stood from her seat in appreciation as the crowd followed.

Rhyker and Scarlett looked again at each other in disbelief of what was happening. Rhyker wished they sat closer so they may decipher what was happening. It almost seemed planned to persuade the voice of the people to back Martis. Scarlett wondered how the normally compassionate and honorable Lanthor could fall for such mockery. She wondered if he could even see what was happening as she looked at him standing there mindless, just gazing into the crowd.

Rhyker was a battle-hardened veteran who had fought for Sanctuary for many generations and was now the commander of the entire Noble army. The very army he and Scarlett had trained to protect the city. He had never seen Lanthor fail to put the people first, even in times of war; he knew something was amiss.

Scarlett was the paladin who ultimately oversaw developments in technologies and medicine advancement and was shocked that none of this news or decisions were brought to her attention before the meeting. She had been directing the exploration of a cure and would never advise or agree to such an irrational decision. She was also the overseer of the paymasters' treasury and knew the ramifications of halting trade could cripple their economy if the gates stayed closed for an extended period of time.

Lanthor called out again to get everyone's attention, ignoring Rhyker's and Scarlett's attempts at speaking to him.

"To ensure the safety of all who leave to Solstice Gardens, I will lend the support of half our army to not only escort the travelers but also to stand guard around the gardens themselves," Lanthor stated, looking to Martis for approval.

The people nodded their heads in agreement and appreciation, but they all looked to Martis as he stood to bow to all the people, a grin spreading from ear to ear.

"Sire, you can't do this," Rhyker pleaded in protest to Lanthor.

"What's done is done," Lanthor said with a dismissing wave of his hand. The people continued to cheer their support as Rhyker stormed out of the chamber, exiting to the rear of the room. Scarlett stood up, visibly upset as well, and followed him through the back.

"Wait up!" Scarlett called out, picking up speed to catch up with Rhyker, who had already made it halfway down the long hallway.

Almost everything was bright white and well-lit due to the multitude of large windows to the sides and clear panels in the ceiling. Rhyker turned back to Scarlett, who had caught up with him. She was so agile, even in her heavy silver and gold Paladin armor. Her beauty was undeniable, the kindness in her eyes and face hiding well her ferocity on the battlefield. She always made him smile. Since she was promoted to 3rd Paladin, they had gotten very close but had to hide their true affections for each other from everyone else.

"What should we do?" Scarlett asked.

"What can we do? Lanthor has made up his mind," he grumbled in response, looking down to the floor in frustration.

"We need to talk to him, surely we can put some sense into him." She tried to meet his gaze while reaching for his hand.

"I talked with him several days ago and although distraught, he wasn't irrational like he sounded today. It was like he was distracted. I am sure he is just overtaken by guilt; you know how serious he takes the protection of the city."

"Martis!" Rhyker blurted out between his heavy breaths. "He must be up to something. The way he played the people and council like that?"

"You know he has to always feel important and center stage, that is nothing new," she said, placing her hand on his arm for comfort.

"Maybe, but this feels like more than his usual ego trips. This feels like he has something else going on and it's giving me a bad feeling." His mind churned with ideas.

"I know you, Rhyker, and you need to let this go. Don't do anything foolish, I am sure it will all blow over soon."

"Then what about the next time? Or time after that? Soon they will be bypassing us and going straight to that sniveling idiot. I am not going to send half my force, right out into the open, just south of ember elves territory." He shook his head repeatedly. "They will see it as an act of aggression and ignite another war, one of which we cannot win with our army split in half. It would be suicide," he said with conviction, worry for his men weighing heavily in his heart.

Scarlett pulled close and kissed him, trying to pull him from his anger. "You go cool off and I will go handle Lanthor. Go straight to the barracks and I'll meet you there this evening," she said with a sly smile and a wink.

She had gotten his attention. "Alright I'll go, just let me know if you find out anything, okay? Otherwise, I might as well get my men prepped for the long march to war."

Scarlett's smile spread as her eyes darted down each side of the halls before leaning in to plant another kiss on his cheek, then turned to walk back towards the court. "Hold onto that for me until later will ya?" she said playfully.

Rhyker nodded, touching his cheek lightly and continuing his walk through the side tower and down the steps, deep in thought. He knew it was his duty to protect the people, and leading the army gave him certain power, but things were spiraling out of control with the plague and now their only army being split down the middle. He turned from the barracks as he approached, knowing he needed to take action.

Martis left the chamber more pleased with himself than he could have dreamed. His grin went ear to ear, the jump in his step, were just the visual signs of his excitement caused from his plans all falling into place. He normally would linger around after such an event, taking notes on the local happenings and chatting with the other nobles, but he had important things to do today.

He cut through the stables off the main courtyard and exited the castle's inner walls through one of the side gates, then into the lower wealth housing where he frequented; it made it easier to slip in and out of the castle without being seen by any of his high-born peers. The buildings consisted of multi-tiered structures to house the ever-growing population. Small, covered ditches ran through the streets and out the castle walls through grates, where the smell of rotten food and waste seeped in where the sewer service exited into a nearby stream. The homeless sat outside the walls, huddled up in patches of hay or foliage, anything to stay warm.

Martis approached a group of sick people, huddled around a community fire. "How do we fare today? What can the creator provide for you?" The men and women coughed and groaned, not wanting to be mocked by a noble.

Martis got a questioning look on his face, for usually people were drawn to his charm. He kneeled into the muddy road, his perfectly cleaned white robe sloshing in the filth, slathered on the street. "The creator has provided for you all today," he stated, holding out his hands and dropping several coins into their laps.

The sickly looked up into his tantalizing stare. "Creator Galigus be praised," a toothless old woman called out, joining the lifted spirits of the others.

Martis chuckled and gave the old woman a loving smile, "Oh dear I fear Galigus has abandoned us to the plague, but our true creator Baladar will save us all."

"Thank you so much, kind sir, your generosity is unequaled," one of the men said, gripping the coins tightly in his unwashed hands.

Martis rose back up to his feet, extending his hand down to the poor people of the district. "My name is Martis, my friends." They all nodded and smiled up to him, hearing of the good deeds that followed his name.

One of the women erupted into a harsh, mucus-laden cough, recoiling from the group. "Martis sir," she gasped, struggling to breathe through the pain in her chest. "Do we have the plague? You shouldn't be here for fear you may catch it." She clutched at her throat.

Martis laid his hand on her shoulder and leaned in close. "No, you do not have the plague, my dear friends, I will do everything in my power to make you healthy again." He placed his arm around another's shoulder in embrace. "Now, let us pray. Please, our Savior Baladar, take these sick and help purge them of any impurities."

One by one, the sick graciously thanked him and pleaded for him not to leave. Martis walked away from the now cheerful group even more pleased with himself than he had been before.

The castle's outer walls encompassed large expanses of land for the different courtyards, markets, or districts inside the city. The main walls dividing the different districts had a tall, central section with different levels of walls and platforms encircling the insides for easier travel during a siege. He slipped through the front portcullis that had been opened to let the merchants leave and continued his way up the road towards Solstice Gardens.

The road was long, inclining slowly up a hill through a divide in the forest before winding its way north. He met up with Feora in the exact place he had chosen as their meeting place outside the city to talk business. He couldn't raise any suspicion amongst the other nobles, for an Arkhunter and a noble working together would raise eyebrows.

Several miles up the road they could hear what sounded like a battle taking place, screams and cries for help echoing down the path. Feora charged ahead with Martis in tow, pulling her twin long swords from her sides.

They ascended a steep, narrow turn in the road to see a caravan, with a merchant frantically screaming on top of an overturned wagon. Several of his under-equipped guards fought bravely against a pair of the salamanders. The closer of the two creatures whipped the old sword out of the hands of one of the guards with its tail, leaving him defenseless. The savage creatures started in on him, cleaving chunks of flesh from his chest, rending straight through his leather armor. The other lizard leapt forward, ignoring a glancing blow from the armed guard, and serrated the arm off the sword-less man, sending him tumbling to the ground. The other two guards backed up into each other attempting to defend one another. The salamanders clawed and slashed in their direction with a shrill shrieking noise, sending the horrified guards into a panic.

The fallen guard at their feet suddenly convulsed, screaming in pain as the shreds of skin left upon his opened chest tore open, his ribcage piercing through. The man called out for help as he attempted to keep himself together with his remaining hand. His body snapped and contorted as his bones tore from his body and the leftover skin shed off. A sleek, black, scaly hide was revealed underneath the remaining tissue as its snout broke through his face. The guards watching in fear at their feet lost all resolve and attempted to flee. The salamanders, being far faster and stronger than a human, quickly caught up and cut them down, standing and watching as they writhed in pain until their newborn brethren tore forth. They exchanged a rattle of shrieks and howls as they turned their attention to the merchant.

The guard laid flat on top of the cart, trying to hide but failing to get into cover in time. He watched in terror as the group of lizards slithered their tongues through gnarled teeth and stared him down, large yellow reptilian eyes narrowing in on their prey.

Feora jumped clear over the top of a formation of rocks and swung her swords hard into the legs of a lizard, knocking it to the ground. Martis cried out a taunt to draw their attention from the defenseless merchant and charged into the group of monsters. They let out a shrill cry as they clawed and slashed at the red-haired woman. Inhumanely fast, with her Arkhunter training she easily out maneuvered their aggressive attacks, cutting and tripping them down as she spun and dodged.

Martis punched at the face of the creature charging him, crushing part of its skull inwards as it swung its long claws at him. Martis was fast, catching the creature's forearm at a dead stop. He cried out as he unleashed a flurry of punches into the beast's chest. It flew back unbalanced and fell to the ground in a roll, its tail whipping through the air in an attempt to catch itself.

Feora swung and stabbed her swords quickly, piercing through the creature's thick hide, lacerating their arms and legs. One of the salamanders let out a deafening howl as it lunged at Martis, coming face to face with him, their eyes locking as he stood his ground. He shouted and threatened the creature, raising his fist to strike as it backed down. They all simultaneously let out small cries of protest, turning to each other for validation and then fleeing into the woods.

The merchant atop the wagon was shocked. "How did you do that?" he called down in disbelief of what he had just seen.

Martis straightened his robe, regaining his composure. "I have the creator on my side to protect me," he answered in confidence, brushing dirt from himself.

"You saved my life … and the lives of my family," the merchant said in appreciation, still uncertain of his safety.

"Are any of you hurt?" Martis asked, Feora coming to his side with a smile as she flicked the green tar from her blade. Her smile faded, turning to a scowl as she watched several children exit the covered wagon.

The merchant slid down the overturned wagon, looking over his children for any serious injuries. "Just shaken up is all, but my guards are dead, along with my eldest.". He turned to look at the empty pile of his son's skin with pieces of his face staring back up at him. He turned to divert his other children away from the bloody mess, trembling from shock.

"You saved my babies, thank you, thank you!" a woman cried out in tears as she exited the wagon, supporting her pregnant belly. She stumbled down in pain, lying on the rocky ground.

"Shyla!" The merchant called out, coming to the aid of his wife.

"The baby, it's coming!"

Martis went to her side, resting his hand on her stomach and closing his eyes. He could tell that these people were tired by the way their horses stood, and had likely been traveling for many, many days. He examined their cloths, features, and expressions. They were all tired, scared, and by the quality of goods and wagon they had, they didn't have enough money to properly take care of their growing family.

"We need to get you to safety and into some proper care," Martis said, looking the woman in the eyes, seeing the stress from the attack overcoming her. "Feora, put Shyla here on the back of one of the horses and escort them to Solstice Gardens." Then he looked over the goods, knowing they wouldn't be able to carry everything. "Make sure you set them up in the best of cabins."

Martis looked at Shayla. "We will take you to my homestead, Solstice Gardens, and see to it that you are properly cared for. It is a community of healers, and we can take care of you and your family and set you up with a small place of your own for the time being."

"But, sir, we have no coin to pay you for your generosity, I'm afraid. We come from Krustallos and Market Town with Aquarian goods for trade. We came all this way in hopes of starting a new life in Sanctuary."

Martis picked up on his uncertainty and reassured him Solstice was the right place for his family. "We will take you in, free of charge. The creator provides and we can assure your family is safe. You must come with us. I will deliver the goods for you myself and send someone to repair your cart. I know the perfect place and they will pay a fair price, so you will have it in case you ever need it."

"Sir, you have done us a great service, but this is all we own, I cannot just hand it over to someone we just-."

Martis leaned in close, cutting him off and looking deep into his eyes. "You will, and you will go with Feora while I trade your goods for you." Martis leaned back from the man's empty gaze. "I am Martis, by the way. And you are?" Martis offered his hand.

The man blinked several times as if waking from a deep dream. "I am Kain, pleasure to meet you, Martis. I will take my family to your community with Feora. We really appreciate your hospitality." He turned and walked back to the wagon.

Martis smiled at Feora and nodded. "Please escort them to safety and I will return shortly, I have business to attend to," he said, unintentionally rubbing his hands together in excitement. He was indeed pleased with how the day was turning out.

"Will do, sir," Feora responded, returning his pleased expression. She turned to Kain and Shyla, gesturing for Kain to lead the children and horse down the road. "Off we go then. Everyone try to relax; we will be there in just a few short hours."

Martis rummaged through the wagon for anything he deemed valuable, putting it into a satchel, and throwing it over his back. Then he turned to return to Sanctuary.

Rhyker stared in disbelief of what he had just witnessed. He saw Feora and Martis effortlessly fight and scare off a pack of the infected manders. Then convince them to hand over everything they owned and follow Feora to Solstice. So many questions cycled through his head he could barely focus on one before leading to another. Why was Martis with an Arkhunter? They were part of a nefarious sect under the reign of Paladin Malik. He knew some of them were still around but were not supposed to be in practice; he thought it odd Martis was somehow associated.

How was Martis so strong to single-handedly halt one of the savage creatures dead in its tracks with a single punch? More importantly, how did he convince the merchant to leave his family's wealth behind? Was he doing the same to Lanthor? His questions only piled higher. He knew he needed to follow, but with the duo now split who would be best to follow? He decided that since thousands of men were about to be stationed in Solstice Gardens, he had better go see what was truly going on in Martis's estate.

Rhyker followed close behind Feora and the merchant's family for the better part of the day until they arrived at Solstice. The entire property was surrounded by a tall, thick hedges that acted like a perimeter wall. He watched them enter the front courtyard area and was surprised to see no gate or guards manning the entrance.

He followed close enough behind the hedges to peek inside, seeing large plots of gardens, ponds, and statues. Several workers could be seen roaming the gardens watering and trimming the plants; they seemed to all be wearing dark green tunics and soft, brown pants. His nerves eased up slightly as he noticed everyone was happy, smiles and laughter had by all he could see. Groups of children ran around playing, trying to catch butterflies or chasing each other. The place actually seemed like a great retreat for the less fortunate.

Several smaller cabins sat along the inside of the wall of shrubs encircling the property providing ample space for a town's worth of residents. The gardens were split into four main quadrants surrounding a central cluster of large buildings. Decorative gates and shrubs lined the various gardens, creating unique and beautiful pathways to explore. Many of the varieties of plant life he didn't recognize, and some of the others weren't normally found this far inland. The corner of the massive estate he was closest to had an expertly crafted and maintained lagoon, complete with a waterfall. To the other corner he could see a light forest outfitted with hammocks, and people spending the nice day lounging with a book.

He watched as Feora led the people to the center of the town and took them into one of the buildings. He decided he would need to go in further to get a better look but was afraid of being recognized in his grand paladin armor.

He removed the big, bulky silver and gold breastplate and pauldrons, stashing them deep under the hedge wall. He then unstrapped his leg and arm guards to wrap up in his blue and golden cloak and stashed it with the rest of his armor. His brown and black padded leather was obviously a noble outfit, but he hoped it wouldn't bring him any unwanted attention. He began walking down the main entry path towards the buildings in the center of town. He could see the biggest building on the far side was a church, beside what looked like a housing facility. On the right was the building Feora had taken the newcomers into, before deciding to go to one of the fancier buildings on the left. From there he should be able to get a better view of what was happening across the way.

As he walked, critters scurried between the different mounds of plants; he looked to see many different types of birds flying around, and he wondered how he had managed to even lure the local wildlife to his gardens. The songs of chirping birds filled his ears as he walked, and fluffy, brightly colored panjams wandered unafraid of the humans. He could see a decorated trellis behind the building he was traveling to and thought it best to head in its direction and see inside the windows.

He approached the black rod, iron trellis, heavily woven with a blossoming ivy, and came across the first guard he had seen. He stood outside what looked like a gate to get inside a fenced area of the garden. He walked up and around alongside, seeing a solid wall of plants blocking view to whatever was inside the fenced area. The only guard he could see was the one in front of the gate behind the manor; he decided he must be Martis's.

"How goes your day, friend?" Rhyker asked the guard, acting as if he was just strolling by.

"Oh, just another fine day thanks to the creator," the guard replied, looking Rhyker head to toe, scanning for weapons.

Rhyker was a tall, imposing person to behold, and a source of nightmare on the battlefield when fully clad in his paladin battle armor. Without it, he was still intimidating to most and in peak physical condition, with black hair tucked cleanly behind his ears. For his age, one might think he had found a fountain of eternal youth.

"Good to hear it," he said, stopping beside the guard as if lingering for a conversation. "May I ask what is in this section of the garden?"

"This is the master's private garden," he remarked, looking up into Rhyker's eyes, his posture shifting uneasily.

"Oh good, is he in there now? I would like to meet with him. I have a few questions about the beautiful landscaping here." Rhyker smiled, hoping to calm the man who was becoming visibly tense.

The guard put his hand on his sword hilt tightly. "Who are you?"

Rhyker took a step back, putting his hands up a little and taking another step back. "I don't want any trouble, friend."

"I don't recognize your clothes and what do you want with the Master? He is the only one who knows who the creator needs." The guard's eyes narrowed, as if gauging how best to take down his threat.

"Who the creator needs? Needs for what? I am sorry, I just got here…" he studied the man's posture, armor, and weapon.

"You are not a follower of the true creator," the guard shouted, lifting his sword from its scabbard.

Rhyker quickly slammed his fist against his elbow, forcing his sword back down into his scabbard as his right-hand balled into a fist, landing several quick jabs into the guard's unarmored throat. The guard coughed, attempting to breathe through his crushed windpipe, his eyes frantically searching for help. Rhyker palmed the man's face and slammed his head back into the metal trellis bars so hard that his steel helmet did little to protect him. His body went limp as he slumped to the ground.

Rhyker looked around to make sure he hadn't caught anyone's attention, leaning over to search through his pockets until finding a set of keys. He scanned the area again and saw a long strip of tall flowers mixed with a leafy Ivy that covered a raised planter. He removed the man's armored vest and helmet and stashed the body in the tall plants.

Flipping the vest over his chest, he shook his head and stretched his jaw as if it were sore from taking a hit. Then he let out a small groan of discomfort and moved his hand to relieve tension from his eyes. After a few seconds, he looked up again to scan his surroundings and his face now perfectly matched the man he had just buried in the planter. He flexed his jaw again, moving it from side to side as he attached his scabbard to his belt. His eyes began to glow a hazy golden color before settling onto the guard's brown eyes, replacing his usual blue.

Martis approached the side entrance to the main castle courtyard and slung the hefty bag of trinkets over his shoulder. He couldn't care less for their value, as money meant nothing to him with what the creator had promised him. But what they lacked in value, they made up for in leverage and a way to sway people's favor. He was able to slip past unseen and uninterrupted as the guards called out for a group of travelers to halt. He slipped past on his way to the less fortunate districts and made his way to a popular stand he liked to preach on.

Because of his busy schedule and plans he had already put into motion for the day, he couldn't linger long. He dumped the trinkets to the stage and called out to anyone who would listen.

"The creator provides for all today, thanks be to him," he shouted gleefully, catching several heads that turned to listen. People slowly began to approach. "Please, my friends, anyone in need please take what you must to provide for you and your family. Buy food, medicines, supplies, anything you need. The creator has given me gifts to give in Baladar's name. Please, take what you need, and remember there is always a safe place for you at Solstice Gardens. Any and all are welcome."

Smiles spread from face to face as the people took the trinkets and rushed off to the markets. "Praise be to you, sir!" and "Thank the Creator!" the people shouted, among other things.

One of the sick he had seen earlier appeared, barely able to walk. "Thank you, Martis, you truly are a blessing," she said to him before erupting into a violent cough, wrapping her arms hard against her stomach.

"Fear not, my friends, Baladar is with you and will guide you," he called out with a smile, before leaving through the gates in haste.

CHAPTER 4

"A LEADER AWAKENS"

Flashes of violence flickered into view; men, women, and children all overcome by an endless torrent of flame. A flash of a large demon terrified him, laughing in a dreadful taunt, rendering him weak and helpless. His chest rose and fell heavily as his forehead dripped with sweat. He saw a man's silhouette in the distance stabbing into a row of mindless people, eagerly awaiting to be next, blood freely spilling out and making his stomach churn. Rivers of blood flowed at their feet with parts of humans, elves, and giants floating past so disfigured they were unidentifiable. He shouted for everything to stop, to leave him alone, but nothing would listen. The demon and the silhouetted man took pleasure at watching him suffer as his breathing quickened and his body convulsed in panic. He screamed out in terror as a bright light washed everything away, then the screaming stopped. A woman walked closer to him, and because he could not move, she drew even closer. He couldn't make out any details except the edges of her small frame and long hair, swaying with her walk. As she got closer, she changed, becoming that of a child, and reached out to him while motioning for his help. She leaned in close before dissipating into shadow, her hand outstretched towards his.

"Kaiden..."

ARKANGEL

Kaiden jolted awake with a deep intake of air, filling his lungs. He looked around the small room, not immediately recognizing where he was. The seat he lay in shook as the door next to him flew open. He saw Gorman's massive fingers curl around the wooden door.

"Yous ok, kid?" Gorman asked, concern etched across his face.

Kaiden slowly shook his head in thought, wiping tears from his face. "No," he said slowly, "I just had a nightmare."

"Your brain be worked out straight?" Gorman grunted.

"No, no, nothing like that, it felt more like a warning. I just saw people... well, more than just people, it was everyone being murdered. There was a demon and something else, or someone else, killing everyone and nobody did anything to stop it. It was awful."

"Hah... I have dem too, they be nothin. Maybe you be a soldier before?" Gorman offered, looking him over. "Na, maybe a squire runt, but ya seen battle before, kid. It be a start."

Kaiden snapped to. What he really wanted to know was who the woman was. His thoughts wandered as he stood up, then made his way outside. The small town had a depressing feel to it after the previous day's attack. People ran around collecting bodies and pieces while others cleaned up bloodstains. Carpenters pounded on small metal spikes, repairing the damaged homes.

"They came for you last night in your sleep, well it did, a thing more like it, just flew right in, at least I believe it was after you, never can tell what is coincidence and what's not these days," Finn called out from the side of the house.

Kaiden walked around, seeing the winged creature stretched out, tied to posts with pieces of wood propping its appendages up.

"What is this thing?" Kaiden asked, afraid of the long-winded answer he was most likely about to get.

Finn merely shrugged. "Well... see it has six appendages, 1, 2, 3..." He counted and pointed with both hands and a foot. "It has six, it's rare, never seen anything humanoid like it, if I haven't mentioned that before?" Finn stared at the creature with a blank look on his face.

Kaiden looked up to see a woman collapse in tears next to a stained patch of grass. "It's not safe here, I need to get away from these people if these things are after me," he said, turning back to look up at the small house. "I don't want them to suffer again because I am here."

Gorman walked back out the front door with his arms full, rolled mats and blankets in one and a pile of spears in the other. "We be talkin while you was out, kid. We gunna take you to Sanctuary." He spouted with a quick glance to Finn, throwing all the gear into the back of a small wagon.

"You been dere before?" Gorman asked Kaiden, walking up the steps to grab another armload of supplies and food.

Kaiden thought for a second, trying to recall anything from his past. The name felt familiar but couldn't recall. "No, I can't remember, at least nothing comes to mind," he responded, still disappointed in his lack of memories.

Finn's eyes lit up at the opportunity to share some knowledge. "Sanctuary is very old in human years and is the largest city of man and constructed by early human engineers along with dwarves which sealed their alliance together against their common enemy, the giants and trolls. Ogres lacked the intelligence to join with the giants…" He stopped, looking for a long second at Gorman, then began blinking repeatedly in anticipation. "Or smart, too smart and often became a wild card you could say, an uncontrollable variable if you will in the ranks of the giants forcing King Stonehammer the Terrible to denounce the ogres and forcing them to flee in need of human protection. That is when the humans found what great laborers and soldiers they could be with proper training. In fact, rumor has it that one of the great paladins took an ogress lover once to strengthen the human lines… but that is little more than rumors and legends."

Gorman winced at what he had just heard, filling his chest with anxiety with seeing his mother again. "Let da boy be, fish, we be dere soon enough," Gorman huffed.

Finn blinked in thought, wondering if he had done something wrong. "I haven't even gotten to the interesting parts yet; the walls are so high that they even tower over the giants and none have ever breached them. The rock they used for the walls were melted by dwarven forges in an old citadel they built in the crafters district. They poured them into intricate interlocking pieces that help to strengthen the walls along with a crystalline powder they add into the mix before it dried, making it incredibly resilient to damage." Finn's voice fluttered with excitement, his little mandibles along his jaw dancing with his smile.

"Sorry, I tend to talk quickly when I get excited," he said, lifting up the rib-like protrusions from his chest to reveal a soft, pink tissue. "Let my gills breath a bit...get it?" he added, chuckling to himself.

Gorman caused a loud clatter as he threw a few pans into the wagon. "Pack yer stuff, Fish," he grunted.

Finn looked around a little. "Oh, I don't have anything, I live completely off the land, so I don't have any personal items and it's just excessive weight that slows down travel." His long finger was pointed up, as if what he'd just said was something greatly profound.

"Not even food?" Kaiden asked, immediately wondering when the last time was, *he'd* eaten. All he could draw, however, was a blank.

"I eat a variety of things that I just pick up whatever is close by," Finn began to explain, before Gorman interrupted him.

"What if dere be nothing?" Gorman asked, completely taken back by the thought of not having food nearby.

Finn cocked his head, not really understanding the question. "Then I don't eat, I only need to eat a few times a month, so I just wait," he said, hopping up into the wagon and laying across the bench with his long legs dangling over the edge.

Kaiden smiled at the thought at how his two monstrous-sized companions would look in such a small wagon.

"Good, den more food fer us, huh, kid?" Gorman said to Kaiden with a wide grin. His single eyebrow lifted up in excitement, with a long entanglement of hairs arched over his tired eye.

"How long will it take to get there?" Kaiden asked, intentionally looking at Gorman for the answer in an attempt avoid another long-winded Finn response.

The tactic, however, did not work.

"Well, it would depend on how many stops we make and our average speed I suppose but it will take up a long day's ride to get to market town and another day from there unless we are delayed by…"

"Wes ain't stoppin!" Gorman huffed as he jumped up onto the front of the wagon, positioning himself for the long ride ahead.

Kaiden followed suit, climbing up the large wheel and settling down amongst all the gear in the back. They set out on the long dirt road that wound out from the forest and away from Hengegrove. Kaiden sat and watched the town get smaller every minute as the overburdened wagon rolled on, the two horses struggling to gain any momentum.

They traveled for several hours, Kaiden taking in the beautiful, grassy hills rolling under the horizon. Patches of vibrant wildflowers dotted the landscape, accompanied only by rare formations of rocks. Herds of large wooly animals he didn't recognize roamed across the plains and grazed in the open pastures. The occasional massive beast could be seen rummaging around in the distance trying to find its next meal or defend its territory. He marveled at the variety of creatures one could see if you only took the time to look. He felt wonderment, as if it had been the first time seeing such vibrant wilderness.

Kaiden was lost in thought, trying desperately to remember who he was or where he was from, anything at all that would help identify himself. He hoped Sanctuary might hold the answer; if it was the largest human city maybe he had family there that would recognize him.

After an unusually long silence, Finn piped up. "Anyone have any stories to help pass the time? I am not used to traveling with others, but I imagine there is more conversing than this, communication often pulls your attention away from the journey itself, giving the illusion that we are traveling faster." He looked up into the cloudy sky.

Kaiden snapped to attention when he heard Gorman respond. "I aint got nothin but war stories, da same ones I be tryin to forget. Da kid ain't know nothin but his name, so no stories," he grumbled, hoping the loud sounds from the wheels on rocks would deter him from sharing.

"Well, I have thousands of stories locked in this here noggin all floating around like a school of fish in the sea, here let me catch one for you," Finn said, gazing into the sky as if searching through the clouds. "Ah yes, this is a good one," he announced as he rambled inaudible words for several seconds, gathering his thoughts in order.

"I was young, about 300 or so, living in the underwater palace of Krustallos with my family of about 100 other younglings. It was the day I decided that I wanted to leave the calm comfort of the ocean and adventure up onto land. I was swimming near the surface when I saw movement outside the water. I came from a long line of explorers and cartographers who made maps to share with us underwater dwellers who hadn't shed their scales yet for surface life. They had found we were the only intelligent life in our land, with much of the surface wild and overgrown with trees and foliage. I swam up to the surface near the beach where I had seen the movement, walking on the hot sand for the first time. It was hard to breathe; our lungs and gills take time and practice to adapt to the abundant air on land and I fell to my knees and saw a small being standing along the rocks looking back at me. It was young looking and about four feet tall with long pointy ears and vibrant blue eyes. Its skin white as porcelain and wore simple grass clothes as it tried to stay out of the direct hot sun, but it ventured closer towards me, curious. I tried to communicate but just couldn't breathe any longer, so I retreated back into the shallow water. A wave washed up to its feet and it back peddled in fear. We locked eyes, coming to the understanding we were both trapped in our own environment, not able to interact. So, we just sat and looked at each other before it ran away, retreating back into the protective shade of the forest.

After that I knew I wanted to go ashore and see all the wonders of the land and would follow in the footsteps of my family to become an explorer. Later we came to realize we were not alone and the first of the elves had been born, the age of the lonely Aquarians had ended." He smiled at the old memory resurfacing; pretty positive nothing had been embellished in the least.

Kaiden sat looking into the far distant landscape, processing Finn's story. "How was the age of your kind over if you are still here?" he asked, wondering what an empty world would be like. Would it feel as lonely as he felt without his memory, he pondered.

"We didn't end you see, just that we were created by the creator in the world how he wanted it at the time. We suppose that he let us be while wanting to take time with the beginning of the other races, like the elves, the moon, ember, water, and the elusive mystic elves. We were just the first, but many more came after them, each new race having time to shape and grow before the next was created and now you humans are here, but it would seem the prophecy was indeed true in that your race will fall at the dawn of the new. The plague has been unrelenting against humans but hopefully we can stop it before you fascinating fragile creatures are wiped out."

Kaiden's gaze turned up to the beautiful, cloudy sky, thinking and processing what had happened the last few days. He began to worry about what would come next and realized just how frightened he really was. He was lucky he'd found the group he now traveled with.

Finn was surprisingly quiet as he wondered what they were actually going to accomplish in Sanctuary. He knew the violent past the humans had struggled with towards any form of arking and wondered how they would react to Kaiden possibly being their only key to a cure. With the signals of the prophecy unfolding, he hoped that they would recognize his importance before it was too late. Sure, there had been bloodshed between the ever-growing races of Allterra, but he hadn't seen any type of plague to be so destructive and so elusive in origin. A tinge of excitement trickled down his spine at the thought of catching one of the quillbacks alive to study.

ARKANGEL

The daylight began to fade as the long day of traveling soon came to an end. Suddenly Gorman snapped the reigns and quickly stood up to scan off towards a patch of forest. Finn jumped from the wagon, looking to see what could have spooked the mighty Gorman. Kaiden rose as well in the back of the wagon, planting a foot firmly on the edge of a sidewall.

A shrill scream exploded out from the woods as the three stood frozen in place, watching for anything. A woman's voice rang out from the woods, followed by cries of what sounded like young children.

"Help! Help us!" the cry echoed from the tree line.

Gorman gave a worried look to Kaiden and then to Finn, not knowing what to expect would come out of the woods. The scream pierced through the thick forest once as more than one voice became apparent. Gorman then readied his dwarven, steam-operated vambrace, pumping the lever several times and placing a long, barbed bolt inside its barrel. He reached back, grabbing several spears and loading one into his massive crossbow. He stood firm on the front of the wagon and looked to see Finn put his fists up in a defensive stance.

"Take dis, fish, yous may need it," Gorman said, throwing Finn a spear and watching it just clang down to the rocky ground. Gorman's face sunk in surprise as Finn just shrugged his shoulders at him.

"I haven't received proper training in that, but it does look like a fascinating weapon," Finn responded.

Gorman grunted, pulling another spear from his back as the first of the women and children poured out of the forest. They saw the wagon with the large-armed ogre and desperately ran for him. Then multiple people burst through the trees screaming as they ran, clawing their way out of the thick brush.

Finn blinked rapidly, addressing the situation. He leapt into action, running to meet them halfway in the field, signaling the others to go to the wagon. "What is happening?" he called out as they passed.

Two men charged out, one covered head to toe in blood-soaked clothes. He called out in pain as he ran but in mid-step Finn watched his knee snap and the flesh from his leg tear off, flailing in the wind as he ran. A slick, black, clawed, limb extended out from the boney leg, snapping off as it charged. Soon his arms followed suit, tearing off to reveal the large, scaled arms shredding through his clothes and skin. His face and chest soon gave way to the transformation as the patches of quills sprouted from its back, leaving piles of flesh scattered across the field.

The man running next to him called out in terror seeing what had happened to his friend, now looking into its yellowish eyes as it snorted in his direction with its newly formed snout. The man fell to the ground when another creature dove on top of him from within the woods. It raked its claws at the man's back over and over while he screamed, looking up momentarily to lock eyes with Finn.

The lizard then lunged forth to meet up with the newly formed ally, ravenously sprinting towards the tall, aquatic creature. Finn put his arm under the last and smallest of the running children, scooping him up protectively against his hard chitin chest. The creatures closed in quickly as Finn made his way back towards the cart.

A long spear sailed past Finn's head, hitting one of the creatures square in the shoulder but barely slowing it down. Gorman reloaded his great crossbow and took another shot, this time hitting it in the lower abdomen, knocking it off its feet. The spear tore out its side when the creature rolled on the ground, releasing a horrible, shrieking noise. The cry was then answered by a wailing, snickering sound, cackling from deep in the woods, revealing that they are not alone.

The creature that had once been a man stood up fully transformed, a pile of loose flesh falling to its feet. The remaining lizard snagged Finn's back, sinking its claws into his hard, carapace back and using its grip to pull in closer. Its clawed feet leapt forward, sinking into his lower back and leg, sending Finn crashing into the ground. The child rolled free, stopping only a few feet from the entangled pair. The lizard's tail wrapped around and squeezed Finn's arm like a python, holding it firmly to the ground. Finn struggled to break free as the creature tirelessly slashed and bit at his chest and shoulder, tearing small pieces of hard scale and carapace from his body. The creature's other arm pinned Finn's second arm against the ground as he lay there helpless.

The terrified people reached Gorman and the wagon pleading for his help, pulling on him to save their children. Gorman managed to hurl another spear but missed, the people interrupting his shot. Kaiden's heart pounded in his chest while he watched the violent reality unfold in front of him so quickly as his new companion lay there struggling to survive. He gritted his teeth and clenched his fists as he leaped from the wagon to race to Finn's aid. He trembled as he ran, fist swinging high in the air as he shouted for the salamanders to stop their attack. As the wounded and the freshly transformed lizard reached Finn, Kaiden lunged high into the air, tackling the one on top of him. An explosive shockwave erupted from Kaiden's body with such force that the one in his arms exploded into a green and black mist, covering the other two that were sent hurling into the air. Finn was sent somersaulting backwards on the ground, slamming up against the wagon, knocked unconscious.

All the people screamed from the sudden burst of sound when they looked to see the dark, grey, scaled armor envelope around Kaiden's body, making him look like some sort of horrific creature. The two lizards sent soaring from the concussive blast crashed hard into the rocky terrain as Kaiden landed on his feet nearby. He grasped the one closest by the snout and, with little effort, tore its jaw completely from its face. It hissed in pain and defensively slashed at Kaiden, though it had little effect on his armored body.

Kaiden grabbed the large lizard by its neck and hurled it up into the air, where it whirled in place, Kaiden's forearms blades filling the beast with devastating lacerations. The creature then landed on the ground, kicking and squirming before stilling. Its companions let out deafening cries, and, in response, five more creatures launched themselves from the forest.

They all held out their arms as they ran, long, scythe-like claws outstretched. Then, with shrill shrieks, all six simultaneously ascended on Kaiden. The first, the apparent alpha of the pack, lunged at him, raking his claws as Kaiden punched straight through the creature's side, sinking his forearm blade deep in its torso. He whirled around and kicked the back of its head, sending it crashing to the ground. Another quickly lunged at him as Kaiden caught both its arms and kicked it hard in the chest, the force of the kick tearing its arms clear off and sending its torso sailing back.

Kaiden swung the creature's arms around to hit another one as it approached, then followed up with a kick to its back, sending it flying forward. With his foot he caught the leg of the falling creature, making it abruptly crash down into the rocky road with such force its jaw slammed shut and its long, slender fangs punctured through its upper snout. Kaiden's other foot spun through the air and landed at the back of the beast's head, crashing it into the ground. Two of the lizards came from the sides, grappling onto his arms and pulling him down, momentarily disabling him. A huge, clawed foot came down hard atop his chest, pinning him where he lay. It dropped to its horn-riddled knee and slashed as hard as it could against Kaiden's chest and face.

Gorman shouted and broke free from the panicked crowd, failing to care for their well-being and trampling through. He let loose the bolt in his vambrace; it sank deep into the creature's chest but still refused to stop attacking Kaiden. Gorman pulled another spear from his back and charged at the creatures still many yards away.

The scale-like armor encasing Kaiden's body held strong, taking only minor scratches from the creature's otherwise deadly lashings. He tried to pull his arm free, picking the lizard up clear off the ground, but it dug into the dirt as best it could to keep hold. Suddenly the blades on his forearms quickly extended and retracted, stabbing both anchors deep into their chests. The blades repeatedly extended and retracted, puncturing them multiple times before folding forward along his wrist and extending out several inches from his fists. He curled his arms up, impaling the two creatures on his arms and slamming them into the one atop his chest. His arm blades cut deep as they fell dead to his sides, and then he began to attack the one on his chest.

Seconds later the creature was severely wounded after taking multiple puncturing punches with the blades tearing away from its sides.

Kaiden reached up, grabbing it by its head as it howled in pain, and with a quick twist of his body slammed it hard into the ground and it went limp.

Gorman finally reached him, wide-eyed and shocked to see Kaiden standing there virtually unscathed by his attackers. He planted his spear through the skull of one of the fallen quillbacks in case it was smart enough to play dead. A golden glow radiated from Kaiden's armor as it retracted into thin air, causing him to faint at his knees. His eyes struggled open, staring at the ground, and then he carefully stood to survey the battlefield, taking note of the multiple dead lizards and Gorman towering above him.

"Yous ok, kid?" Gorman asked, surprised that he was still conscious written across his face.

Kaiden continued to look around, then saw Finn laying on his side against the wagon. "Yeah, I'm fine, Gorman. Did I do all this?" he asked, looking in disbelief. Gorman nodded and reached down to help him up off the ground. "Yes... Yes, I remember," Kaiden recounted slowly, walking to where Finn had been attacked.

Gorman followed, glancing a worried look to the fish man just lying in the dirt road.

"I remember a flash of bright light, then darkness, and quick movements, here, and then there. It all happened so fast." He motioned to where he had transformed and gently holding his hand to his chest as if it was sore from pain. "I remember being attacked repeatedly... then somehow breaking free and attacking back." He looked up in excitement to find Gorman back at the cart lifting Finn up off the ground and holding him up with his arm slung over his shoulder.

"Is he ok?" Kaiden called out, his excited mood shifting to worry.

"I ain't no fisherman but me would say he be hurt real bad," Gorman said, lifting him up to lay across the wagon.

Kaiden approached as Finn let out a startled moan, putting his hand to his chest. He felt around with his webbed fingers and lifted his flaps, where a human's ribs would sit, to check his gills. Small droplets of blood pooled underneath on bright pink flesh.

Finn's head tilted in thought. "Well upon inspection, gills are ok for the most part, interestingly enough they were unable to pierce through my thick carapace, though it will take some time to get these damaged ones repaired." He sat back up and held his chest. He took several deep breaths, watching as the flaps of scale rose and fell as it sifted the oxygen from the air into his three gills on each side.

"Well, it looks like you're the only fleshy one here soldier," Finn announced to Gorman with a smile, patting his shoulder several times and pressing a long finger onto his skin. "Even the kid's got you beat," he added with a chuckle as Gorman just shook his head with a dissatisfied grunt.

Gorman slammed the back of the wagon closed, causing Finn to fall over on his back. Kaiden laughed, relieved he was okay, and walked over to the crowd of people at the other end of the wagon.

"Is everyone ok?" Kaiden called out to the fifteen or so people who had made it out of the forest safely.

"Our Savior!" A woman called out as they rushed over to him.

"Who are you?" someone else asked. "What are you?" Another shouted.

Gorman approached them; the crowd suddenly intimidated by his hulking size. "What happened to yous?" he asked, taking a knee to get closer to their eye level. The children huddled behind the adults as they all questioned Kaiden, eyeing him over, never having seen or heard of anything like what had just happened.

An older man looked at Gorman, leaning heavily against the wagon. "We are refuges, traveling from our small village just west of here, Sandsran. Ever been there?" he asked wearily.

Gorman shook his head with a grunt. A woman piped up, "The plague struck, it's started with a traveler passing through and then the next day…" The woman began to tear up. "The next morning the place was tearing itself apart. Most of the fishermen stayed to fight them off so we could escape but I fear they have all been killed." She sniffled and wiped at her cheek, trying to be strong for the kids.

The elderly man nodded slowly in agreement, a tear streaming down his cheek. "We have no place to go, we have nothing but the clothes on our backs, nowhere to stay, no food, and no supplies. What do we do?" He hung his head, looking down to the children. His old, skinny fingers sifted softly through his granddaughter's hair. Her little hands clenched his tattered trousers as she looked shyly at Kaiden, her stained, pink dress almost torn into shreds from their escape through the woods.

"You can take our wagon and our supplies, we are almost to our destination anyways," Kaiden offered, pointing to all the stuff stacked in the cart.

"Hey! Dats my stuff!" Gorman shouted, glaring at Kaiden with his eye.

"Stuff which we do not need, for we are well on our way to Sanctuary and can manage the walk, these people can't." Kaiden gestured to the children and elderly to climb aboard.

Finn tapped Gorman on his stomach. "I think we could all use the walk," he said with a sly smile.

Gorman slapped his hand away. "Fine, take da cart, we just take food."

"No, leave it, Gorman, we will buy more when we get to Market town, they need it a lot more than we do," Kaiden commanded.

Gorman's mouth dropped, staring in disbelief that he was to be taking orders.

Finn got out of the wagon and helped one of the women up into the driver seat, his side feeling the pressure from his wounds. "Go to the shore and head south until you get to the water tunnel to Krustallos, it is in the rocky alcove within a shallow cave underneath the waterfall and tell the guards Finn Worthington sent you and they will make sure you are taken care of," Finn said with a smile as one of the children played with one of the mandibles bouncing along his jaw. He rolled his eyes wide and, in a circle, to entice a giggle.

"Fine take it all!" Gorman grunted as he loaded the pile of spears he had brought in his back satchel, making sure his grumbling was loud enough for all to hear.

"Thank you, young man. You have saved us, thank you, thank you," the woman said as the rest of them piled up into the wagon. The elderly man handed the reigns to their driver. "Southwest, you say?" he asked again.

Finn wobbled his head with a smile. "You are indeed correct, good sir," he said with a wave to the children.

The party said their goodbyes and continued up the path towards the trade center of Market Town. Kaiden kept a step back, expecting a sour reprimand from Gorman.

"What yous did be noble, kid, I's not be likin it but all da same, gave em a chance…" Gorman trailed off, outpacing the much shorter human.

Finn paced himself to accompany Kaiden. "I don't think giving comes easy for the Ogre, especially when it comes to his food." he chuckled. "That may just very well be the kindest thing he may ever admit to, but he is right, though, you saved them, or at least gave them a fighting chance. Krustallos is my home, and they will help resupply and relocate them to one of the other southern fishing villages or possibly Fort Bastion or let them live in in a pod of their own, it's hard to say at least until the elders expire and they rebuild elsewhere but at least we know there is a low chance they will be eaten." Finn rambled on, shrugging his bulky shoulders.

The sun was setting and the light from Market Town emitted a soft glow in the distance. They soon entered town, exhausted from their unexpected hike, and decided to find an inn to stay at for the night. Kaiden watched as they passed by a variety of merchants, blacksmiths, fletchers, leather workers, apothecaries, general goods and about everything you could think of. One could truly find anything they were searching for from all corners of the land.

ARKANGEL

Gorman approached a tavern called The Slippery Goose but turned up his nose before entering through the door. "We stayin somewheres cleaner," he grunted with a look of disgust.

Finn's eyes lit up. "I know of just the place and the innkeeper owes me one, funny story really, so there was this woman that was visiting with lonely travelers late at night, one by one sneaking into their rooms and I was curious as to what they were doing so I followed her into one man's room and..."

"Enough!" Gorman scoffed, with a wave of his hand to dismiss him. "Just be leadin da way."

They followed Finn deeper into town; Kaiden was in awe of all the detailed statues in what looked to be a maze of gardens. The sun had set too low to be able to enjoy the view, but he hoped to have time in the morning to explore further. Finn led them to a smaller inn attached to a long stable. The tall building went several stories into the air and stretched over the entire stable, allowing for many guests. As they walked past, Kaiden noticed the wide variety of mounts other than horses; he wondered what use a wolf would be. There were other, larger creature types he didn't recognize, but they looked incredibly slow. Everything was so new and strange; he was beginning to forget his stresses of not remembering who or what he was.

Kaiden and Gorman waited outside as Finn went in to inquire about a room for the night. A webbed hand waved them in and Kaiden looked up to see the sign, "The Rested Wanderer" tacked to the side of the building. Inside was a large seating area with a bar and waitresses walking around with trays of food and drink. The smell of roasted meat wafted past their noses, causing Kaiden's and Gorman's bellies to growl.

Gorman motioned for the other two to go upstairs and find their room. "I's be gettin da food, yous be gettin da room, no trouble ya hear?" He warned with a look of desperation spread on his face as he eyed the slabs of meat on a grill.

Kaiden and Finn went up through the long, wooden staircase to their room. Kaiden thought it looked rather nice: two large straw beds with actual cloth sheets and stuffed feather pillows, a chest at the foot of each bed for storing belongings, a small table, and a bench in the corner furnished the spacious room. Finn walked in and lit the four torches on either side of the room for light before sprawling out on one of the beds.

Finn twisted and turned on the hard surface and looked to an empty corner where a tub might go. He sighed and turned to Kaiden, who was looking through the dirty window. "You know they usually equip the rooms with several bed options, unfortunately not all get a tub, but I will have to make do." He lifted his head to point over at the cabinet against the wall. "There, yes in there, I suppose there might be some bedrolls for you to lay on unless you're planning on taking your chances with the big guy? Although you may end up on the floor either way once he begins to roll around," he said with a chuckle. "I'd offer to share but I'd wake up to half your skin stuck to my scales. Aquarians prefer to sleep in the water unless sleek skinned." He dragged the corner of the blanket on his hard, crustaceous shoulder, tearing it into shreds.

The door swung open, quickly ending Finn's lesson as Gorman stomped into the room, ducking under the low door frame. He attempted to stand straight but was forced to slightly hunch to the side. "Need a bigga room," he stated, tossing the tray of various meats and veggies on the table.

"Eat up an get some rest, be a long day tomorrow," Gorman grumbled, taking a large leg of meat off the platter and falling into the bed with a loud crash as the legs gave way to his weight. "Much betta," he said, barely audible through the sound of his chewing.

Finn took a handful of the veggies and berries, lying back into the bed and flipping the pieces up one by one, trying to catch them in his mouth.

Kaiden leaned back in the chair, nibbling on several small pieces of food; he couldn't remember the last time he had eaten, and his stomach wasn't taking too kindly to it. He looked out into the dark sky, staring out at the flickering lights in the sky, wondering if anyone was thinking about him, or searching for where he was. His hope with each passing day faded for ever getting his memory back, and he hoped that after they reached Sanctuary, he might be able to find meaning in his life again. His thoughts went to the nightmare he had the night before, hoping they wouldn't return, and then remembered the woman. Was it his mother? Sister? Was he married? Other than the small, round rock around his neck, he didn't have any personal belongings, nothing to help him piece together where he was from.

His thought began to blur as he thought about the girl; he awoke several times, startled from the brutal battles he had seen already and the many people he had seen killed by the plague, if you could even call it that. He wondered what would come of the people they had given their cart to, and if they would ever make it to a safe place.

He was startled once more by a soft, whirring sound coming from Finn, followed by Gorman's long, heavy breaths. Rays of light came through the window, inviting him outside to take in the beauty of the rising sun. He stood up, taking a few bites of food, his stomach still unsettled from the meal he had the night before. He stretched his arms up into the air, fingers poking into the hard thatching at the ceiling. He had wanted to see the gardens and decided to take advantage of everyone still sleeping.

He walked down the old, wooden staircase and cringed at every creak from the boards, as if they could somehow be heard over Gorman's breathing. Warm light shined through the cracks in the wall boards, lighting his way down into the main dining hall, filled with folks getting breakfast or just waking up from their night of drinking.

Stepping through the front door, he was met by a cool breeze along with the blanket of sunlight filling the air. He walked to the entrance of the Garden Oasis closest to the inn, glancing around at all the people walking around preparing for the day's barter. The sounds of hammers on metal began to ring through the air, along with talks of trading news from all over the land.

He walked onto the path exploring, taking in all the beautiful types of flowers and foliage along the sides of the pathways. Statues of beings from all shapes, sizes, races, and professions could be seen along the trail, immortalizing their lives for all to see. Small plaques lay at their feet, telling their stories, making Kaiden wish he had the time to go through them one by one to see what great things these people had done to better the world.

He could hear the sound of a waterfall splashing into a pond ahead, drowning out the sounds of the town, immersing him in the secret garden. Trellises filled with ivy and flowers arched over the path, making him feel like he was in a whole different world than everyone else. The small dirt path opened into a hidden bench area that sat empty, not a soul around. The benches separated to other paths that went off in all different directions. There was a pile of rocks intricately placed with blooming floral vines wrapping around a miniature mountain scape.

There was a water wheel continually spinning in place, lifting water up onto a wooden ramp that fed the rocky mountain with trickling streams of water. A statue could be seen crouched over a ledge facing the opposite direction. He walked around to the front of the waterfall, where it fell into the pond with cool mist billowing out from the constant splashing of water.

As he circled around, he realized he wasn't alone, and through the mist he saw a girl sitting along the rocks, her legs draped into the water as she skimmed the rippling surface of the pond with her fingers. He had never seen anyone with such vibrant, shimmering blue hair that almost sparkled in the mist, barely draping over her shoulders and along fine silver armor. Long, pointy, white ears reached behind her head; she wore a graceful, blue and black skirt that hugged the curves of her thin frame.

"Excuse me…" he managed in shock at how exotic and lovely she was.

She turned around quickly, and for a split second their eyes met, her big, blue, radiant doe eyes looking into him. His heart immediately stopped, and his knees threatened to buckle as he struggled to breathe. All time slowed to a halt as he took in the beauty of her face, the soft curves of her jaw, and her pillowy lips tantalizing him with an overwhelming sensation of attraction. He felt drawn to her, an unrestrainable urge to get closer to her, to feel her touch, and it sent his mind spinning like he never could have thought possible.

"What are you doing here?" she yelled, jumping up onto the slippery rocks with the mist swirling around her.

He tried to speak but was unable to find his voice.

"Who are you? Are you a hunter?" she demanded.

Not a second later, a bolt shot through the air, narrowly missing the beautiful elf, and plunged deep into Kaiden's shoulder. His eyes went wide as he returned to his senses and cried out in pain. His eyes met hers for a moment longer as he saw her brows furrow in panic.

A sonic boom erupted through the air, sending her flying off the rocks, but her elven agility allowed her to twist and land on her feet. Another bolt flew from the other side of the mist, this time shattering against his armor as it instinctually materialized to deflect the blow. His armor continued to materialize, encircling his body with a golden glow sparkling in the mist. Black scales lifted from his shoulder and around the lodged bolt, pulling it out and sealing over the open wound. His shouts of pain became muffled as the armor's helmet sealed around his head.

A woman's battle cry filled the air, sword held high as she jumped toward him, swinging it down with all her might. Kaiden's armor instinctively raised its forearm blade to defend against the blow. The sword struck hard against his, throwing sparks into the air as they clashed. She followed up the attack with a kick, knocking him back several feet. With incredible speed she whirled around with another attack, swinging her sword to his side, which he easily parried with the blade jetting from his forearm. She stepped in close and slammed her fist against his armored face with all her strength and momentum.

His head jerked to the side, then rose up to glare back at her, his eyes glowing such an intense white they seemed to steam into the air. She stopped for a second in shock at his strength, hesitant to attack again before her anger raged through her blood, lifting her sword high into the air. His eyes followed her movement and body language, scanning and adapting to her movements. She flung her blade through the air with speed and accuracy, which he followed easily, meeting her wild thrusts

ARKANGEL

and swings, sending showers of sparks through the air with every clash of their weapons. Their battle intensified as he parried her attacks, becoming one step ahead, spinning his body low with his leg and sweeping hers out from under her. She fell hard to the dirt, and he reached down, grasping onto the open top of her bronze breastplate and lifted her into the air, clamping his other hand around her bare leg. He held her high into the air helplessly and threw her hard into the rocky ground, the impact sending dirt and debris throughout the small clearing.

The woman stood up, her chest heaving in both exhaustion and rage. "Oh honey, you're going to wish you hadn't done that," she warned, turning to the elven girl and lunging at her. She arced her sword through the air to slash across her abdomen as the elf backpedaled from the woman's ferocity.

The elf clasped her hands together, weaving her fingers as her eyes began to flicker a bright orange flame. She screamed and she tore her hands away from each other, drawing an arc of flame between them; the unleashing of a burst of fire, engulfing the woman in a searing pyre. The fire quickly dispersed, having little effect on her but distracting her long enough for Kaiden to jump high into the air and kick hard into her back. She flew forward uncontrollably and crashed into the rocks along the side of the sunken pond.

She stood back up without pause, her long wet hair whipping back with a slap on her back. A smirk spread to her face as she eyed Kaiden with a hint of lust in her eyes. "Oh, aren't you the gentlemen?" she taunted. "I love a challenge, sweet thing, and you must tell me who you are. The name is Vixis, but you can call me whatever you wish, love." She slammed her sword back into its scabbard.

Her seductive smile faded as she looked to the elven beauty. "She is coming with me; she is inflicted and must be taken in for processing. You understand, don't ya, honey?" She looked back at Kaiden with a wink.

"What say you, warrior? Why don't you make this easy on everyone and just let me take her?" she asked, taking a step cautiously in her direction.

Kaiden's armor straightened his arms to its sides, the blades along his forearms extending further.

"Oh, the silent type, huh?" Vixis said playfully, then chuckled. "I like that in a man."

"Nirayus, what did I tell you…" A man's voice called out as a tall, expensively dressed elf sprinted in from one of the paths, coming to an abrupt stop. He drew out two ornate, curved blades from his sides with ancient etchings carved intricately along their metal that began to glow a faint golden color.

"Back away from my daughter," he commanded, his eyes darting between Kaiden and Vixis, unknowing which was the bigger threat.

"Oh my," Vixis said, eying the noble elf head to toe with a playful smile spreading across her lips. "Why aren't you just a cute little thing? Your daughter, you say?" Vixis teased.

"Tell me the meaning of this right now, I demand it!" Valryn commanded.

"Oh, we're just having a little fun, aren't we?" The bruised up Vixis replied, looking to the barely visible Nirayus behind the stoic Kaiden.

Valryn took a few steps closer to the showdown. "Nirayus, come here, we are leaving," he said angrily as he eyed the uniquely armored figure with intrigue, its glowing gaze staying fixed upon Vixis.

A scowl came to Nirayus's face as she looked down and began to step closer to her father. Vixis raised a small crossbow, light enough to wield with one hand, up to aim directly at her heart, causing her to freeze in fear.

"Ah, ah, ah, now you know I can't let an inflicted go. Even a beautiful princess like yourself doesn't get preferential treatment, unless you find yourself in my bedchambers." She winked.

Valryn sprung forth swinging his blade in a wide arc at the weapon, attempting to knock it from her hand. Despite his enhanced elven speed, Vixis brought her blade up, deflecting his attack and planting her foot hard against his chest, knocking the air from his lungs. Valryn coughed, staggered, and toppled to his knees, struggling to draw in breath. In the blink of an eye, she whirled her leg around and kicked the kneeling king, sending him sliding into the dirt below.

Nirayus let out a gasp and reached her hand out from behind Kaiden. "Father!" she cried out.

"I'm sorry, honey, but this has to be taken care of first before we can play," Vixis interjected with a vengeful smirk. She raised the crossbow and fired; the razor-sharp bolt flew through the air towards Nirayus's frightened face.

Kaiden lurched forward, snatching the bolt midair and rammed Vixis into the side of the rocky waterfall. His weight crushed her deep into the rocks, shattering them as his momentum continued to press her in deeper. He pushed back with a solid kick to her stomach, folding her over as he spun in place with his blades lacerating through her leather armor. He grabbed her head, slamming it into his armored knee, then picked her limp body up over his head.

He jumped clear across the clearing and smashed her into one of the many marble statues, shattering it into several large pieces. Her body fell at the statue's base as it continued to crumble apart, burying her beneath its rubble. The bottom half of the statue remained firmly attached to the ground as a fresh coat of blood dripped down its legs.

With a flash of golden light, Kaiden's armor retracted. He collapsed to his knees, breathing heavily, his body and hair wet from being trapped within his armored prison. Nirayus leaned forward and grabbed his shoulder so he wouldn't fall as he wobbled unconsciously. Her eyes widened in shock to see the place where he had been shot in the shoulder was little more than a small healing scar with the blood still fresh on the arm of his shirt.

"How?" she asked softly to herself, looking to her father as he pulled himself from the ground.

Kaiden shivered from shock, then jolted awake, his reality slowing down as the world came back into focus. "Are you ok? I didn't hurt you, did I?" he asked the elf, trying not to stare into her eyes too long. He looked away and saw the elven king holding his chest, struggling to stay on his feet, a look of intrigue spreading to his face.

"I will be fine, young man," he answered, "I have suffered far worse over my many years. But what I have seen today, I am at a loss for words."

Kaiden stood up, his hand instinctively going to tend to his nonexistent wound.

"I don't know what it is, I can't control it," Kaiden offered, attempting to explain and affirm to himself the reality of it.

"Who was she?" Kaiden asked, pointing to the pile of marble crumbled over Vixis's body.

"She has been hunting me," Nirayus responded shyly, her hand pulling strands of bright blue hair from her face and tucking it behind her long ear.

"Her name is Vixis," Valryn said, the commanding tone returning to his voce. "She is an Ark hunter, and little is known to me about them or where they come from. The human paladin Malik formed their sect to seek out beings with the gift, cursing it to be a blight upon the land. Human's fear what they cannot control and fail to understand, so they created a handful of these Ark hunters who do nothing but travel around, hunting down anyone who might possess the gift. Naive creatures they are… No offense."

Kaiden shook his head. "No, I don't remember anything beyond a few days ago so it's all new to me, and I have nothing against anyone with any abilities." He gestured to Nirayus, then stole a glance at her, his heart leaping up into his throat to see her looking at him.

He gulped for breath. "I mean I ark too, right? Maybe that's what is happening to me?" He'd hope to finally get some answers.

Valryn got a baffled look on his face. "Human's fail to possess the fortitude to be able to ark; it would tear your body apart from the inside. But with the golden light it would indeed make sense." He looked at the muscular Kaiden without a trace of his armor present. "I believe you have... something else," he said softly, his voice trailing off.

"Something else? I mean, there has to be someone with this ability before, right?"

Valryn looked to the female statue atop the waterfall in silence for several seconds. "I have been a part of this world for many centuries, young man, and have never seen anything like it myself. There have been writings of an end to a new race and a hero rising, but the writings had turned into nothing more than mere stories. Paladin Malik feared it and, with the Ark hunters, tried to stop it and anyone with the gift. Malik died, though, several years ago, and his Ark hunters were exiled and banned from hunting, although they work for themselves now trying to finish what they had been created to do. Now there is you, your abilities are different, born as a response to the plague from the Creator perhaps? Rare relics have been forged by the creators themselves for many different reasons and this could be one of them." He pulled forth one of his twin daggers. The thin, long blade came to a sleek, curved end with the handle made of some sort of silver, lined and encircled with different types of runes and markings.

"This was a gift from our Creator, a blessing to my family, and a mark of our responsibility to our people to keep them safe and lead them into prosperity." He held it out as it began to glow a vibrant golden color, the etchings gleaming a bright blue. "Though I admit that this has not happened before."

Nirayus stepped closer to Valryn's side. "Father, what is this?"

The blade got brighter as Kaiden began to emit a golden glow himself. He stepped back from Valryn, and the blade pulled out of his hand and flew through the air towards him, his armor materializing around his legs and slowly spreading up to his waist and half his chest. The other blade at Valryn's side glowed brightly and lifted itself free, making its way towards Kaiden. His eyes went wide in confusion as the blades spun slowly in midair before slamming down against his shins with a deep echoing *click* as the armor around his leg adjusted and altered to form scabbards, holding the blades firmly along the front of his legs with the thin handles stretching out from his knees as the pommels transformed into a sharp point.

The glow around the blades and armor diminished, the armor retracting into thin air along with the two blades. A single, longer ornate blade was left fastened firmly against his side. Kaiden drew it free as a dim glow emitted from its sheath and blade.

"What is the meaning of this?" Valryn demanded.

"I'm not sure, this hasn't happened before," Kaiden responded, confused. He then tried to hand the blade back.

Valryn glanced to Nirayus, then turned his attention back at Kaiden "No, it has chosen you, Kaiden, it is not my place to question the Creator's design. It chose me when our people were desperate for a leader and I stepped in as King, and now it has chosen you, my friend." He leaned forward in a bow.

He slowly raised back up. "Kaiden, I believe this is no chance meeting we have had here today, and I believe you have a great destiny ahead of you, young man. If the words written were true, then you will have great challenges ahead of you, and the land is now in greater danger than we thought."

Valryn's eyes expressed a hint of sadness as he looked to his daughter. "You may not understand this now, Rayus, but you must go with him and aid him on his journey." He put his hand on her shoulder in comfort, somehow managing a warm smile.

"What? Why, Father?" She protested, glancing over to Kaiden briefly, hoping for aid in objection.

"My companions and I are traveling to Sanctuary, on a journey to see if someone has an answer to my loss of memory and see if we can be of help with the plague. We gave our wagon away to some refugees and I'm afraid we can't meet the needs of an Elven Princess." Kaiden said, looking down from Nirayus's glare.

Valryn chuckled. "This is excellent. Rayus, you will travel with Kaiden and his company to aid them in your journey and help protect him, for you are very gifted and they will need you." He tried to put a hand on her shoulder.

"Protect him, Father?" she asked, brushing his hand off her shoulder and taking a step back. "Did you see what happened? He doesn't need my protection; I would just be a liability," she argued, gesturing in Kaiden's direction.

"You must go. I will lure the hunters away from you and they will not be able to find you where you are going. He can protect you far better than I am capable of. It is time for you to grow up, my daughter, and show the humans how special you really are." He smiled at her with pride, then turned to Kaiden.

"Will you keep her safe, my friend?" Valryn asked, looking deeper into Kaiden's eyes.

Kaiden looked back and could almost see into his ancient soul, finding great honor and power deep within. He felt a sense of pride in what he was being asked to do. And, admittedly, he wouldn't mind getting to know the fiery beauty as well.

Nirayus huffed and crossed her arms around her thin waist, sulking about. A tear rolled down her cheek as she grasped her compass delicately in her hand.

Kaiden sensed her sadness and looked to Valryn. "She may travel with us if she would like. I know her skills will be useful to our cause, but I cannot force her to go if she doesn't want to," he said, hoping to ease her stress. "It has been a dangerous path so far and I will do what I can to help protect her."

Valryn put his hand on Kaiden's shoulder and nodded in agreement. "Thank you," he said to him softly. "You must hurry, the Arkhunter will not be out long and I will lead her away from here. You are welcome at our table any time, my friend. For now, however, your destiny awaits, and you must go."

Nirayus turned to her father, shaking her head and throwing her arms around him, gritting her teeth while trying not to lose her composure.

"I love you, Nirayus. Be safe and be smart. I know you will find what you have spent your life seeking, my daughter. You are stronger than you realize, and you make me proud."

Nirayus squeezed tightly around her father. "Thank you, I love you too," she said, turning to see Kaiden walking down the path he had come from. She looked at Vixis one more time. "Be careful, Father," she said softly as she slowly walked to catch up to her new companion.

"How can someone survive that?" Kaiden wondered to himself, hearing Nirayus's reluctant steps behind him.

Valryn watched as they walked out of sight and down the path before covering their tracks behind them. He took another look at Vixis and sprinted away down the path he traveled from, knowing the long road ahead of him weighed deeply on his shoulders. He realized the icy grip of time was slowly tightening their grip about him. He thought he would have more time, but events had started to unfold and were beginning to set into motion. He needed more time to prepare. His pace quickened as his thoughts wandered, knowing full well what was to come.

Mist sprinkled down from the crash of the waterfall, blanketing the gardens. The rising sun intensified as rays of golden light passed from behind the statue of the elven woman atop the waterfall. The pile of marble rubble atop Vixis lit up brightly from the warm morning sunlight as it began to move slowly, and the sound of stone grinding against stone echoed through the empty clearing.

CHAPTER 5

"THE MISGUIDED ARCHER"

Arcusbane crept down the dirty streets of Muckton, his home for as long as he could remember. The small, poor section of town held the dump and sewage passages, directing it away from the rest of the settlements. If someone was desperate enough, they could set up a tent and live for free in relative safety from the miscreants of the town. For now, that's what he would have to live with despite the toxic fumes permeating the hot air. The heat of the desert didn't help with the stench, or the thick air filled with sand swirling around like a constant cloud of dust. He didn't let that get him down, though, for he knew he was destined for more.

One day he would prove himself worthy of being an Akarian, then rise up and change their way of life for the better. He knew he couldn't change everyone; murderers, rapists, and thieves can't be changed overnight, but maybe he could show them a better way? Life expectancy in Amid was sometimes just a few days, where only the truly strong and clever survived.

Being a greenhorn, an unwanted child left to die in the streets that had somehow managed to survive, he knew he was alive for a reason. Most children born into their violent society were used as food for pets or discarded for lack of responsibility shown by the men and out of control of their enslaved mothers.

He passed through the garbage dump and around the perimeter of the small wooden wall that protected the inner town from the filth of the Muckton area. The normally reddish, sandy ground was stained brown with the feces that lay scattered throughout the area. His little hovel was made out of an old, tattered canvas and broken chunks of wood barely stitched together at its fragile seems.

Arcus approached his home to hear the familiar deep growl of Saber, his mountain wolf he had rescued several years back on a hunt. Saber eyed him through the slats of wood and stood up to expose his massive, seven feet tall body behind the flimsy shack. He playfully shook his tail and bore his huge teeth in a smile that would strike fear into anyone else.

Saber was big for a mountain wolf at over twenty feet long and taller than a man; his massive paws were the size of a human chest, with eight-inch claws designed for tearing through thick hide and rock. Mountain wolves were generally white and brown to blend into the snowcapped peaks where they roamed, but Saber was a silvery white with dark grey patterns down his back to the tip of his tail. Their thick fur protected them like armor with patches of a strong carapace, which grew on their haunches and shoulders that jutted out like sharp rocks.

Arcus ran his hand through his thick hair lovingly to greet his most loyal companion. "You ready for a ride, boy?"

Saber stood up tall to stretch his legs and attempted to circle around in excitement in the small, confined area to the side of the shack. Arcus led him out to the path along the edge of town, looked both ways in caution, and then pulled back a loose section of wall to let Saber out.

There was little keeping crime from occurring in town other that the fact that nobody wanted to deal with the odor or the mess it created within the walls. Outside was a completely different story and everyone and everything was fair game if you had the strength to take it. Arcus had to be careful leaving so close to sundown, as some prided themselves on stealth kills alone.

It was worth the risk tonight, though, and with the greenhorn hunt being the next morning, he would need to do whatever it took to win. He held tight onto Saber's long hair and steadied his feet into the wolf's rocky armor before he took off. The massive wolf leaped and bounded over the terrain much faster than any horse and could leap over small walls or rivers in a single bound. Not many creatures could outrun a mountain wolf, and even fewer could outmaneuver one.

Arcus dismounted several miles from the city Amid and knelt to the ground, running his fingers along the mud and dirt while slowly examining the foliage for signs of wildlife. He was a gifted hunter, tracker, and marksman, having to build his skills in order to survive and eat. Tonight, he wouldn't be hunting food; this night he needed to hunt something much larger.

It was rare that a greenhorn such as himself would have a bestiarius, so having Saber was a huge advantage. The winner of the greenhorn competition would not only get him the honor and respect for having the biggest and most dangerous beast but would also qualify him to possibly rule the entire tribe one day. He was going against all the other younger Akarians, including newcomers to their tribe, so he felt he had a good chance. Most new to the tribe were prisoners and degenerates sent from Sanctuary who had served their time for crimes and banished from the great city.

Tonight, Arcus was trying to hunt a carnitor, very rare and dangerous desert creatures, but he had heard people in the market talk of attacks on a lionel village to the east next to the forest. If he could cross the desert and pick up on its trail, he might be able to find it in time for the competition the next day.

Most Akarians had little respect for rules or authority, so he most likely wasn't the only one getting the early start. The faster he was able to track it down and capture the giant formidable creature the better off he would be.

After some searching, he found what looked like a trench that had been dug into the sand. The long, deep grooves came from some sort of rock formation or cave he had passed and continued many miles to the edge of the desert. As he approached the thin forest, he noticed a pathway of downed trees twenty feet wide with nothing left but destruction. The earliest rays of dawn had set in, allowing him to pick up the pace and maneuver faster over the forest terrain.

He hadn't seen one of these creatures before but had heard tales of them devastating entire villages and even small towns, unprepared to deal with a beast its size. Akarians trained to hunt large prey as part of their contribution to their society, and even their army was composed of various beast riders of all shapes and sizes. The thought of going toe to toe with such a beast was merely everyday life and his talents would be all he had to keep him alive. Compared to the plague of caiman tearing down people left and right, he liked the idea of being the hunter again.

The trees thinned as the beginning of the forest gave way to a large field littered with massive formations of rock. He made it to the outskirts of the Lionel territory and had to make an extra effort to be stealthy so as to not be caught by one of them.

The Akarians had been at odds with the different tribes of Lionels for decades. With the Akarians love for fighting beasts they would often take these native humanoid lions and tigers as slaves or to be slaughtered in the arena for sport. The Lionels were such a peaceful, nature loving folk that would refuse to fight suffering animals, laying down their lives just to provide food for them. A trait not understood by the Akarians but an act they took great pleasure in watching.

Saber ran to take cover beside a stone bridge that crossed a shallow ravine and stream. Patterns of stone formations dotted the landscape here with meanings long forgotten. Arcus never went to any sort of school so he figured someone must know what they meant. Maybe from the sky, their meaning could truly be seen.

Saber tensed and the hairs on his back rose up, almost hiding Arcus completely within his thick fur. The wolf's lips curled as a low rumbling growl expelled slowly from his lungs. Arcus stood up and jumped down to the side of the rustic bridge. He looked across the field and could see a small mountain sized creature lurking near a pond by the far tree line. From this distance the carnitor looked thirty feet tall and with long claw like hands he guessed could stretch almost as wide.

He was taken aback by the sheer destructive power of the creature. It was like the Creator couldn't decide on what to do with it, so it was a mix of different offensive and defensive features. It had a massive thick carapace back with spines that jut out longer than spears, all the way down to a long, spiked ball tail. Its head was rather small for its body except for the helmet-like plates that stacked down its forehead to its neck. Its rear squat legs, equally as deadly with spines coming from its knees slowly side stepped as it bent down looking to attack its prey. It was able to claw down several trees with a single swipe of its long scythe-like claws.

It was hunting something, which seemed like the best time to take it by surprise while its attention was elsewhere. It swiped with its long claws in attempts to catch its prey, lifting them high in the air and revealing a second pair of smaller arms folded up against its torso on its sides.

Arcus had never seen anything like it before and decided to sit back and watch what it was capable of. With its unique features he didn't want to be taken by surprise and fail, or even worse, be killed. A sound like thunder struck in the distance as it smashed its large claws into the trees furiously. Its tail rose up over its back and whipped around, destroying a small patch of trees in its path and sending a cloud of leaves to rain down below.

His attention was so dead set on the creature he had failed to notice the small band of horsemen approaching it from his left. It looked like an Akarian raiding party by the shabby clothes and shoddy horses they rode. Horses were considered the weak man's mount, so these guys were probably going to try and capture the fearsome beast like he was.

Arcus jumped up to the side rail of the bridge and ran down its length, jumping up into the air and landing on the back of Saber who had been matching his speed. They darted off into a full sprint and with how fast Saber was he wouldn't have much time to formulate a plan even though they were hundreds of yards away.

It was dangerous taking on a beast this size alone and he knew this from personal experience, seeing his only friend savagely killed just a few months ago in his last hunt. He wouldn't make the same mistakes again and was determined to persevere in his friend's honor.

As they closed in, he pulled out his bow, attaching a reel to the hard leather harness on Saber's back. He would need to tie up the carnitor's powerful legs and get it to lose its balance and fall to a more manageable height. He unraveled his quiver with his assortment of specialized arrows he had created, snapping it in place across Saber's back. Saber knew the drill and started to circle the beast, keeping a safe distance away that only arrows could reach.

Arcus shot six large arrows in rapid succession attached to a strong, thin rope and sunk them all deep into the trees of the forest line. These would hopefully keep it from straying much farther than the trees if he needed a chance to flee. Three to the left and three to the right, the other end of the rope held clips to attach onto the thick barbed arrows that would be shot at its legs.

Saber whirled around as Arcus let loose the long-barbed arrows. Before the first hit there were three more following closely behind, already sailing through the air. The carnitor let out an enraged roar but didn't draw his attention away from the forest, still swatting and swinging its deadly tail around frantically.

The next set of lines were shot into the ground behind the creature, Saber getting close by the swinging tail as Arcus shot the other end with the arrows deep into its legs and pinning it to the ground. The end barbs of the arrows were like a one-way pulley; the farther Saber ran away from it, the tighter the tail would be forced down.

The carnitor tried to turn and engage Arcus but was unable to move its legs from all the rope tethering it to the ground and trees. Its large claws started raking at the ground to try and sever the hold from the ropes.

That is when Arcus noticed the flashing of a bright green light in front of it. The rapid bursts were hitting the creature and somehow subduing it. A small slender figure jumped out of the forest, running around to the back of the beast. It reached down with a gesture and flicker of light, pulling up massive root tendrils from the ground. The thick vines shot up, entangling the carnitor and pulling it swiftly to the ground. It struggled as it fell backwards onto its back with the huge spear like quills sinking several feet into the ground.

By this time the Akarians had reached the beast and began throwing spears into its less armored underbelly. It bellowed out in pain, flailing its limbs trying to break free and right itself over in defense. Arcus's chest heaved in panic, these guys were here to kill it, not capture it. He had to stop them before they took his prize.

While facing the creature he pulled Saber hard to the left to go intercept the other Akarians, knowing full well what he had to be prepared to do. Before he could get Saber into a run he collapsed to the ground, whimpering in pain. Arcus flew off Saber, the momentum sending him flying into the grassy field and rolling several times before coming to a stop, his vision spinning in circles before coming to focus. He saw a female Lionel hesitantly approach him with a short bow in hand, arrow drawn.

"I don't want to harm you, human," she purred.

He could see in her step and shaky hand on the bow that she was frightened.

"Tell your friends to back away and not kill this creature," she said nervously.

Arcus tried to lift himself up, measuring his injury from the fall. "They are not my friends, now put the bow down before you hurt yourself," he replied with a scowl, noticing her cat-like ears pinning down. Her eyes widened in fear as she started looking side to side for a place to flee.

Arcus cringed when he heard the horses come to a stop behind him.

"What you got there, little kitty?" A man said patronizingly.

Arcus knew this was going to take a turn for the worst very quickly. He was not in a good place to be laying almost flat on his back without his bow. He looked to Saber, who was pulling the arrow lodged in the bottom of his foot with his teeth. Saber suddenly stopped to look at Arcus, sharing a worried expression. Looking deep into Saber's eyes Arcus was somehow able to momentarily see a blurry vision as if somehow looking through his eyes. He was able to see the three men armed with spears and machetes, with a fourth back beside the Lionel, bow in hand, and pointed directly at the unaware tigress. Arcus shook his head from dizziness and felt to his side, pulling out his small hunting knife, noticing his bow only a few feet away.

"Put your bow down, filthy cat," an Akarian demanded.

Her ears pinned further as she let out a frightened hiss.

"Just give us the boy and you can leave," He demanded, anger raging in his voice.

As she began to give in to panic, she raised her bow to the man, her mind racing to figure out what she should do, not wanting to hurt anyone. Arcus heard the ringing sound of their weapons freeing from their sheaths. She quickly dodged to the side, narrowly being missed by an arrow flying right next to her head from behind. She let her arrow fly, slamming deep into the man's shoulder; she winced in instant regret.

Arcus rose up and threw his knife at the archer behind the tigress, hitting him in the chest. He then rolled on the ground, simultaneously picking up his bow and knocked an arrow to shoot the wounded man. His arrow released and pierced through the man's side, knocking him to the ground motionless.

The two men behind Arcus ignored their fallen companion and lunged at the tigress, swinging their machetes wildly at her, lacking any form or skill. She dodged and parried with her bow, backing up and pulling a knife of her own in a panic.

Arcus noted that she was very fast and skilled in her abilities but was unprepared to deal with the unpredictably wild men. She slipped, taking a glancing strike to her shoulder by the old rusty blade, beads of blood now dripping through the fur on her arm. She cried out from the pain, dropping her bow to protect the wound with her hand.

Arcus let his next arrow fly, it quickly punctured through one of the attacker's neck, his eyes widening in shock. He grasped for his throat, the uncontrollable flow of blood now draining from his body. He started to choke as he frantically gasped for air, clawing at the arrow to dislodge it. The spray of his warm blood splattered across his companion's face, distracting him long enough for the tigress to reluctantly plunge her knife into his heart to end his suffering.

As the Akarian went into shock, the tigress grasped onto his torso and cradled him as she lay his head gently onto the ground in a pool of his own blood. The tigress moved her hands softly along his body and up to his face to close his eyes. A flash of soft green light burst from her palm as the man slipped peacefully into the darkness of death.

Arcus stood spellbound by what he had just seen, his guard down as the archer he had hit with the knife rose up to his knees to shoot another arrow. The tigress instinctively flicked her wrist as her forearm burst into a thick weave of vines and leaves circling into a defensive shield. The shield formed just in time to catch the arrow in a nest of woven twigs before it could hit Arcus in the chest.

Arcus pulled out another arrow and landed it squarely between the man's eyes and sent him tumbling back. He let out a sigh of relief to see the man twitch several times and go still, unable to retaliate. He watched in confusion and intrigue as the tigress went to the other two men who had just tried to kill her and lay them to rest. The same green light from her palm put to each of their faces.

He was snapped out of his thoughts, his chest still heaving from adrenaline as he looked to see the giant carnitor lay dead on its side. Several spears sunk deep into its underbelly still spilling a thick ooze of blood onto the ground. He would have thought a massive creature would have been harder to kill, but despite all its armored plates and defenses, it fell victim to the thoughtless Akarian raiders. He realized he had failed and shouted out in frustration, lashing out into the air in a fit. Saber limped up beside him and howled into the air to share in his master's anger.

The tigress knelt beside one of the bodies and was ill prepared for the net that she all of a sudden found herself enveloped in. Arcus pulled a lasso from the pouch on Saber's side saddle and tightly bound it around her.

"I saved your life," she hissed.

Arcus scowled. "I can handle myself and because of you I lost my prize," he responded harshly.

"Your prize? You mean that creature? No creature belongs to you, human."

"I needed it!" he shouted, tying the end of the lasso to Saber's saddle. "You have no Idea what you have done."

"You can't expect me to carry this heavy net and walk, I'll collapse from exhaustion."

Arcus tugged hard at the rope. "You will live long enough for me to show as my prize or I sell you, then I could care less what happens to you after that."

She lurched forward holding onto the rope around her neck in hopes it would help her breath "Please take my knife, I can't lose it."

Arcus looked to see the finely crafted knife lying in the grass beside one of the bodies. He picked it up, wiped the blood off in the grass, and held it in his hand for several seconds as it balanced on his fingers. "It's good enough," he proclaimed, slamming it into the empty knife holder on his side. He then walked and cut a small section of rope from the net and bound her hands. "So you don't get any ideas on flashing that green light at me," he said behind clenched teeth.

"I don't like to ark," she stated, looking to the ground. "It's a curse and brings nothing but trouble." she said.

"It is a curse. Just look at you, you're all tied up now, so keep it to yourself. The only reason you're still alive is because you got lucky in blocking that arrow. Otherwise, your pelt is worth just as much as your services will be," Arcus shouted as he tugged on the rope again and jumped into his saddle atop Saber's back. "Let's go, we have a lot of ground to cover."

She hissed at him in disgust and started to shuffle her feet forward, her eyes dripping with tears of fear. Arcus yanked on the rope to quicken her pace, but she refused, taking the pain over her pride of letting the monster control her. Arcus's brows lowered in frustration; he knew just crossing the rolling dunes in the forsaken sands would take at least a day's walk. His heart weighed heavily with failure from his hunt, his frustration surged, and he pulled harder on the rope.

The tigress fell to the ground, ears pinning in anger. "I do not deserve to be treated like this, what gives you the right?" she cried out in spite.

Arcus looked back to her. "You are nothing but a talking animal, you have no rights."

Her whiskers quivered with anger and his lack of compassion. "I am the same as you, human, my name is Taja, who are you to treat me so cruelly?"

Arcus lifted her up, pulling on the rope and pulling her forward. "My name is Arcusbane, and you are just an animal, Taja, nothing more."

"You are the animal, hunter, I grew up same as you and I had a family and have lived free, same as you. I do not force others against their will mindlessly and that makes you the animal." She spat in disgust, refusing to let him seep under her skin any longer.

"Shut your mouth before I feed you to my wolf, you're beginning to be a bigger hassle than you're worth," Arcus growled.

They continued to make their way through the plains and into the deep sands of the desert, leaving the forest far behind them. The rocky patches of carapace on Saber's body helped to dull the sting of the harsh sun, keeping him cooler. They needed to find water soon, Arcus hadn't planned on the trip back to take much more than a few hours.

Taja began to grow weak from the weight of the braided net rope that draped over her like a poncho. She began to stumble and slide down the endless desert dunes.

Arcus, still sore from the loss of his beast, looked back to the tigress. "If you dislike your ark, or whatever you inflicted call it so much, then why were you even fighting the carnitor?" he asked.

"It is none of your concern, human," she shot back, looking away, the strength in her legs returning from anger.

"Oh, so I hit a nerve, did I?" Arcus grinned in delight. "I hope it wasn't important and I'm keeping you from it? Like you kept me from my prize."

"What exactly have I taken from you, hunter? That beast is better off dead than to be in the hands of creatures like you. You and your people are all the same, no thought or care for the destruction you cause around you," she shouted, her dry throat causing her voice to go weak as she coughed.

Taja struggled to pull air into her dry, hoarse throat as she swallowed what little saliva she could produce. "They say the plague upon humanity will wipe you all out but if you ask me, it is the humans who were the true plague in the first place," she shrieked, barely able to project her voice as her knees gave out, collapsing into the sand.

"You are relentless, aren't you, doing everything you can do to slow me down," Arcus yelled, bringing Saber to a halt and jumping down from his back. He grabbed the rope to the net and whistled to signal Saber to freely go drink from the small stream they were about to cross. Taja continued to cough and gasp for air as Arcus lifted the heavy net from her small slender frame.

"There is water just over the mound, get what water you need, and I'll fill up a skin," he said, throwing the net onto the sand to roll up, before pulling out his worn leather water skin.

Taja stumbled weakly towards the water as best as she could with her hands still bound, rolling down the back side of the dune and coming to a stop in the hot sand at the edge of the stream. It was four to six feet across and only a few feet deep at most, only days away from drying up for the rest of the year. She dipped down, lapping up water to rehydrate herself, then let out a sigh from the nice, cool water flowing around her feet.

Arcus stepped up onto the sand mound, inspecting the river and terrain around them. A strong breeze had begun to blow through, making it hard to see very far through the sand.

"We need to hurry this up, it looks like a storm is brewing up north, we don't want to get stuck out here when it hits."

Taja just glared at him angrily, for Lionels hated violence and always thought to take the higher road on many things, but she had been forced to survive in the wild alone after banishment and did not uphold such values all the time. She bent down into the water, washing the dirt and sand from her fur as her strength began to return. She knew she could outrun the hunter but not the wolf, so she would need to outthink him to escape.

She let her eyes wander as she took her final sip, gathering her resolve to flee, when she heard something. Her ears perked up as she looked up the river, startled. She also saw the wolf take notice, long before Arcus had heard anything.

Arcus drew his bow from off his back and knocked an arrow to let fly if need be. Minutes later a small crate approached them, just drifting down the stream.

Taja walked out to retrieve it. "Just let it be," Arcus commanded, recognizing the familiar cries of a baby. In Amid, the only cries from babies were the unanswered calls right before it was about to be eaten or discarded, usually followed by the mother's tears. Arcus looked up stream, unable to see anyone that it may belong to.

Taja ignored him, a wide smile spreading to her face to reveal the long fangs of her kind. She pulled out a small baby girl, screaming and crying, kicking and hitting the best it could to escape the leaking crate of water.

She looked to Arcus.

"I told you to just leave it and we have no way of taking care of it, it's better off getting a quick death," he said.

Taja stroked the small child's hairless head with her silky-smooth paw, trying to calm it down. It continued to cry but held on tightly to the ropes bound around her arms as she struggled to support it properly. She had seen cubs born before, but they were different, less fragile than humans. A being completely defenseless for so many years after birth, she wondered how they had ever survived. The little girl's fragility humbled her and made her heart weep for the young one, filling her full of purpose to protect it.

A strong gust of wind sent a steady spray of sand against them. "We will never get out of here like this. Drop the baby now, we need to get out of here and find shelter."

Taja's ears pinned as she hissed, the hair atop her head and shoulder rising slightly on end as her tail flicked side to side. "NO," She threatened. "I go, the baby goes." She hissed, baring her teeth at him.

Saber picked up on the threat and hunched down in a low, pouncing position to protect his master, a deep rumbling growl rolling out from between his exposed fangs.

Arcus kicked the sand at his feet, raising up his hand to block the stinging wind from hitting his face. "Come on, we don't have time for this," he started in protest as gusts howled over the dunes. "Alright then, fine, come on, let's just go." He pulled on her rope to get her to start moving.

Taja whipped her tail and bowed her head, trying to shield the baby as she was pulled. Arcus helped lift her on top of Saber at the end of the saddle and tied the rope to a large metal ring on the side of the saddle.

"Hold on tight, I ain't stopping for anyone who falls off," Arcus shouted as he strapped himself into the saddle, bringing Saber to a blind sprint, unable to see more than a few feet ahead from the torrent of sand.

Saber's thick tufts of fur around his eyes, designed to relieve the winds from blizzards, helped him see, even though his riders couldn't as they pressed on. The wind howled as the gusts became more violent, stinging their exposed flesh. Arcus bent over, holding the flap of his saddle over his head, unable to see anything, his eyes burning from the dry, hot sand.

Taja held the baby tightly to her body and swirled her fingers in a small circle as green light sparked and twisted from her fingertips. The light began to wrap around the baby and harden into a thick bark wrapped in leafy vines that helped guard her from the vicious gusts of the sandstorm.

Arcus's vision blurred into the darkness under the saddle flap and shifted into a foggy grey color. This had happened before earlier in the day when he first met Taja, and they were attacked by the raiding party. He could see monstrous paws out in front of himself and the bridge of a long snout. He looked side to side, the sand blowing hard against his face as he sprinted forward. How was this happening, he thought. He had been very close to Saber over the last few years and developed a tight bond to where they could almost read each other's minds, but nothing like this had ever happened.

He noticed an outcropping of large rocks and attempted to will his paws into changing direction towards them. Slowly against the harsh wind they forged ahead as if moving against a strong current. He clenched his eyes shut against the piercing sand and a few minutes later it suddenly stopped.

Taja lifted her head, her ears flicking off the red sand as her body twitched, shaking off the rest. She tossed the wooden shield she had arked down to soft ground as she examined the dark cave they had entered.

Arcus emerged from his sand-filled, leather mat as well, looking around as his eyes adjusted to being himself again in the dark room. The pile of large rocks provided decent shelter from the sandstorm, with only small gusts of wind circling its way around the entrance. He jumped off the saddle into the warm, soft sand and walked deeper into the cave to find it only a few yards deep. Strands of cloth and rags tangled into a pile of bones lay mounded in the back of the cave against the far wall.

"This must be a creature's burrow," Taja stated, the cry of the baby becoming noticeably louder in the enclosed cave despite the whistling wind outside.

"Make it stop crying," Arcus demanded, with a wince of pain in his ears. "Can't you feed it or something?" He was frustrated by the never-ending complications he had faced throughout the day. He paused for a second and realized the day was coming to an end by now, putting them back in Amid late afternoon the following day. Best case scenario, if the storm let up, they could make it by early morning.

Arcus yelled out in anger, kicking the sand and bones at his feet.

Taja blinked several times, trying to replace the moisture the sand had sucked from them as she tried to examine the tracks at the base of the cave. "What now?" she asked, equally as frustrated, now being stuck with two children.

Arcus turned to her, his chest rising and falling with his heavy breaths. "You just wouldn't understand," he said.

"Is this about that carnitor again?" she asked sarcastically.

Arcus sat back against the inner wall of the cave. "It's not just the carnitor," he said, snapping his fingers and motioning for Saber to lay down and guard the cave. "I needed it for a competition. Like I said, you just wouldn't understand."

Taja followed suit, spinning in place several times to kick the sand into a comfortable pile to sit upon. "Is this another human competition where your beast will tear apart another as you bet on the winner? Will it be forced to slaughter innocent lives, again for more money?" she asked in a harsh, disgusted tone.

Arcus picked up a pile of sand between his fingers and watched as the grains fell to a pile one by one. "No, it is to prove myself as a hunter, so my voice can be heard," he said as his tone trailed off. "Things aren't just as simple as you think, and I don't gamble." Arcus gritted his teeth, the baby's cry dueling with the last of his nerves.

Taja lifted the baby, trying to get it to stop crying. "It is easy, it's your people that make it difficult on themselves. If your voice is not heard, speak louder or leave."

Arcus let out a manic chuckle. "Just leave? I was... my best friend and I were just days away from leaving and starting over somewhere else, only days away," he said as his tone changed to an unresolved sadness.

The death of the only friend he ever had still weighed heavily upon his heart. "He was killed, killed by the plague. It got him just as we had taken down a beast and he was unable to move out of the way as it fell." A horrified look washed over his face as he recounted the most tragic day in his life to her. "I was lucky I suppose, he wasn't able to turn into one of the caiman creatures and forcing me to take him down, I don't know what would have been worse." Tears started to well in his eyes and stream down his dirty cheeks.

"I had to just leave him there, I was too afraid I would catch the plague. I didn't even get to say goodbye. Suddenly the whole forest became overrun by caiman, and I had to flee before it was too late." he said with a sniffle as his eyes gazed at nothing.

Taja felt bad for the human, for despite his harsh exterior and complete lack of manners, he had heart. She knew what it was like to lose a friend too. She watched as he sat silent, trying to regain his resolve.

"I lost someone special to me too. She was both my friend and teacher, and even worse a close and trusted friend to my family," Taja recounted, trying to fill the awkward silence, letting him know he wasn't alone.

"After my mother and father were taken and killed by..." She paused, her eyes flicking up to Arcus and then back to the baby. "Humans, I was taken in by my friend's family. Rexah was a little older than me and had already been trained to Ark. She was to teach me to use my gift but there was an accident."

"About a year later, we were in the forest where she liked to train with me, and we were attacked by Akarians. I tried to defend myself but had trouble using my abilities at first, lacking concentration after the loss of my parents. She was able to subdue three of them, not realizing that a fourth had circled around back of us. I tried…" She trailed off, her eyes welling up in tears and soaking into her fur. "I tried to stop him, I really did, but I saw something no one should ever have to see."

Taja broke down into a sob at the memory like she had been reliving the moment, burned so vividly into her mind. She began to rock back and forth both for the baby and herself, struggling with the pain. Her face turned to horror as she continued to sway. "I saw my mother's skin atop the man's shoulder. He had even stitched the part of her face together where he had crushed her skull."

Arcus's grim gaze turned to that of compassion, for he knew full well the brutality of the people he had grown up into and could understand her pain and anger. It was the sole reason he fought so hard to rise in the ranks to change their ways.

"I am sorry you had to see that," Arcus began, only to be cut off by her sobbing.

She let out a wounded growl and hiss at the memory. "That is not all. I felt so enraged that I attacked him with everything that I had, anger consumed me and I arked all my power to kill the human. I unleashed a storm of sharpened roots and vines, stabbing him in every place and every way that I could think of, letting the rage take control of me. Then I fainted from the strain and awoke hours later to find Rexah impaled through her stomach and chest by the vines I had created."

Taja's breathing became heavy and labored as she choked down her tears. "I killed her; I killed the only person who had cared for me after my family was taken. That is how I repaid her kindness."

Arcus felt a deep pain in his chest from the great sadness she had to endure in her life, the pain so great it kept him from speaking about his own past. They both sat in silence for a long while, the baby's cries filling the cave with an even more disheartening tone.

Arcus spoke up first in an attempt to relate and break the silence. "I never knew my family; my mother was probably killed after she gave birth to me or during. My father could be any number of men who had raped and tortured her. Such is their way, and the babies are just left to die. Someone had to have taken me in, as to who I have no clue or memory, but I grew up on the streets alone, no family or friends until I found Saber as a young pup in the same situation as I. Hunters had killed his family for fur pelts and I claimed the sickly cub, too small to even get a decent pelt from. He eventually got better and grew up to become my companion." His eyes set on the alert wolf as he guarded the cave with pride.

"Most people come to Amid as rejects from other cities or prisoners Sanctuary doesn't want to deal with, but those born in the city, the greenhorns, have to earn our respect as if surviving wasn't hard enough. This competition was my chance to prove myself and earn my place amongst the ranks in hopes of changing Amid for the better." He needed to put an end to their ways and for the first time since meeting Taja, for he could see the damage they had caused to the other races. He needed to put an end to their slaughter and slavery.

"But you are no different than them," Taja stated. "You captured me, are going to do creator knows what with me for the sake of personal gain. Also, the baby, you would have left her to die at the stream like they had done to you." She looked him in the eyes as he sat against the rocky wall. "In order to make the change you must become that change," she said sternly, her gaze falling back down to the baby that had finally fallen asleep from her rocking.

Arcus failed to come up with a response or argument, instead only sat in silence before drifting peacefully asleep, his eyes heavy from the tears that had filled them. Taja stroked the baby's forehead gently and relaxed, surprisingly calm despite her current circumstances. She piled up the warm sand against her chest as she lay down, holding the baby close beside her with her tail wrapping around it to keep her warm.

Arcus awoke to the early morning sun beaming down into the cave. He got up and stretched, waking up Saber with his movements. He prepared his saddle, wiping the thick layer of sand from his seat. He let everyone else sleep for as long as he could before waking them up when he was ready to leave. He knelt and touched Taja's shoulder to wake her up.

She lurched awake with a hiss. "Get your hands off me, human," She warned, searching his face for intent.

He stood up startled by her warning. "We must be leaving now," he said as he walked over next to the restless mountain wolf. "Come, I'll help you up." He offered while patting the back of Saber's saddle.

"So, you are allowing me to burden your beast now?" she said sharply, looking down to the hungry baby, taking comfort that they would make it to a source of food much faster this way. "I can get on myself."

Arcus shook his head, put off by her reaction to him trying to be friendlier. No matter, she would be gone soon. They rode for several hours north towards Amid before coming across a covered wagon with malnourished horses tied to the sides. Various items littered the ground in the surrounding area like it had been ransacked. A struggle could be heard from within, along with a muffled cry.

The side of the canvas wagon shuttered with a crashing sound, followed by laughter. Arcus's heart sank and he winced at the muffled cries for help, knowing what was happening and that it was too dangerous to interrupt. He looked back at Taja, whose eyes were fixed on the wagon and her long teeth visible from her protective growl. Arcus took a deep breath in thought, trying to decide what to do; his already bad streak of luck could easily turn further for the worse.

Taja, seeing his hesitation, hissed at him. "Be the change, hunter," she pleaded.

Arcus scowled and reluctantly approached the small door of the wagon and pulled it open. The shouts of protest and the shrill cries of the woman flooded out. Taja's hair stood up on end as her adrenaline surged, the baby in her arms and rope around her wrists making her feel helpless in the situation. Arcus reached in, pulling a man from the wagon and throwing him out onto the ground, his almost naked body slamming down into the mix of sand and dirt from the road. Arcus kicked into the cart hard with his foot as it rocked back in place. Seconds later he was tackled by another man from the inside of the wagon. They fell out onto the ground as the man punched at Arcus, pounding on his sides as his arms raised up against his face.

Arcus cried out in pain and with a surge of fear kicked the man off, his tattered pants around his ankles preventing him from standing. Arcus jumped up and repeatedly punched back at him, his head jerking left and right with his furious blows. The first man ran to the horses and drew a sword from the saddle. Saber hunched over in a pounce position as Taja hissed, the baby letting out a wailing cry from the wolf's sudden quick movements.

"Arcus, he has a sword!" Taja shouted in time for him to draw his knife and parry a swing towards his chest.

The man repeatedly chopped his machete over and over, Arcus barely keeping his footing as he retreated into a better attack position. Saber let out a fierce growl to threaten the man, causing him to startle, looking back for the attacking beast. Arcus managed to dodge and roll away to get closer to Saber. He reactively rolled again, narrowly being missed by the man's rusty blade and sending his knife like a dart directly into his shoulder. He shouted out in pain and pulled the knife from his flesh. Enraged, he swung his machete at Arcus as he rolled on the ground, coming mere inches from the blade's edge.

Arcus was light on his feet as he frantically rolled away to get closer to Saber for protection, but not fast enough as the blade came down directly at his face. He winced as suddenly a long tendril of green light intercepted the blade and hardened into a thick mass of vines tearing from the ground. The machete sank deep into the vine as it raised up, yanking free from his grip. The vines lashed and whipped out, encircling around the man's chest and waist. Its long thorns tore into his flesh as it wrapped tighter around his body, streams of blood beginning to run down his legs. The vines pulled him off the ground and held him high into the air to restrain him.

Taja's hand weaved around in a circular motion as she commanded the vines to pull him closer to her, sitting atop saber. "You will never harm another innocent again," she threatened, hoping that he hadn't killed anyone within the wagon already. The baby let out a shrill cry, pulling her from her angered trance, still distraught, recounting her parents' death the night before.

"How did you get out of your restraints?" Arcus called up to her, thankful for her aid.

A slight smile came to her face. "I could have escaped at any moment, hunter, binding my hands does nothing to stop my curse," she mocked, chuckling and sliding down Saber's back. "You have a lot to learn."

Arcus frowned and turned to go check inside the wagon and was met with a tied and gagged woman, her plain dress torn to shreds. She kicked frantically at him in defense, streams of tears falling down her young face. Her eyes went wide when she saw Taja's furry face peek in from around the door as she tried to scream through the ball of cloth in her mouth. Arcus pulled the knife he had retrieved and cut the ropes around her feet. She planted her bare bloody foot against the ground readying to kick with all her might until she saw Taja step up into the wagon.

Arcus struggled to get the knife into the ropes around her hands and finally cut her free. She pulled the blood and saliva-soaked cloth from her mouth. Tears of joy began to roll off her smiling cheeks at the sight of her baby in Taja's arms.

"My baby, you found my baby and she is ok?" she cried in hopeful joy.

Taja looked down at the whimpering child in her arms with a smile, her heart set at ease at finding the mother. She approached the woman and handed her the child, which instantly began to calm itself.

The relieved smile across the woman's face was more than enough to make Arcus's heart fill with pride with being able to help, and that Taja had pushed him to it. He looked back at the tigress, who just purred peacefully beside the pair. She looked at Arcus with a reassuring smile and nod of her head, acknowledging his good deeds.

"Be the change," she said under her breath with a smile.

The woman held her baby closely to her chest, ignoring her injuries and lack of clothing and just gazed at her child, thankful to have her back. She lay against the wall of the wagon and looked to Arcus and Taja. "Thank you so much, I can never repay what you have done for us, I owe you my life," she said in tears.

Taja reached for a blanket spread over a wooden chest in the tightly packed wagon and draped it over the woman and baby. She gently glided her furry hand over the woman's shoulder and arm, inspecting her wounds.

"What happened?" Arcus asked, now feeling obligated to comfort the woman somehow. He had spent most of his life alone and on guard, making small talk and compassion difficult and awkward for him.

The woman pulled the blanket tight around her baby as she looked to Arcus. "My husband and I were traveling when these men approached us begging for supplies. We didn't have much but shared what we could. They used our kindness against us and attacked us when we least expected it," she said, beginning to shake with the memory. "My husband kicked the one from the wagon and we took off as fast as the cart would go. They regrouped and caught up to us." She trailed off momentarily, trying to regain her composure.

Taja rested her hand on her shoulder to calm her. "If it is too difficult you do not need to recount what happened, just take comfort that you are safe now."

She nodded in understanding and her voice cracked as she tried to talk through the tears. "They killed my husband, and our wagon came to a halt. I ran for my life with my little girl and found a stream and had no choice. I feared what they would do to her, so I put her in a small crate and pushed her down the river," She recounted, squeezing the child close. "I had no idea what fate she would find but you saved her, you saved me. I have no way to repay you but with my services, anything you need doing and I will do what I can."

Taja shook her head slowly with a compassionate smile spreading to her thin lips. "No need, we are just glad we were able to help you. For now, you need to get up north and away from Amid, anywhere but there, it is a dangerous place, especially for a lone woman traveler."

"Where were you headed?" Arcus asked.

The woman choked down her tears. "We were headed for Sanctuary and had no idea the roads had gotten so dangerous," she answered.

Arcus nodded his head, knowing full well how dangerous the surrounding land was around Amid. The killer heat in the desert was the least of your worries. "I would stay away from the south. The Akarians are very dangerous and ruthless people," he explained.

Taja gently laid her hand on the woman's leg near an open gash, meeting her worried expression with sympathy in her eyes. The woman flinched in pain at the touch of her cuts and bruises, Taja displaying a loving smile as a bright yellow and green light emanated from her hand. The light pulsated in waves under the blanket as tendrils of arked energy wrapped around her leg, traveling throughout her body.

The woman gasped in shock and began to breathe heavily from the rush of panic. "What did you do?" she asked, looking over her blood-stained legs and arm without a trace of the bruising or cuts, staring at her in disbelief.

Arcus's face contorted in confusion; he learned more about this mysterious feline all the time.

Taja lifted her hand. "I am no master, but I arked my essence to you, healing some of your wounds to the best of my ability. I apologize if it wasn't enough, but you should be strong enough to travel now and take your baby to safety," she explained while standing up to admire the woman in front of her, little girl held tightly in her arms.

Arcus left the wagon to wait for Taja outside, helping to get the horses ready, and checked the wheels for any damage from the chase. He pulled free several arrows stuck into the side of the wagon and added them to his own quiver. He motioned for Saber to come and retrieve him for the rest of their journey and called out to Taja. "It's not far from here, get on and let's move."

Taja listened and made herself comfortable amongst the roll of supplies and weapons attached to the back of the saddle. She lifted her unbound wrists to him. "Do I need to be tied again, Hunter?" she asked timidly.

Arcus was taken back and expressed a look of confusion on his face, not knowing what he was really doing now. Everything he had planned for had changed so much and he hadn't thought his next actions through yet. "I suppose not, but don't you get any ideas about running off, my arrows are much faster than you can run," he said, looking back towards their path.

Taja let out a chuckle as she watched the woman come out and climb up to the driver's bench. "Be safe and take care of your little one," she called out with a wave of her hand.

"Thank you and you too, please find me if you are ever in Sanctuary, you are always welcome at my table. My name is Shara Evermore."

Arcus grabbed onto the saddle and dug his heels into Saber's sides. "Let's ride," he called out as Saber sprinted ahead towards Amid.

They passed through a small oasis of forest and twisted more west, staying to the harder ground for faster travel when available. The far reaches of Amid's beast enclosures looming off in the distance. There was a massive canyon on the east side of Amid that they had learned to use as a stable for all their giant beasts of war. Walls of long pikes and spike barricades lined the upper walls of the canyon to keep the creatures from crawling out. Akarians had little to fear from anyone sneaking into their territory, for it was scary enough looking from the outside that nobody was stupid enough to try and get in.

They traveled along the canyon until it deepened, and the large canvas tents became visible, dotting the ledges of the cliffs, leading to primitive looking structures built into the sides of the steep ravine walls. Long suspension rope bridges passed over in several places alongside giant wooden lifts of multiple sizes.

Taja was amazed by the sounds of the pent-up creatures below, moaning and growling amongst each other. She had feared for their care and well-being but from what she could interpret the creatures sounded happy and content to her amazement. She was relieved, the Akarians may not care for humanoid life, but they took pride in their beasts of burden and war, taking decent care of the lot. She could see massive skulls raising up over the tops of the wooden walls amongst the tips of the canvas teepee structures before losing the view of the canyon as they circled around the city. By the massive size of the city, she wondered how many of the savages there really were compared to the small prides of lionels she was used to.

Before getting to Arcus's usual entrance by Muckton, a group of riders approached and circled around them, forcing Saber to a halt. One of the men adorned in fresh pelts and leather straps came in close. "Nice catch, greenhorn," he said with a vulgar smirk towards Taja and motioned for them to head towards a massive crowd of people.

Several angry and scared creatures were tied up or netted, laying in a row next to the crowd and pinned down by long pikes hammered deep into the clay of the sand. Taja could feel a swelling fear deep within her heart as she clenched onto the saddle straps tightly at her sides.

"I'm not participating in the competition. She is mine and I am taking her to my hovel," Arcus called out in a deepened tone, hoping to misdirect them. He attempted to move Saber forward through the ring of horse mounted men and was met with the ringing sounds of rusty metal swords being pulled from their scabbards. Taja could tell by the way they were dressed that they were more than just hunters and a lump in her throat arose in anxiety.

Arcus glanced at his secret place of entrance only a few hundred yards away and back at the men, deciding whether it would be worth the chase to get lost inside the city. "Alright, we will go your way," he said with confidence in his more commanding tone of voice.

They followed up to the mass of people, all talking about their catches and kills for the event, trying to determine who was to win. Taja could hear people debating and betting on which of the restrained beasts would be most formidable in the arena and boasts of how they too could have caught them if given a chance. Arguing broke out here and there in the crowd along with fights that led to more bloodshed. Besides the vile stares and smiles she received from the dirty hunters she also witnessed an argument over which creature was the deadliest that quickly ended with one man losing his limbs. Her whole heart and soul ached for these people and their disgusting way of life.

Arcus froze in place momentarily. He recognized Aldair coming his way and his ego laced eyes glaring directly at him. He gulped. "Aldair, I am not participating in the competition and am just trying to make it home when these men interfered," he said, eying the ornately dressed man approaching.

Aldair was Radagar's younger, more sophisticated and clever brother, and being brother to the King gave him almost limitless power in their society. Aldair ignored Arcus's request and walked his horse directly up to Taja. "What do we have here? An offering perhaps?" he asked with an awful smile spreading across his lips.

"No, she is mine. I caught her today. As I told you, I was not competing," Arcus said firmly with a threatening glare through his long, wavy hair.

Two men flanking Aldair's sides approached Arcus, staring him down and watching with hope of altercation lingering in their smiles, just waiting for the slightest excuse to cut him down. Aldair reached up and with a single tug pulled Taja down from Saber's back and landed across his horse's back. He yanked her head back by the scruff of her neck as she let out a growl in pain, and her ears pinned back. He tossed her body forward off his horse as she crashed face first into the rough sand below at his horse's feet. "I believe you are smart enough to know the rules, greenhorn, you cannot own slaves until you earn them," he shouted, kicking Taja back down on her side as she tried to stand up. He then dismounted his horse and pulled out a knife, reaching down and pulling her roughly to her feet. His eyes traveled down her fury body and back up, licking his lips with desire.

He thought for a second if he should spare her life, his hands caressing the soft curves of her body. "I believe I have some uses for you," he smiled, motioning for the men to get rid of Arcus.

ARKANGEL

"No, she is mine!" Arcus shouted, the look of horror of what he knew was going to happen to her washing over his face. The men poked and prodded at Saber with the tips of their swords, ushering him forward. Arcus's plea went unheard as they forced him further away towards the edge of the crowd.

Taja stood trembling in place, terrified as she saw Arcus's worried look before he disappeared out of sight, powerless. Aldair's hands traveled up and down her backside. "We are going to have some fun tonight, Kitty," he said, with another foul smile spreading across his face. Taja could feel her tail wrap tightly down and around her leg as her hair stood up on end from fright. She had never felt so dirty or violated and feared for her life that it was only going to get worse.

CHAPTER 6

"BEGINGINGS OF A BOND"

Kaiden and Nirayus exited the Gardens together with a clear and uncomfortable distance between them. Nirayus drug her feet, lingering behind her forced companion and wasn't happy to be away from her father, feeling the anger of a wrongful punishment in her heart. Why did she have to go with this person they had just met? Let alone a human? She despised humans for the most part even if he had just saved her life, what made him different than any other? He had saved her from Vixis and possibly even her father but even still, she didn't like the idea of traveling so far away from her homeland with someone she didn't know. She had never been past Market Town, it wasn't safe for the gifted the closer you got to Sanctuary, but at least her new companion had abilities of his own, so in a way she didn't feel so alone and decided to pick up her pace.

    She watched Kaiden walk up to a monstrous man, easily standing a foot taller than the door to the inn behind him and almost just as wide. The heavy scars on his face and ugly patchwork of skin over his right eye made her feel timid. An aquarian stood beside him, his webbed hands resting atop his jagged carapace hips as they scoured the area for something. She had seen aquarians before and had always been envious of the vibrant and wildly colored hair of their females.

    "There you is, runt," Gorman sighed, nudging Finn with his fist, who was lost in thought and staring down an empty alleyway.

An intrigued grin spread to Finn's face. "Look, he found an elven maiden, interesting and unexpected for a journey such as this," he said with a bounce of his mandibles, walking uncomfortably close to her.

Nirayus's light blue eyebrows furrowed at the breach of personal space. "May I help you?"

"Interesting," he said, bending down closer to her level. "Long ears, white skin, no, very white skin, short, even for an elf, almost child-like, and with such shiny blue hair. Yes, very soft blue hair," Finn stated, putting his webbed fingers through her hair. "No golden eyes?" he asked, cocking his head to the side in puzzlement.

Nirayus batted his long arm away, unconsciously taking a step closer to Kaiden for safety. "Please keep your hands off," she stated with her hands beginning to glow a fiery orange as embers slowly swirled up and around her. "I do have golden eyes, but only at night."

Finn clapped his hands in excitement at meeting the young moon elf and that she had the gift to ark. "You have the gift. You know that abilities like yours are getting few and far between over the last few centuries? I suppose the fact that you're hunted constantly doesn't help either I suppose but it is fascinating all the same."

Gorman smacked Finn on his back. "Give da girl some space," he said with a stern look.

Finn looked from Gorman to Nirayus, trying to understand what he did wrong. "Oh, my apologies, I get caught up in the moment sometimes. I am Finn by the way, and I will be your guide on this adventure so to speak." He took a step back with a wide grin.

"This is Gorman," Kaiden said with a gesture to the hulking half ogre. "She is coming with us. Hunters are after her as we speak, and I have made a vow to her father that we would keep her safe the best we can. I killed one in the gardens but there may be others, so we should get moving." He realized he had just killed someone and felt a wave of guilt settle heavily in his heart. He wasn't sure if he had ever done that before, but it still didn't feel right. At least when his armored form killed, he was unconscious and not in control, so it made it feel a little more bearable amongst all his other worries.

Finn and Gorman exchanged glances. Gorman's face showed the dread of the extra responsibility and the frustration of Finn's obvious excitement about the situation.

"Excellent, welcome to the family," Finn exclaimed as he watched Gorman's hands reach up to caress his own temples to relieve stress.

"We's already walkin, how we to be carryin more food?" Gorman asked in frustration.

"I will hunt for my own food and can take care of myself," Nirayus said sternly. "As for the wagon and supplies, all I have to do is ask and any merchant will be glad to put it on my family tab." She straightened her dress and walked towards a stable.

"Excellent," Finn said again as the grin on his face stretched even further.

Gorman's eyebrow raised slightly. "Family tab?" He mumbled to himself in thought of who this girl could be.

Kaiden began to walk quickly to follow behind her. "Alright let's go, we need to leave before any more show up." he said, his hand moving to his shoulder that had been shot by the crossbow bolt, finding the wound now completely undetectable.

Finn walked up into the lead. "We shall stop at the Wayfinding Wanderer, and there we can get all the supplies we need. They have everything ready for adventurers just like us that are in a hurry. I suggest we get the wandering warrior package so we can get a cart with more than one seat this time." He pointed to a large building surrounded by wagon parts and stacks of crates and barrels.

Kaiden nodded his head in agreement, trying to keep pace with the agile elf. "That sounds great, Finn, lead the way," he said, finding himself looking at the beautiful elf in front of him.

ARKANGEL

They entered in through the side of the building with Gorman approaching a pair of the biggest horses and started to cinch down their harnesses.

Nirayus eagerly dealt with the shop keeper and sprinted excitedly to the new horses, petting and running her fingers through the white one's long, black mane.

Finn hopped up into the sturdy cart and lounged across the far back bench, ready for the day's journey.

Kaiden helped the workers finish loading crates of supplies into the side of the wagon and hopped in to take his place amongst the supplies since the two overly large companions took the entire benches for themselves.

Nirayus, feeling more comfortable by herself, mounted onto her new favorite horse, her almost weightless body settling into its comfortable saddle.

They set off down the road east to the grand city of Sanctuary, the wide-open road unfolding ahead of them through rolling hills and grassy plains. Hours into the journey they came up on a small lake surrounded by tall grasses and scattered trees. Finn started sniffing hard into the air, waking up from a deep sleep after being rocked by the constant swaying of the cart. He let out a shriek and jumped from the wagon, sprinting towards the small lake. Gorman grabbed his crossbow from beside him as Kaiden perked up alert. Nirayus stood straight up onto the horse's back to get a better vantage point, her ears spreading slightly to pick up any sounds of warning.

Finn's eyes went wide from amusement as he dove into the crystal blue water, the ripples spreading over the calm surface and causing an array of creatures to scurry away from the sudden intrusion. He swam deep, pulling the fresh clean water through his chest gills, revitalizing his system and jump starting his body's healing to repair the damage done in the salamander attack from the day before. Skimming across the bottom of the lake, he waved at the small schools of fish as if being reacquainted with old friends. He even took the time to stop and pet a large creature resting at the bottom, its wide mouth stretching and unfolding open to trap any unsuspecting fish that swam by. A few powerful kicks with his webbed feet sent him up soaring into the air and splashing back down, throwing water over the surface of the lake.

"He be a fish an a dog. Only seen dogs splash around like dat," Gorman huffed, resting his crossbow back down and steering the horses off to the side of the path.

Kaiden stood up and stretched. "I guess this is as good a place as any to rest."

Gorman stopped to think. He was a military man, point A to point B, no messing around. He had decided that Finn quite possibly was his exact opposite until his thoughts traveled to the realization, they were to be in Sanctuary soon, and decided that stalling may not be such a bad idea. "I's be castin a line," he said. "Maybe catch me a big stupid fish," he added with a grin.

Kaiden jumped down from the wagon with the fishing pole and handed it to Gorman. "Here you go, I am going to go bathe over there," he said, pointing to the far end of the lake where large flat rocks lay scattered along the bank.

Gorman nodded, eyeing the elf as she stood tall on the horse's back, scanning the grasses like a falcon. "I think it's time to feed," she said softly to herself as she leapt from the horse, landing into a full run. She darted into the tall grass and vanished from sight, off to hunt her prey.

Gorman's gaze turned to Kaiden. "Where you find dat one?" he asked with a hearty chuckle.

A smile came to Kaiden's face as he turned his attention from where she disappeared and headed towards the rocks, completely zoned out in thought. He made his way to the other end of the lake and dove into the cold, clear water. He took his tattered clothes off to wash and wring them out, laying them across the warm flat rocks to dry in the hot sun. He swam around in the tranquil water surrounded by trees, relaxing his stiff muscles.

Kaiden jerked to the side, startled, arms raised in defense as the intimidating Finn quickly swam up beside him from the deep. Finn smiled, his mandibles bouncing water drops from his face as thick, protective lenses folded in from over his big, black, glossy eyes.

"What do you think the odds are our big friend will catch anything?" Finn asked in a playful tone.

Kaiden looked to see Gorman reel in his line to find a wad of water fern tangled in. He grabbed it off and threw it back into the lake and recast the line. He then watched as Finn disappeared into the deep water and only moments later saw Gorman's pole bending again.

Gorman reeled it up again to find his hook sunk deep into a dense waterlogged branch full of runny sediments. He broke it off and threw it down to the ground, before recasting the line.

Moments later Finn returned with a huge mischievous smile spread across his face in anticipation. Kaiden watched Gorman reeling the pole as hard as he could, bending as it neared its breaking point. He lifted and cranked at the pole in building excitement to see his victory catch only to find a large stone at the end. He held the stone in his huge hand in confusion until he noticed the neat bow tied around the rock with the fishing line.

Gorman's death gaze settled on Finn as he shouted, "I's kill you, fish!"

Finn let out a gurgled laugh before diving back down into the water to safety. Kaiden laughed at the banter, feeling bad for the always serious half ogre.

Gorman reluctantly cast the line a final time and immediately got a pull on the pole, then threw his arms into the air in frustration. "Fish if dis be you I will eat you!" He shouted as the pole pulled from his hands and disappeared into the deep water.

Kaiden grabbed at his stomach in laughter, his breath getting harder to draw into his heaving chest. He collapsed back onto one of the flat stones as tears rolled down his face watching Gorman's temper fly.

Gorman started shouting and waving his arms in the air in anger, cursing Finn as a massive wave splashed over him and a fish almost half his size knocked him back on his ass. He struggled to hold onto the slippery fish as it tried to flap and flail its way back into the lake. He reached back and grabbed one of his spears and stabbed it through the fish's body, pinning it to the ground. He stood up and brushed the slime off his pants, a rare smile of satisfaction spreading to his face.

Finn returned to the laughing Kaiden to share in the short, joyful moment amongst the hardships they had endured so far. He set the pole down beside Kaiden and jumped back into the water to play before they would inevitably have to leave.

Nirayus peered over the tall grass, holding a big fluffy panjam in her arms. She stroked its long, soft hair as it nervously shook in her cold grasp. She watched the display of Finn messing with Gorman and chuckled at the daft ogre's plight. She had never met an ogre before and found his simplicity amusing. Her hand suddenly flickered a bright white and blue glow of energy with a sudden jolt to the panjam before it went limp.

"I thank you, friend, for your sacrifice. Say hello to my mother for me," she whispered before opening her mouth, exposing two longer fangs to the sides and sinking them deep into the little animal. Several seconds later she had sucked most the blood from its body, her eyes glowing into a bright golden color, before taking a deep breath of air and sighing contently. She then drew her dagger and skinned the small, rotund animal as she walked over to the edge of the lake.

Without thinking, she passed through the long grass and came face to face with Kaiden, who was still getting dressed. She noticed him pulling up his pants and her eyes immediately darted down as her cheeks begin to turn a bright pink in embarrassment.

Her eyes shot back up at the realization of what he was wearing. There was a familiar, one of a kind, smooth, circular rock dangling from an old string around his neck. Her chest tightened as she froze in place, unable to blink or breathe. Could this really be him? She struggled to remember to breathe, her eyes blinking rapidly in thought and in search of grounding herself back in reality.

"Is everything ok?" Kaiden asked as he pulled his shirt over his head.

Nirayus gulped in an attempt to answer but her words failed to come out, her heart racing and pounding so hard she feared he may hear it.

"I'm fine," she managed, looking away to gather her thoughts. How could it be him? Does he remember her? How could he? She tried to sort out the best thing to say in her mind. She felt so relieved that she had found him but remembered that he had no memory. Her heart sank, she felt bad, so bad for how rude she had been to him. She wanted to embrace him and remind him of the encounter they had shared and how he had saved her life, giving her strength to be the woman she was today. But it was too much, she couldn't burden him with that right now. A feeling of loneliness washed over her, she had finally found the young boy she had searched for but without his memory he really wasn't there.

"Are you sure?" Kaiden asked again, gathering the fishing pole and walking up the grassy bank to get closer to her. He looked into her eyes and could sense sorrow. She must really be missing her father and still coarse from having to leave with complete strangers. He felt allured by her, there was a tension he could not describe, some pull he felt but didn't know how to act on it.

"Yeah sorry, I was just reminded of something from when my mother passed, but it is of no concern, we should be on our way," Nirayus quickly remarked, brushing her hair back out of her face and behind her ears. She looked at him from the corner of her eye, wanting so badly to let him know who she was and how much he meant to her and how she had thought about him every day. But she feared what he would think if he didn't remember, he may just think she was crazy.

"I can imagine what you must feel like," Kaiden responded, stealing a glimpse of her beautiful doe eyes. It made him feel bad that she was clearly so sad, and he found it strange it affected him so much considering how little he knew of her.

"I have no memories of my family, at all, no matter how hard I seem to try. It is hard not knowing if they are still out there or if they are

ARKANGEL

looking for me." he chuckled. "I could pass right by them and not even know." He looked back up to see her sorrow turn to understanding and the spark return in her smile, listening contently.

"I know it may sound strange, but I think I can feel my father somehow, it feels like we are getting closer and that he is still alive." Kaiden brushed his brown wet hair to the side, out of his face, to better look at her walking next to him. "I can't feel anything from my mother, nothing is there at all; I fear something has happened to her and I'm scared that if my memories return it will be like reliving her death all over again." He sniffled slightly, keeping back any tears.

"Maybe she is just far away?" Nirayus offered. "Or maybe you just have a strong connection to your father like I do?" looking back to meet his eyes as they approached the wagon. "If you don't remember and she is gone, the only thing left of her in this world are her memories and it would be sad to lose those forever," she said, clenching her golden compass in her hand. "Sometimes that's all we have of the ones we love, and you should fight to not lose them. Don't give up," she added as a tear rolled down her cheek.

Kaiden saw her tear and wiped his own away before it could stream down his face. She was right, though. After they did what they had to do to help with the plague in Sanctuary, he would seek answers from his past. He climbed up into the back of the wagon and found a comfortable spot amongst the gear and was surprised when she leaped into the back beside him.

They watched as Gorman made his way up to them, carrying his catch with a smile of pride spread across his face. Finn sprinted up as well, hands full of dry sticks and branches to set up a fire.

"Dis be a good meal here, I's like cookin fish," he said with a hearty chuckle, looking to Finn while attempting to spark a flame. He struck a stone against a cylinder of black metal several times. Weak sparks danced around the wood shavings and twigs, failing to light.

"Need a hand there, Finn?" Nirayus called out, holding up her glowing hands as a tall flame flickered from her palm. Finn stood back as she snapped her hand; the ball of fire splashed on the pile of sticks, igniting instantly into a blaze. "Here, I caught this in the field too," she said, throwing the panjam over to Finn as he marveled at the fire. Gorman reached into the cart and pulled out a metal spit and stabbed it into the ground.

"We be eatin good here soon," Gorman said as he pulled a pouch of spices from a bag and began to cook the fish. Finn pulled a skewer and prepared the panjam, its little rotund body full of meat and fat. They quickly ate what they could, Kaiden eating more than he thought he could, his stomach twisting in pain again from the food. Nirayus took a few nibbles of meat but left the rest to Gorman, who downed anything that was left in front of him.

"Let's get going, we should really be getting to Sanctuary as soon as we can, and while it's still light out preferably so they are more likely to let us in the gates after we explain to them what we have seen, the high paladins will want to hear of the plague if they haven't already," Finn said as he put out the fire.

Gorman grabbed the lead of Nirayus's fine white horse, looking back at the two sitting close to each other in the back with a small grin. He pulled the leather lines up from their horses to add her in and froze momentarily, realizing that adding the third horse would only get them there faster. He slowly finished tying it up and pulled himself onto the bench in the front seat to make himself comfortable, setting his reliable great crossbow beside him for safety.

Finn jumped in and laid across the entire center bench again and crossed his webbed fingers together across his chest for a long nap. The wagon inched forward and began to slowly pick up pace as they made their way closer to Sanctuary. The rolling hills turned to forest and open pastures as they got closer. Small villages and farmsteads lined roads; the people working hard tilling and plowing the fields.

The scenery turned ever grim as they continued to get closer to Sanctuary. It became all too common to find blood-soaked patches of grass or dirt littered with skin and clothing. Streaks of blood staining the ground with body parts strewn across the ground recklessly. It was clear the plague had only gotten worse and more frequent as they approached the massive human capitol.

The ride was depressing and mostly silent as the main talker Finn slept and Gorman kept to himself as usual. Nirayus squeezed her hand tightly around her compass, wanting so badly to talk to Kaiden but not knowing what she should say. They awkwardly caught each other looking at one another and away again, trying to see who would speak first.

"Do you remember anything?" Nirayus asked shyly, immediately regretting asking such a stupid question.

Kaiden was startled out of his own thoughts of her and managed, "What? Oh, No, I don't". He used the opportunity to adjust himself so he could better look at her. "The first thing I remember was laying on the ground with Gorman here shouting at me; he thought I was one of the plague victims turning salamander." He gestured over to the back of the giant half breed, shadowing them from the glare of the sun.

"Luckily, he steadied his hand and allowed me a chance to come to my senses. I was unconscious, my body was riddled with pain. I couldn't move at first. But then I got up and we fought our way to his home in Hengegrove where we found Finn and found my… armor. I guess you would call it armor. We left right away and then I came across you; it has all happened so fast." He recounted everything he could, remembering everything over the last few days easily enough but absolutely nothing prior.

"That must be frightening not to even really know the company you're with. Do you know if Kaiden is really your name?" Nirayus asked, looking for signs of his necklace, which was under his shirt.

"That's the only thing I remember, my name. At least I am pretty sure it's my name," he said with a chuckle and a grin, thinking of how pitiful he must sound.

She let out a smile, the first real smile she had actually given him as she had finally come to terms with them traveling together. "I'm sure you will get it back eventually; it may just take some time." She softly placed her hand on his knee for reassurance.

    Kaiden gulped at her touch, feeling so uncomfortable, his emotions creating a tornado in his chest as his breath quickened. Her hand was so gentle, he wasn't sure how to reciprocate what he was feeling, so he put his hand over hers in thanks of her support. Her skin was slightly cold but very soft, and he found himself fighting the urge to curl his fingers up into hers.

    The cart hit a worn dip in the road, jarring the whole wagon, and her hand slipped free to brace herself. Kaiden sat unaffected by the disturbance and wanting nothing more than the comfort of her hand back in his. His mind raced for what to say or ask to get her attention again.

    "Where did you get that compass you wear around your neck?" he asked, examining all the details he could see in the intricate etchings along the rim. "It is beautiful."

    Her hand quickly went to grasp it tightly. "I," she started. "It…" There was a pause in her voice as she thought deeply about what to say in this moment she was unprepared for. "Someone very special gave it to me many years ago," she said, looking away and forcing herself with everything she had not to shed a single tear. Her eyes met his again and there in an instant that seemed to last forever in her mind was an internal war waged over what she could and should say to him. Maybe it would help jog his memories a little? Or maybe he would think she was crazy. She tempted herself with her next words. "I noticed earlier you have one too, do you remember where you got it?"

    Kaiden's hand moved to his shirt as his finger traced around the edges of his own necklace. "I can't remember," he said, looking back into her eyes as a small smile spread on her thin, pink lips. His head lifted up. "But I do know it is special to me. I feel it, and a strong connection to it." he chuckled lightheartedly. "Maybe that seems silly since it appears to only be a simple rock?"

    Nirayus's heart raced faster. She was so tempted to throw her arms around him to hear how much it meant to him even though he didn't know why. "No, not at all," she said with building excitement. "I find it gives me peace to carry something special with me and hold onto it when I need strength. It's like a special memory locked away into this little object and it will never be lost," she said reassuringly. She decided to see if she could find something close by and now, with more control of her power, make another smooth rock for him and see if it would help him remember. Then a booming voice interrupted her.

"We be here," Gorman announced as the view of the gigantic castle gates centered between three white, stone towers rising up over the hill; rings of towering walls all connecting to each other defending the center with hundreds of soldiers patrolling the tops of the high outer walls. The three central towers deep within the walls towered over the already overly tall walls with bronze, mechanical contraptions attached to the sides of the towers. Long, sharpened logs sunken deep into the ground lined the base of the walls to keep the largest of intruders at bay.

As they approached the gates, they noticed two balconies above them with archers armed and ready watching their every move. Guards poured through a brief opening of the gate and surrounded them with weapons drawn. Their big, bulky sets of plate armor glinted off the rays of the sun.

Kaiden shook Finn awake, looking alarmed. "Finn, are they always this aggressive to newcomers?" he asked, looking to the anxious Nirayus in hope of answers.

Nirayus leaned in, her voice trembling, thinking that somehow, they knew right away she is gifted, that this display of aggression was all for her. "I have never been here before, they don't exactly like my kind," she said as her body trembled in fear.

Finn sat up blinking his eyes repeatedly to adjust to the dry sun. "No this is very unusual, this city, at least its outer mercantile districts are always open to travelers and people looking to move in, this is both bothersome and yet very fascinating and I would suspect the effects of the plague may largely be at work here," he said in wonder, looking over all the armed archers above. He looked to the side of the castle and pointed to a crowd gathered around the other side of the castle towards another main road. "It looks like we are not the only ones," he said, watching the armed guards march out the far gate, holding a mob at bay.

Gorman pulled on the reigns, bringing them to a halt several yards from the gate before the approaching guards. He searched the city over once again with his limited field of view. He felt a sense of home in this place and missed the safety inside the walls with his family. He couldn't help but notice the demeanor had changed so much that all he felt was cold distant memories.

"Are they going to let us in?" Kaiden asked Gorman.

Gorman turned his head to eye Finn. "You got this, fish?" the half ogre asked in hope of not getting involved with the guards. Having grown up in their ranks under his father's command, he had gotten to know many of them, but this new generation of guards wouldn't recognize him and hopefully leave him be.

Finn eyed the situation for a few moments. "One would assume they have barred the gates and are turning away the newcomers until whatever they are scared of is solved, although if we know someone important inside maybe we could get a message inside for them to let us in, it's been many years since I have been here and do not know anyone with enough pull to get us on the inside which is unfortunate because the info we have pertains to what is most likely the dilemma in the first place," Finn said, laying his long fingers on Gorman's shoulder, implying he may be the only one with connections on the inside.

Gorman quickly brushed his hand off and snapped the reigns. "I may know someone," he said hesitantly.

"Halt, come no further!" a guard yelled out from above, holding a bow with a knocked arrow.

"Turn back, gates are closed," another guard with a spear said as he approached. His knuckles turned white from the hard grip on his spear and his knees began to tremble together at the realization of Gorman's size.

"I's need a message into da castle," Gorman said gruffly in a commanding voice.

The guard turned back to see more men coming to aid him if there was any trouble. "Ah, yes, sire, I can get a message inside for you or I can let you just deliver it yourself?" he said as his apparent nervousness turned into excitement. Moments later the other guards came to his side in a rumble of chatter, all looking to the half ogre in awe.

Gorman turned back to see his companion's blank stares and then turned back to the group of guards. "Yes, inside good," Gorman said with a confused expression.

The guards each bowed at him and rushed to open the doors almost as if it were a competition. "Yes sir, whatever you say," one of them said, fumbling to get his spear up to his side to let them pass. One by one they lined up in a row with the gates open and bowed their heads excitedly to Gorman as they passed through the growing group of guards.

Gorman drove through the gates, barely able to squeeze the wagon through the mass of people to get into the courtyard. The inner courtyard behind the main walls had a secondary lower section of wall with tiered ledges and archery stands lining almost the entire inner courtyard for defense. Many men stood post, all watching the single wagon pass through.

Kaiden was transfixed by the massive white stone towers soaring high into the sky. "What is that building?" he asked Finn, pointing at a structure suspended in midair between the three towers.

Finn cocked his head slightly in thought, reminding himself that Kaiden had lost his memory and wouldn't know of the most legendary human structure in Allterra. "That is the High Paladin's chamber which holds the important meetings and courts of the Paladin's and nobles of the city and is where the war room is for planning city defenses and military strategy and campaigns," Finn responded, noting the lack of peasants in the courtyard and alleyways.

They rode up to an empty stable where Gorman jumped off the cart to tie the reigns to a post buried into the ground. Gorman looked around the city that he hadn't seen in ten years in dismay of how bleak it looked. Nobody walked through the yards or in the market alleyways, only frightened guards lining the walls.

ARKANGEL

"What are you doing here?" an elderly man blurted out dumbfounded, hesitant to leave the inside of his home near the stable.

Gorman looked around again into the empty courtyard. "What be happenin here? Why no people?" he asked with a worried expression.

"It's the manders," he said in fear. "Everyone is hiding in their homes, it's only a matter of time until the plague makes its way inside the castle walls. It's not safe here, I would travel north if you can to Solstice Gardens, I hear that's the only place left safe by them wretched Salamanders," he said while his eyes darted around in alarm.

"Solstice Gardens?" Gorman asked, having never heard of such a place before.

The man began to point out directions before being interrupted by dreadful screeches and screams that echoed down the alleys. A loud crashing and banging sound began to drown out the screams, followed by shrill cackles of laughter.

Gorman reached to grab his crossbow off the wagon and motioned for his alert companions to get out and behind the cart. Kaiden watched as the guards poured from the barracks building beside the gate and lined themselves along the inner walls, several stories up and drawing their bows.

The screams got louder and louder, drowning out the clanging of armor as the soldiers filled the courtyard. They formed a line to the main entrance deeper into the district, pulling free their large heavy swords and standing shoulder to shoulder, shields raised in a solid wall of steel. A woman stepped out of the barracks gate; her long strawberry blonde hair almost glowing in the sunlight as she took her place behind her men. She put on an ornate looking gold steel helmet with silver trim and detached a curved, bladed glaive from her back.

"Scarlett?" Gorman said in a huff under his breath in disbelief.

"Alright, men, the time is now to stand against this evil. We must purge our streets clean in the name of High Paladin Lanthor. Stand firm, strike true, and for the creator's sake give em hell!" She raised her weapon high into the air and with a flick of her armored wrist the glaive extended into a deadly polearm. The men followed suit, raising their weapons high and shouting to raise their morale in a symphony of battle cries.

Nirayus backed up behind Kaiden, who was crouched behind the back of the cart, peering past the soldiers towards the continuous cries deep within the alleyways. The men all planted their back feet firm against the hard dirt holding their shields up. Finn lowered his body so he could see over the cart while staying as unseen as possible, while Gorman rested his giant crossbow against the top of the wagon, ready to fire at whatever came into view. The creature's shrieks reverberated through the buildings, causing them to shake as they flooded in closer.

"Ready!" Commander Scarlett shouted, standing center behind her men, the archers around the walls all pulling arrows from their barrels and drawing them in their strings.

The echoing of their relentless hissing and breathing drew nearer with a thunderous boom striking as the wave of lizards slammed themselves against the wall of shields, clawing and snapping their teeth as whatever they could see. The men swung their swords repeatedly at the horde, unable to aim at a target in the flurry of their bodies scrambling to break through the line.

"Back!" Scarlett yelled as they began to march steadily backwards, bringing them further into the courtyard at a controlled pace.

The archers let loose a volley of arrows hitting the horde and filling them with arrows like pincushions, with little effect to slow the beasts down. Their claws continued to slash and grab, attempting to tear down the thick steel shields. Another volley of arrows blanketed the crowd, followed by another. The well-trained aim of the archers aiding in trying to place the razor-sharp arrow points in the vitals of their former human brethren.

Gorman could see fear begin to take hold on the soldier's faces as the onslaught only grew more and more desperate as the creatures tired out their victims. He looked back to Kaiden to give an order but was met by a look he hadn't seen in the kid before, a purpose to protect.

Kaiden stood up, fists clenched at his sides. "Let's not let these men fall today, Gorman. Get on the cart and put that crossbow to use. Finn, stay back here and help Nirayus," he shouted, building up the courage to take action, knowing full well he had no idea how to use his armor.

Finn looked back at the shaken Nirayus and blinked repeatedly, coming closer to pull her further behind the cart. Gorman stood looking at Kaiden for several seconds in disbelief that just a few days ago this was the boy who ran from battle when he could.

"You don't have to do this, stay back here with us," Nirayus pleaded, the fear of seeing such hideous and violent creatures for the first time paralyzing her.

Kaiden let out a roaring cry and ran in behind the men looking for an opening to get through. His adrenaline made his body tremble and chest pound as he charged the back of the armored men and leapt several feet into the air, soaring up and over them, landing deep in the mass of scales and talons. A sonic boom blasted, sending the lizards hurling through the air and splattering against the sturdy stone walls of the castle. Rays of golden light radiated from inside the chaos and the heavily armored guards were thrown back several feet.

Standing in the center clearing stood Kaiden in his dark grey suit of intricate armor, golden light encircling his body with his eyes glowing, a silky white smoke softly billowing. Gasps could be heard around the courtyard as all the soldiers caught a glimpse of him standing stoic in the dangerous courtyard. Scarlett, still standing from the blast in her heavy paladin armor, unshielded her eyes with her hand and stood in awe of the majestic knight.

Kaiden flicked his forearms out and forward, causing the blades from his arms to extend as he reached down and pulled out the thin curved blades from his shins. With a blurred speed he began to whirl and spin, his arms slashing forward with his short swords and following up with another slash from his arms. Spinning back and forth like a whirlwind of blades they slashed repeatedly at the salamanders, who still struggled to get up from the explosion.

One lizard leapt forward from behind the growing number of casualties, its mouth agape and claws outstretched to pierce into prey. Kaiden stepped to the side, landing a deep gash with his short sword as he spun around and quickly impaled it with his other sword, deep into its side. The momentum of the attack completely disemboweled the lizard as it fell into a bloody pile of scales.

Cries and shrieks continued to fill the air as more flooded forth from within the town. Kaiden flipped back and out of the pile of corpses into the courtyard with the other swordsmen. He motioned for them to separate, five to each side of him to create a wide "V" shape with him being the inside point.

Gorman jumped forth, spear in hand with loaded crossbow in the other to join the men to Kaiden's left. Commander Scarlett motioned for her archers to draw their arrows and ready a volley as the rushing horde screamed and cried their demoralizing call.

Moments later two dozen quillbacks tore their way through their fallen kin and burst out towards Kaiden, savagely clawing at the air like madmen preparing to tear apart their victims. Arrows flew over the swordsmen's shoulders, sinking deep into the creature's scales, only making them angrier. Another round of arrows flew down, hitting their marks as the lizards continued their attacks unhindered, the arrows protruding from their sides and backs, barely visible among their quills.

As the mass of creatures neared Kaiden, he signaled a charge as the men closed in from either side. The lizards bounced and funneled their way along the walls of steel shields right into the flurry of spinning blades with Kaiden slashing and stabbing at his attackers with his four razor sharp blades.

Scarlett circled around the back to the right, along with Gorman from the left, blocking any possible retreat. The swordsmen continued to slash their swords at the heads of the towering creatures while pinching them together with their shields.

Nirayus and Finn, watching the tactical execution, stared in awe as the soldiers all worked together against their foes. Nirayus hopped up onto the wagon for a better view, getting overwhelmed with adrenaline herself and unleashing a blast of lightning. Electric blue bolts crackled out from her fingertips, arking between her hands. They swirled and spun into a glowing ball of electricity as she pulled her arms out wide, blasting the ball out into the center of the attacking swarm. It exploded into a brilliant burst of lightning that bounced and whipped bright blue energy between them, paralyzing them in their place. The tendrils of crackling energy crawled all over and jumped from creature to creature, Nirayus standing tall, weaving her hands around, pulling the energy to and from its victims. After several long seconds it dissipated, and the electrocution whip marks lashed all over their bodies began to steam with a pungent smell of burnt scales.

Kaiden stopped and paused inside the suit where he usually sat catatonic, his senses briefly awakened to see Nirayus standing atop the wagon. He managed a smile from within his helmet as he saw the beautiful elf swirling her arms around in a vibrant blue glow. He raised his sword to her in cheer before his mind drifted back to darkness.

Kaiden's armor stood firm, blade high in the air as Nirayus unleashed a long, liquid splatter of fire that found its way to his short swords. The swords erupted in sparks, tossing out embers as it sheathed the blades in a liquid fire.

Two of the creatures tore through the wall of shields, clawing and biting their way free as the men's fatigue began to take hold. Kaiden swung his flame swords hard, easily cutting through their thick scaled hides repeatedly. They swiped and clawed, unable to even make contact with their slayer as he swirled around in his dance of blades.

Scarlett sunk her glaive deep along the neck of a creature and kicked it off against the growing pile of limbs scattered along the ground. With both hands she spun the long pole of her weapon, its heavy blade gaining momentum as she twisted and slammed it hard into the chest of the lizard, ending its miserable existence.

A massive roar bellowed out from behind the garrison of men, its deep shout reverberating through the ally and into the armored frames of

ARKANGEL

the men. They all simultaneously looked towards the noise and instantly broke lines in terror. The leftover lizards pushed through the wall, pinning some of the soldiers against the ground as they tore at their prey.

Gorman looked back behind him and briefly saw a man deep within the ally, masked in an unnatural darkness, his vibrant red eyes piercing through its dark veil. Then a massive, spiked hand broke forth from the darkness and wrapped around Gorman, who pushed Scarlett out of the way just in time. The hard-pointed spike sunk into his skin as its claws wrapped around his body. Gorman let out a cry of pain as he raised his only free arm, holding his crossbow and firing it into his fleshy captor.

From the shadows came an ogre, its skin tearing and shredding as it walked, blood flowing freely from its wounds. It stood several feet taller than Gorman and only continued to grow as massive taloned feet tore their way out of the ogre's fleshy legs. Its knees popped and snapped, breaking its boney caps and bending backwards unnaturally. The ogre's brutish face expressed an overwhelming fear as a massive beak with long serrated teeth broke forth from the ogre's detaching jaw. Long spines pierced their way through the thick tan ogre flesh, encasing almost its entire back and backsides of its arms, which continued to extend its muscular black scaled form. The newly formed beast bellowed out a mighty roar into the air, causing all the archers and solders to fall victim to panic.

Finn's normally cheerful expression of excitement fell into pure horror as he watched petrified at the transformation. For its size it moved with terrifying speed, its long talons cleaving the heavily armored soldiers in two. With ease it picked the half ogre completely off the ground and threw the battle-hardened warrior across the courtyard as if he were a mere doll. Gorman's body slammed hard against the castle gate, sending shudders up its steel hinges. He flopped motionless to the ground as Finn and Scarlett raced to his aid.

The archers encircling the courtyard on the inner wall began to fire repeatedly at their target, standing almost level with the massive beast. Hundreds of razor-sharp arrows hit the giant lizard, pulling its attention from the soldiers below. It leaped into the air, grasping hold of the stone ledge, its long fingers cracking and sinking into the white stone with ease. It swiped at the men who fled deeper into the main wall as its long talons raked at the stone, sending a shower of rock and debris raining down below. It caught one of the archers, tripping him onto the hard, cold stone as he balled up in his chainmail armor in fear, trapped between its claws.

Streaks of blood from the shreds of ogre flesh stuck onto the scaly hide, leaving streaks across the white walls. It opened its giant jaws to expose its long, twisting and curved points of teeth and swallowed the archer whole, its eyes stricken with an evil enjoyment. It bit repeatedly into the air, forcing its prey further down its throat and gulped as the cries from within ceased. Its head pulled back, and its round bulbous yellow eyes narrowed in on a brave archer and lashed out like a snake, its long fangs closing only inches away from the woman's body.

Kaiden gave another pull on its tail, pulling it down from the ledge as it landed steadily on its two hocked legs. Kaiden immediately jumped up onto the side of the giant lizard and stabbed his daggers deep into its arm, stabbing over and over as he climbed his way up to its shoulder. The creature snapped and clawed at him, trying to knock him off. It spun in the courtyard, its tail slapping hard against barrels and wagons, the sharp quills on the back scraping into the stone.

The remaining soldiers grouped up and began to hack at the creature's legs, trying to knock it off its feet. Despite their heavy long swords, they struggled to do any real damage to the creature's thick scaly hide.

Nirayus watched Kaiden climb up the side of the giant lizard and failed to notice the handful of salamanders still in the courtyard leering eagerly at her. Finn from across the courtyard crouched alongside Gorman, prodding his skin for broken bones or signs of internal bleeding. He gazed up in time to see the quillbacks arise for feeding on their prey and lunged at Nirayus. At the last second, one of the fallen swordsmen let out a gurgled warning and with his last bit of strength swung his sword, clipping the salamander's knee and making it fall just short of Nirayus.

ARKANGEL

Nirayus leapt in surprise as a vortex of burning flame began to consume her within its torrents of fire. Her hair and skirt flapped violently in the wild orange and red storm that spun around her, searing and throwing the creature several yards back. The wagon behind her caught fire and almost instantly turned to ash wherever the flames touched. Her eyes glowed an intense golden orange color as she twirled her arms around like she was gathering up some sort of tangible ball of fire. Once gathered, a globe of molten orange brimstone spun wildly between her outstretched hands and with a shout of rage she unleashed it towards the crowd of approaching quillbacks. The ball exploded on impact and completely vaporized everything it touched and smashed into the stone wall behind them with a splash of liquid magma. The red-hot stone sagged and warped from the high heat and began to pool at the base of the wall. She fell to her knee breathless and gasping for air, her body trembling from the expelled force.

The monstrous creature, writhing in pain from Kaiden's repeated stabbings, turned to see the explosion below and saw the charred remains of his minions. It let out a deep shriek of anger and its wild arms thrashed through the air as if it was dragging itself closer to the exhausted elf. It lunged forth into the air, ready to grasp her tiny body within its spiny grasp when Kaiden swung his entire body down from the creature's shoulder into its lower jaw, his dagger dragging and tearing through its scales.

The creature's jaw shattered on one side, hanging broken as it let out a cry of pain. Kaiden used its jaw to swing down onto its chest, frantically carving into its scales to get at its vitals. It reached down to grab him, but Kaiden was too quick, launching himself up and onto its swinging arms and jumping up onto its snout. It madly shook and clawed at its own face while Kaiden crawled up the bridge of its snout, his back taking blow after blow from its talons strikes.

Kaiden's armor held true, taking subtle damage against the brutal blows as he forced his way up its head, doing anything he could to take down the creature before it had a chance to cause any more harm. A talon went to rake at him once more as he rolled out of the way and was able to puncture both of his daggers into the creature's sickly yellow eye.

It stopped and thrashed in agony, trying to snap at the air with its broken jaw in panic.

Nirayus stood up weakly, and breathlessly limped over, away from the charred wagon along the inner wall of the courtyard. She saw the beast clawing and tearing at Kaiden, trying to crush him as he slashed and carved at its face. She tried to dig deep within her to summon up anything she could do to help.

Scarlett retreated into the castle walls shouting orders to any soldiers who may be left standing, leaving Finn to watch over Gorman. Finn grasped onto the ogre's arm and struggled to drag him inside the barracks door to safety. He hooked his leg over his shoulder and was able to pull him over the rough dirt just in time as the beast's spiny tail whipped through the air in its frenzy.

The creature finally made enough contact with Kaiden's armor to wrap its talons around his legs, and with a tear of its flesh ripped him free from its face. Kaiden dangled upside down powerless, with his legs firmly within its grasp. The warm red blood splattered down his armor as the remainders of the ogre's flesh draped off its forearm. The giant lizard used its body as a whip and slammed him repeatedly into the inner stone wall of the castle as giant chunks of stone broke free from the impact. His body lay limp from the repeated bashing and the creature threw him across courtyard, sending him crashing hard into the wall on the other side before his body flopped lifeless to the ground.

The realization and shock of what Nirayus had just witnessed caused an adrenaline filled panic and rage to surge through her body. She alone was left standing to face the creature in the courtyard with soldiers and companions scattered through the area either wounded or worse and unable to help. Her eyes began to glow a sickly golden green as drips of dark green and black ichor gushed from her eyes like tears running down her cheeks. The veins in her porcelain white skin emitted a green glow as her arms spun around subconsciously in an upward motion. The ground around the monstrous beast's feet started to liquefy into a thick tar. Long, slimy green tentacles lashed up and pulled at its legs and torso, restraining it firmly in place.

Her hands went up into the air as green bolts of light arked from her fingers as she clenched her fists tightly and slammed them down towards the ground. The creature roared threats of anger through its broken jaw as the tendrils wrapped tighter and tighter around its body and started pulling it into the tarred ground. Nirayus fell to her knees again, her fists outstretched as she dug deep within herself, she had to overcome the struggling creature. Her breath quickened in panic, fearing she may not have enough energy to overtake its sheer size and strength.

Scarlett shouted for her soldiers to charge as she pointed to the restrained beast who had sunk almost halfway into the ground. The black tar hardened, rendering it helpless against the humans' attacks. Soldiers poured out of the gate, swords and spears drawn to finally take down the monstrous creature. Finn followed suit and ran over to Nirayus, picking her up as she slipped into unconsciousness. He took her next to Kaiden and knelt beside him, laying her next to him as he turned to watch the humans' final thrusts of spears into the creature's heart. The ground began to move like violent rippling waves inward that enveloped what was left of the beast. The thick tar hardened into place as it returned to rocky dirt that had been fused together, stained a dark green and black.

Finn turned up to Scarlett, who stood victorious with her soldiers. "We need a Cleric!" he shouted urgently.

CHAPTER 7

"SECRETS BELOW"

Rhyker walked through the locked gate behind the biggest house in Solstice Gardens, using the keys from the fallen guard. Finely crafted tables and chairs sat in the center of the secret garden, along with statues of Martis.

"This guy must think awfully highly of himself," he thought aloud while taking in all the intricately carved statues in various heroic poses.

A wire net hung overhead with baskets of flowers and intertwining ivy to keep out animals, or was it to keep something else in? The back of the manor shared a wall to one side of the garden with no windows to look in or out, and the only door had been barred shut.

He slowly walked the stone paths gardeners had carefully placed for the ease of travel through the dense garden landscape. Three barrels were stacked in the corner, and he decided to check its contents. He wasn't sure what he hoped to find in there but thought the guard had to be protecting something.

What could be so important in here? he wondered. The entire place itself just seemed off somehow. Martis was up to something, he could feel it deep inside his being. The man was so popular with such a grand ego that he knew it was to compensate or conceal something. If he was really that charitable and compassionate, then why would he be trying so hard to get people of the city to come here? Overthrow the paladins perhaps?

The barrels were stacked in a pyramid shape with the smallest one on top. He lifted it up and, despite his great strength, could tell it was heavier than it should be. He popped the lid off as his nostrils were assailed with a warm, iron smell. He lifted the lid higher to see it move like a thick gel, immediately recognizing it as blood. His heart lurched in his chest as even more questions came to mind as he attempted to make sense of it.

From the side of the garden, he could see lines dug into the soil where the barrels had been dragged from. He followed them to the other side of the gated area and under some thick, low-hanging foliage. Tucked away in the corner was a cleverly placed hatch, hiding behind some bushes.

Rhyker stood up, checking his surroundings and feeling anxious from what he had found. It was only a matter of time before someone found the unconscious guard by one of the hundreds of people walking around in the gardens. Despite his concern, he decided to open the hatch to see what was inside but was stopped by a steel latch lock sealed shut. He eyed his surroundings again but was unable to tell if anyone was on the other side of the garden walls to hear him break the lock. He considered the contents of the barrels and decided he needed to know what was being hidden below. Grasping the lock in one hand, he pulled hard, forcing the locking pins inside to collapse and give way without giving the appearance of the lock being forcefully broken.

He pulled up the sturdy, wooden door and saw a stone staircase descend deep underground. Cold, foul-smelling air wafted up the staircase, making his nostrils burn. He decided that he had to know what was inside in case anyone needed his help and would need to report this right away to Lanthor and have it shut down, but he needed some sort of proof to back his claims against Martis the great.

Ever since Martis came to Sanctuary in his youth he was immediately showered with lands, titles, and gifts from Paladin Malik, which he had always thought was strange suspicions. What Lanthor saw in him after Malik's defeat was beyond his understanding, so he just tried to keep an eye on him as much as possible, but now realized it wasn't enough.

After traversing down several stone stairs the air became thick with moisture. The darkness overcame any light from the hatch above, so he closed his eyes very tightly. Several seconds later he reopened them, and his eyes started to emit a soft golden glow. His eyes had changed to almost twice their original size and took on a long slender pupil, his eyelids now closing outwards away from his nose. His vision had changed as well; the entire room was almost just as bright as a sunny day looking through a golden filter.

He slowly walked down the wet stone corridor until he came to an entryway with a dim flickering light. Several walkways started to branch out at this point, heading deeper in and now off to the sides. He peered into the room and saw several cages lining the back wall with blankets of rotting straw on the cold ground. The room reeked of urine and feces with buckets of it lining up by the door. He saw movement and jerked his head back around the doorway, his chest beginning to pound as adrenaline began to surge through his system. Rhyker had lived a long time and not much scared or surprised him anymore, but he had yet to see something as foul as this place. He knew he didn't have to fear much from humans but was more worried about what sort of corruption he may find in the dark dungeon.

A woman's voice called out breaking his thoughts. "Guard, guard, is that you? Please, you promised, you promised," a weak voice pleaded, barely having the strength to form a sentence. "I don't want to live anymore, please kill me before he returns!" she cried out in an old raspy tone.

Rhyker peaked around the corner again and saw the woman hunched over, her bones clearly visible under her thinly stretched skin. He felt terrible that someone could be treated this way and needed to help, but how? He thought, there wasn't much he could do here by himself, he shouldn't even he here without Lanthor's approval first and without any military support things could escalate out of control very quickly.

ARKANGEL

He decided it was unwise to keep the appearance of the guard above and was better off appearing as someone new. His hands went to his face and his fingers massaged his jaw and cheekbones. He shook his head slightly and stretched out his jaw side to side. The pinching feeling of his muscles contorting on his face was always painful; he much preferred just being Rhyker.

He took the guard helmet off and walked in through the door with a commanding presence and sat the helmet down on an old table full of rotten food and scraps.

"I don't know you," came the weak voice, followed by a cough for air.

Rhyker pulled a stool closer to the cage and sat down, unsure of what to do at this point or if he could even be of help at the moment. But information was key, and he needed to find out all he could before going back to Lanthor. He especially needed to know if there were more of them.

"I am new to this shift," Rhyker stated, attempting to see the woman's face through her long tangles of matted black hair.

"How long have you been down here?" he asked, realizing there was no way of telling day from night in the deep damp, stone dungeon.

The woman shook in sorrow and fear. "He comes to cleanse me monthly so at least 5 years," she sobbed shamefully.

Her head leaned back quickly, and she gasped for the air in the empty cell. "Glover, is that you? Glover, are you there? Have you finally come back for me?" she cried out. She managed to stand for a few seconds before collapsing into tears, wrapping her long, bony arms around her curled knees, weeping.

Rhyker watched her, seeing nobody or anything in the cell beside her. She must have lost her mind down here; the poor woman had been completely broken. A tear rolled down his cheek for the abused woman, his heart aching for her.

"My sweet Glover, please take me with you!" she pleaded, rocking side to side on the ground.

He decided he would have to come back for her in her current state. He knelt down beside the gate and put his hands on the rusty bars. "Is there anyone else down here?" he asked softly, hoping not to upset her further.

She rolled onto her side, lifting her hand up to his face and gently stroking his cheek, her eyes rolled mostly back into her head. Rhyker's heart stopped at the realization of who the woman was, his eyes wide and his breathing difficult as if he had just seen a ghost.

"Trinity?" he muttered, grasping her hand in his against his cheek.

"Oh, Glover, is it really you?" she whispered before collapsing back against the wet straw.

Years of heartache swept over him like a hurricane ravaging a small town of emotions, a whirlpool of sorrow threatening to drown him where he knelt. "Trinity, it's me…" He trailed off, remembering at that moment he wasn't Rhyker. "Where have you been? Where did you disappear to?" he asked impatiently, wanting answers he had been searching for so long.

Trinity gasped and retracted her hand into her cage, terrified, tears flowing freely from her eyes in panic. "It's the red woman!"

Rhyker's head smashed into the bars as fingers grasped his hair and yanked his head back, ramming his skull into the bars again and again. He struggled to remain conscious and held firmly against the bars to stop the attack, the sheer strength of the threat causing the bars to bend inward. With inhuman strength, he was pulled back, crashing against the table as old food spilled all over him.

"What are you doing down here?" a familiar, strong female voice commanded.

Long reddish orange hair swirled in his vision as she grasped the back of his armor, picking him clear off the ground and throwing him face first in the cage beside Trinity.

Rhyker wheeled around in place to see Feora standing there behind him, slamming the gate shut. A grin spread across her thin lips at the chance to display her power. A golden amulet lightly glowed on a golden chain dangling down against her chest.

"How did you get down here?" she demanded.

Rhyker realized she didn't recognize him, and although the steel bars would do little more than slow him down, he couldn't risk his identity or to scare the fragile-minded Trinity. He curled up into a ball, grasping at his head like it was severely hurt, and refused to answer.

"Never mind you, I'll let him deal with you," she said with a smirk, brushing her hands off on her tight, dark red pants. Her fiery orange eyes pierced the darkness of the room, making her seem almost gifted. She smirked at him again, trying to taunt her new captive, and walked out of the room, followed by a group of rough voices.

Trinity sat wedged in the corner of her cell in terror, eyes wide open staring into the air with a worried look on her bony face. "She killed you," she said eerily, swaying back and forth while trembling. "She took you from me." She began to mumble softly to herself repeatedly, struggling to hold onto an ounce of sanity.

Rhyker's heart ached for her but was glad he was at least still in the room with her. He wished he could've taken the form of himself, Rhyker, but was afraid she would be terrified and give away his secret. At this point he wasn't even sure her fragile psyche would be able to cope with the extent of his abilities, or who he really was, but no human, especially her, should find out until the right time came.

He studied the room while trying to come up with the best way to handle the situation. He lay down and stretched his arms out and was barely able to grasp onto the wooden table leg he had been tossed into. He then used it to leverage against the old, rusty steel door. In the act of prying the door open, he was able to discreetly crush the old lock in his hand, its metal mechanisms destroyed inside. The cage door flung open, but he was able to catch it before it slammed against the next cage over.

Setting the board down, he knelt beside Trinity. "There are people looking for us, I will get help and come back for you, I promise," he said with a sad look of worry upon his face.

She stopped rocking momentarily and sat up on her bony knees, her tattered rags of clothing looking almost too cumbersome for her fragile figure to bear. "Please don't leave me here," she begged, her face elongating into a display of dread and fear. She pleaded again for him to take her, melting his heart to see his lost love this way, but fearing what could be happening above ground.

"I promise, I will be right back, Trinity, I will get your father and we shall storm the gates and set you free, and you will never have to see him again," he promised, sickened by the monster Martis had been to her. Maybe he was using her as leverage to force Lanthor into doing his bidding, he wondered.

She protested again but succumbed to her insanity, quickly beginning to rock back and forth, murmuring to herself. He gently placed his hand against the bar, pausing for a few extra seconds to see what had become of Lanthor's daughter and his wife-to-be, taken from him so many years ago. It pained him to think he had given up on her and his chest filled with rage for the man responsible.

He peered around the wall to see if they were alone and made a right, going deeper into the stone hallway. Removing his armor, he placed it back out of sight beside a stack of barrels. He wished he had more time to search but knew he needed to get back to Sanctuary quickly.

He shook his head and braced his face within his hands, focusing on the last time he had seen Martis. Although it wasn't that long ago, he had watched him on the road, he feared the small details would be lost. Rhyker did his best to take Martis's face and would just have to make do with the fancy padded clothes he wore underneath his paladin armor.

Several paths led off from what appeared to be the main hallway, and although the fact that Trinity had been locked down here would be more than enough to convince Lanthor to allow his men to raid the place, he searched for proof of Martis's involvement. Somehow Martis only needed to mutter a few words and could convince anyone to take his side. It had been about twenty years since Trinity had gone missing;

having her back was really going to change things in Sanctuary. He tried to chase his thoughts of her away and focus but he couldn't help but think of what Scarlett would think. With Trinity's disappearance only weeks before their wedding and the single night they had shared, he wasn't sure how Scarlett would take her coming home. He wasn't even sure how he would feel about it after she had disappeared on him.

He committed his mind to the task at hand and slowly crept down the hall, coming up on another room and peering inside. Small, metal towers with metal discs spaced apart sat at either side of a table. Leather straps and chains lay across the blackened table where human appendages could be fastened down. Smaller tables of various tools and unknown metal devices lined another wall with metal wire branching from the tips of the towers to what looked like a helmet and spiked prods, stained heavily with blood. Other odd contraptions sat on top of a shelf attached to the back wall beside more cages, and a pile of decomposed bodies were stacked in the far corner.

He continued his search, finding a locked door will a small, barred window about eye level. With a glance, he could see a table with pens and parchment along with cases of books and scrolls. Attached to the walls were charts and notes on a waxed canvas with depictions of the human body and different organs located inside, each with notes on the manipulations and tests done on each.

Rhyker heard voices echo down the hall and hurried to the next junction, slipping into an unlocked room. He turned to see several of the Salamanders that had been responsible for all the attacks strung up in chains with several dissected bodies across various tables. Each of the bodies had been maimed and taken apart in different ways with unidentified contraptions attached to their bodies for tests. The floor was so thick with stains of spilled blood that the cobbled stone floor appeared to be a nice flat surface in many areas. Through the crack in the door, the voices diminished down the hallway.

Rhyker turned around to leave and saw even more cages against the opposite wall, noticing a large pile of torn flesh piled high against a cage, with blood slowly dripping from a hanging flap. He heaved and choked, the visuals becoming too much for him to take in.

After a few minutes of slow, labored breaths in the thick stench of death, he decided to leave the room and go further in before turning back for Trinity. He approached the area where he heard the voices coming from and peered slowly around the door. It was a small room with a ladder going up into a small, wooden hatch door. Beside the ladder was a closet rack of white and tan robes with a table of books stacked high atop it.

He heard the voices again, a male and female, but the male's accent was unmistakable. He silently rushed, peering into the window of the door on the other side and noted it to be a large room with more stacks of barrels, possibly hundreds of them. He raced down as silently as possible and crouched against the wall to look through the barely open door where the voices were coming from. He gulped in shock when his suspicions were confirmed. There stood Feora, along with several bright orange ember elves. She was addressing a particularly large elf whose skin was almost completely covered and stained in white ash.

Rhyker recalled the wars in the north with the ember elves and their relentless hate and savagery of the other races. They were a warring nation only driven by bloodlust and the conquering of the other races. They had waged war against the aquatic elves in the west and the majestic elves of the mountains of the north, nearly wiping them all out. Then humans had gotten thrown into the mix when their land became the center of their tireless fighting.

The embers mark themselves to show their great battle prowess and earning the right to raise up their ranks. After burning their victims, they mark their bodies with a handprint of hot ash from the fires to permanently mark their victory. The beast before him must be a veteran killer to have earned so many handprints of ash melted on his body that he could hardly see any of his orange skin underneath. Streaks of sparkling light blue glinted from the torchlight, meaning he was also adept at killing the aquatic elves as well.

"Feirun, listen to me now," Feora demanded, standing her ground and commanding the savage brute. "We must stick to the plan and wait for the right time to strike. If you attack now, you won't stand a chance and we are so close!" she yelled in frustration, balling her fists in outrage. Her hair was so long and fine, its orangey red color almost matching the elf's skin.

The large, muscular brute Feirun let out a growl and reached out, forcefully grabbing her shoulder. His enormous figure completely diminished her slim frame in comparison with his large hand encircling her shoulder and back. "I am tired of your games, human. We only wait because you are small, weak, and scared. With no Lanthor, they will not stand against us this time," he grunted, surprisingly well-articulated for an ember elf and leaning in to intimidate her.

Feora reached her slender arm up and easily moved the brute's giant hand off her body, throwing it down to his side with such force it caused him to backstep to keep his balance. He scowled at her attempt to challenge his strength as his muscles went tense. His men all reached for their large cleavers, but he raised his hand to stop them, not wanting to risk their fragile alliance. He knew what was coming and from the ashes of the humans he would build himself a mighty army for the coming age.

Feora saw him seething for a fight and raised her hands to calm him, laying them upon his heaving bare chest. "Calm yourself," she said, feeling the heat on his chest from his burning blood within. "I will help you get your revenge, Feirun, for your beloved queen Queliss, but first..."

"Don't you mutter her name human," he said, enraged in anger, cutting her off. His heavy breathing caused her hands to recoil as he swatted her hands aside to force her away from him.

She caught his arm midair with one hand and pulled his lumbering body in close to her, their faces barely inches apart. The other elves began to draw their cleavers, loosely fastened to the sides of their furry loincloths.

"I give the orders here!" she said in a stone cold, steady voice. Her grip tightened and forced Feirun down to kneel, his face wincing in pain and shock. "If you wish to do your part in this and live to lead your men than I suggest you follow my orders," she said in a calm, clear, and sharp voice.

There was a moment of tension as the elves looked at the two, debating what they should do. Besides the massive hulk, Prince Feirun, ember elves were slenderer and more relied on their speed and agility in battle. Although they were stronger than most humans, it was their speed and agility that made them more than deadly.

"If you question me or force me to show you who is in charge again, I promise you, your people will be searching for a new leader," she threatened, eying him down and thrusting his body back as he tumbled to the floor. The beautiful, golden amulet around her neck shined a radiant light that pulsated to a dull glow as her anger subsided.

Feirun lunged up quickly, his giant muscular chest rising and falling in such rage that his body trembled in place, his hand at the side of his oversized Khopesh. He reluctantly calmed himself as his stature began to relax. His head darted to his men and nodded to them to relax, with a look of defeat weighing heavily on his face.

"Forgive me, Red Queen," he said through gritted teeth.

"No matter," she stated casually with a flick of her wrist, walking around them with her back now to the door. "You will gather your men and wait for my orders. Set up camp at the edge of the Wither where you won't be seen, and everything will fall into place shortly. We will house the soldiers in the tents being constructed to the north so they will be defenseless if they try to flee and leave the rest to me. Understand?" she asked politely, eying them like they were halfwits.

"Yes, my Queen," Feirun growled hastily. The thought of being controlled by a tiny human female disgusted and tormented him, especially with her display of superiority in front of his men. Every fiber in his being told him to crush her to bits. When the siege started, he knew where his slaughtering would start.

Feora walked casually around them, her back strategically placed to invite attack if they dared, a game of control and dominance she loved to play. "And Feirun," she started with a smile. "If all goes well and your men perform as promised, I will see to it myself that your revenge is gotten on the Spirit Queen Lu-Sea," she said as her gaze became dark and cold. "When our Lord arrives, she will be nothing but a confused elf who can perform nothing but tricks. She will be all but helpless before him." she said as an evil tone of laughter came from her dark smile.

Another figure on the other side of the wall turned and ran as Rhyker suddenly threw the door open. Feora's narrowed eyes quickly locked onto Rhyker and sent her into a fiery rage. Rhyker leapt back and ran down the hallway, the noise of sprinting footsteps heard closing in behind him as he navigated back through the maze. He ran past several corridors and decided to turn multiple times to cut off their pursuit, turning down only the darkest of hallways. The elves were fast, running at full speed almost completely silent and unhindered by the dark, their elongated pupils drew in more light than any human.

"Find him and bring him to me!" Feora shouted, racing down the hall after them, attempting to cut him off by going down other hallways. "How did you find us? What are you doing down here?" she shouted as she ran, knowing full well her inquiries would go unanswered.

Rhyker's heartbeat rapidly as he ran. How was he going to get back to Trinity and get her out safely? Who was the other person in the room that he couldn't see or even sense? But the biggest answer eluding him the most was if Feora recognized him? Was Martis not the mastermind behind this, he thought? Was he just a puppet? Or was it possible she had seen straight through his disguise the entire time? These unanswered questions bothered him deeply and put him at a great disadvantage. He found an odd door and opened it slowly to find an open, well-lit room. Without thinking, he moved inside.

The weighted door slid back closed with a thud, then he turned to find there was no door at all. Segments of identical panels lined the entire wall. He spun around again to see a confusing and troubled sight, row after row of bunkbeds. Hundreds of stacked beds filled the room with children's clothing stacked and scattered about on the floors and beds. Small statues and blocks for toys lay in piles to be played with, along with other knick-knacks.

ARKANGEL

Rhyker stood dumbfounded as he looked around the room wondering what children were doing down here, and where they all were. He decided to change his face back into the guard he had knocked out earlier and find a way out.

Against the far end of the massive room was a door He walked through confidently to not raise alarm and found another lit hallway and staircase. He decided not to press his luck in search anymore, and instead just leave in hopes of finding an exit. At the top of the stairs, he found a small, nicely furnished room with several doors. He noted carefully placed holy relics and symbols decorated around the room. He walked through the center door to find a stage overlooking hundreds of pews capable of seating thousands of people. There was a single podium sitting dead center in the middle of the stage with several books piled high atop it.

Rhyker retracted back into the smaller room and decided to open one of the other doors, finding a small bedroom full of robes, documents, and books piled beside a desk. By the looks of the bed it was hardly used, unlike the table with fresh ink and parchment stretched flat across it. The room was small but there was a window to the outside that could be easily opened. He stood on the desk and pulled himself through, landing softly on the green grass below.

His relief to be outside was short lived as he looked up and across the building to see the Garden entrance he came in swarming with armed guards. His brows furrowed in frustration at the delicate situation at hand. He could overtake the guards with ease but didn't want to risk any unnecessary bloodshed, for most of the guards were just young men playing soldier. He felt his heart sink at the thought of Trinity still being locked in the cage and breaking his promise to set her free. It may be difficult to convince Lanthor of what was happening here and now, not being sure if Martis was even to blame complicated his accusations without any proof. If he didn't get Trinity back to safety and something happened to her, he would be devastated, aside from what it would do to Lanthor.

He decided to exit the facility by sliding through the tall hedge wall against the side of the church, making his way back to the front gate. He recovered his paladin armor and fastened himself back inside its solid steel shell, the weight of it resting familiarly back on his shoulders. He clenched his teeth, returning his face back to the Rhyker everyone was familiar with, and reattached his sword and glaive. Entering Solstice like this would bring a lot of attention but the guards would think twice before questioning him.

Several guards approached as he walked between the tall hedge walls and through the front. "Hail, Paladin," one of them said, cheerfully approaching with two others.

Rhyker lifted his hand and motioned a hello with a silent nod.

"Is there anything we can help you with, Sir?" another soldier asked attentively, the third anxiously looking back across the gardens.

"I am here to inspect the accommodations set up for my men who will be stationed here temporarily," Rhyker said, trying not to keep his eye on the secret garden. "I fail to see with this many residents that there will be enough suitable places for all my men," he followed up firmly, gesturing to all the people walking through the gardens.

The first young man looked back and side to side, trying to come up with an answer. "I don't know any of the details but I'm sure there will be plenty of room for them to stay," he said, itching his scalp with a finger and a hint of concern coming to his voice.

Rhyker intimidatingly stepped closer to him and leaned down to look him straight in the eyes. "Is there something troubling you, young man?" Rhyker asked the soldier as he dodged eye contact.

The guard looked back nervously again to the garden's center buildings, then back to Rhyker. "No, Sir, nothing is the matter," he managed with a subtle gulp.

Rhyker put his attention to the other two guards who were getting antsy as well. "So, you are telling me that there is enough room in those small buildings for five thousand troops I am sending up here?" he said, agitated with their stalling.

The first guard stumbled over his words to answer. "Oh, that is a lot, maybe they plan on setting up tents outside the garden area?" he said with a wince. "I am sure Feora has everything under control," he added, barely able to utter her name.

"Why would a disgraced Arkhunter have any say on where my men are staying? Isn't Martis in charge here?" he asked, prodding for information, watching the boy begin to panic. "Wasn't it Martis who requested the soldiers? Why would he be trying to get people to move here if there wasn't enough room to begin with?"

Rhyker grew impatient with the guards when he needed to hurry and find his way back down to Trinity and leave as soon as possible. He waved his hand to them in dismissal and walked past the trembling guards.

"Sir," the guards muttered, almost in unison.

Rhyker turned to face them, their hands now resting on their sword hilts.

"Yes? I am going to just go look for myself," Rhyker stated impatiently.

The men nervously looked at one another and back to the daunting Rhyker.

"We have orders, Sir..." one of the guards said, trailing off.

"You have orders? What orders? You are not part of my guard or my army, you are peasants holding weapons and armor, nothing more," he said in a threatening tone, resting the palm of his hand on the pommel of his sword.

With hesitation, all three men drew their swords and took several steps back, barely able to hold them upright in fear.

"I see," Rhyker said evenly. "And who gave you these orders?"

"We were told not to let anyone in or out of the gardens, Feora's orders, Sir," one of the men said, looking over to his other two silent companions.

"Where is Martis in all this? I demand to see him right now."

All three men shrugged their shoulders, feeling confident they had answered Rhyker's questions enough to get him to leave. "You need to leave, Sir. Feora will take care of your men," one of them said as the other two soldiers separated to Rhyker's sides.

Rhyker attempted to call their bluff, not wanting to hurt these untrained kids who could barely even hold their swords straight. "I am going to have a look for myself and talk to Feora," he said, turning his back to the men, inviting their attack if there was to be one.

The men saw their chance to strike and lunged with their swords. Rhyker drew his sword and spun around with inhuman speed, deflecting all three blades at once. He leaned forward, using their momentum, and punched one on the left hard with his armored gauntlet, knocking him clear off his feet. He spun around and kicked the legs out from the one in the middle, slamming him down into the ground with the flat of his blade. He stared down the other closing in, his sword held high to strike, and leaned a little to the side. The sword blade rattled as it wedged itself stuck in Rhyker's massive pauldron. Rhyker twisted his body, pulling the sword completely out of the boy's hands, and raised his foot to kick at the shocked guard, hitting hard, doubling him over on top of his friends as they all gasped for air

Rhyker reached up and removed the stuck sword, throwing it down to the ground with a loud clang. "How dare you attack a Paladin of Sanctuary?" Rhyker shouted in a booming voice, looking down to the terrified young men as they began to sob from fear. Something was clearly wrong here and he didn't want to draw anymore unwanted attention. "Your offence is punishable by death. Why should I spare your lives? Answer me."

"Please don't kill us, we aren't allowed to let anyone in or out, no matter who it is and that is all they said. With Feora any little mistake gets you killed or worse," one of the boys cried out, struggling to hold any composure.

"Then what of the Army being sent in? Are you supposed to send them away as well? To what end?" Rhyker demanded.

"All they said is we are to send them north to the end of the gardens and them to set up camp at the base of the mountains until they are taken care of."

Rhyker held no ill will towards these kids, pawns in a much larger conspiracy, and let them go. "Do any of you have any family here?" Rhyker asked in a calm tone.

The boys all shook their heads. "They were killed by those creatures, I was the only one to survive until Martis found and brought me there to safely," one of the other guards sobbed.

"This place is about to become unsafe real soon, and I would suggest you run to Sanctuary, all three of you. It's a long days walk south down this road here," Rhyker gestured, pulling a few golden coins from a satchel on his belt and throwing them to the ground by their feet. "Listen to me closely. Go to Sanctuary and find Paladin Scarlett, tell her Rhyker sent you and show her these coins. Tell her to stop the men from marching north and that I have found something. That is all, can you do that? Keep the coins and that should be plenty to start a new life in the city where it is safe, do you understand?" Rhyker asked, looking deep into the boys' eyes.

It was important he get to Scarlett in time, but more so that he rescue Trinity from the cage and get her to safety. Something just didn't feel right here, even beyond the hidden labyrinth of torture devices. With the troops coming and being stationed at the base of the mountainside, not far from the Wither, it would be the perfect place for an ambush, leaving the castle pressed for trained troops if the Embers followed up with another siege.

His eyes began to water as he looked across the busy gardens with new understanding. He not only saw it as a threat, but whatever Feora was planning didn't sit well on his heart. The Wither was not far and was the very location where so many souls were killed by the ember elves that the land was now dead. It was cursed with strange creatures that spawned from the blood-soaked grounds of soil and bone. It was truly an awful place and should stand as a beacon to prevent such war, not a place to start another. His eyes welled up slightly at the memories of all the battles and men he had lost there.

Rhyker shook away this thoughts, tossing them to the wind to focus on the important matters at hand. He had made his way directly to the garden area from before and found another set of guards now blocking the closed gate.

"Hail, Sir!" they shouted at the Paladin approaching.

Rhyker aggressively walked right up to their faces and stood only inches away. "Step aside now," he demanded, his hand resting heavily on this sword handle.

The boys began to quiver, not wanting to quarrel with a Paladin, and stepped aside. Most knew better to never ever question one, let alone pick a fight with one. Rhyker pushed through the gate, finding it unlocked this time. He ran over to the trap door, which was also left open. He drew his sword and reached on to his back to detach a thin shield that snapped perfectly into place from the back of his breastplate.

Armed and ready, he entered the cold dark chamber, his eyes swelling and emitting its golden glow again. As he descended further down the stairs and into the damp stone tunnel he could hear voices, most likely more soldiers, now guarding their prisoner. He raced forward into the room to catch them by surprise and found Feora standing silently with two reddish ember elves standing to her sides. Their powdered white patches around their chests stood out in the dim torchlight.

"No no, Demons, Demons please no more, leave me be please," Trinity's weak voice pleaded behind them.

"Rhyker? Has it been you playing tricks on us down here this whole time?" Feora teased, her hands resting on her hips.

A sudden lump rose in his throat. Could she see through his disguise somehow? His mind swirled with questions and panic as he tried to reason what she knew about his identity or not.

"It had to be you, I always knew something was different about you and knew it was only a matter of time until you or whoever lingered down here returned. Silly boys, so predictable," she says with a playful smile, looking over his bulky silver and gold plate armor dancing with brilliant colors from the torchlight.

She snapped her fingers and the embers to her sides lunged at him, swinging their long, curved Khopesh's in unison to either side of him. His shield and sword easily deflected their blades but forced him to take a step back from their unexpected force. He stepped back into the hallway for more maneuverability.

The elves were very fast, their eyes glowing an intense orange color in the low light as they slashed their swords like a well written dance across his shield, sword, and shoulders. Rhyker was a trained expert swordsman with countless years of battle and could tell these attacks weren't to wound, they were meant as a distraction. Their speed made it difficult to get the upper hand, each elf wielding two of the deadly blades and swinging them with incredible skill. He blocked and parried, sparks bouncing off his blade and shield from the blows.

With his shoulder he lunged forward, slamming his bulky pauldrons, bringing their blades to a sudden halt. He spun around to the side while their arms still worked to gain momentum and stabbed his blade deep into one of their sides. The blade cleanly tore through its flesh as its skin flapped open to a stream of blood. The strike did little to slow the elf, who furrowed his eyebrows in rage and continued his attack.

Stories told that the ember elves enjoyed fire because the heat was the only thing, they could feel on their orange skin. An opponent who could not be slowed by pain or feared its sting was dangerous.

Rhyker spun back around, kicking at the wounded elf attempting to break up his attacks. He continued to back down the hall as their whirling blades sent out an ear-splitting ring from clanging on steel and stone. He decided to focus on the wounded one in an attempt to disable or disarm it. After deflecting against his shoulders, he lunged again at the injured elf, now too close for him to recover enough for a swing, bringing up his knee into its chest as his armored knee punctures its skin. He slammed his forehead against the elf's nose, temporarily blinding it and causing it to stagger. An attack from the other elf disrupted his assault, but he was able to parry it with his sword, using the momentum to swing the tip of his blade around through the air and sliced the injured elf's arm clean off.

The arm fell heavily to the ground as the elf let out a roar of anger, kicking Rhyker square in the chest and forcing him back several feet. The uninjured elf used the opportunity to hit Rhyker right across the face with the pommel of his blade and grasp onto his shoulders. With a leap it was high in the air, and with both legs kicked off Rhyker's breastplate, sending him sailing through the air. The elf landed gracefully into a roll and was back up onto his feet with ease, turning to watch his fearless companion charge in with his one arm.

Rhyker fell back hard against the ground as his attacker reached him, bringing his sword down hard against Rhyker's arm guard and sending his blade far to the side. He kicked up with his armored foot at the elf's chest and followed up with a quick stab with his sword as he rose to his feet, burying the blade deep into its abdomen and lifting its body off the ground as its head smashed into the low stone ceiling.

Rhyker let out a victory cry as the limp elf fell dead to the floor, simultaneously turning to face his next attacker. It leapt at him with the tips of his swords pointed straight at his face, but he narrowly dodged to the side, slamming his shield in its chest. The sudden impact sent a shower of blood spraying from the elf's open mouth and Rhyker continued to slam harder and harder with his shield, sending his assailant into a daze. It had been many years since he had fought an ember elf and he had always admired their endurance.

He pushed the elf off his shield and slashed with his sword, opening a long tear across his bare chest. The elf's arms surged as it went wild, hitting Rhyker's sword repeatedly, knocking it from his solid grasp. Rhyker tossed his shield at the elf to buy himself the second he needed to unclip the glaive from his back. He grasped the long-handled shaft and flicked the blade down as it spun open and snapped into place. He thrusted the long weapon at the elf's chest to keep distance in between them as he watched the elf quickly adapt to his new weapon.

Suddenly, he heard Feora's cry for battle as her foot landed square on his back, sending him flying through the air, crashing and rolling over the ember. The elf quickly recovered and positioned to strike, looking to Feora for the okay to finish him. Rhyker turned to see her flick her wrist, motioning for the elf to leave.

"I have been waiting a long time for this, pretty boy," she shouted, spinning and kicking him again as he tried to get back on his feet. He slid several feet across the rough stone, his pauldrons sending sparks showering in the tight corridor before coming to an abrupt halt, breathless. He flipped up to his feet just in time to block her blade with his forearm, her sword sinking into the thick, metal bracer. They struck each other repeatedly, both matched closely in speed, his fist hitting her and slamming her into the wall, unphased before she struck back against his armored chest, buckling the steel beneath her fist.

She was fast and unbelievably strong, and in his bulky armor he wouldn't be able to match her speed no matter his strength. He noticed between attacks that the fiercer she became, the brighter the amulet around her neck would glow. Getting desperate, his blows turned to holds, trying to subdue her attacks. She moved with such speed her form became almost a blur in the dark. Rhyker managed to restrain her arm under his as she repeatedly struck at his arms and shoulders, making it harder to move with his damaged, armored joints. He slammed her down on her back, following up with his knee to her face, his slams pushing her body harder to the ground and her fist out of striking range. He kicked her to her side and reached down, grabbing the back of her leather corset. He lifted her off the ground and with all his might slammed her harder and harder against the stone walls. Back and forth, rage overtook him as her body crushed and snapped from the deadly strikes against the stone.

His rage overtook his senses as he failed to detect the remaining ember elf charge in and attach two heavy shackles to his arms, forcing him down. Feora sprang free, barely able to move with her broken skeleton refusing to obey, her shattered rib cage heaving for breath. She stood, ready to strike despite her body's broken state, with chunks of cement and stone imbedded in her hair and clothing.

The ember elf pulled against the chain. Despite all his kicking and flailing in his damaged armor, Rhyker was unable to break free. He was ruthlessly dragged into one of the side chambers and a loud *clank!* filled the room, followed by a ratcheting sound from a metal contraption on the table. Feora came to the elf's aid and together they twisted his heavy armored shoulders backwards in place and chained them to the table. The elf did the same with his feet while Feora slowly turned a wheel at his side, stretching his body and limbs to the edge of detaching.

Feora came to stand in front of him, blood dripping down her forehead and mouth, with wet stains barely visible through her red, leather armor. Her pants were ripped in several places and her corset so torn up it struggled to keep her covered.

A victorious smirk spread to her face. "Thank you for that," she said playfully while wiping drops of blood from her lips with her finger. "It's been a long time since I've had a good challenge," she added while grasping at her golden amulet in her hand. As the amulet grew brighter, her exposed cuts and bruises appeared to rapidly heal and vanish in mere seconds.

Rhyker struggled against the chains at the sight, trying to break free and enraged at what had just happened. How could he have been captured? Especially one as ancient and powerful as him? What about Trinity? Had they hurt her? What were they going to do to her now that he was captured?

"Let me out of here, you monster!" he shouted in pain as every joint in his body threatened to give out. "Just wait until Lanthor hears about your treachery. You are a demon and a blight, and you Arkhunters should have been destroyed a long time ago."

Feora let out a chuckle. "Demon, no. Blight... well maybe." She smiled at the sight of his pain. "You know we are not that different now, handsome. I once lay on that very same table. Although the things I will do to you may be a little different, you will learn to enjoy the pain, I promise you that."

"What are you? How can a human have such power if not demonic?"

he asked, gritting his teeth in pain and anger.

She lifted her almost bare leg up onto the table and leaned in closer, her lips traveling up his damaged breastplate, up his neck and onto his chin. Her lip had torn from the twisted metal of his armor, and she planted a bloody kiss on his lips.

Rhyker moved his head and spat at her, trying desperately to stop her from making her advances. "What is that amulet you wear? I have seen it before!"

She sat up, giving him a seductive smile as her fingers caressed his face. "Oh, this old thing?" she asked, moving her hand to the amulet resting on her chest, pulsating a deep golden glow. "This is a gift from the creator, a power he sent us to be extracted from the only human known to be born with the gift. It has been harnessed to give me limitless power, though you gave me a rush today," she said with a wink. "Despite the torturous tragedy its original bearer endured to give it to us, we will put the power to a good use. Soon enough, though, I will have to let him know we have a special guest first.'

Rhyker struggled again at his chains. "Let who know, Martis? Is he behind all this?" Rhyker demanded.

Her eyes rolled around as she looked up to the low ceiling. "You honestly have no idea what is going on, do you?" She chuckled while looking down to a dark cage against the wall next to the table. "Wake up!" she yelled, kicking the grated door.

A raspy breathing stirred awake, followed by wheezing gasps for air. "What do you want from me?" the course, male voice questioned.

Feora stood up from the table edge and looked down with a pleased grin. "Look who I found. It's one of your little paladins," she mocked, kicking the cage again. "You know, you should really keep a closer eye on them. Well, you boys, it's been fun, I have a lot to do, and I am sure you two have a lot of catching up to do. It's been, what? A few months?" She gave a small laugh and walked out the door, the badly wounded elf following close behind and slamming it behind them.

"Rhyker, is that really you?" the voice called out, coughing to catch his weak breath.

Rhyker struggled against the chains again, unable to better his position to see the figure. "Who is asking?" he demanded, straining to see the origin of the voice.

"Thank the creator, Rhyker, it's you. I was taken who knows how long ago. The days all blend together. With the beatings and experiments, I never know how long I've been out or if I will ever wake up at all." The weak voice began to turn to a sobbing cry as tears rolled down the man's face. "Rhyker, it's me, Lanthor!" he spat out before erupting into a fit of coughing.

Rhyker's eyes lit up and his face twisted with confusion. His memory retraced over the past weeks as he suddenly noticed a trend in Lanthor's strange behavior, and his almost treasonous decisions at the council meeting. His thoughts were interrupted by Lanthor's voice.

"How did you find me down here? Is anyone else coming?" Lanthor asked with a hint of hope in his voice.

Rhyker ignored his questions as he worked out how all this could even make sense. More importantly, what was Feora planning?

"So, if you have been down here this whole time, who is the imposter running Sanctuary?" Rhyker asked, knowing that without him, Scarlett was now in great danger, along with all of Sanctuary.

CHAPTER 8

"THE JOURNEY NORTH"

The cleric recoiled away from Kaiden as a flash of golden light emanated from his body after he had gotten close. The cleric had learned his lesson the hard way after the last time he tried to lay a damp towel over Kaiden's forehead and his armor reacted, threatening him with a long slender blade from his forearm that had risen to his neck. His armor was still actively trying to protect him even though he wasn't conscious.

Another medic came to try and feel for a temperature but was blocked by the scaled armor quickly wrapping itself protectively around his body. They eventually gave up and went to tend to Gorman, who was sprawled out over two beds pushed together, his legs dangling over the ends. He lay there comfortable while wrappings were applied to his side where his ribs had fractured from his impact against the wall. Finn stood beside Gorman as his eyes slowly started to flicker open to realize he was in the infirmary.

Finn grabbed a bone saw off the table of tools beside the bed and held it up. "Is this where I start sawing?" he asked, grasping onto Gorman's arm. A slight smile spread to his thin lips as he looked at Gorman from the corner of his eye.

Gorman pulled his arm away and sighed in pain from his ribs. "Hands off, fish, or you be dinner," he said gruffly as he moved his hand to his grumbling stomach.

Finn's mandibles bounced in laughter before heading over to Nirayus, who was awake and eyeing everyone nervously as if at any second, she would have to defend herself from someone. He sat down on the foot of her bed, his smile turning to an odd sympathetic look.

"You are safe here you know? The hunt for arkers has been officially disbanded after Malik's death, other than the few renegades who act on their own behalf and are not part of Sanctuary or any of the Paladins, I might add," he said, his awkward expression attempting to curl back in an uplifting smile to reinforce his information.

"I still don't trust the humans," she said in a sour tone, her arms folded across her chest, eyes still darting to anything that moved. "How is Kaiden?" she asked in a hopeful tone as her eyes lowered down to her knees shifting under her blanket.

Finn looked over to see the fourth cleric attempting to get close to him, this time with some sort of concoction in his hand. Finn tapped the bed beside Nirayus's elbow and gestured. "Look and see." He was just in time for a shockwave from Kaiden's body to throw the cleric and his medicine flying across the room in a mess.

"HAHAHA!" Finn laughed with a hearty gurgling sound while another medicine man gave him a foul stare. "I thought you didn't care for the humans?" he asked, his smile hinting as a tease.

"Well, I... I just wanted to know because he is in charge of keeping me safe and he would be very sorry if he let Father down, I don't care how thick that armor of his is. Plus, the sooner he wakes up, the sooner we can leave." She glanced at Kaiden, laying there motionless. "I wonder what is wrong with him?" she asked under her breath.

Gorman sighed and grunted as he leaned up, putting more pillows behind his back to sit upright. "He does dat, it be da armor, it weakens him," he piped in, looking over at the defensive Nirayus and Finn.

"What are we even doing here?" Nirayus asked, ignoring Finn, with her ears perked up and alert.

Gorman grunted as he shifted in pain, a frustrated look upon his face. "We be here for da Paladins, no plan after dat. We be here to help with da plague. But I's sees we be too late." He looked around the room to see where exactly they were. It had been a long time since he had been here and even longer since he had been in the infirmary.

Several large windows lined the walls slightly above the height of the beds. The daylight helped make the place feel open and uplifting despite the screams that came echoing down the wall every so often. Shelves holding labeled bottles of various liquids and medicines were all over the walls with racks of tools and instruments. The white stone walls made it feel clean except for the faint red stains of blood, hinting at the many deaths that had occurred here.

"We be leavin soon after da kid wakes," Gorman said with a lift of his chin in Kaiden's direction.

Nirayus stood up on the bed, her weight barely making the mattress dent where she stood. She silently jumped down; alert, she eyed the people in the room to monitor their actions. She felt weak from the energy she had arked in the battle and felt a little lightheaded as well, needing to feed her thirst soon.

The main cleric who had been tending to them approached to warn her she needed to lay back, but quickly retreated without a word at the promise of pain that glared in her eyes.

"I wouldn't go near that one," the cleric offered before getting dismissed with a wave of the elf's hand.

Nirayus wasn't used to being told what to do except by Father; being the only princess in her land, no one would dare to challenge her actions. She slowly crept up to Kaiden's side and waited, eying his body from top to bottom, looking for wounds. She found herself intrigued by his lean, muscular build and caught herself staring too long at his bare chest before darting her eyes away as her cheeks flushed red. She fought the temptation to look again and distracted her mind with the fact she couldn't see even a single wound despite the battle being only hours ago.

Finn walked up behind her; in case the impact threw her back; he would at least help soften the blow to her small figure. Female elves of most breeds were generally very slender and tall, though Nirayus was unusually short standing a little under 5ft tall at best, making Finn feel like an awkward giant at little over seven feet tall.

Nirayus dared to get a little closer and sat on the bed beside him, her hand resting mere inches from his as he lay there unconscious. She looked into his peaceful face and got lost in memory. He looked so similar from how she had remembered him from her childhood, the same kind boy wrapped up in years of stress and hardship. She found her eyes traveling down to the ringed stone amulet that lay upon his rising chest and came to the realization that she was grasping the compass he had given her in her other hand. Without thinking, she lay her hand gently on his chest, her finger tracing the edges of the smooth stone amulet she had made for him when they were young. She felt a warm tear roll down her face, pulling her from her distant memories.

She didn't know what was wrong with him, but she wanted to find a way to help him like he had for her. If she could help him get his memories back and remember who she was, she dared to think what his feelings might be for her. Her head hung in sadness for finally finding him after so many years and being so close but really in many ways so far from him at the same time.

Gorman and Finn stood in silence, watching her sit beside him, both taking notice that whatever protected him from the outside world somehow let her in close. She had even been able to touch him when the clerics who were there to tend to him failed to even stand beside the bed. Gorman looked over to Finn and saw a tear roll down his greyish blue scaled cheek, his bulbous eyes nearly shut with their protective lids, holding back anymore tears.

Nirayus lifted her head and let her gaze settle on his closed eyes. His skin was dirty from the long road they had traveled. She cupped her hand to his cheek with her thumb softly rubbing against the dirt.

Suddenly his eyes flickered open. "Nirayus?" he asked confused, his hand going to hers and holding it against his cheek. He held her soft, cool hand momentarily before coming to and sitting up, her hand falling from his as she stood in shock.

Kaiden looked at her with a big smile then down to see his legs under a blanket. He quickly scanned the room, settling his gaze on Gorman and Finn. "What happened?" he asked, confused at where they were.

"She just woke you up from a deep sleep, nobody knew what was wrong with you and not a single person could even get close to you except the little elven princess," Finn responded with a small, sly smile.

Kaiden looked to Nirayus with a slight blush, realizing he wasn't even wearing a shirt and grabbed for his torn-up tunic beside him. "No, Finn, what happened? How did we get here?" he asked before noticing the bandages wrapped around Gorman's waist. "Are you ok, Gorman? Did I hurt you?" he asked in hesitation.

Gorman shook his head, touching his ribs with his giant hand to test its sensitivity. "Nah, kid, da beast got a good swipe at mes." He huffed with more enthusiasm than usual, thankful Kaiden had finally awoken. "But mes ok," he added, pulling the blankets off and gently getting out of the bed.

"A creature attacked us. More quillbacks? Or something else?" Kaiden asked, eager to learn what happened to everyone and why they were in some sort of medical room.

Finn came over to the opposite side of the bed from Nirayus. "Well to start at the beginning, we got here right before an attack, the plague has ravaged through here as well I fear and from what I gather it may be getting worse not ever seeing so many at once and something much bigger, maybe a leader had formed or a newer generation that had infected an ogre so it was a lot bigger, stronger even," Finn recounted, his voice gathering excitement as he explained.

"It not be dere leader," Gorman grunted as he walked closer. "But I's saw it wit da red eyes in da darkness, it be makin dem, I's see it before in Hengegrove." he added

Finn looked at him briefly in thought. "So, there was something commanding them or controlling them from the shadows? I find that exciting news as well because as you were all sleeping off your injuries I studied the lizards' remains as best as they would let me and they are the exact same as the ones from Hengegrove, whatever it is has spread this far north and possibly further, especially now that we know something is spreading the plague purposefully and there is intelligence behind their attacks though that makes this foe even more potent and dangerous since they always seem to be several steps ahead of us," Finn said, slapping Gorman on the shoulder. "You waited until now to let me in on this insightful detail?" he added, clasping his long-webbed fingers together and twirling his fingers around, deep in thought.

Kaiden gave Gorman a smile and a nod of acknowledgement. "Good work, Gorman, now let's go find this Paladin you were talking about, maybe he knows more and whether we can be any help to the cause." He got out of bed, his body feeling strong and limber from his sleep. "Was anyone killed?" He pondered aloud, looking to the distracted half ogre.

"I lost ten of my best soldiers," a woman's commanding voice interjected, resonating above all the other noises in the infirmary.

A tall woman with long, wavy strawberry-colored hair approached wearing highly decorated silver and gold plate mail. The curves in the bulky armor hugged her shapely body and moved fluently as she walked quickly towards them. The long waves of her hair bounced along her high pauldrons and a long blue cape billowed behind her. She stormed through the room taking little notice of the many clerics walking around, hands full of potions and bandages clearing way for her entrance. She was a paladin with very little time on her hands, they would move or learn the hard way if they didn't. She came to a halt and her face, although very beautiful, was cold and stern as if the weight of the kingdom rested on her shoulders.

An odd look rested on her face as she looked at Kaiden in the light. "Martis?" she breathed, feeling herself tense up.

Kaiden looked at Nirayus and then to Gorman, searching for answers and coming up empty. "Who is Martis?" he asked excitedly, a small glimmer of hope that someone may recognize him from his past.

Scarlett shook her head at her misjudgment. "No, my mistake, you look like someone I have seen before," she explained with a hint of confusion lingering in her voice. "Do you have family here in Sanctuary?" she added, her words flowing quickly like the small talk was a quick attempt to change the subject.

Kaiden perked up thinking he may have family close by. "That's actually one of the reasons."

"Is that you, Gorman Vaylen? Paladin Darvish's son?" Scarlett interrupted in shock. "I remember you from training; Gorman Mad Fist, they called you." A smile of fond memories spread across her face. "Where have you been? We thought all of you died after the attack in the Pride Fields."

Gorman's face turned to sadness, his normally unreadable expression turning to clear discomfort as his memories began to surface. "I's only survivor, most of me," he said, tilting his head and tapping the thick fold of skin stapled across his missing eye.

Scarlett stepped closer to Gorman and reached up, setting her hand gently on the side of his face in empathy. "I am sorry to hear about your loss, Gorman, I truly am. We all lost people in the war and your mother has taken it very hard," she said, looking over to the rest of the party and retracting her hand to place on his forearm for reassurance as a soft apologetic look washed over her face. "Lady Tomba will be thrilled to know you are alive and I can take you to her. I promise, she has been well taken care of since your fathers passing." Her gaze uneasily looked at the others before settling on Kaiden. "I have a lot of questions for you." she said

Kaiden opened his mouth to speak but was interrupted by Gorman's weakened voice. "He be Kaiden and we be here to see Lanthor," Gorman said as his face returned to its permanent scowl.

Scarlett tossed long waves of hair back over her shoulder as she spoke. "Well, Kaiden, then I will call an audience with Lanthor, and he will want to ask you questions about what happened in the courtyard, along with a personal thank you, I imagine," she smiled.

Nirayus noticed she barely looked her direction and took offence, struggling not to lash out considering she played a big role in defeating the quillbacks, but being deep within the biggest human settlement just made her feel on edge and uneasy. She wasn't here for glory but would feel more accepted amongst the humans if they at least acknowledged her existence.

Scarlett turned and motioned for them to follow as she led them through the wide-open infirmary and into a long hallway with tall, rounded ceilings. The smooth stone walls were a clean, pearly white that almost sparkled in the light from the tall windows that ran almost the entire distance of the hallway. They turned out into an open field crowded with people going about their daily lives, all dressed in fancy colorful cloths. A crowd had formed outside the infirmary with everyone wanting to see the hero who had taken down the plague monster and the group was showered with praise.

Nirayus felt homesick seeing all the large castle towers and walls, soldiers marching atop the walls with archers posted in groups in the towers. The humans had clearly stolen their superior defensive strategies and modeled them after another race, and a sly smile spread to her lips at the thought.

Kaiden was awestruck by the massive stone towers in the center of the enormous grand walls, erected so high they would easily tower over most trees. He wondered if he had lived here before and thought he would surely remember all the grandeur and craftsmanship of such magnificent buildings.

They followed Scarlett though the courtyard and through an open courtyard of gardens at the base of the white towers and onto a large circular platform. Scarlett looked up and signaled to an unseen person who started the giant steam lift.

Finn fell to the ground and crawled to the edge, looking down at the ever-shrinking land below them. He had passed through Sanctuary several times during his travels but had never had the privilege to ride the platform before, for it was rarely used by anyone but the highest of nobles. He watched as they rose high into the air and became queasy, looking back to Kaiden and Nirayus, his eyes widening with panic.

"I think Finn is afraid of heights," Nirayus whispered to Kaiden, using the excuse to step a little closer. She hadn't been further than two feet from him since he had awoken, somehow feeling protective over her protector.

Kaiden chuckled, briefly taking his eyes off the towers to look at Finn, crawling back to the center as the lift took them higher than the walls. Kaiden looked out to the top of the noble buildings covered in bronze and silver-colored rooftops of the inner noble district and the beautiful architecture.

Gorman watched Finn scramble around with a rare smile spread across his rough face as he walked over to the floundering fish. "Dis one be bad, let's toss it back," he said, looking back at his companions as they erupted into laughter.

Finn managed to get up to a knee before a loud hissing noise sprayed from the lift down below them as the disk inched up higher, locking into the bottom of the paladin council building. Finn blinked rapidly in excitement, taking in all the finely sculpted statues and decorations that lined the place. He noticed several guards stationed around, with one to either side of some large wooden doors. A long blue carpet with golden embroidery around the edges ran along the floor and stopped at their feet.

"This way, follow me," Scarlett announced as she waved her arm to the guards in dismissal and led them down the central inner hallway, which branched to either side of the central chamber. They followed her through several different hallways and into an open foyer with seating and a table. "Wait here, I will go get Lanthor and he will be able to see you shortly," she said with a warm smile before motioning for Gorman to come closer. "Are you ready to see your mother?" she asked

Gorman momentarily turned to return to his friends but reluctantly looked down to meet Scarlett's kind eyes. His face expressed the desperate dread of someone trapped in a corner with no way out, needing to decide what path to take. He feared his mother's rejection more than anything in life and it piled on the responsibility he took for his father's death. He looked back to the door to the small council chamber and remembered high paladin Lanthor, who would be waiting behind that door. He knew he would be faced with a line of questioning about what had happened on the battlefield so many years ago and still wasn't ready to relive the memories. He looked back at Scarlett and then back to his friends as Finn laid his hand on his shoulder for reassurance.

Kaiden responded with a nod and a smile, prodding him to go as he watched the half ogre shrug off Finn's hand with a groan, strengthening his composure before turning back to Scarlett.

Gorman nodded slowly at Kaiden. "Wait for me," he said, struggling to talk with the lump in his throat. Scarlett and Gorman walked out of view and around the hallways to the right of the chamber.

Finn sat down and spread his arms on the tops of the chairs beside him, relaxing. "I have traveled through Sanctuary on several occasions and always wondered what was inside the giant white and gold towers but never thought I would get a chance to be in here and wish we had a chance to explore but I guess we should see what it is that is happening in the kingdom, they should have some of the answers we seek, don't you think? I am sure the Paladin's are the first to get all the important information." His eyes never stopped their gaze as he took in all the fine detail work of the tapestries and decorations in the room.

Kaiden watched Finn tapping his fingers on the armrests of the chairs. "It seems like they are just as lost as we are, I only hope we can be of some assistance. Maybe someone here will have answers to what has been happening to me," he said hopefully.

Nirayus's eyes narrowly squinted together as she inspected the doors, her ears perking up. "I can't wait to leave this place. Besides the fact that this place is crawling with humans, something doesn't feel right," she said, leaning to peer further down the hallways with a look of worry weighing heavily on her face. "If they have no need for us then what is next? What do we do then, Kaiden?"

Kaiden picked up on her nervous behavior and stood from the chair to stand closer to her. "I was hoping that something here would help me remember my past, but so far it all seems so foreign to me," he said as he thought about Scarlett's reaction to seeing him. "But I agree with you, something does feel off and there is a presence nearby that fills my soul with great caution. It feels very strange."

Scarlett walked Gorman down the hall, constantly looking back over her shoulder to make sure the quiet and suddenly timid ogre was still behind her. "She has been doing well, Gorman. We took care of all her needs after your leave. Most importantly, though, she is healthy, and I know she will be overjoyed to see you." She came to stop by a sturdy wooden door to the side of the hall.

Looking at all the other doors down the hall, Gorman could tell this was the place, for it was almost twice as tall as the others and had been painted purple. Planters sat along the wall and floor, carefully planted ivy wrapping up and around a half trellis around the edge of the doorframe.

"Ready?" Scarlett said with a warm smile, looking up into the half ogre's panic-stricken face. She found the great warrior's fear endearing, for she had heard stories of how valiantly Gorman had fought in the war but facing his mother nearly bringing him to his knees made her see the hero in an entirely different light.

Gorman looked down and took a deep breath, trembling at the thought of facing his mother after so long. Waves of guilt and fear washed over him, and for the first time in his life he felt the need to flee from an enemy within that he couldn't see. Sweat beaded upon his forehead as his fingers shook, wiping them off. He suddenly realized it was himself, he feared his own choices and regretted them. He knew it wasn't his fault his father had fallen that day but struggled to truly believe it.

"Ready?" Scarlet asked again, her small hand in comparison held onto his forearm by the rim of his steel bracer, pulling him out of his thoughts.

Gorman cleared his throat to answer but was interrupted by the door flying open.

"Oh, Scarlett darling, dat be you?" a loud, feminine voice called out as a tall organ woman stepped through the door.

Gorman's eye went wide as his heart stopped still and the memories of his childhood ran through his simple mind. He saw his mother, her long, light tan arms grasping the door and frame. She wore a beautiful purple dress covered with pockets that were overflowing with various tools and flowers.

Tomba froze in place as she looked over to the tall half ogre standing at eye level with her. Her jaw slackened and her eyes welled up instantly with tears. As if in disbelief she put her large hand to the side of her cheek in shock while the other grasped harder onto the doorframe to hold against her legs, threatening to give way.

She was breathing heavily and leaned against the door for support. Gorman reached down and put his hand on her arm, having trouble seeing through his tear-filled eye.

"Baby dat you?" Tomba cried out, daring to let out a smile despite knowing deep inside it was truly her son that had finally made it home.

"Look who I found," Scarlett said lovingly, giving her friend a small hug on her side.

"It be me," Gorman said, fighting a losing battle through his tears.

"Creator be blessin, you come back to you mama," she cried out as petals of flowers fell from her pockets as she struggled to regain the strength in her legs.

Scarlett took several steps back and watched; with all the struggles in the world it was moments like these that made them all worth it. She, too, struggled to hold her professional paladin composure and turned to give Gorman a pat on his back. "I'll go check on the others, big guy," she said, her hand wiping a tear rolling down her chin.

Scarlett approached the foyer right in time as several guards opened the door and stepped out. Their ornate silver and blue armor gleamed in the light. She hastened and waved her arm, "I will escort them in," she commanded before coming to a halt before two crossed spears.

She turned her head to address the soldier in shock to be argued with. "Excuse me? I will escort them in, soldier," she said in a threatening tone as sharp as a knife.

"My apologies, Paladin, we have our orders," the guards said almost simultaneously without even looking their commander in the face.

"Who are you? Who do you think you are to command me?" she shouted as her words landed on deaf ears.

Kaiden, Finn, and Nirayus tensed up and stood back, for they had not counted on a fight and were unsure how to deal with the politics of nobility and order.

"On whose orders, soldier?" she shouted, her freckled face turning red with anger as she lay her hand on the pommel of her sword.

"Martis's orders, Ma'am, now step back," he warned as another soldier motioned for the companions to enter.

They hesitated. "We are with Paladin Scarlett," Kaiden announced as he tried to take a step closer to her, behind the crossed spears. Finn and Nirayus followed Kaiden's lead, moving away from the door, Finn cocking his head to the side in confusion.

The guard turned and disappeared through the door only to appear moments later and say, "Very well, you all may enter." His eyes darted to Scarlett, his emotionless face cold as iron.

Scarlett saw the odd expression of the soldier and looked to the two spearmen and noticed the blank stares as if frozen in place. She scowled and moved closer to Kaiden, motioning them inside the chamber so she may have a stern word with Martis. As she entered the dimly lit room, she quickly noticed Martis sitting alongside Lanthor in the judging balcony with a wide smirk on his face.

"What is the meaning of all this?" Scarlett demanded, looking to Martis, who gestured for more guards to enter the room. She could see something physically wrong with Lanthor sitting lazily on his throne, a golden locket glowing on his chest as beads of sweat freely rolled down his forehead. The normally proud and strong Lanthor being reduced to a sickly-looking husk of a person with the same empty stare in his eyes, completely disregarding Scarlett's demands.

The room was normally used for single trials where one of the Paladins could easily pass judgement and sentencing upon a subject with a few witnesses or family for support. There was a stage at the end of the long narrow room with a chair higher up in the middle so that they could sit above the accused. A steel grate fence was in front of the group so they were forced to stay to the one end, and only a few people at a time could step forward onto the stand. The stand where Lanthor and Martis sat, about a dozen guards all mindlessly glared at the companions, spears and swords ready at their sides.

Martis stood from his chair. "Lanthor is feeling ill today and so I have been given authority to help answer any questions and address the… incident in the courtyard," he said smugly.

Scarlett ignored Martis and looked to Lanthor. "What happened here, Lanthor? This is unlike you, you were fine only a few days ago, please explain," she demanded, feeling betrayed that the High Paladin wouldn't turn to his fellow Paladins first before relying on a sniveling noble priest.

Martis smiled at the unresponsive Lanthor and stepped down the stage to get closer to the dividing grate, his smirk of confidence almost sickening to look at. "With all the problems with the plague going around, Lanthor needs to keep his strength, but has accompanied me by the good graces of his heart in case he is needed. Baladar be blessed," he said, looking back to Lanthor for recognition.

Scarlett scrunched her nose in confusion as the mention of the unknown Creator.

Lanthor raised a finger to continue with his gaze unmoved, his chest rising and falling rapidly as if having a hard time breathing. He looked upon the companions with the slow glowing of the amulet highlighting the darkness around his eyes.

Martis knew his presence would anger Scarlett and he had hoped she would be left outside without argument so he could interrogate the new heroes in private, but he really knew better than that. He looked at the well-traveled Aquarian, for he had seen sleek skins before but never one that chose to keep their thick scale and carapace armoring over fitting in with the humans. He discounted him, he would not be of any use to him in his future plans with his need to be tethered near water, although he could be useful if he was indeed a skilled cartographer as most traveling Aquarians were. He changed his mind on Finn and ultimately found him expendable, but useful for plotting out dangerous and uncharted areas of Allterra.

Martis looked to the pale skinned elf with vibrant blue hair and was intrigued. She dressed in fine silks and armor like a noble of their kind yet her muscle tone and athletic build for a female elf suggested possibly a hunter. He liked mysteries and took interest in the exotic elven beauty, though his mind wandered to more personal uses. He decided excitedly that she would do nicely to entertain him on the occasional evening when he grew bored of his other girls.

His gaze moved to the boy and his face squirmed and froze in a stare of disbelief. He looked upon the young man as he came to the stand, his heart beginning to race with anxiety and his blood pumped with anger. Was it possible? He thought. His eyes went to the floor then searched the almost empty room, scanning his mind frantically trying to piece together the possibilities of Kaiden standing before him alive. He scowled at the boy; he had changed, he looked different somehow and, in his panic, he couldn't figure out the details and it angered him, the details were always the most important. He looked into his eyes, judging his gaze upon him and noticed his calm collected demeanor.

"What is your name?" Martis managed, the single second he stood waiting for a response lingering for years in his mind.

"My name is Kaiden," he responded. "These are my companions, Finn and Nirayus, and we come to offer our help to the cause," he said, gesturing to his friends.

Martis was clearly preoccupied in thought and his stoic features turned hysteric, unable to believe what he was seeing.

"No, it isn't!" Martis shouted like a crazed man, smashing his fist through the stage railing as splinters of wood shattered through the air.

Kaiden looked at Martis, then to his companions in puzzlement.

"No, it can't be you, it can't be you, you are dead!" Martis seethed in anger, letting out a bellowing shout, raising his hands high into the air as the faint light in the chamber dimmed even darker. He turned and left the room, slamming the heavy door in an enraged fit as he exited, his frantic shouts echoing into the rooms beyond as if he had snapped and gone insane.

Scarlett, confused by Martis's uncharacteristic actions and the unsettling black mist looming in the air, shouted her pleas up to Lanthor. "Sir, there is something terribly wrong here, let me in there so I can help you," she pleaded as she frantically shook the grates in between them. The guards moved in with their spears to force her back and started to cry out in pain, falling to their knees before getting close to her. "Please, Sir, you are not yourself, let me help you," she called out again in alarm just as the face of one of the soldiers tore off in a solid flap and a long black snout outstretched, snapping and chewing at the scraps of ripped flesh it could catch. Claws began to tear through limbs as the cries of pain intensified and entire limbs were thrown against the grate, sending showers of hot blood into the air.

Scarlett let out a terrified scream when a splatter of blood slapped across her face. She turned to flea with the companions and pushed the two guards to the side, knocking them to the floor to embrace the burning pain swirling within their stomachs. She looked back to see Lanthor erupt into a fit of coughing, clenching at his chest, his gasps for air getting more and more desperate.

Nirayus turned back to see the stunned Scarlett and grabbed hold of her arm, pulling her out through the chamber doors, noticing the deep golden glow of the necklace around the High Paladin's neck like the hunter Vixis had worn. She saw the man's arms begin to flail wildly as his face began to swell.

Kaiden's arm wrapped around Nirayus's slender waist as he scooped her closer. "We must go," he said, pulling her and Scarlett through the doors.

Nirayus turned back surprised and nodded at his bold gesture, moving to follow close behind him.

Finn slammed the heavy brown door shut behind them with a worried expression on his face when the door began to shake from desperate clawing within. The screams and cries of the soldiers died out and were replaced by shrill shrieks and cackles of the quillbacks communicating with each other.

"I apologize. Things here are far grimmer than I had believed, and it is not safe for anyone in here," Scarlett said, gesturing for the group to go around the wall towards the exit. A wailing cry echoed down the hallways, followed by more screams of men and the sounds of swords being pulled from their scabbards. Their screaming became louder and louder, more intense before several loud snapping sounds punctured the silence. Scarlett's eyes went wide with dread as the group froze in place, looking back towards the sound coming from behind the chamber door.

Gorman walked through the large open door of his mother's house, admiring all the flowers and different arrangements she had organized around her living room. Tomba gripped his hand as if he were her only tether to life and could never let go, dragging him in and sitting him on the couch. She put her big hand on the side of his face, her short tusks lifting up past her bottom lip from her smiling.

"My baby want a tea?" she asked, her cheeks still wet from tears. She felt like she had died and had been delivered to the creator itself, her wait finally over and the weight on her shoulders no longer dragging her down.

Gorman nodded, relieved, his heart lifting from its usual burdens of guilt. He forced down a gulp of relief that his mother wasn't furious with him but still dreading the inevitable questioning.

Tomba gathered a handful of logs from the stack by her front door and threw it into an oven before lighting it on fire. She came back and sat across from him in her favorite chair overlooking the castle's districts and markets. She found herself looking out the window as usual and had to remind herself that her wait was over and the person she searched for was now only feet away. Her heart leaped again in shock as her eyes welled up, looking at her young boy.

"Baby where you been?" she asked softly, her hands fidgeting on her dress and armrest.

Gorman struggled to choke back his tears, barely able to look his proud ogran mother in the face. "Mes Warden of Hengegrove now, Mama," he tried to say in an uplifting tone.

Tomba nodded with a slight smile of pride. "Why you gone so long?" she followed up softly, as if scared of the answer.

Gorman shook his head slightly, struggling to find the words for his guilt. "Mes scared, Mama," he said with a sniffle, his eye struggling to stay open through the tears.

Tomba placed her hand on her chest in sorrow for what she may have done to make herself unapproachable by her son. "Why yous so scared, baby? I be waitin fer yous, waitin fer long time, I's scared yous gone forever." She broke back down into tears and moved over to embrace Gorman, pulling his head against her side, her hands holding tightly onto his shoulder.

Gorman was very big for human standards, and being half human made him look less brutish than a normal ogre male but was considered to be a runt in size. Tomba stood about the same height as Gorman but had the bigger proportioned appendages and limbs like a pure ogre. She was also greyer and tanner in tone, and it made her stand out in contrast to Gorman's more peach colored skin.

Gorman put his war-torn hands on his mother for support. "Mes scared you mad about Pops," he said, hunched over and looking up into her face as if he was groveling. "Mes not save him, Mama."

Tomba's eyes clenched tightly together as she slid off her chair, kneeling beside him in embrace. She had feared that was why he hadn't come home but she was relieved that he finally did so she could be the one to tell him. "No, baby, yous did good," she said looking into his face.

ARKANGEL

"You's Pops alive baby, alive," She added with a joyful smile.

Gorman's heart wrenched in sorrow, not only for his mother's denial but the memory of seeing him bleed out from the brutal wounds he suffered at the hands of the ember elves. He moved his head to the side in pain, sniffling back his tears. "He be, dead, Mama, Mes see it happen," he stated with final confirmation.

"No, baby, he be alive," she said, trying to pull him closer as he recoiled away. "Baby Lu-Sea save him," she added.

Gorman quickly regained his composure at the sound of her name. "Lu-Sea?" he muttered, his body stiffening as his pain gave away to anger. "Lu-Sea be bad, Mama, she no help," he argued.

Tomba gently moved her hands to his and caressed them in reassurance. "She be good, Baby, she save Pops," she said as her eyes lit up. "He be ogre now."

Gorman's jaw opened in disbelief; he knew she had a unique arking skillset but couldn't understand why she would so willingly help, when all that woman wanted was destruction and power.

"Why she help Pops? She kill many many humans."

Tomba regained her composure as well and the great relief she felt for her life finally turning around gave her tremendous joy. Her face hardened slightly. "Oh she be a danger, baby, but it be true, she save yous Pops," she said, her voice turning very serious.

The guilt that weighed so heavily on Gorman's heart for his father's death dared to lift slightly but he still knew there had to be a catch. "Where be Pops, Mama?" he asked, afraid his mother had lost her sanity and he was afraid of what answer she may come up with.

Tomba nodded her head in thought. "He be at her tower, baby, he lives there now." She wrapped her arms around him for a long, sturdy hug.

Gorman pulled away slightly to look into her eyes for an answer. "Why yous not with him, Mama?" he asked slowly.

Tomba's face turned warm with love as she looked into his eye. "Baby, mes wait for yous, waitin for yous to come home," she whispered.

The genuine love in her voice tore at his conscious. How could he have been so selfish, hiding from the truth while his lonely Mother sat and waited for him instead of being with the man she loved? His heart broke in sorrow and wrapped his arms around her to embrace her tightly. They sat holding each other for several minutes, the small fire she had made withering into ash.

Being with his mother and finally coming to terms made him sad for being selfish but he was relieved it was over, and it was only to get better for her now. Now she could return north and the forbidden love between a noble and his organ servant would no longer need to be secret; they could finally live together happily.

Gorman's head shot up alert at the sound of loud screaming. He recoiled from his mother and went to the door to investigate. A dreadful sound of snapping bone ended the tortured cries as he knelt beside the door to reclaim his spears.

Tomba came up behind him, resting her hand on his forearms, the same way she used to do before he had to leave for battle when he was young. "Be safe, Baby," she said, giving him a kiss on his forehead. She stood in the doorway watching her soldier run down the hallway towards the sound of danger.

Gorman rounded the corner to see an oversized quillback crash through a stone wall and lunge at Kaiden. Its long talons outstretched at him, slashing and clawing through the air to its victim. Gorman could see the hosts flesh stretch and tear over the creatures big, scaled body with its quills jutting several feet behind its back. It turned slightly and Gorman saw the human face still intact as its jaw broke away, flopping to one side. "Lanthor?" he breathed in shock.

Scarlett gasped at the sight of the creature wearing her high paladin's face and sprinting towards them, barely hindered by the foot of solid stone wall it had crashed through. Kaiden pushed Nirayus into Finn's arms and jumped in the opposite direction just to be snagged by the creature's claws. The two collided through a window and fell over thirty feet down into the busy courtyard below.

On impact the sonic boom blasted the ground apart beneath them, causing a crater to span almost twenty feet in diameter. Lanthor was thrust high into the air and whirled around to attack as he descended back down towards Kaiden's armored body.

The townspeople screamed in terror at the sight of the hideous creature, its long spiney tail curling around as it crashed into Kaiden. It stood tall and bellowed a terrifying scream, Lanthor's torn face draped across its snout as it jerked to the side to devour it.

Cries for help filled the air when the nobles and merchants fled every direction in panic. On the ground Kaiden spun with his legs, ripping the creature's legs out from underneath it and sending it crashing into the dirt. Kaiden flipped out of the crater, his arm blades gleaming in the bright sun as he jumped up and plunged into its shoulder. He pulled them free as hot green blood sprayed out for an instant before the wounds completely sealed shut. It reached its arm around and encircled Kaiden's torso with its claws and leapt high into the air. As it began to fall it threw Kaiden's body hard into the crater below, landing atop him again and again as it slashed at his armor.

It continued to jump and slash wildly as Kaiden got beaten deeper into the hard soil. He raised his forearms to guard and the blades along his arms shot out several inches, catching the lizard's claws. It dragged his body out from under its weight before its arm recoiled from the pain. Kaiden flipped up to his feet and readied for his next attack.

Large claws lashed out at him, sweeping side to side in a flurry of attacks. Kaiden dodged back and down, easily evading its recklessness. He drew out his short swords from his shins and slashed at the creature's palms and arms, jumping up and over the swipes as the creature attempted to circle around him.

Several of the townspeople filled the nearby buildings, watching the battle unfold while others took to the stairs to see a safer view from the top of the inner walls. The lifting platform began to raise up into the air to retrieve the other companions who watched helplessly above.

Gorman, anxious to help his friend, drew his spears and hurled one down, sinking it deep into the creature's back. Loud shrieks of pain erupted from the creature, hardly slowing down its onslaught of attacks.

Kaiden stayed ahead of it and began to maneuver around the beast to where its attacks were wilder and desperate to find their target, confusing the creature. The spears in its back fell to the ground as the wounds sealed up. Gorman saw that the second Kaiden struck into the beast the wounds were almost instantly healed as well. He held tight to his last two spears and ran, jumping out of the broken section of wall high above. He slammed down seconds later, landing hard onto its back and his spears piercing straight through and out its scaly chest, pinning it down to the hard soil. It flailed and pushed trying to lift itself up, its snapping snout never taking its evil glare off its prey. Its tail swung up, wrapping around Gorman and sending him spinning through the air, crashing into the side of the massive tower several yards away.

The lift locked into its bottom position with a loud clank before a loud hiss of steam filled the air. Finn ran over to Gorman as Nirayus snuck up quickly behind the stuck creature, the hunter inside her stalking her unsuspecting target. Scarlett drew the glaive from her back and unfolded it into battle position for better reach and sprinted to aid Kaiden.

Nirayus's eyes lit up a brilliant blue as electricity lashed out from her face; she raised her hands together into the air and pulled them apart with a massive arc of lightning dancing between her hands. She ran up and threw the bolts onto the beast to see them immediately dissipate. She scowled, cocking her head to the side in confusion. She arked her hands into a bright fiery glow but decided against the destructive power of her fire, not wanting a stray blast to hurt the growing crowd of people around them. She focused her energy again and started swinging her hands around as if she was wielding two long whips. Long lashes of electricity snapped and cracked at the creature's back, still having no effect. She then caught glimpse of the golden chain now stretched across its neck, glowing a warm golden color, recognizing it to be like the one Vixis wore.

"Destroy the amulet it is wearing," Nirayus cried out, her warning falling on deaf ears as Kaiden remained catatonic within his armored shell.

Scarlett and Kaiden took turns parrying the creature's slashes while the other one stepped closer to land an attack at its face, working together in unison as if they had trained together their entire lives. Even though the creature was pinned it was just as dangerous with its razor-sharp claws and teeth, and massive barbs jutting out of its violently lashing tail.

Nirayus's heartbeat quickly as anxiety took over with panic; her companions would only wear themselves out, eventually being overtaken by the beastly lizard. She gulped in fear and noticed Finn rush up from behind with Gorman, who was loading a barbed bolt into his forearm contraption attached to a rope.

Gorman fired the harpoon into the creature's tail and planted his big feet firmly against the bank of the crater, holding it at bay. Finn took the small opportunity to run in and leap onto its quilled back, forcing his way through, his thick carapace skin getting torn and pierced as he tried to pull himself further up the creature's back.

Nirayus saw the rope begin to fray from quills of the tail striking against it and made a split-second decision. She sprinted full speed and leaped into the air, clearing the quills and landing gracefully on Finn's shoulders. She jumped off again as Finn dragged his way through the forest of quills. She landed onto its shoulder and pulled her curved dagger free, stabbing it into the creature's skin and under the stretched golden chain. She pulled with all her might, trying to stand and balance against the flailing creature's attacks.

Finn finally reached her, teal streams of blood running down his injuries as they both reached down through the quills to pull at the chain. The two of them screamed, Finn pulling on the chain with his webbed fingers as Nirayus pried with her dagger. The chain finally snapped with a loud booming sound that rippled through the air, rupturing the magic barrier protecting the creature. The wave of energy washed over everyone like a burst of thick, hot air.

The creature used the momentum to spin around, un-planting Gorman and throwing him across the crater, while Finn grabbed Nirayus and hurled her off the creature's back to safety as he struggled to hold on. The creature reared up with a roar, pulling the spear through its body and reaching around to tear Finn from its back. It held Finn in its hand, its other raising to strike through his aquarian body.

Suddenly, long blue arcs of electricity enveloped the beast's face and torso. It released Finn, falling several feet into the dirt as it reared up, its body beginning to convulse and twitch uncontrollably. Nirayus's hair stuck straight back in the air as if caught in a violent wind with electricity cackling from her eyes. Her outstretched hands held a rope of pure blue energy tightening and grasping around the creature. The blue tendrils of electricity burned and seared into the beast's thick scales.

Kaiden moved over and grabbed Scarlett's glaive from her hands and jumped into the air in a spin. He whirled around and struck the blade deep into the creature's chest, dragging it all the way down the belly of the beast and unleashing its green and yellow stained organs all over the ground.

Nirayus stopped arking as the creature fell to the dirt, its electrified entrails popping under its weight. The companions took a second to acknowledge everyone was ok as Kaiden collapsed to the ground, his armor retracting into thin air. Kaiden gasped, reaching up to the sky, coughing and struggling for breath. He pulled himself up to his knees as the world spun around him, trying to focus and stabilize against the vertigo of his sluggish mind.

Gorman and Nirayus raced to his side for support. "Yous ok, kid?" Gorman asked, sheathing his spears on his back.

Nirayus bent down and lifted his arm around her shoulder, helping him to stand. "Are you ok? You're awake?" she questioned in confusion while he breathed heavily, his hand pressed against his chest.

The strength returned to his legs as he looked around at the aftermath of the battle. "Did I do all that?" he panted.

Scarlett retrieved her glaive from the ground and folded it back together, snapping it to her back. "You don't remember killing it?" she asked in concern.

Kaiden shook his head, his eyes glossed over in thought, still trying to piece together the events leading up to his blackout. "No, I black out, but this time was a little different, I remember flashes and impulses like I needed to do something but was unable to move. There was something else, or someone else present, I could feel them close by like in a dream before waking up here on the ground."

"Dat be how I's find him too," Gorman said, his hand releasing the steam pressure from his dwarven arm guard.

"I have never seen anything like that in my entire life," Scarlett said in surprise, looking over his sweaty shirt draped over his tense muscles. "You must have some sort of Arking ability but nothing I have ever heard of. Where did you learn it?" she asked, still sorting out where the armor could have gone.

Kaiden finally snapped out of his deep fog; he had caught a glimpse of control for the first time and needed to hold on to it, tame it, analyze what he had just felt within. He wished he was alone to concentrate. "I don't know, I don't remember anything past last week when Gorman found me, it's just blank. That's one of the reasons we came here, in hopes of finding my memory or someone who may recognize me," he said as his voice trailed off.

Nirayus slipped out from under his arm, making sure he was strong enough to stand. "We will keep searching," she said, hopeful. "I've heard you humans have taken residence all over the land, you are bound to be from somewhere." She realized too late that her word choice hadn't come out quite as intended.

The group's conversation was quickly interrupted as the crowd of onlookers huddled around closer since the apparent danger had passed. Everyone erupted into shouts of praise and gratitude for saving them and their families. Cheers of shouting went out for the victory over the creature. One of the merchants came forth to shake the hands of the heroes to thank them and express his gratitude.

"What is your name friend?" he asked while shaking Kaiden's hand.

Kaiden stood confused, not used to being put on the spot in front of so many people. "My name is Kaiden," he said hesitantly.

The man raised his arms to the sky in cheer, "To Kaiden!" he shouted. "Kaiden the beast Slayer!" he called out over and over as he was joined in by hundreds of people. Others called out praise for the "Elven Ark Master!" or "The Ogran Warrior!" or "Kaiden the Sword Master!" People shouted praise.

Gorman came up behind and lifted Kaiden high into the air as the crowd erupted into even louder cheers of praise for Kaiden and his companions.

Nirayus felt completely overwhelmed by all the human attention and went to check on the wounded Finn staying away from the bulk of the crowd on the other side of the slain beast. "Here is the Amulet from around the beast's neck. What should we do with it?" she shouted as she got closer, trying to be heard over the cheering.

Finn took it from her and held it on his open palm as it began to glow. He shuddered and was surprised as the resonating glow pulsed through his body, healing the wounds he had suffered from the creature's sharp quills. "Incredible!" he stated. "There is an enormous amount of power locked away in here, it is best to keep it between us that I have it and we will find a time to research it further, it is truly fascinating how this works and yet feels so familiar but I cannot put my finger on it exactly," Finn said as he pulled a rough patch of scales away from his hip, putting the amulet inside. He looked up at her with a grin. "I have things hidden all over this scaly body of mine, the last place anyone would think to look." he chuckled.

Nirayus smiled ear to ear, her gaze going back to see Kaiden being praised by the crowd. "It seems like he is getting stronger and recovering a lot faster when using his armor. Do you think it will help him get his memory back somehow?" she asked hopefully.

ARKANGEL

Finn bobbed his head for several seconds, his eyes scanning the crowd while his mandibles bounced joyously. He could see the deep admiration the elf had for the boy in her eyes, and it brought on a wide grin. "You know you very well may have saved us all; it seems though our party was missing something after all and I am glad you are with us because if you hadn't known to remove that amulet I fear it may have eventually overrun us if my calculations are accurate, and they almost always are," he said with a chuckle.

Nirayus's heart felt warmed by Finn's kind words, she felt tired from her arking but somehow felt accepted by her new companions in a way she never had before. She found her hand gently caressing the small compass hanging on her chest. She watched all the people praising them and hoped one of them may know recognize Kaiden and help to recover his memory. She was glad he had attracted all the attention, keeping the human's gazes off her.

Their attention was pulled to Scarlett as she escorted Gorman and Kaiden back on top of the lifting platform, gesturing for them to follow. They stood there on the raising disk overlooking the continuously growing crowd as thousands of them waved, calling their names in praise until the hiss of steam drowned them out.

They found the main room lined with Paladin guard, an elite group of guards that were stationed within the tower to respond to greater threats. Their heavy black and silver plate mail created a wall of shields as they stood firm with piles of lizards slain at their feet. Scarlett gave a nod of thanks to their captain as their formation shifted into a column before marching away to their remote barracks.

Tomba rushed towards Gorman. "Baby you be a Hero," she said, the pride she felt for her son ringing in her deep voice.

Finn tapped Gorman's shoulder with his webbed finger and nodded to his mother. "I couldn't agree more, Ma'am," he said with a smile and bounce of his mandibles. "You must be his beautiful mother, you know, I can tell where he gets his likeable personality and charm from," he added as she wrapped her arms around Gorman in a hug.

She looked back from the hug. "Oh, who be yous friend, baby? I's like him," she said with a warm smile to Finn, whose smile only widened in delight.

Gorman huffed and shook his shoulder loose from Finn's grasp, stepping over to Kaiden. "We's need a plan, kid," he said, eying Finn talking to his mother.

Kaiden looked over to Scarlett, the adrenaline of battle wearing off as he came to the realization that the reason they had come was to speak to the now deceased Lanthor. "What is there to do now Scarlett? What happens now that Lanthor is gone?" he asked, searching for a purpose.

Scarlett looked down the council hallway where she had just talked to Ryker only days before; he hadn't shown up at the barracks like he had promised, and she feared he had traveled north alone. She wished he was there with them, not only because he was her superior and needed to help make decisions with Lanthor gone but mostly she missed him and worried for his safety.

"I am in charge until Rhyker comes back and we will vote upon a new Paladin, so I am stuck here, to command what army we have left," she said in a wounded tone.

"Army yous left?" Gorman asked.

"Yes, last week Lanthor sent away half the army north for Martis to help protect his estate at Solstice Gardens, the last safe place from the plague they say," she recited with a worried expression crossing her already shaken appearance. "This is bad. This is getting out of hand. If Lanthor wasn't in his right mind when he sent away those soldiers, they could all be in danger." Her eyes darted around in search of what to do. "The city could be in even greater danger with whatever Martis is planning."

Scarlett closed her eyes and shook her head. "I should have listened to Rhyker, we should have stopped this before it got out of control, we must find him," she said, looking out the broken window and across the city. "When the people find out they are leaderless and now mostly defenseless we will have a mutiny and mass panic on our hands, the city will chew itself apart with the plague unchecked." she said.

Kaiden stepped closer to her and rested his hand on her great pauldron. "So, you are in charge, now lead, that's all it takes. Trust in yourself and your training and your loyalty to Sanctuary. You have us at your disposal. What would you like us to do?" he said confidently in a supportive tone.

Finn's eyes gleamed when he realized he had the perfect excuse to finally lead the party further north and spoke up, raising his hand. "I have this from the creature's neck and from what I can tell it resonates a unique golden ark energy I have never seen before and may have the answers we seek inside of it or may lead us in the right direction but we need someone familiar with such trinkets and power, through my trials there has only been one with such a gift and she lives far north by the name of Lu-Sea, alas she may be able to help and unlock your mystery as well Kaiden but I warn that she often is led only by her own agenda and ulterior motives, is very unpredictable and very very dangerous," he said, his eyes widening to further prove his point.

Gorman looked to his mother and began to speak but was quickly cut off by Scarlett. "She is very dangerous but also a legend, a hero to many and a terror to a great many more. In the days of the war with the ember elves she was the one who finally put an end to it, striking such a brutal blow to their army that they had no choice but to retreat. She used her power to corrupt their forces, turning them on one another, and even was able to pluck their queen right from under their noses. They took the defeat very hard and haven't been seen since."

"We are told stories of her as children to make us behave or she may steal your body," Scarlett chuckled.

"There are stories about her in our history as well, but Father would never let me listen, I only know what little I was able to pick up in rumors," Nirayus whispered to Kaiden.

Scarlett watched as her men dragged away the corpses of the fallen guards, who had been violently turned to quillbacks, feeling responsible for not catching on to Martis sooner. She looked back out the window towards the looming mountain far in the distance, deep in thought.

"Nobody as far as I know has ever been able to find Lu-Sea. The stories say she is locked up in an obelisk of pure power, constructed by the creators and surrounded by an impossible maze. Others say she is one of the creators, still living amongst us," she said, entranced in thought and regret. "Though they could just be stories, she struck down hundreds of our own in the war as well. Finn is right, she plays with life like it is a game that only she can win, someone like that cannot be trusted."

"I's know her," Tomba said, catching Gorman's gaze. "She be a hero to me and be good help," she added in a defensive confidence.

Scarlett looked at Tomba in shock. "You know her? You have seen her? She isn't one that you just know," Scarlett snapped.

Tomba looked up in thought with a smile spreading across her face. "She be savior an got me's husband back from da dead," she said joyfully, despite Gorman's worried expression.

Nirayus, hearing the argument of Lu-Sea being her ticket to leave the city, decided to pitch in her input. "From what little I have heard of her I know she is an elf like I am and a distant relative from my people. It is true that she may be the most unpredictable and destructive force when given a reason to be, but she is inherently good and only destroys unbalance. There are no sides for her war or loyalty, only good and evil."

Nirayus looked up to Kaiden with a smile on her face, with a sudden newfound purpose to go. "Finn is right, though, she would be able to help you get your memory back if anyone could. She has unique arking abilities that no one quite understands and is even rumored to be able to haunt and inhabit another's body." Her tone had shifted to more of a convincing statement while a tingle ran down her spine at how terrifying the woman truly was.

Kaiden returned Nirayus's smile, for it meant a lot to him that she thought about what could help his memory and find the answers he was seeking. "Scarlett, it's up to you, should we travel north in search of Lu-Sea in hopes to get answers about the plague or help you find the other Paladin and secure the safety of Sanctuary?"

ARKANGEL

Scarlett continued to stare blank faced and silent out the window over the city, her head sinking down along with her heart. She worried so much for Rhyker and the city, but she didn't want to be selfish, for ultimately the city and its people came first and if the plague was stopped then her people would be safe. She looked at each of the companions, her gaze settling on each with sincere gratitude for stepping up to the cause.

"Alright, what is best for the people is that we do what we can to keep them safe and the best way to do that is to end its suffering from the plague. If each of you are willing, I need you to travel north, find Lu-Sea and tell her of our plight. Tell her we will forever be in her debt and can arrange for any supplies or payments she desires from us."

Gorman straightened his hunched posture in pride, resting his massive hand on Kaiden's shoulder. "Me's be followin you, kid, you be needin mes," he said with a gruff smile and nod.

Kaiden looked up to the tall half ogre and pushed at his arm playfully. "I need you too, big buddy, thank you," he said as his gaze went to Nirayus and then to Finn. "I cannot guarantee your safety but would be honored to travel with you once more," he said as his gaze traveled back to the elven princess.

Finn perked up in excitement. "Yes, onward to adventure we go, though I am not as familiar with the northern areas, I can get us most of the way there my friend," he said as his mandibles bounced in anticipation. He knew they would reach her and that she would see to it that they were found quickly.

Nirayus's heart lurched into her throat as she searched for words. She knew she would travel with him to the end of the world, memory or not, and would overcome any danger in hopes for the day they could reunite, and she could freely tell him her heart. She reached her hand out shyly and grabbed his, gently pulling him closer without realizing what she was doing. She looked up to him, her big doe eyes gazing into his. "I, too, will follow you, Kaiden."

CHAPTER 9

"RIGHTING A WRONG"

Arcusbane rolled to his side, the rough and rocky ground digging into his shoulder blades from under the burlap sack he used for a bed. He rolled again, now the noise from the late-night celebration party echoing through the city and keeping him awake. He heard Saber's heavy breathing and whine who was also unable to fall asleep with the loud noises unsettling his nerves.

Arcus's thoughts kept going to Taja no matter what he did to divert his thought to something else. He hadn't had many friends in his life, and she would be the second taken from him. He wasn't even sure if they were friends, what was a friend really, other than someone to lose? He thought of how great it would be to stand above Aldair and cut him down, victorious and praised as a mighty hero. That would teach him and all the others for taking what wasn't theirs.

He shook his head again, she wasn't his, nor was she Aldair's and his heart kept worrying for her. He had heard what some of the slave owners did with the lionel woman and it made him feel sick. Just thinking of what she would be put through night after night brought tears to his eyes, even if she did drive him mad. But what could he do? Where was she now? Maybe she found a way to escape somehow? He felt a little rise of hope before remembering her aversion to fighting, but maybe she would save her own life?

ARKANGEL

His legs became restless, and he rolled back over, lost in an internal battle over what he could even do. He had only known her a few days and had all intensions to turn her in or sell her but had no idea he would feel so bad about it, plus he didn't even get anything for her. He sat up frustrated with himself, it wasn't about the money or his compensation, she was innocent, and he brought her here against her will.

His fists clenched and slammed into the sandy dirt beside him. Saber lifted his head alert, listening to his master's discomfort. Arcus's mind went to his friend Kaiden and how much he missed him, his first and only close friend his whole life. Arcus imagined it was the closest thing to having a brother he could get, a family, they had been inseparable since the first day they met. They both had violent and terrible pasts and vowed to watch each other's back no matter what.

Arcus felt tears of sorrow and loneliness stream down his face. He had lived on the streets, starving, no family and barely a will to survive until he met Kaiden. He had told him stories of his rough childhood of endless running, never settling in one place for long until his brother betrayed their family for money and power. Kaiden was weak and fragile, always sick but his brother told someone of power that he could Ark which made him a product of mystery to be studied.

Arcus didn't know what arking even was until he had met Kaiden who explained what little he had been told before spending half his life being the victim of experimental procedures and torture. His body and face almost unrecognizable as human under the layers of scars but Arcus didn't care, he would be his new brother and was supposed to protect him. The stories Kaiden would tell him of their experiments made his stomach turn into sickness, all the different ways they would bring him to the edge of death just to nurse him partially back to health and do it again. They hooked up metal contraptions to test the limits of his body in an attempt to harness any power he was unlucky enough to have.

Arcus winced in pain and started to cry aloud, his thoughts traveling back to what those monsters were now doing to Taja right now as he lay here in his bed. As his hands wiped away the tears they brushed against the handle of the dagger at his side. He drew it free and studied the unique curved craftsmanship. It was simple and sharp, designed as a tool as opposed to a weapon. He wondered why it was so important to Taja for him to grab it when he captured her and started to feel bad for how mean and arrogant he was to her, even though she had saved him.

He went to his knees, regaining his composure and searching for purpose within, he replaced regret with anger as he slowly repeated to himself. "Be the change."

He slammed the dagger back in its sheath and went to his feet knowing he needed to act. He needed to do something but was unable to think clearly and come up with a proper plan. Taja was so meek and gentle but never hesitated to act when defending others, he wished she was with him right now. He went to saber and stroked his thick fur along his face and behind his ear, his favorite place to be scratched.

Arcus grabbed his lead and tied Saber to the sturdiest post of his hovel and attached it securely to his harness. "I am tying you up, so you don't follow me Saber, stay here," he said while petting the side of his massive snout. "But loose enough that you can escape if I don't return, ok? You will need to leave and find a new home if I don't come back, ok? Do you understand?" he asked his friend.

Saber shook his big body of fur and lay down on his side as a big breath of air escaped his lungs. Arcus walked down the street and turned to see Saber sit up to watch him leave, he didn't go anywhere without him but hoped he somehow understood. He turned and walked slowly down the dirty pathway past several other hovels that reeked of piss and rotten trash. He understood what it was like to be poor but didn't see it as an excuse to be filthy.

As he entered closer to the interior of town, piles of bodies littered the streets, most likely passed out from overindulgence of rum or the ingestion of drugs the addicts never failed to accumulate despite their lack of money. He found one of the men, mouth open as a pile of drool pooled into the dirt below him and noticed the man had a nice blade tied to his belt. Arcus was an expert marksman and usually had no need for a sword but tonight his bow would be of little use. He remembered most of his gear was still packed away safe on Saber's saddle and thought it would come in handy if he needed to escape quickly.

Arcus reached down gently and started to untie the sword's scabbard from the man's belt. It would be much easier to kill him where he lay sleeping which was always a big possibility in this part of town, but he didn't like taking life unless completely necessary. The man's body jolted as he drew in a deep breath of sandy air and let out a groan.

Arcus's heart started to pound in his chest, and he stood up quickly, surprised by the man. He looked down and watched to see if he would wake. His plan would be to run so he looked for the slightest cue to sprint away until remembering this may be his last and only chance to free his friend. He needed to harden his resolve and face the fact he may have to kill this night.

He withdrew his foot from over the body and attached the sword to his side. He could hear the shouts of laughter from the feasting tent far up ahead, he knew that would be where the king and his men would be celebrating along with their new initiates. Greenhorns weren't allowed at the celebrations, so he had no idea what to expect inside but spent his fair share of time digging through compost to get the leftovers.

As he approached the massive tent covered in animal hide, yelling erupted in a smaller canvas tent beside him. Startled, he jumped back and hid around the corner as two men slammed through the opening. They were punching and kneeing each other as they rolled on the ground shouting. Neither wore more than a small loincloth as they rolled over and over wrestling. They were arguing over a woman from what he could tell and who got to have her next. A third man came out, holding his leather trousers up around his waist with one hand and a machete in the other and started to kick at one of them.

Arcus breathed heavily from alarm and was shocked when several women rushed out from the tent wearing very little or nothing at all, screaming in terror as they fled. One circled around right next to him and froze in place. They both stood startled, looking at each other, the woman's young face covered in dirt and blood, tears rolling down her dirty cheeks. She whimpered and began to plead for him to let her go, one hand attempting to cover her chest as the other held up a handful of rags, resembling an old patchwork dress.

Arcus nodded at her, trying to advert his eyes from her mostly bare body and turned to watch the man with the machete call out in anger when he noticed the women fleeing from the tent. Arcus watched as the two men on the ground stopped fighting, realizing neither of them would be getting a woman as the man with the machete started shouting at them. The three men begin to drunkenly brawl with each other, dirt and blood splattering out onto the dusty ground. One reached for the machete and swung it hard into the neck of the other, killing him instantly and kicking his body off his blade. He was then instantly tackled by the third man, holding onto his back momentarily before getting thrown off and slammed into the ground.

Arcus startled again when he heard chains rattle inside the tent and a woman cry out, "No!"

He had thought they had all escaped, but he was wrong. The vision of fear in the poor girl's eyes he came face to face with filled him with sorrow, he hated these people and decided he needed to interfere.

The man gasped for air from the impact against the sandy floor as the machete came down hard into his chest, easily breaking through his chest cavity. His cries of pain gurgled with blood gushing from his chest and mouth. He squirmed as the blade came down several more times before he fell still. Arcus's eyes went wide as he watched the brutality of the savage but was unprepared for the feeling of terror he felt when the man turned to look at whoever was still inside. The man's chest heaved hard with adrenaline; his grip tightened on the machete handle, a crazed look of madness upon his face. The chains rattled again; the woman's cries grew with desperation.

Arcus waited for the man to enter the tent while he built up the courage to follow him in. If he had his bow, he would have shot him down already but having to rely on the sword left him at a huge disadvantage. Tonight, he would need to use stealth over honor.

The woman screamed again, and Arcus burst through the flaps of the tent and sunk his sword deep into the man's back. The man spun around in an adrenaline filled rage with the blade still stuck in his back. He shouted at Arcus who froze in place momentarily before drawing Taja's dagger. Arcus's attacker was slowed from the blade lodged in his back, but repeatedly swung his machete at the nimble Arcus who easily dodged out of the way. Arcus lunged in close, dodging an attack and thrusting the dagger at the man's bare chest several times, slashing as he moved around him, thin lines of blood appearing to drip down his body.

The savage flinched in pain and swung his sword high, Arcus ducked out of the way, only to be met with the man's knee to his face. His vision blurred to the point he could barely focus on the now hazy figure in front of him, tears welling up in his eyes. The man began to spin with a cry of rage, his swing narrowly missing Arcus's face as he tumbled backwards, deeper inside the tent. His vision began to correct itself as the man lunged at him, machete held high into the air. Arcus kicked his leg, throwing him clear over the top of him, using the man's momentum to send him flying.

Arcus scrambled up to see the man crash face first into the hard dirt ground, reaching out to retrieve the blade still stuck in his back. He lifted it high into the air and kicked him, using his weight to hold him down. He hesitated before bringing his sword down into the back of his neck and held it tightly until the body lay still with the releasing of his last breath.

Arcus turned to see the disheveled naked young woman chained to a small metal cage, her thin face and body suggesting she was on the verge of starvation. The stains of blood and worn skin around her wrists and ankles telling her life story of living inside the cage for many years. He went to one of the shoddy dressers and pulled out several furs and a long shirt to hand to her.

"It's ok, you are safe now," he told her as he scanned the room for a key to release her shackles.

Atop a table was a ring of rusty keys, with most of them bent almost to the breaking point. There was a small pouch of coins spilling open on the table, with various items of garbage and food. Several half-eaten legs of animals and loaves of bread lay scattered across the table amongst enough mugs of rum to feed a small clan. He handed her the clothes, trying his best to keep his eyes away from the poor girl and free her restraints. He fumbled and dropped the keys, like a fool he patted around looking for the key and touched her leg. He froze and apologized to her. She was very confused and chuckled at his shyness. He found the keys and managed to unlock her, tossing the heavy chains onto the bed.

He noticed the girl's wrists were so heavily scared by the constant scraping of the heavy shackles that he thought he could see bone coming through the thin skin, memories she will be forced to endure for the rest of her life.

"Take this food and coin, go back down this path, the streets are usually clear and get out under the wall. Do your best to travel northwest to Sanctuary, I hear it's full of much better people than here," he said, adding another layer of fur to her back to help disguise her. The scorching heat was almost unbearable during the day, but she would have a much better chance if she could increase her small size and look like another raider wandering around.

She looked at him with a tear in her eye and a smile on her face that could send his heart into the clouds. "You are the only man to ever show me such kindness and I thank you with all my heart. I hope we meet again, and I can somehow repay your kindness," she said with a genuine smile and kissed his cheek.

Arcus's face instantly turned red with embarrassment. "I am Arcusbane, but you can just call me Arcus," he said to her, worried for her chances to make it to Sanctuary alone but unable to leave without Taja. "Please, you must hurry. If I ever make it there, I will look for you, ok? What is your name?" he asked with pride.

She thought for a few seconds looking confused at the question, "You can call me Lily," she said with a sudden smile. "Lily Freeheart."

Arcus watched her leave to make sure she passed into Muckton unhindered. She paused and looked back at him, briefly locking eyes with a sweet smile before slipping under the wall. With his spirit and confidence soaring he looked at the scene around him. This sort of thing was common, especially during celebrations so he needn't worry about covering anything up.

His eye caught a sword hung on one of the posts of the tent wall, its unique blade was long and curved instead of a standard straight blade. Hung beside it was another short sheath holding some sort of contraption he hadn't seen before. From what he could tell it was a small crossbow strange forward-facing arms, along with a satchel of bolts. He decided he was running out of time and the fallen men would have no more use for the weapons, so he strapped them to his belt. This being the first time he owned anything more than his bow and simple dagger, he felt quite accomplished.

Arcus made his way in the dim torchlight to the side of the main feasting canopy and went around the side where the compost was tossed. The smell alone usually kept all but the most desperate away, though he was used to the smells by now and unfortunately the taste.

The noise coming from the inside of the building was loud and boisterous, he couldn't decide if everyone was fighting, laughing, or dying. With the torches inside the room, he had learned that he could see the shadows of figures up close against the canvas walls along with various pieces of furniture. He crept quietly, though questioning the need for silence but still feeling more comfortable with his attempt to stay hidden.

He took Taja's dagger and sliced a small hole in the canvas to peer inside, alongside all the stitched-up patches from the harsh desert winds nobody would ever suspect it. He could see hundreds of men around tables slamming down jugs of rum and waving legs of meat into the air. He felt bad for the women who were serving the food, wearing nothing but the food that had been flung or spilled on them. The savages were harsh, pushing and pulling them where they wanted while laughing and throwing their food about.

Arcus realized he was relieved he was never allowed to come to one of these, the loud, belligerent activities disgusted him. Games and pieces of all shapes were scattered across the tables, some with boards and others with knives, challenges of reflex and skill. He watched as a drunk man's hand got stabbed straight through into the table, everyone laughing as he struggled to pull it free. Over in the corner he spotted cages of dogs with limbs of slain animals scattered around the cages for them to feast upon. From this side of the room, he was unable to see the entire area and would need to go to a different side to see around some of the taller pieces of furniture.

He circled around the back and found a loose piece of patching he was able to look under and could see a stage with several people playing instruments. From the looks of their thin frames and tattered clothes, they were slaves. He felt a surge of worry and anger go through him as he thought that even the dogs were being treated better with all the meat they could eat while these people went hungry. A lionel was part of the band, his face covered in scars with his fur matted and burned.

Arcus watched as large brutes took turns coming to the stage to act completely crazy, attempting to sing or make lude gestures to the crowd. One pulled a female lionel slave up onto the stage, forcing her to stand in front of the crowd as the man walked around her, poking and prodding at her. The lionel's ears pinned, a sign of disapproval that went ignored. He forcefully tore the rags from her body for everyone to mock.

"You are an animal and don't wear clothes," he shouted, causing a roar of laughter from the crowd. He collected her bent tail in his hand like a rope and tugged on her tall thin body as she let out a painful cry. He then kicked her legs out from under her, forcing her on all fours as he put his leg over her back to sit on.

"Now this is what animals are for. Am I right, boys?" he shouted, swirling his giant mug of rum in the air with a drunken grin.

The crowd erupted in laughter again as he continued to publicly torment the young tigress. Arcus struggled to see much against the side of the building he was on but was able to catch a glimpse of Radagar and Aldair sitting atop throne like chairs raised on a wooden platform. Iron bars lined the bottom of the platform, and he could see hands and tails moving from within the dark cage.

He was startled by cheers as he looked to see the man on stage kick the lionel hard into the ground below, too scared to even try and catch herself. The men pounded their jugs on the tables as the man left the stage and was replaced by a large, armored woman.

It was rare for a woman to be treated as anything other than a slave in Amid but the ones who weren't, commanded respect and everyone gave it. The woman on stage began to dance, pulling one of the staggering brutes up with her as the crowd cheered in protest that it wasn't themselves.

Arcus circled around the building to the back, its canvas wall pressed close to another building, making it hard to slip through. He found a grouping of holes, likely caused by stray arrows, and looked inside. Under the platform was completely barred off to create a big cage and he could see several women stuffed inside the small area along with several lionels.

He moved to the side and saw a young lionel against the back of the cage leaning on the bars, her patterns and facial markings unmistakable as Taja's. She looked miserable sitting under the platform in the dark with chains wrapped around her arms. Arcus's chest tightened as he thought of what to do next, she was at least in the corner and away from direct sight of the crowd. "Maybe she could ark the bars loose or something?" he thought, not really understanding how the gift worked but was still hopeful.

He circled around to the corner of the tent and started a slit from the bottom of the canvas up a few feet, just enough to slip through. Arcus gently tapped on the bars to get her attention while holding his finger up to his lips to signal her to stay quiet.

Taja, along with three other human girls all shuttered, startled to see him behind the cage. Taja's eye lit up in surprise, her other swollen shut and puffy with blood caked in her fur all the way down her shoulder. She had several lacerations along her arms, shoulder and face. Her armor had also been removed and replaced with filthy, loose-fitting rags which were more than most of the other girls got to wear. The other girls pressed themselves at the far end of the cage in fear of what this guy may do to them, not wanting to go out on stage to be humiliated or worse in front of the crowd.

"What are you doing here?" Taja hissed.

"I have come to take you out of here, we need to go now," Arcus whispered as best he could with all the noise.

"No, you got what you wanted, hunter, I am not your concern anymore," she spat back angrily, feeling betrayed by him.

Arcus was so glad to see she was alive that he ignored her temper. "Oh, come on, I know I can get a much better price for you elsewhere," he said with a smile, drawing her into a slight chuckle.

"Next time I will be the one selling you, see how you like it," she replied, moving closer to the bars. "Well? Are we escaping hunter or what?" she whispered, straining her neck to watch for any interruptions from the drunk savages.

Arcus looked around at the construction of the cage. By the looks of it, its builder had intended to hold in much more powerful and aggressive animals. "I was hoping you could just zap the bars out or something, you know ark the bars into powder?" he said with a blank stare as if the answer should be so obvious. "I know you don't like to use your gift but right now would be a good time for an exception," he added with growing worry in his voice.

Taja scowled at him. "Is that how you think it works, hunter?"

Arcus looked around the bars again, searching for any sign of a weakness he could possibly break or manipulate without the men sitting up top noticing. He ran his fingers against the bars and the boards by which they were attached and found simple wedges of boards that held the bars separate from each other. They were heavily nailed together with long spikes of steal except for one which had been bent and broken off before sealing the wedge down.

He drew Taja's simple knife and pried at the spacer board, trying desperately to lift it out but failed. Arcus handed the dagger to Taja and drew his new sword to stab deeper into the spacing to get better leverage to lift out the block.

ARKANGEL

Arcus had a strained look on his face both from worry of being caught and struggle of getting his plan to work. "A little help here?" he said strenuously between pulls.

As he pried down and lifted, Taja was able to get the thin blade of her dagger down enough to get under the wedged piece of wood. With a snap the wood shattered and came free as a smile returned to their faces. The other women became antsy, shuffling around, deciding if it was worth the punishment if they were to get caught.

Arcus motioned for them to get back as Taja hissed, her tail whipping around like a warning slap to get back and not cause a commotion. Arcus put his shoulder to the loose bar and slide it sideways until it was able to be lifted out, allowing a wide enough gap for the slender women to slide through. In excitement he reached for her and grabbed her hand to help her through, but she refused to move.

"We must wait and release all of them," she said stubbornly.

Arcus scowled at the women but nodded his head, afraid they will slow them down but fearful of what their punishments would be if they stayed and were silent while they escaped. He motioned for the others to follow but was blocked again by Taja who pointed at the girl being humiliated on stage.

"We need her too," she said firmly, watching in disgust as the lionel on stage was groped. She was forced down to her knees next to one of the brutes sitting in a chair, a chain wrapped around her neck to hold her down.

"How are we supposed to get her out Taja?" Arcus asked in frustration. "We can come back for her later."

Taja shook her head. "No, they swap us out when they are bored of us, we must all be in here when she is tossed back in and then we can leave," she hissed.

Arcus slammed his sword back into its scabbard, frustrated but was suddenly alarmed as a drunken man stumbled and collapsed into the front of the cage. The commotion drew the attention to the man with the other lionel who yanked at her chain to get up. "Get away from there," he shouted to the man passed out with his head now wedged between the bars.

The brute drug the lionel over near the cage, kicking the man on the floor until he came to. The drunk tried to stand but fell face first into the sand and rolled to the side of the cage, out of the way of the gate, mere inches from Arcus.

Arcus's heart raced as the cage was opened. With a hearty chuckle the brute threw his pet inside, staggering back and forth where he stood. Taja caught the slave and pressed against the back of the cage bars as the man's hand rummaged around to pull out his next victim for entertainment. Taja grabbed the wrist of another girl and moved her into the back so she wouldn't be taken and moved forward to take her place. The man's hand firmly gripped onto her as she was drug out, she turned and locked eyes with Arcus and motioned with a nod as she whispered, "Go."

Arcus's chest heaved with dread to see her violently yanked out. They were so close to escaping, why did she sacrifice herself for these other girls who would just end up going back to their masters for food in a few days' time if they couldn't make it themselves.

"Damn her, why was she so stubborn," he breathed, slamming his fist down into the dirt as he pulled the girls free one by one, sending them through the flap in the tent.

Taja was put up on stage as the crowd cheered and shouted for her to dance. "Do a sexy dance for us, give the men a good show of it," the man chuckled as he pushed her, prompting her to dance, but she refused with a prideful hiss. The drunk let out a chuckle to the crowd as he balled his fist and slammed it hard into her thin stomach, folding her almost completely in half as she gasped for air. The men laughed and clapped as they cheered louder for her to dance.

Arcus clenched his own fists and grit his teeth, completely powerless to do anything but sit and watch what they were going to do to teach her a lesson in obedience. The man grabbed the chain collar around her neck and pulled her bloody face close to his. "Do a sexy dance or I'll gut you where you stand," he shouted threateningly, his face turning red with anger.

A calm voice was heard talking over the crowd and settling them down almost instantly. "That one is mine, let me have a try," the voice said as the floor above him creaked. Aldair jumped down into view only a few feet away from Arcus who was still hiding behind the cage.

Aldair walked slowly and gently caressed Taja's shoulder as he walked behind her to the other side. His face moved in as he took a long sniff of her neck and circled back around her. His hands came around to her chest, caressing her as she trembled in fear and humility.

Taja's eyes betrayed her defeat as they lowered down at the floor, her tall ears and tail going limp from the embarrassment.

Aldair's hands began to slip under her shirt and caress her while kissing her neck, causing the crowd to explode into cheers and whistling. They began to chant and slam their jugs of rum repeatedly on their tables or chair arms shouting, "Tame the beast, tame the beast, tame the beast."

Arcus's blood boiled in anger and hatred for Aldair and these people beyond all disgust. For that moment he didn't care what happened to him, only that he must stop what was being done to her. Without thinking he pulled out the small crossbow contraption he had stolen from the tent earlier and fondled with its spring-loaded levers, attempting to make it work. Instead of having a bolt sit on top there seemed to be a stack of them inside that pushed up into a chamber as it fired. He pulled on some sort of release and took aim right at Aldair's head. He was an excellent shot with a bow but had never used a crossbow or any other weapon like it before. He took a deep breath and held it, steadying his aim, pulled the trigger and nothing.

He frantically pulled at the different pieces of the contraption trying to figure out how to make it work until he found a small lever on the side that spun around. A lever unfolded to the side with a snap as another gear aligned up against the spinning gear and he began cranking the lever around. As he continued to crank it let out a small hiss as a bolt clicked into firing position.

He aimed again, making sure not to hit Taja and pulled the trigger. Suddenly the main gear started to spin wildly releasing bolt after bolt hurling through the air. Startled by the weapons operation he failed to hold it steady and sent a shower of bolts into the crowd. Shouts and moans cried out as the party turned into a stampede of panic. Several seconds later it stopped firing with a loud clicking noise and Arcus stood in shock at what had just happened.

He quickly put it back into its pouch at his side and ran into the fray of terror to retrieve Taja. The men fled the stage, pushing over tables and slaves, leaving food and drink to litter the floors. Arcus grabbed the frightened Taja's arm and pulled her back towards the cage. She tried to follow but was stopped dead in her tracks, unable to move with him.

Aldair stood in place behind her, two of the crossbow bolts sunken into his steel pauldron with a terrifying scowl across his face. Several of his men caught a glimpse of Arcus attempting to flee with the tigress. Aldair walked closer, yanking hard at her chain again, forcing her towards him.

"What's the matter, greenhorn? Did I take your plaything?" he asked sarcastically, his hand reaching up to Taja's bare shoulder.

Taja's eyes closed tightly, looking down at the stage floor, she felt like things were escalating out of control and didn't want anyone to get hurt. She struggled with what to do next, feeling Aldair's vile fingers on her body again, sifting through her fur.

Arcus stood firm, meeting Aldair's taunting gaze. "She was not yours to take or mine to give, she is her own person."

Aldair's hand traveled up her neck and onto her mouth, gripping her snout firmly he shook her face. "I'm not free, my life now belongs to Aldair and wouldn't know what to do with my meaningless life without him, I live to give him pleasure," he said mockingly, in a poor attempt to copy her voice. All of his men erupted in a hearty laughter, completely enthralled in the show, scooping up the scattered jugs of rum to drink.

Aldair smiled at Arcus and turned to Taja with a sly smirk on his face. "Come now, your master is lonely and wants to play with you in his room," he said, throwing her face to the side and yanking her chain again to follow. He turned from Arcus, showing he didn't even consider him a threat, then paused to the sound of ringing steel.

Arcus drew his sword and swung it hastily at Aldair, narrowly missing his shoulder as he dodged to the side. "Funny, who would have thought you had the balls to attack someone such as myself?" he said arrogantly.

Aldair threw Taja to the side and into one of his men's filthy groping hands. Aldair slowly drew out two short swords at his sides as if keeping everyone in suspense. Arcus swung again, Aldair easily parrying while pulling his blades free.

Taja's adrenaline started pumping as she noticed just how skilled her captor was with a sword and realized her friend didn't stand a chance.

Aldair slowly spun and slashed with his blades as if he were reciting a dance followed up with an elegant stabbing motion, mocking Arcus of his unskilled swordplay.

Arcus tried to parry the moves, confused by what Aldair was doing and unfamiliar with his new sword. He brushed Aldair's blades to the side and landed a hard kick into his stomach as the men all readied to join in on the brawl, flipping tables and slamming their fists into their open palms.

Aldair recovered quickly, taking several steps back and speeding up his attacks. Arcus held up his sword to deflect his swings, but his arm quickly grew fatigued as Aldair's sword repeatedly clanged against his blade.

Aldair's conceded smile returned, seeing Arcus tire, "Now isn't this fun greenhorn, fighting for your pet, you're almost acting like a real man," he mocked, watching Arcus's growing panic.

Arcus shouted in frustration and swung his sword hard and fast at Aldair with everything he had, only to have Aldair move out of the way and swing at the back of his sword, using its momentum to send Arcus crashing to the ground. Arcus was a decent fighter, never trained but had learned to survive and fend for himself. He was quickly disheartened by Aldair's superior show of skill, fearing the worst for Taja.

Arcus rose to his feet, blade firm in his tired hand. He swung just in time to hit hard against the twin short swords, ripping the blade free from his grip. Aldair followed up with a kick to his leg, sending him back to the ground. Arcus cried out, Aldair's sword tip stopping inches from his face.

"I want you to think tonight of your failure as you lay in chains. I want you to think about what I'll be doing to your animal here," Aldair said with a wicked smile, eying Taja's body up and down. "I might even leave a little life in her for you to enjoy."

Three of Aldair's men came from behind Arcus to restrain him when a green burst of light flickered brightly in the room, making it difficult to see. Taja's eyes lit up as she raised her arms slightly, still hindered by the chains, while thorny vines slithered up through the sand to tangle the men together. She panted heavily from the strain against the chains, trying to lift and subdue the men in the air.

Aldair jerked on the chain with a look of shock and terror flowing over his smug face. Taja cried from the pain as Arcus rolled across the stage to retrieve his sword. He swung it hard, hitting Aldair against his thick armored pauldron and followed up with a strike to his back. Aldair cried out, trying to reach back and remove the blade, struggling to move his wounded arm. Arcus swung again, his rage boiling deep within as he hit Aldair repeatedly with his sword, Aldair struggling to bring a single blade up to deflect.

Aldair's sword slipped from his grasp from Arcus's constant attacks, his chest heaving heavily, continuing his assault. Suddenly his focus of rage shattered with a familiar yelping sound, his best friend was in serious pain. His eyes glossed over grey, and he saw flashes of men with ropes and chains pulling at him, a feeling of terror washing over him. He snapped out of it to see the canvas open, and several men drag Saber into view.

ARKANGEL

Chains, ropes, and a net, forced his companion down helpless as he yelped, his teeth showing through his muzzled snout. Saber was vicious and in most circumstances was equal to a small army in ferocity but against a team of skilled beast hunters was little more than an inconvenience to subdue.

Taja struggled to turn, hoping to be able to help the wolf from harm only to feel a massive fist batter her already beaten face over and over until she slipped into unconsciousness.

Arcus's heart shattered, the battle quickly shifting from his favor and shouted almost in tears for his friend to be left alone. The last thing he saw was Aldair's bloody smile before he was restrained, and his vision went black.

Arcus awoke in a dark, rusty cell and could sense he wasn't alone. He felt around in the room to find several bodies piled behind him, most of them cold while the others still dripped with warm blood. Minutes turned to hours, struggling to recount what had happened and how he had gotten where he was. He could feel the ground shake while it moved, light beginning to peak its way into the giant room from above.

The shaking came to a sudden halt as reddish orange dust began to blow in at his face. He raised his hand to block out the blinding sun, noticing Taja's body laying still on the blood-stained floor. He tried to reach over and shake her in an attempt to wake her when he became aware of his ear-splitting headache, reaching back to find his long hair caked in blood.

Taja woke up to the same discomfort and pain, crying out briefly in shock and fear, confused of how she got into the cage. She turned to see the bodies and panicked with a yelp until she met Arcus's fearful gaze.

Arcus leaned over in an attempt to calm her, but she quickly crawled over and behind him in fear. He then noticed beyond the bodies was Saber, muzzled and heavily restrained to the steel floor, his tail trying to wag at the site of his master's awakening. Arcus saw the thick patches of blood, soaking his fur and feared for the worst.

Arcus went to his companion and began checking him over while removing his restraints, motioning for Taja to come help him. They were interrupted by a booming echo of shouts so deep it shook the walls of their cage. Thousands of voices all started to call out with cheering and clapping, violently rattling the cage until the door broke free and fell flat on the dusty ground.

Arcus and Taja looked out of the cage to see an enormous wall completely encircling them, covered in large spikes and blood with the grounds littered with bones. Thousands of people sat atop the walls in seats, causing the commotion and filling the air with a roaring plea for entertainment. They saw a brilliant crystal floating high in the air at the center of the wide-open structure, the sun gleaming bright from its reflection. Then a booming voice brought the crowd to a silence as King Radagar shouted, "Welcome to the arena and let the carnage begin!"

CHAPTER 10

"BETRAYAL"

Martis took a deep breath as he forcibly willed his hands to loosen their tight grips in his palms. He had spent the last several hours fuming, his mind racing and calculating to formulate a reasonable explanation for what he had seen. The last time he had seen his brother was two thousand one hundred and twenty-five days ago and he had been told he died on the table, his body disposed of properly, fed to the other prisoners, which was more than he deserved. Martis even checked and inspected what he was told were the remains and followed through with witnesses.

A vortex of fury built inside him, and he struggled to keep himself in check. He remembered to breathe, slow and calculated breaths.

Martis approached the entrance to Solstice Gardens and felt slightly relieved to be home, he could finally get back to his work. Doing the creator's work was all he needed to stay sane, and he knew he would one day be rewarded for it and that day was coming very soon. His work put his mind at ease to relax.

He went into the chapel and walked the long isle in between the benches counting them as he passed. He entered his room, which he rarely stayed in, to inspect his ledger. Upon entering he immediately noticed his desk wasn't in order and not the exact way he had left it. His nerves were sent into alarm; another stress he did not need at this moment. Chances were, it was one of the new students or choir volunteers thinking this was the bathroom again. He was about to dismiss the organization disaster when he noticed the footprint on his desk.

After inspecting the trail of light steps and orientation of the prints he judged his desk was used to exit through the window up top. He clenched his already sorely indented fists, his nails resuming into their positions of digging into the skin of his palms. His breath quickened as his chest pounded, he desperately needed to work, to relieve stress, then he would seek out Feora for answers; he wouldn't stop until the trespasser was found, and he knew the best ways to get the truth out of people.

He hurried through the back of the chapel and down his ladder to his preferred office and came upon a locked door. He entered the room taking a deep breath of its sweet aroma that instantly stilled his nerves. He let out a big relieving sigh and went to his favorite chair to relax his tired muscles. The ambiance and chatter in the room added to its allure and brought his mood to a euphoric high as he started to hum. He prepared everything joyfully, starting to feel good about the long night of work ahead of him. He needed to put in extra hours to achieve the level of progress he desired due to recent events.

He eagerly pulled on a lever and swayed back and forth to the music in his mind. He hummed and whistled to the melody as he worked, pulling the lever as hard as he could to further entice himself into the hummed melody to the point that made him sweat with lust. He reached for his favorite tools, the tools only he knew how to properly use and which he alone had such impeccable skill in, which he should be for all his pain staking work he had done. He pulled at the lever again but was met with resistance, and he really disliked resistance.

He moved the heavy barrel, which he was proud of filling so quickly, and set down his tools. He took a step back to investigate the problem and was yanked out of his entrancing tune of screams and torture. He lifted the lever to raise the heavy block off the body and long narrow spikes pulled free from the skin, causing the blood to pour forth from the punctures instead of his delicate lacerations he so lovingly carved below.

The young, naked man screamed in terrified pain, pleading for him to stop at the sight of blood oozing forth from his exposed chest cavity.

Martis was careful not to waste and normally took great pride in his ability to inflict just enough pain for his offerings to sing their songs of sorrow for the creator for hours before passing out. He was so skilled he had mastered keeping his experiments alive long enough to see their final drop of lifeblood drip out.

The man strapped to the table begged and pleaded to be freed, promising services, gold, anything to be let go. Despite the offers he was usually presented with he was proud to admit that he was never tempted once because he knew his work would be rewarded soon enough. He double checked the man's restraints, making sure they were tight and inspected the free-flowing blood down the table in the specially carved grooves, where it trickled down into the barrel below.

What could possibly be causing him so much grief, he wondered? He looked into the man's eyes with a big bright smile. "Good news, we are almost done here. Just a few more minutes and I can send you off into the creator's arms," Martis said with a joyful smile, looking up as he tried to control his excitement to the point of trembling. "Though don't get too attached to him, he will be spending all his time with me soon."

Martis lovingly placed his hand gently against the top of the man's head and dragged his fingers through the man's hair. "No need to thank me, I know how grateful you truly are deep down, don't you worry about a thing," he said reassuringly.

Martis continued to look over the multitude of punctures from his heavy press and gasped. "Oh, I see the problem, how could I have missed that?" he chuckled, looking to the man with such delight he could barely stand it.

"You know, this is really the guards' fault," he giggled. "I will make sure to talk to them on your behalf, they must have broken some of your ribs dragging you in here. Oh, and what is this?" he asked as he reached his fingers deep into the gashes in his chest and pulled out a section of rib that had completely broken free. "These were in the way," he said

ARKANGEL

playfully as the man convulsed on the table, screaming in agony.

"See? There we are all set. Now shall we continue?" Martis asked politely as he lowered the block of spikes back down into the quivering body.

Martis continued to pull on the lever that forcefully pressed all the liquids from the man until it stopped flowing. He knew once the seductive songs of torment ceased his job was done. He reached over and placed a lid on the barrel and grasped the rope handles to move it along with the stack of others. He took a deep satisfied breath in accomplishment as he looked across the room, down the multitude of rows filled with barrels. He then turned to fetch another sacrifice from the cages in the other room but froze in disgust.

He looked down to his bright white sleeve and saw small droplets of blood near its cuff. Martis screamed, suddenly filled with rage, and grabbed a hammer off his table of tools and began to beat the dead man's body lying upon the table. He struck and shouted at him for ruining his robe until there was nothing solid left to strike at.

"For that I will make sure to bleed your wife next and I will not be as patient or generous as I was to you," he threatened as he stormed off to go back to his room.

After reaching the top of the ladder he could hear all the chatter of his followers gathering for their daily word from the creator. Martis's smile and zest quickly returned as he hurried to his room to change.

Feora caught up with him as they entered his room. "We have a problem," she said with a playful grin as she watched him untie his robe.

Martis looked at her confused of how she could know about Kaiden. "Yes, I am aware, so we need to accelerate our plans. We will do the conversion today," he said, turning to face her as his robes fell to the floor.

Feora pursed her lips as she eyed his perfectly sculpted figure, her finger unknowingly going to her lips in intrigue. Martis was tall and muscular with the body of a perfectly trained athlete, which was only secondary to his hypnotically charming, frosty blue eyes. She gasped for air, almost forgetting to breathe as she stepped closer to him, her hand softly gliding along his chest.

He straightened the golden amulet around his neck and pushed her away. "Not now, like I said, we need to prepare. It is happening tonight," he said firmly, the raw sexual energy he felt for her being subdued by urgency to his creator.

Feora let out a whine of disapproval and stepped away from him. "So, you found him?" she asked in frustration.

Martis slammed his elbow to her neck and pinned her hard against the wall. "How long have you known? Why didn't you tell me?" he demanded as he pressed harder and harder against her throat.

She struggled to breathe, clawing at his arm to release her. "Know about who? Rhyker?" she gasped.

Martis released her from the wall and looked at her in confusion. "Paladin Rhyker? What does he have to do with this?" he commanded.

Feora scowled at him, even more attracted to him now that he was enraged. "I found him lurking down below with your mother," she said panting. "But don't worry, I restrained him after toying with him for a while. He put up quite the fight you know," she added, reaching her arms around his back to pull him in closer. She had known Martis for several years and never had she seen him loose his temper this often. Her need for him grew almost out of her control. Something must have really made him angry, and she didn't know what it was, but she hoped it would continue.

Martis just stared at her, his mind calculating what Rhyker could know and what it could mean for their plans with the army arriving at any time. "Rhyker is locked up down below then?" he asked in confirmation as he formulated a new plan.

Feora leaned in and began kissing his neck and chest as she pulled his body close to hers. "Yes, who did you think I meant?" she asked between kisses as she tried to fulfill her need for him.

"I know who it is," Vixis said, walking into the room as her face lit up to see Martis disrobed. "Oh, I am sorry, am I disrupting something?" she asked playfully, hopping up to sit on his desk. "Keep going, you know I don't mind watching," she said with a mischievous smile spreading to her lips.

Martis turned to face her, remembering his robe was indeed off, grabbing one of the freshly washed robes off his rack. "Where have you been, Vixis? We have been in need of your assistance. I can't have you running off on fool's errands anymore." His tone became more irritated.

Vixis gave a pouty scowl as Martis tied the robe around his waist. "I found your... not so little brother," she said, regaining her smile as she recounted. "I can tell you he is traveling with a powerful little elven arker, too," she added.

The rage returned to Martis's eyes as he slammed his fist down into a box of scrolls, shattering the thick wood into splinters. "How can this be? He was dead!" he shouted as his veins protruded from his skin as it discolored into a dark red tone. "The last bit of his power was drained and put into this," he shouted at the top of his lungs as he stepped closer to Vixis to slam his finger down on her golden amulet. "I know, I was there," he recounted, throwing his arms down and spinning in a wild rage of thought.

Vixis grasped her amulet and twirled it between her fingers. She had never seen Martis so angry and knew he only wanted the best for humanity, which is why he gave the power to the Arkhunters, to finish Paladin Malik's honorable quest.

"Well, he isn't dead now and his abilities have grown far past these little trinkets you made us. I tried to fight him and kill his little elfling for you, but he knocked me out within seconds. He has some sort of armor that protects him, enhancing his speed and strength further than even ours. I've never seen anything like it." She recounted their battle as if there was something irresistible about him that really caught her attention, aside her need to kill him for being inflicted.

Martis shook in anger, physically trembling to the point he had to fight to control it. He had to be careful what he said and not let his anger allow a slip in his words in fear Vixis would learn the truth of his plan, because he still had need of her. He gave his anger over to the creator and was able to come to an unsettled peace.

"You did what you could, child," Martis said empathetically. "The creator has faith in you and your work, and I am sure he will provide us with what we need to rid this world of its inflictions. Foul creatures such as him do not belong in this world as you well know."

Martis knew he needed to be extra careful with the information he let out, not wanting to cause any more upsets to his plan. He needed to find a way to get her out of solstice immediately if he was to execute his plans properly and a lot quicker than he had anticipated.

"Vixis, I have another errand for you," he stated politely, struggling to keep the anger of his brother's return at bay.

Vixis unfolded her legs and hopped up from the desk, throwing her long ponytail over her shoulder, batting her eyelashes at him. "Anything for you, Martis," she said sweetly.

Martis couldn't deny his attraction to the breathtaking Vixis, but despite her attitude she was naive, and her misguided morals would certainly conflict with his own plans. He couldn't risk letting her get closer in fear of losing an Arkhunter despite the insatiable desire he had for the young beauty. "I need you to go to Sanctuary and find Kaiden and his companions. He is helping them fight against this dreadful plague, which he may very well be the cause of. Even though he may have the best of intensions we can't let a group of inflicted wander free," he said in a compassionate voice, staring intensely into her green eyes as if he could see into her soul. "But I need him alive. Just follow him and let me know where he is going," he said with a warm smile, ushering her out the door.

She turned back to catch his gaze one more time. "Can you do that for me?" he asked.

Vixis shuddered at his touch with a look of passion on her lips. "Sure thing, whatever you need of me. I wouldn't mind keeping an eye on him anyways," she said with a playful wink before turning to walk out of the chapel.

Feora leaned in close to Martis. "I don't like or trust that girl," she said, the upset in her face almost matching her red hair.

Martis dismissed her obvious jealousy and simply stated, "We many need her, so you need to play nice until he arrives. Then you can do what you wish with her."

A wide grin spread to Feora's face at the thought. "What shall I do with the Paladins?" she asked, already missing his fiery temper.

Martis got a satisfied look on his face, not wanting to play with the pieces he was given, only sprint for the finish line. "Just let them rot," he said carelessly, unable to calculate any useful gain for keeping them alive. He didn't really care for either of them in the first place, and he knew by now Lanthor was his grandfather. Though he was weak and didn't deserve his position of power, having no place in Martis's brave new world he was about to create.

Feora took a step to leave but stopped abruptly. "What about your mother? Shall I have her moved?" she asked.

Martis took a long second to think, already lost in thought, plotting what he would need to do to prepare for the day. He brushed his fingers through his thick black hair. "I suppose it would do her good to watch as her weak father rots in front of her eyes," he responded softly, deciding it to be the best end for her.

Martis paused. "On second thought, no goodbyes for her. I want her full attention finally on me when I rise to power, and my destiny fulfilled. Finally, she will see me in all my grandeur and power and know that I, Martis, was the better son and I am a power that shall be feared and bowed down to by all the other races, not her perfect little Kaiden," he stated in an ominous voice. "I want the last thing she sees before she dies is me ripping Kaiden's heart out in front of her and serving it to her like the dog she is," he added in a cheerful tone, turning to skip down the hallway, pleased with his new plan.

Martis walked up to the podium to address the crowd in his newfound happiness and smiled wide for all to see his excitement. Row after row of people all lined up to praise his generosity and listen to his hope inspired words. "Welcome, everyone. Now let me share what the creator has planned for you today," he said aloud with a grin.

Rhyker kicked as hard as he could, attempting to break free of the straps around his legs. He let out a roar of frustration, waking up Lanthor from his weary sleep.

"I fought too my first few days," the weak voice of Lanthor admitted. "But it was all for nothing," he said in a grim tone, barely able to project his voice. He struggled to move into a better position in his cage, his muscles deteriorated and weak. His skin stuck to the stone with dried blood, too firmly for his weary state to move his bodyweight. "They leave us here to break us, to take away our pride and honor," he said in his raspy voice, wheezing to draw in the pungent wet air.

Rhyker pulled hard again on his leg, struggling to make any progress. "They will not take anything from me, and I won't let them take any more from you," Rhyker stated firmly, his mind still hesitant whether he should end his show of struggle and reveal his true identity to Lanthor. He feared he would likely have no choice.

"Rhyker?" Lanthor moaned.

"Yes, Sire?" Rhyker responded, resting for a second so he could hear his friend.

Lanthor coughed, blood splattering forth from his throat. "I have always thought of you as a son," he said in pride. "Even though we were never bonded by family I have always hoped for it to be so, despite my daughter's foolishness." His head collapsed to the cold stone floor in tears. "I don't know what I did wrong or why she left us! What did I do?" Lanthor cried.

Rhyker was unexpectedly struck with emotion, a tear welling up and rolling down his face to the table. He remembered the pain he felt when Trinity had left right before their marriage, after he had finally found a strong woman that he cared for and that made him feel, almost human.

Her leaving left him feeling both guilt and anger, though he never stopped to think how Lanthor took her abrupt rejection to the marriage.

"Thank you, sire, I am honored by your words," Rhyker responded, trying to hold strong. "Hold on just a while longer, we will make it through this, I promise you." Rhyker, with a display of great effort, snapped his legs free and flipped his legs up and over his head, taking care not to shatter the steel armor strapped to his body.

Free from the table and his arms now moveable, he released the restraints on his wrists. He adjusted his armor and knelt beside Lanthor's cage. "I will come back for you, sir, I will be back with help shortly. There will be thousands of men arriving soon and we will seize the city," he said in high spirits, hoping he could get aid to Lanthor before it's too late.

Lanthor let out a wheezing cough and nodded before laying back down against the stone to regain his energy.

Rhyker ascended the stairs to the garden he had come through earlier and found the place free of guards. He peered through the gate and saw a massive crowd of people all waiting outside the largest building in the estate. He walked cautiously across the gardens, looking for signs of what was happening. As he got closer, he could see the people all gathered and expressing their excitement and praise, lifting their arms up to Martis.

Rhyker paused as a young lady walked towards the chapel. "What is happening?" he asked, puzzled, still looking over the growing amount of people.

The girl barely slowed to answer, overcome with excitement. "It's Martis, he going to save all of us and the soldiers from the plague." She picked up her pace to catch a glimpse of Martis.

Another man overheard his question and piped in. "He has the cure, the creator blessed him with it for all his glorious deeds," the man said as he helped his injured wife closer to experience the miracle.

A knot formed in Rhyker's stomach as his feeling of dread almost

ARKANGEL

overwhelmed him. He could feel the end approaching and he had done little to stop it. His guilt mixed with the fear of imminent danger made him pick up his pace, crossing to the center of the gardens and onto the main road through the estate.

He recognized Vixis jogging the opposite direction, out of Solstice. His adrenaline surged as he prepared to force an answer from one of Martis's Arkhunters.

"Vixis!" he shouted in a commanding voice, stopping her dead in her tracks.

She spun around to greet him and completely caught him off guard with a smile rather than an attack.

"Hello there, handsome. It's a pleasure seeing you way up here, Paladin Rhyker," she said, eying him up and down. She reached her hand out to place it on his heavily dented breastplate. "I'd hate to see the other guy," she flirted with a wink.

Rhyker grabbed her hand and pushed it away. "I demand answers, Vixis," he shouted at her as her little nose scrunched up in confusion. "Don't play with me, girl, what is Martis planning? Tell me about this cure of his," he commanded as his eyes seethed with anger.

Vixis took a step back, unprepared for his questions. "I don't know anything about a cure, I am just supposed to go find his brother," she said, finding nothing wrong with her current task that would warrant secrecy, something which she was never very good at anyways.

Rhyker was taken back as if he had just been punched in the gut. "Martis has a brother?" he asked, unaware he even had relatives.

Vixis's smile curled on her face. "Yes, and I would say he is a bit cuter too," she said with a slight giggle. "But unfortunately, he is inflicted, so…" She hesitated. "I am just supposed to go find him, though, that's all I know."

Rhyker's face contorted with even more confusion. "Vixis, humans can't be inflicted, our bodies are too weak to harness the power required to ark," he said, not picking up on what should now be obvious to him.

Vixis furrowed her brow. She was an Arkhunter, how could she not have realized this before when she saw him. "So does that mean he isn't human?" she asked, her nose still scrunched in thought. "He was protected by some sort of armor that made him change somehow." The thought filled her with feelings she had never felt before, had she somehow fallen for an inflicted? Impossible, for her sole purpose since she was trained as a child was to hunt down the cursed creatures, to protect the people. This she was taught. She felt very confused, questioning what she was supposed to be doing.

"So, does this mean Martis isn't human either? Can he ark?" she asked softly under her breath, not sure if she really wanted an answer. Why would Martis want her to hunt down all the other inflicted and bring them their bodies to purify if he was one himself?

Suddenly the giant doors to the chapel slammed open with an echoing bang as soldiers and people alike spilled out of the giant room. The soldiers struggled to walk, clinging their arms to their armored torsos, pleading for help.

Rhyker snapped out of his thoughts on Martis and his brother to watch in horror as thousands of his soldiers stumbled out of the great chapel. Rhyker and Vixis both stood transfixed over the sheer number of armored bodies all throwing themselves down on the ground, moaning and crying out in pain. Some of the soldiers quickly tried to remove their armor, attempting to ease the burden of their weakened bodies, unable to move as the throbbing shock of the plague overtook their bodies.

Rhyker grabbed for Vixis's arm and pulled her with him as they ran to the chapel doors. They managed a glimpse inside between the stumbling bodies to see Martis on stage, his eyes glowing a deep and vibrant red, his facial features greatly exaggerated and transformed to look like some sort of otherworldly horror.

Vixis gasped, holding her hand to her mouth, struggling to breathe with the tightening knot in her stomach.

"Sir, is that you?" one of the soldiers pleaded, recognizing Rhyker as his commander.

ARKANGEL

Rhyker reached for the boy's outstretched hand. "What has happened here?" Rhyker shouted over the growing sounds of agony among his troops.

A dreadful echoing laughter erupted from Martis as magenta and black tendrils of smoke arose from the floors around him and began to swirl into the air like a giant tornado, tearing the place apart. The whirling vortex spun violently, tearing the glass from the windows and decorations from the walls and hurling them around like projectiles. Martis continued to laugh aloud as he rose his arms up from the crowd, commanding them to follow him to their creator.

Several soldiers, barely able to crawl on the ground, reached up pleading for Commander Rhyker to help them. "Oh, the pain, please help me!" they cried out, rolling onto their backs in excruciating pain.

Rhyker stood steady, jaw open wide as he tried to process what was unfolding before him. Thousands of men all piled in the room clamoring over the top of one another for help.

Vixis pulled hard on Rhyker's arm. "We need to leave. Now!" she shouted, dragging him further from the door.

Rhyker didn't resist, letting Vixis pull him out. He stood in a daze as his heart was breaking for his soldier as he drowned in the tides of his own guilt that he was powerless to stop. He should have acted, should have seen what was going on and trusted his gut, which had been his sole purpose was to prevent the prophecy from starting.

The people outside ran around frantically in fear as chaos began to ensue with so many screaming for help as the smoke billowing out of the chapel doors encircled them.

"The plague has found us," a woman cried.

"We are all doomed," shouted another.

As Vixis and Rhyker ran away from the building the moans turned to wretched, stomach-churning shrieks and screams. They looked back to witness troops on the ground spilling with blood, their skin tearing off where exposed from within their armor. Men bent over wailing as long sharp quills pierced through the backs of their armor, pulling strands of skin and bone along with them. The heavily steel armored soldiers erupted like bursting sacks of blood, splattering high into the air. A small wave of blood rushed out of the chapel doors filled with torn flesh and bone.

Vixis and Rhyker both gagged in disgust and turned to flee in terror, knowing within seconds the place would be overrun with the Salamanders.

People ran in hysteria, trying to get out of the winding trails of gardens, screaming and shouting in an attempt to recover loved ones. The lizards tore through the masses of people attacking anyone and everything they came upon.

Rhyker led Vixis towards the gated Garden, hoping to get down below safe from the creatures momentarily while they collected their thoughts. "Come follow me, let's go below, I need to rescue Lanthor and Trinity before it's too late," he shouted behind him.

Vixis followed suit, not knowing where she was going but not wanting to be alone either. Her expression went wide eyed in shock as she gestured to the far north of the gardens. "Look over there," she shouted.

Rhyker looked to see the tall, orange, elven soldiers march through the entrance. He then quickly peered to another entrance to see it guarded with the heavily armed ember elves as well. "We just can't catch a break," Rhyker shouted as they dodged and weaved around the mass of screaming people.

Rhyker busted through the gate and waited for Vixis to follow before slamming it shut and locking it behind them.

"I have never been in here before," Vixis said, looking around at all the statues of Martis amongst the delicate flowers. "Martis said this was his private garden, a peaceful place to pray to the creator."

Rhyker ran over to the hatch, motioning for her to follow. "Oh Vixis, it is so much more than that," he said as he motioned her down below and closing the hatch tightly behind them.

Rhyker grabbed her arm and raced down the hallways he was unfortunately now well acquainted with until they got to the first set of cages. "I found this only days ago, I suspected Martis to be up to something since the last council meeting and had to come see for myself and accidently came across this place," he said, breathless as his heart raced in panic.

Vixis gasped when she saw the frail starving woman in the cage. "What has he done? Is she inflicted?" she asked in confusion. "Who is this?"

Rhyker didn't hesitate and tore the steel bars from their hinges. "This is Lanthor's missing daughter, Trinity," he responded, reaching down and gently picking up the skeleton of a woman.

"Oh, Glover, it's you. Are you here to take me away with you like you promised?" she rambled as tears of joy streamed down her thin face, wrapping her arms around Rhyker's neck.

Vixis peered around the entryway. "Who is Glover?" she asked, trying to keep her mind focused and not racing into panic. She was more than a match for a few of the salamanders but didn't want to see if her amulet would actually keep her from getting infected or not.

Trinity pulled her thin strands of hair over her ear to look her best for her Glover. "Where are you taking me, my love?" she asked, unaware of the outside massacre.

Rhyker thought it best to end their conversations until they were somewhere safe, not wanting any distractions. "Vixis, we need to get Lanthor before we can leave. "Follow me!" he shouted, leading her deeper into the underground maze.

Vixis followed close behind taking in the smells and peering into each room that they passed, taking note of the various cages and sickly torture devices. She had done her fair share of killing, but the thought of what Martis did down here to innocents sickened her. Faint flashes, remnants of old memories, hazily resurfaced in her mind as they ran.

This place seemed familiar for some reason, feeling a deep torment being introduced to her mind, terrifying her. As if their panic over the situation wasn't bad enough, being below gave her an earie sickening sensation in her stomach.

They rounded the corner and Rhyker entered a room, kneeling in front of one of the cages. "Lanthor, are you awake? Wake up, Sire," he pleaded as he rattled the side of the cage.

Lanthor let out a weak cough as Rhyker sighed in relief. "Sire, we are here to get you out, but we must hurry," he said as he effortlessly shattered the hinges of the cage to remove the door.

Lanthor looked at him dumbfounded. "How did you…?" He began to ask but was interrupted.

"Rhyker, we have company," Vixis shouted, glancing down the hallway.

Familiar wailing cries from the creatures echoed down the long tunnels as the stragglers descended in search of food.

"Grab him," Rhyker shouted to Vixis, realizing how glad he was to have run across her. "Brace yourself, Trinity, we will need to move fast."

When they reached the surface, the breath of fresh air easing the burden on their lungs just in time to smell the thick stench of blood. Looking through the vine riddled gates, Rhyker momentarily watched the massacre taking place. Armored Salamanders traveling in packs, hunting down the last remaining humans and violently tearing them apart, only to leave their chest cavity behind for another to spawn from within. Shredded flesh and puddles of blood now lay across the once serene gardens, the fresh planted soil now a dark red sponge.

Vixis smashed her fist through the back door of the house and tore it free from its hinges.

"What are you thinking?" Rhyker shouted as he looked to see her mischievous grin.

"I'm not dying out here. This way, we will have cover all the way up to the wall of hedges," she said, pushing through furniture and doors.

"Yeah, but what will be waiting for us on the other side?" Rhyker questioned, fearing he knew the answer already.

Vixis approached a closed door and kicked it open so hard it shattered to splinters, sounding like rain as they fell across the ground. "I'll tell you when it's safe, Paladin, if you're that worried about it," she chuckled, securing Lanthor to her shoulder with her other arm as she sprang off the ground and over a large table, punching the door to the edge of the estate.

Rhyker caught up with Trinity, inquiring why the road was so bumpy today. "Moment of truth," he said aloud as he pushed through the thick wall of hedges, covering Trinity's back and neck as best he could from the lashings of branches.

Vixis followed him through and quickly scanned her sides and the ground for tracks. "That way," She pointed towards the forest. "The horses must have made it out before being added to the menu," she said with a brief chuckle, scanning her surroundings for traces of ember elves or lizards.

Rhyker glanced up north and noticed all the tents his men were to stay in during their stay to protect the gardens. His heart hurting for their suffering and how many children would be left parentless as the result of Martis's greed.

They arrived at the edge of the forest with Rhyker following closely behind Vixis, who was tracking a stray horse. The sound of voices could be heard, shouting from inside the hedge wall, pleading for help from the outside. Rhyker only shook his head to dismiss them, for there was nothing he could do but get to Sanctuary and warn them of what had happened and prepare for the worst.

They came to a clearing with several horses wandering in a small field once used for farming. When they approached the horses acted unsettled, able to sense the great danger around them. They sat Lanthor and Trinity on the backs of one still equipped with a blanket and saddle, strapping them in to keep them on.

Vixis let out a sigh. "So, what now, darlin?" she asked, glancing nervously to the edges of the field.

Rhyker stopped to think. The urge to keep going until they were safe weighed heavily on his shoulders. "Where is Martis's brother? Do you think he has any part in this?" he asked while tightening down the saddles and reading the reigns.

Vixis shook her head. "No not at all, there is something different about him, more noble like. Martis hates his brother and until recently thought he was dead," she said, thinking about how guilty she felt for attacking him and his companion. "Should I track him down and let him know what is happening, so he doesn't get swept into Martis's schemes?" she asked, wanting to see him again.

Rhyker looked over the two on the horse and back towards the Gardens. "Help me get these two down to Sanctuary where they will be safe then I will do what I can to help you Vixis." He turned their horses around to get out to the road quickly.

Vixis nodded her head, mounting up onto one of the saddleless horses. "Agreed," she said, eager to find Kaiden. She had unresolved apologies and feelings she needed to get settled. She dug her heels into the side of her horse, and they were off, south towards Sanctuary.

Martis stood at his podium, shaking in excitement as he saw all his hard work coming to fruition. He watched as his lands became saturated in blood and knew the time would be short before he could unleash his grand finale. Once and for all, he would bend the living to his will, and all would bow down before his greatness. His self-pride was short lived as he noticed Feirun entering the chapel with some of his finest, ashen covered elves.

"Your vision has come to pass, now we must strike at them," the elf said impatiently, slamming his fist into his other palm.

"Patience," Martis commanded in a deep ominous voice with an unnatural tone as his eyes glowed a fiery red, his veins glowing to match under his skin. He came down from his swell of power and jerked his head awkwardly to the side and gazed around briefly like he had just now awoken. His eyes faded to their normal icy blue and his skin returned to its normal hue.

"I have one more task for you before we march," he said, returning to his podium.

Feirun growled in anger and drew out his large, curved sword. "I am done with your games, human. We attack now before they are prepared for us," he shouted, approaching Martis.

Martis's head flicked back, his demonic glare returning to his face. "You will do as I ask or I will wipe you from existence like the stain you are, Feirun," his monstrous voice boomed throughout the destroyed chapel. "Do as I command, and you will be rewarded a place in our new reality. My new reality." He beat his chest with his fist, ready to strike down the mighty king in a heartbeat.

Feirun looked back to his men with a glare and back to Martis, before settling his gaze on the floor. "What shall I do?" he asked with hesitation.

An evil smile spread unnaturally wide across Martis's deforming face as long sharp fangs began to expose themselves through his lips. "You will bring me my brother... alive."

CHAPTER 11

"THE SPARK IGNITES"

The journey to find Lu-Sea in Shiver Spire Coast had just begun and the companion's morale was high despite the attack in Sanctuary and the danger of the journey they were undertaking. Nirayus had become closer to Kaiden and was warming up to him quickly as more than just her protector. Gorman was happy to have his mother with him and he felt at peace for the first time in many years as they recounted old stories, and he filled her in on the last ten years he had been missing. Tomba was delighted to have her boy whom she had waited for, unwavering for so long and all things considered was excited to see her husband again. Finn was excited for adventure and to have the chance to travel again with his newfound band of companions feeling a part of something big and important, he hadn't journeyed north in many years.

 For Kaiden everything was new, he was pleased with the connection he was forming with Nirayus despite the weight of responsibility beginning to increase in volumes on his shoulders. He had been given a power he had no idea where it came from or if he even wanted it, but it had a way of continuously moving him forward towards the unknown. He tried to focus on the future rather than searching for his past as he was finally becoming comfortable in his new life.

 Finn leaned across the entire center bench of the wagon, his legs dangling off the edge the way he liked. His long fingers pointing and pinching up at the clouds above, amused with little noises escaping his thin lips as he worked his hands around for entertainment.

Nirayus huddled next to Kaiden, her knees up against her chest as she rested her chin atop them staying fully aware of the times her shoulder would bump against his on the untraveled road. "What are you doing Finn?" she asked curiously.

Finn continued, his fingers moving as he answered. "I was thinking of a world where you could gather your favorite animals all together and watch them live their lives like the clouds in my mind I pinch and pull at their ends, it looks like a school of fish back home when they all swam around in circles, going about their daily lives. See like that one and that one," he said, making a dripping sound as he pointed to another. "See, I am creating an entire sky full of my best fish friends, now if I could only gather them all up in something like a see-through bowl then I could watch them all day, it would be like home wherever I go," Finn said with a smile.

Nirayus just stared blank faced, processing what he was trying to say without laughing but she did know what it felt like to miss home.

Kaiden looked up with a laugh, wondering to himself where the clouds were going. "Finn?" Kaiden asked to get his attention. "Where do all the clouds go? What lies out past the water?" he asked.

Finn smiled at the chance to tell another story but was abruptly interrupted. "There be nothin kid," Gorman answered from the front of the wagon.

Tomba hit him in the side with her elbow, "Yous not be knowin that," she said with a laugh.

Gorman let out a grunt. "Da boats just stop, there just be nothing," he stated again.

Finn lifted his head up from looking at the clouds. "You know what, big guy? Interestingly enough you are right," he said, trailing off and gathering his thoughts. "And on the other hand, you are wrong, stories say before the races were made the creator created the ocean to keep all his creations in one place kind of like a giant bowl," Finn said with a smile, leaning back to watch the clouds again.

Gorman looked to his right as the elevation of the road began to rise up into the base of the mountains. The road breaking down into nothing more than faint wagon impressions in the tough dirt the further north they got, it was far too dangerous to maintain a proper road with very few travelers risking the journey.

"Dat be da Wither," Gorman warned, a hint of fear in his voice as he pointed to the far right.

Kaiden, lost in his own thoughts of the oceans, looked to find the Wither. Nirayus laughed at him and put her hand on his head to turn it to the right direction. "Over there," she said, pointing with a giggle. "Father has told me stories of the battles that have taken place there. The land has been tarnished century after century with blood shed between the Aqua and Ember elves followed by the humans. That is where Lu-Sea struck down her great wrath to end the war." She recounted, watching the look on Kaiden's intrigued face, rather than the devastated lands.

Her tone grew darker as she continued. "The immense power she unleased upon the land destroyed all life and is now unable to produce any new life," she commentated ominously. "Father said the things that are born there are of living death too," she explained as everyone else stared silently at the black, barren land.

Layers of dark rings encircled a permanent burn in the soil with skeleton like trees lifting from the reddish ground, their trunks looking like they were pieced together with the bones of the fallen. Their skinny branches raising up high into the air as if reaching up for help.

The landscape turned into a beautiful grassland kissed by light blankets of snow that traveled up the side of the mountain. Large, sharp chunks of rock jut out from the one side of the mountain as it raised higher into the sky like they had been peppered down from the creator.

Finn blinked rapidly, preparing to tell a new tale of intrigue as they headed into the less known areas of their land. "They call that shattered peak," he said, pointing to the mountainside of sharp scattered rocks. "It is the home of the Shalings and as it be, nobody knows where they come from or much about them as they have perfect camouflage blending within the rocks they are touching and could be anywhere or everywhere, they do not speak so not much it really known about them but every morning if you look closely the rocks will all be in different locations and different shapes and sizes, not so great for making shelters against I suppose," Finn explained, being clever as he pointed to the different formations of sharp rocks sunken deep within the mountain side. Long icicles and solid streams of ice cascaded down from the mountain peaks in front of them.

"Aren't you cold?" Kaiden asked Nirayus, who had spent almost the entire trip curled up next to him.

She couldn't get cold; moon elves had a harder time with heat, but she wondered what he would do if she had said yes. She decided she liked where they were in fear of him leaving to try and find a blanket. "No, I am fine, are you? The few humans I have seen are almost always in thick clothing or furs of some kind," she asked, holding up her hand as it went up into a swirling glow of flame, dancing upon her open palm.

Kaiden smiled at the gesture thinking the patterns of fire were beautiful as they whipped higher and higher off her hand. "Thank you but oddly enough I have noticed that I can't really feel the difference in temperature. I first noticed when we stopped at that lake but thought that maybe it was just warmer than normal." He looked around at the growing amount of snow and ice on the grounds. "Now as the ice thickens around us, I still can't feel a change, is that strange?" he asked as she extinguished the flame on her hand.

Their attention was drawn to Finn as he slowly sat up, his body making small popping sounds as he moved. "Now I remember why I rarely travel north, the water retained in my scales thickens and freezes, making it hard to move along and with a general feeling of discomfort," he said as only one of his mandibles was able to move, slightly.

Gorman gleamed with a big smile spread across his face, "Serves da fish right, maybe your mouth be freezin soon too" he chuckled.

Tomba turned to Finn with a motherly look of worry in her eyes. "Oh, dear boy, here be a blanket for ya," she said as she reached in one of her bags and pulled out a thick, hand stitched blanket she had made back home.

Finn's mandibles tried to dance in excitement as he wrapped himself up in the blanket tightly. He looked up to Tomba, the corner of the blanket flapped partially over his face. "Thank you, Ma'am, for the blanket, I hope you don't mind it getting a little wet," he said with a hint of play in his voice.

Tomba waved her hand in dismissal. "No, baby, it be ok, an yous call me Mama for bein such a good friend to me Gorman baby," she said, looking to see Gorman wince.

Finn took his golden opportunity to place his hand on the back of Gorman's shoulder with a squeeze. "Thanks, brother," he mocked.

Gorman was startled as his eyes went wide and he unintentionally snapped at the reigns, lurching the carriage forward as everyone shifted in the cart.

Tomba's face, full of joy, as she settled back down, looking forward for the beautiful journey up the mountain. "We stoppin for da night, boys?" she asked, leaning back with a big stretch.

Gorman looked back, intentionally ignoring Finn's eyes looking at him from under the blanket. "We stoppin?" he grunted back to Kaiden who was transfixed up ahead in the sky by the vibrant orange and red sky.

Nirayus perked up, her head lifting off Kaiden's shoulder where she had drifted asleep. She had felt a sharp pain in her stomach and knew it was time to feed before she became too weak. "Let me scout ahead quickly, I will find us a good place to stop," she said as she grabbed at her aching stomach, trying to stand.

Without a sound she leaped from the cart and was off into a full sprint over the side of the mountain, her vibrant blue hair and white skin almost glowing in the failing light.

ARKANGEL

Finn's awkward gaze from within the loose blanket-stitching landed on Kaiden who glanced his way and then looked to catch a glimpse of Nirayus run out of sight. He blinked several times in envy of her speed and stealth and realized his lips were curling into a smile, until he noticed Finn again.

"Are you going to mate with the elven beauty?" Finn asked, a playful sparkle gleaming in his big bulbous eyes.

Kaiden froze in place. "What kind of question is that Finn?" he asked with an embarrassed scowl.

Finn's smile revealed his delight in the latest gossip. "She clearly takes interest in you and has already entered the age to mate, although it would be interesting to see what concoction your seed would make being half moon elf and half human," he said with a smile.

Kaiden's eyes went wide from embarrassment. "Finn, there is more to it than that," he blurted out quickly, his mind racing for some sort of answer to get him to stop. "We have our task Finn, I am not going to think about that or myself while Sanctuary is under threat, Ok?" he followed up, finding his mind drifting right back to how excited he was indeed getting closer to her.

Finn let out a playful giggle and turned his monstrously long body away from him in thought, his long fingers grasping tightly around the soaked through blanket.

Nirayus sprinted around the side of the mountain, her eyes glowing a bright golden color as she scanned the grounds for movement. She saw the head of a deer lift up alert to the feeling of not being alone. The creature didn't even see her coming as she leaped onto its back with a jolt of electricity down its neck, knocking it out. She raised its head and held it in her lap as she sat in the frosty grass. Her hand running up and down its long thick neck to comfort it. She knew it was knocked out, but she still felt the need to thank it before grasping its head in both hands and sending Arks of lightening through its head until it passed.

"At least it was painless," she whispered to the deer. She ran her fingers down its neck looking for its main artery before sinking in her two long fangs hidden amongst her teeth. Her body felt a wave of warmth as she drained its blood, rejuvenating her own with its nutrients. She stood up feeling revitalized and content, the essence of the creature now flowing through her veins.

She pulled her knife and ran it along the creature's belly and legs, pulling the hide free. With most of its organs charred from her blasts of electricity and its blood almost all gone the creature was almost ready to be cooked. She rolled up the hide and grabbed a long stick to fasten its legs to with the thin rope she kept in her hunting pouch. She then lifted the heavy beast up on her shoulder, her body now pounding with energy and adrenaline as she took off towards a nice flat area she had spotted, not far from where she was.

She arrived long before her companions caught up to her and set up a spit next to a grouping of rocks, placing the ends of the stick firmly into place off the ground. She gathered some tree limbs and fallen sticks and arked them into a strong, steady flame below their next meal.

Nirayus's long pointy ears picked up the sound of the wagon wheels far down the path and decided to scout the area before running down to guide them in. She found a small pond only footsteps away from the grassy field she had set up her roast. Rocks formed into large groups along the mountain side created a safe, defendable area around most of the perimeter of their camp. A hint of glow caught her eye as she ran towards the fire. She sprinted up the hill to find a small cave through the wall of rocks, she peaked inside to be met with a warm wave of sweet-smelling air. There was a small pool with bright colored flora as if she had stumbled into a wild garden, lit by the bright moon in the sky. She knelt and brushed her hand lightly in the warm water as a big smile came to her face, she knew who she wanted to share her secret discovery with. She left promptly and listened for the rattling of the wagon wheels grinding against the frozen ground and sprinted off in their direction.

"There you be," Gorman said in relief. "Thought a quillback had got ya." he said

Kaiden's head perked up hearing the elf had returned. "Find us a good spot?" he asked, stretching his limbs from the long bumpy ride.

"Sure did and got a fire started with some food cooking, hope you're hungry," she responded back to him with a bright smile, hoping for a chance to bring him up to the cave she found. A part of her wanted to share their past together and she tried to work towards the courage to tell him, thinking a special place would help with her confidence.

The tired group's spirits lifted at the promise of food and Gorman flicked at the reigns to speed up the horses. They arrived shortly at the camp, a fire flickering out from behind a wall of rock, glinting off the fresh ice.

Finn slowly made his way like molasses to get warmed up by the fire as Gorman readied poles and canvas to prop up a tent.

"Know what Fish? Yous aint half bad up da mountains," Gorman said with a grumbling giggle, putting his hand on Finn's icy shoulder.

Finn would have had a comeback but decided to wait until he was thawed out a bit first.

"Oh Finn, there is a pond over through the trees there," Nirayus pointed out, bringing a childish grin to his frozen face.

Tomba sat next to the fire, her bare feet exposed as she warmed them up by the heat of the flames, "Dat be smellin amazin," she said, rubbing her hands together, before taking a turn at the spit rod.

Kaiden began to set up a small square of canvas, completely unaffected by the freezing chill in the night air. He couldn't help but wonder where Nirayus planned to sleep through the night and made sure there was room next to him if she wished. He looked up to see bright dots of colored light scattered throughout the night sky, realizing some of the patterns matched parts of her starry skirt.

Gorman and Kaiden finished the tents while Tomba finished dishing out dinner. Nirayus ran over from up the hill, doing some evening scouting in case any danger had lurked their direction towards the fire.

She ran up with a look of fear spread across her thin face. "You guys need to see this," she said frantically, motioning for them to follow her further up the mountain side.

After several minutes they came to a flat area, peppered with large boulders. She jumped atop the massive rocks and offered a hand to the others as they gathered closely on top. They peered across the distant land and could see the entire countryside with the forest hiding Solstice Gardens far into the distance along with the Wither towards the base of the mountain range.

"Look there, do you see it?" she asked, both amused and terrified at the same time.

Kaiden squinted his eyes trying to focus from so far away, letting out a gasp, never seeing anything so hideous before. "I wonder if Finn knows what they are?" he asked, looking back to see if he had followed along with them.

Gorman looked down and couldn't see any details despite the bright moon in the sky, only dark black with patches of a sickly green color, glowing off in the distance. "What you be seein, elf?" he grunted in frustration at his inability to see very far.

Nirayus looked to Kaiden and then over to Gorman with a look of confusion. "Well over there are the piles of bones surrounded by swamps of a hazy green liquid. The mounds of bones look like piles of hay scattered around that has just been sewn from a farm," she explained with a shudder.

Gorman nodded his head, knowing exactly what lye in the dark mists of the Wither swamp. "Those be da dead," he said eerily, having heard stories of the haunted soil that could turn knots in your stomach.

Nirayus leaned closer to Kaiden as they all stared off in the distance. "Have you ever seen anything like this before?" she asked, watching the tall thin trees sway in the breeze.

Kaiden shook his head. "I don't think so, something like this would be hard to forget I imagine." he said, squinting his eyes closer together to see if what he was witnessing could possibly be real.

Nirayus gasped, clenching her compass in her fist for comfort. "Did you guys see that?" she whispered.

ARKANGEL

Kaiden and Nirayus watched as the closest mound of bone began to move. The bright glow of the swamp flickered on their wide eyes despite how far away it was. The bone pile reared up as if on short stubby legs as a massive claw came out the side like the pincer of a sea crab. It stretched its long boney arm out and raked it into the soil, digging around. Another pile reared up to expose and unfold its claw, stabbing it into the ground and unfolding several legs from underneath it. Its legs scraped at the dark soil, dragging its massive body weight as it stopped to dig like the other. Wailing sounds of sorrow echoed up through the air against the side of the mountain.

Gorman heard the lonely wailing sounds and turned to usher Kaiden and Nirayus back to their camp. "Der be evil in da Wither, best not be listenen," he warned, turning back to the blur of green and blackness that left an unsettled feeling in his stomach.

They all settled around the campfire and reluctantly ate their food. Their appetite spoiled by the bone horrors of the Wither that they had witnessed below. Their moods had shifted to depression and sorrow, a strange side effect from the mere glimpse of the devastating battlefield from the past.

Tomba retrieved another roll of blankets from the wagon and set it up in one of the tents and walked over to Nirayus. "We be sleepin in da woman's tent tonight darling," she said warmly, gesturing to the one behind her.

Nirayus nodded with a smile, capturing a quick glance at Kaiden before leaving to go roll up in the blankets for the night.

"You sleep out here in da puddle, Fish," Gorman said to Finn with a chuckle as he retreated back to his tent.

Finn perked up from staring into the fire and remembered the warm spring behind him. "I will be fine out here in my pond, don't you fret big guy, I won't be far if you need me to sing you to sleep," he responded mockingly. Finn reluctantly moved from the warmth of the fire and food to go slip into the steamy water as he let out a relaxing sigh, slipping under its murky surface.

"Well kid, get rest, an no dreamin of da bad," Gorman said to Kaiden, trying to comfort him from the slew of disturbing dreams he had every night as he threw a group of logs on the fire. Gorman lowered into the tent to lay down and found his long legs sticking out the opening flap of the canvas. Exhausted from the long day of travel he barely managed to grunt in disapproval before drifting off into sleep.

Kaiden went to lay down in his own tent as he stared over into the flames of the fire. The mention of his dreams echoed through his mind as swirled in thought of what they had seen. He had learned so much so fast about the world around him and seeing the High Paladin turn in front of him seemed to haunt his thoughts the most. His heart felt heavy, he felt like he was missing something, or someone close but he didn't know who. There was a bond he felt was missing and replaced by another, his soul felt muddled, he could feel inside him something he couldn't pinpoint was different but felt as if he wasn't alone, something was watching him.

The closer they traveled north the more he felt the pull, he knew he was on the right track but a big part of him wanted to slow down, afraid of what he might find at the end of the road. He was thankful for his new friends and their support, they had already been through a lot together and he could feel their friendship growing stronger, but there was still something missing.

His mind went to Nirayus, the moment she popped into his mind every inch of him longed to have her close and suddenly he remembered the image from his dreams, the woman's figure off in the distance filled out as the elven princess. It was her, he had no doubt in his mind, pieces finally came together, and he battled the urge to wake up and go tell her. He decided that she didn't know about his nightmares and was afraid she would think him nuts and decided to just hold his tongue. He couldn't deny his growing feelings for her and felt that his dreams were a good sign she was important, and he felt the calm she had always brought him in his dreams.

The terror of the violence in his nightmares hit him hard in the realization that if Nirayus was there with him, the violence and death may soon come to fruition as well and it brought him fear, a dead reality he would have to face. Did this mean that no matter what he did that he was destined to fail? He pushed the fear aside and decided to think of Nirayus, deciding she must be the part of him that was missing, the companionship he felt loss for. The last thing he remembered seeing was her smile and the curl of her lips when she looked at him, even when she thought he didn't notice.

Kaiden awakened to Nirayus's hand on his shoulder and her finger against her pursed lips. She leaned in close. "I have something I wanted to show you," she whispered softly.

She took his hand and led him up the side of the mountain, carefully stepping to sneak out of camp.

"Not those bone horrors again I hope?" he joked half serious, wondering what could be so secret that she waited for everyone to fall asleep to show him. After Finn's awkward inquiries he had been thinking a lot about her and what she meant to him. Without his memories he couldn't be certain he didn't have a wife and kids waiting for him somewhere and that fear slightly persuaded him from pursuing her. Though he struggled against what it meant for her to be in his dreams all this time or if he would ever get his memories back at all and would be forced to start over. She was beyond stunning and her quirky, yet supportive personality helped keep him sane in their journey. There was something that really pulled at his heart for her but the thought of hurting her or someone from his past scared him to death. He couldn't be certain if she had the same feelings for him but hoped she would still be around when he was ready to let go of his past life.

She led him up to the entrance of the cave she had found earlier, the inside radiating a soft greenish blue glow in the darkness. She took his hand and led him inside, he was awestruck to see the small secret lagoon, waves of warm air washing around him. The water's edge and beautiful flora encircled the inner cave were all glowing multicolored greens and blues, reflecting from the moonlight between the cracks in the rocks. He had never seen flowers or plants so breathtaking in his life along with the symphony of water spilling into the lagoon from a small waterfall

ARKANGEL

trickling down the back of the cave wall.

Nirayus looked back at Kaiden, a sly, playful smile on her lips. "Like it? The water is warm, I thought it would be nice to relax after all the long days you have spent in wagons," she said, releasing his hand to go to the water's edge.

She slipped her long boots off and dragged her foot through the luminescent water, kicking it up at him with a splash. She let out a playful laugh as a smile spread to his face.

"Hey," he said grinning as he reached down to splash the water back at her.

She raised her hand up to block the splash as her hand erupted into flame, hissing and evaporating the majority of the spray.

Kaiden's grin only widened as he laughed. "Oh, come on, that's not fair," he said as her foot kicked more water up, into his face.

"Oh, that's it," he threatened playfully, reaching out in an attempt to catch her as she easily out maneuvered him, only to end up behind with another splash to his back.

Kaiden turned to see her standing there, her big beautiful blue eyes glowing in the dancing lights of the lagoon. They paused momentarily entranced in each other's stares before he lunged as a fake to maneuver to her other side just in time to wrap his arms around her waist and pull her in tight. She let out a long breath and put her hand on his chest as he pulled her close. She looked up into his eyes and began to raise up onto her tip toes for a kiss.

Kaiden realized her body was firmly pressed up against his own and released his arms just in time to have her shove him back, sending him splashing into the warm pool. He stood up and flipped his hair out of his eyes in shock that she had just pushed him in.

Nirayus stood there with her hands on her thin hips and a playful expression on her face as she marveled at his surprise. "Lose your footing there hero?" she giggled.

Kaiden laughed aloud and moved his arm under the water, lifting a big wave of water to splash her. She quickly spun to the side, completely missed by the funnel of water. She dipped her toe in again to splash at him as he dove under the water. He raised up for breath several seconds later with a smirk, proud of his cleverness.

When he stood up a beautiful teal glow radiated from under the water, making the rippling water's surface project a colorful parade of patterns on the cave ceiling. The plant life around unfolded to project a beautiful pink glow into the mix of greens and blues. The water that trickled in from the ice above the cave dripping atop the newly opened leaves causing them to shudder with light.

Nirayus looked at the back of the cave, taken back by the spectacle of light, completely unaware of Kaiden's advancement. Her pearly white skin reflected the vibrant colors of the cave, complementing her wavy blue hair.

Kaiden grabbed her foot, causing her to leap into the air in surprise as he pulled her splashing down into the lagoon. She surfaced with a scowl, causing his victory smile to fade. Her long wet blue hair stuck to her face as he reached over to brush it from her eyes. He pulled it back and tucked it back behind her long slender ears as her eyes locked into his. They spent many long seconds gazing into each other's eyes as the beautiful reflections of light danced across their faces.

Kaiden wrapped his strong arms around her slender waist and pulled her in against him, peering deep into each other's souls for what felt like an eternity. His vision began to glow a soft golden color as he started to somehow see into the depths of her heart, the core of her being. Opening like a book in front of him, sensing her hopes, fears, dreams, and him. He could feel as clear as day her intensions and love for him as if she had been in love with him her entire life.

Kaiden pulled away, afraid of what had just happened, he had never seen someone so clearly as he just had and had no idea how he was able to do it. He looked down at the reflective water and saw himself, ripples of light glistening on his own face that he could not recognize.

Nirayus put her hand lovingly up to the side of his cheek, "What's the matter?" she asked, her heart fluttering with the overwhelming emotions she had only ever dreamed of.

His hand met hers and he looked back into her eyes, his heart aching in confusion but finding it difficult to resist her captivating stare. "I don't know," he said solemnly, his hand caressing hers on his face.

Her warm smile dissipated into worry for him. "What's wrong? You can tell me; did I do something?" she asked gently.

His gaze lowered a bit but was followed by her worried eyes as she tried to comfort him. "It's just that I don't know anything prior to these past few weeks," he said hesitantly. "I don't know if I have a family waiting for me somewhere out there or not." he added as his heart sank into sadness and regret of ruining their romantic time in the lagoon.

Her expression turned to puzzlement as she herself hadn't thought of that before either, she had only thought of him as hers because of their past and the fact he still wore his neckless from her.

He could see the disappointment spread across her face, "It doesn't mean I don't have feelings for you Nirayus." he said, hoping for her smile to return. He held her tightly in his other arm as he moved his hand to her cheek, lightly stroking her porcelain skin. "Before I found you in the garden, I felt lost and other than Gorman and Finn, I was alone. When you came with us you started to awaken emotions inside me that I didn't know I was capable of," he said softly, looking at her beautiful face.

They stood there silently in the glowing water holding each other tightly as a battle raged within her, whether she should tell him or not of their past but feeling selfish for wanting to use it in hopes he would overlook the possibility of his past life. She was a princess and had grown up getting what she wanted, when she wanted. But she found deep down she cared for him too much to possibly cause him any regret.

She felt a tear roll down her cheek, struggling to speak. "You have changed a lot in me as well, I see all the good you are doing for these people, putting your own needs aside as you solve the problems of others," she said, realizing it to be true in how much she felt needed and had a purpose. "You are so selfless in your actions, and I don't know the man you used to be but who you are now has stolen my heart," she whispered, daring to allow a hint of her sly smile to return.

Kaiden swelled with happiness, knowing confidently that he could have never felt this way for anyone else before, she somehow broke down the barriers he had and decided to take a leap of faith and follow his heart. "With you being next to me I have been able to find confidence and purpose in what we are doing and in finding myself." he said pulling her closer. "Whatever we have here, I would be honored to explore and grow it with you. We don't know what tomorrow brings but I do know it is you I want to be by my side," he whispered back.

She reached her hands and gently wrapped them around the back of his head, looking up into his eyes as their hearts pounded in unison with each other. She pulled him close and kissed him with her soft lips, their hearts overflowing with emotion that neither could have prepared for, the love they felt for each other. They had finally found something they had been missing and were now finally whole.

Kaiden ran his fingers through her hair and embraced her back as he softly kissed her lips. Nirayus's heart longed to share how long she had waited for this moment but couldn't bring herself to say anything until he was able to share in the memory with her together. She laid her face against his chest, living in the moment before drifting off into the first peaceful night's sleep she had ever had.

Kaiden felt her body slacken as she drifted to sleep in his arms, and he scooped her up and carried her back to hold her by the fire until their clothes had dried. He held her close while gazing into the flames that flickered up into the moonlight. He felt free and relieved to have someone close and for the first time he felt he was ready to take charge and live out his destiny, whatever it may throw at him. He thought about the day after the plague was over and their foes were dealt with what it would be like to settle down and share their life together.

He found his gaping smile was hurting his face when he snapped to, and his thoughts moved to what they would have to do to end the plague and find whatever was behind it. He wondered about Sanctuary and who the man was with Lanthor. Why had he reacted when he saw him and how it was possible that they resembled each other so much? He thought that it was possible his family was from Sanctuary but had been already taken by the plague, his thoughts raced around trying to piece together the riddle of his past. His eyes grew heavy, and his head slumped down atop Nirayus's shoulder as they lay against each other by the open fire.

Gorman awoke to his own snort startling himself awake and noticed the first rays of the morning sun piercing through the clouds. He crawled out of the tent to find Kaiden and Nirayus passed out in each other's arms and decided to wake Kaiden up with the gentle shove of his foot.

"Get up, kid, wes need to move," he said in his usual gruff tone.

Kaiden woke up along with Nirayus as they were pushed into the grass. Gorman tossed them a couple dried out bars of rations and went to wake up his mother.

Nirayus looked over into Kaiden's eyes. "Good morning," she said with an embarrassed smile.

Her infectious grin struck Kaiden as he wrapped his arms around her with a squeeze. "It's the best of mornings," he responded as he took a hesitant bite into the dried chunk of food. Nirayus got up and doused the pile of ash beside them in water and helped Kaiden roll up his unused tent and bedding.

"Have you seen Finn?" Nirayus asked Gorman, watching him toss the bundle of canvas into the back of the wagon.

Gorman let out a grunt and briefly looked side to side. "Nah, I's say wes leave em," he said with a smile.

Nirayus and Kaiden shared a chuckle as she led him to the small pond off the edge of the field to search for him.

Finn laid on his back with his hands clasped behind his head. "You know I can really respect a man in your dilemma but I believe in you and that you are doing the right thing, but you just need to give it time, let her cool down a bit and just ask your questions, be direct and honest, females really appreciate that especially when you say you have 12 hatchlings and another 8 on the way. I think that's just fantastic," Finn said looking up into the crisp blue sky of the new day.

"Who are you talking to Finn?" Nirayus asked before stepping through the trees.

Finn sat up and patted the split tailed newt atop his head. "I believe in you," he whispered as the newt continued to slowly lap up the water of the pond.

"Just one of my new friends," Finn answered as he got up to meet Kaiden and Nirayus.

Nirayus gave the aquarian a puzzled look as she followed him and Kaiden back to the wagon. They saw Gorman and Tomba sitting in the driver's bench as Tomba opened another ration of food they had packed to add to the other two she had eaten for breakfast already.

Kaiden climbed up and reached his hand down to help lift up Nirayus who leapt into the cart with minimal effort. "Too slow," she mocked playfully as Finn's webbed fingers encircle around Kaiden's.

"Thanks, Kaiden, awfully generous of you," Finn said sweetly, mocking him with the batting of his eye lenses.

Kaiden took his place in the back against the end of the wagon amongst the luggage followed by Nirayus who squeezed herself in beside him. She pulled her hair over to her side out of the way and rested her head on his shoulder in content. Both looked forward towards the horizon with smiles sweeping across their faces.

The companions arrived at the top of the mountain pass, only to look down at the steep unforgiving decent down the backside. Far across the frozen countryside they could see an Ivory Obelisk raising high into the air, so high that its peek was lost in the clouds. The narrow pillar like structure widened at the base, keeping it firmly in place against the strong, howling winds. The bottom was masked by what looked like an endless maze of thorns, barely visible through the torrent of fog. Tall stems of monkshade outstretched towards the sun readying to strike unsuspecting travelers with their poisonous sting if anyone was stupid enough to attempt the maze.

The horses struggled to keep the weight behind them in the cart from spilling over and down the dangerous cliff as the trail switch backed down the mountain. They reached the base after a long day of travel, both dreading the tower getting ever closer and eagerly leaving the eerie land overlooking the wither behind them.

In the distance, Nirayus spotted an odd grouping of beings. Two tall giants, lumbering over an array of brightly colored aquarians, elves, and ogres. They were all standing at attention, very aware of their approach as they slowly made their way over the rocky hills to the base of the mountain. As they approached, Finn perked up to see some of the female sleek skins and their illustrious, colorful hair that could be seen shimmering from so far away.

In the center of the group was a bright white covered coach, pulled by several ember elves wrapped in metal and leather strappings. The two giants off to the sides gestured for them to approach from across a small stream with a long stone bridge spanning the distance many times the size of the rapid stream.

"They knows we comin?" Gorman asked aloud, wondering who could have made it there ahead of them to give warning of their arrival.

Tomba, patted at her knees in excitement to see her husband Darvish for the first time in many years and even more so to reunite him with Gorman. "It be ok, baby," Tomba said to reassure her son. "Lu-sea be knowin everything," she added with a smile of anticipation.

Kaiden and Nirayus shared a look, unsure of what to expect. "I see a moon elf," Nirayus said, leaning in close. "I wonder what he is doing so far north, away from our people?"

"Anyone you recognize?" Kaiden asked as he squinted to see who she could be talking about, envious of her eyesight.

Nirayus shook her head, looking at the long straight raven black hair of the skinny half elf man with more of a light grey complexion than her own, pale white. "No, he doesn't appear to be from my family line," she replied.

The cart leveled off onto flat gravel soil with little to no grass or plant life as they approached the stone bridge. By the look of the path, it was rarely ever used, if ever, at all, as few would ever dare to approach Lu-sea's dangerous tower. As they approached, the giants immediately stepped closer, pulling their massive, spiked clubs up into view and setting them roughly back into the damp soil, a gesture of momentary truce putting their weapons down in sight.

Gorman slowed the wagon to a stop and jumped down to the frozen dirt. The normally intimidatingly large Gorman was dwarfed by the giant's enormous size almost doubling his.

Never losing his charm, Gorman shouted, "Yous need to move, we be travelin to da tower." he stated gesturing for them to move off the only passible path. He felt a sting of anger rise within at their refusal to listen until he noticed everyone's eyes ahead of him were a solid glossy black. He was taken back, alert, and then was startled when the door to the white wagon slowly began to open.

A tall, beautiful, sleek skin with thin fins running the lengths of her forearms hurried to the door and offered a hand up to the person inside. A tall, muscular woman stepped out and grasped the open hand. Her light orange colored skin was encircled with streaks of powdered white in intricate patterns loosely covered by a glimmering pitch-black skirt trimmed in silver. The woman's eyes commanded attention brightly yellow in color with long fine slits for pupils that brought her crowd of followers to their knees with a simple glance. Her face was stoic and undeniably unique in beauty as she locked eyes with Gorman like a viper homing in on its prey.

Gorman's knees started to wobble in fear, looking into her icy stare. He tried to look away, looking past to the kneeling giants or the stream at his feet but found himself compelled to look back, getting lost in her trance. She walked closer, her limbs seeming to fade in and out of existence in a blur as she moved at an unnatural speed. Within a blink of an eye, she stood in front of Gorman who steadied himself with a hand on the side of their wagon, his other hand trying to reach for a spear but without a response from his own arm.

"I have been waiting for you and it is I in which you seek," came a sharp voice, echoing through the air like the sound had originated from all around them.

Her eyes flicked towards Kaiden, completely ignoring his other silent companions. "Kaiden, we have much to discuss, please tell your driver to follow close behind and follow me into my tower," she commanded.

Kaiden blinked once, to see her standing right next to him momentarily, her eyes blazing like fire, peering into his soul, then blinking again to see her back across the bridge, elegantly walking back to her wagon. When she walked, a thin, dark blue cape streamed from her back, hovering along the rocky floor. Kaiden sat in thought, feeling like his very being had just been forcibly entered, like a crate that an intruder had just tried to rummage through. For an instant he somehow felt like he had somehow resisted her and forced her to retreat but what did she find while she was inside?

Tomba jumped off the cart and hurriedly walked towards Lu-Sea, searching through her crowd of escorts. "Lu-sea is me Darvish with yous?" she shouted in hope.

Lu-Sea turned to see Tomba, a forced smile spreading to her face as she gestured for her to get into the covered wagon. "Come, sweet Tomba," she said before returning inside the confines of her wagon.

Gorman stomped his way up to his driver seat grunting. "I's think this be bad idea," he announced to his companions as he flicked the reigns for the horses to proceed forward across the bridge.

They watched as one by one the beings on their knees all stood and followed unflinchingly behind the white cart as it turned to lead towards the entrance of the maze. Before the entrance they veered off to the side to follow the long wall of thorns filled with monkshade spines. Rising high above the thick maze walls the plants turned slightly, as if they were prepping to strike. Before they could run into the wall of bramble the ground beneath them shifted into a ramp that slowly lowered down into the dark ground below. They hesitantly followed, sinking into the tunnel beneath the surface as the ground behind them began to lift back into place.

Finn looked back to Kaiden and Nirayus in excitement, finding only blank stares struck on their faces. "That is awfully clever, what better way to keep your home safe than a maze with no way out and full of traps and dangers, though I would bet she doesn't get many guests." he stated aloud, wondering how someone would not want guests to come over to visit all the time.

"Did you see her suddenly appear right next to us? Kaiden whispered to Nirayus, unable to shake the eerie feeling she left him with.

Nirayus looked at him confused. "No, she stayed by the bridge the whole time, but she warned me that we needed to talk, alone. Something isn't right with her but at the same time she feels very familiar somehow, yet I've never seen another elf like her," she said, completely disregarding Kaiden's question.

When the ground behind them lifted back into place the tunnel cast itself into complete darkness for many moments before blasts of light erupted from the sides of the passage. Thin streams of fire funneled through vents in the floor several feet into the air at either side as they passed. Rows of guards stood by, watching as their solid glossy black eyes reflected at the pillars of flame.

They pulled up next to what looked like an underground stable with all manner of beasts tethered to rails or caged against the wide-open ledge. The ember elves pulling Lu-Sea's cart, wheeled her into place as she descended from the stairs of her carriage door. She gestured commands to several servants that approached her without ever muttering a single word aloud. The servants nodded and went about their duties without question as one of them retrieved Tomba politely from the wagon and helped her down the stairs. The aquarian servant bowed to her with a nod and escorted her down a hallway, looking back Tomba followed with a gleaming smile on her face.

An echoing voice haunted the companions; they all looked across the room to see Lu-Sea glaring at them. "Come, leave your belongings behind, you have no need for them," she said as her voice resonated in their minds.

Gorman looked to the thick damp air around his head in agitation as her voice said, "Bring your weapons, you will be needing them," she warned.

The companions shared a look of uncertainty as they listened to their commands while walking over to her standing majestically atop a platform, surrounded by rings of steps. Her form seemed to shimmer and shake from the light above like she was fading in and out of the world.

Kaiden smiled at Nirayus, calming her nerves, he had noticed her ears were lowered slightly when she was alarmed or frightened and he wanted to let her know they were in it together. All he had been able to think about was the time they had spent together in the cave but had to push it from his mind as he felt his thoughts were not alone. She smiled back and reached her hand out to grab his, his fingers gently interlocking into hers for support.

"It's ok, she is on our side," he whispered reassuringly, even though he hardly believed it himself. He wondered why all the silent communication and why everyone he had seen stood mindlessly staring off into the distance with blank, glossy stares.

Once they were all on the platform, Lu-sea nodded to a bluish grey elf standing below next to a pedestal with an orb fastened in the center. The elf placed his hand upon the orb, causing it to glow brightly under his palm. The lift began to glide silently upwards, quickly passing floors in mere seconds. They traveled up several floors underground before reaching the surface and rising high into the air. They could see thousands of beings all going about their daily lives, working and walking about. They passed what looked like plantations, schools, libraries, homes, and common areas. The obelisk was tall and cylindrical, reaching high into the sky with the very center of it being hollow for the lift. Staircases could be seen going up and down through the levels which was the usual method of movement between the different levels for its inhabitants.

Everything was pearlescent white and or transparent making the whole place seem cold and clean as one could see through the whole building out towards the dark blue ocean or over to the snow-covered mountains. Somehow the fast movement of the lift wasn't disorientating in the least and it slowed and halted into place at the top of the tower. The room at the top of the tower was shaped like the inside of an upside-down diamond with glass walls surrounding the entire floor and raising into a sharp peak at the top.

Lu-sea walked off the platform and towards a door leading outside of the glass walls to a clear staircase that went out and around the outside of the peak. She looked back to the group who were eyeing the bright white and blue interior.

"What we be doin here?" Gorman asked, not taking a step from the platform.

Kaiden nodded his head in agreement while squeezing Nirayus's hand tightly. "We traveled for several days to get here to," he started to say but was quickly interrupted by her ominous voice.

"I know exactly why you are here, and you will all have your answers regarding your misguided plague, but you will do something for me first. If you refuse you will be sent back where you came without the answers you seek, and I care not but you need to decide quickly as the problem at hand is growing ever dire." The voice said as she turned to look at them, her eyes staring back unblinking.

Kaiden looked to each of his companions, his eyebrows scrunched together in frustration while deciding what was best for the people of Sanctuary. They had come all this way to possibly be led astray, but at the possibility for answers he couldn't refuse her offer.

"So, you will help us if we help you first?" Kaiden asked, without a response beyond her icy cold stare.

Finn was completely captivated by the glass architecture of the obelisk and its rooms within and raised a finger in an inquiring gesture.

"How many beings live here? I counted levels somewhere around one hundred with each floor contains approximately 200-300 beings, what are they all doing here? Why are all their eyes…"

"Silence," she yelled, her echoing voice throbbing in Finn's head.

Lu-sea turned and moved through a glass door, nearly invisible to the eye that a door even existed there and walked quickly up the stairs.

Kaiden looked at his confused companions. "We do need her help and as long as she will give us answers, I say we help her out, it couldn't hurt to have her as an ally, it is clear the stories about her power pale in comparison though," he stated.

Gorman shook his head. "No good, why mes need weapons?" he asked, guessing it had to do with whatever dangerous task she couldn't manage to do herself.

Nirayus looked up to Kaiden, getting closer to his side. "Maybe the two are related and once we complete her task it will help with our own?" she added in hope. "But I do sense a strange power here, like we are all under a blanket of sorts, with the true nature of what is going on here on the other side of it," she commented with a shiver.

"I say we do what she says and get out of this place," Finn said with a nod of acceptance, still sore from being cut off from his questions.

They followed Kaiden outside, the ground so far down that it was hard for all but Nirayus to make out the details below. Looking across the landscape they were almost as tall as the shortest of mountains in the range. The wind swirled and howled violently past them, creating a force seemingly pulling them away from the glass structure.

They ascended to the very tip, a small platform sitting on top of the glass diamond point. They came to a stop on the platform that was only a few meters in diameter behind Lu-Sea and were taken aback by the sight of a magnificent crystal. Before her sat a long-jagged crystal sitting several feet off the platform hovering in midair. As the wind lashed around it the colors emanated brightly, pulsating with more colors than one would think possible, like a brilliant prism.

ARKANGEL

"Take the leap of faith Kaiden and touch the stone but you may only take one other person with you," the voice echoed in his head. "I do not know where the crystal will lead you but take care in your choice as I have sent many warriors through and none have returned," she warned in a heavy tone as she looked upon the crystal, her eyes reflecting the same prismatic refractions.

"Why must I choose only one?" Kaiden yelled against the violent wind.

Lu-Sea's face scrunched up into an angry scowl. "You must do as I say and the time to choose is now. Return to me shards from the opposing crystal and I will tell you everything you need to know if you return," she said in a tone of building urgency.

Kaiden looked upon his companions, frantically trying to decide what he needed to do. He hated splitting up the group and needed each one for their support they bring to their team. A worried glare came to his face as he tried to find the best solution. Finn could help him travel back if he were lost or solve any situation where Gorman would be of the most use if the danger was truly enough to scare even Lu-Sea which he could never subject Nirayus to such a fate. Gorman was already armed to the teeth holding his spears and crossbow like he had planned for the journey already.

Kaiden turned and looked at Nirayus, putting his hand on her cheek and leaning in close. "I can't put you in this unknown danger," he said, losing himself in her bright blue eyes. "Wait here with Finn, I will return as fast as I can," he shouted, even though they were only inches apart.

Nirayus started to shake her head in protest, giving Lu-Sea a scowl of her own. She could tell something was going on and she couldn't help but feel a wave of panic wash over her. She didn't want to leave his side; the world was even more dangerous than she had grown up to believe and struggled at the thought of letting him go again. She looked down and pulled him close to her in a hug, hoping it would last forever. She went to her tip toes and gave him a brief kiss, "Hurry back to me," she pleaded as her long blue hair flew wildly around her.

"Let him go Nirayus, it is not your time yet," a crystal-clear voice rang in her head as her eyes opened alert, in shock of the sudden intrusion.

Kaiden let her go and reached out to Gorman. "Let's go," he shouted, grasping onto his big metal vambrace.

Gorman gave out a grunt of satisfaction "Good choice kid," he said with a halfcocked smirk.

Kaiden stole another glance at Nirayus with a warm smile as he reached towards the crystal and in a blink of an eye, vanished.

Nirayus blinked several times in disbelief that they could just disappear. Finn reached his hand out in awe but was smacked away by Lu-Sea.

"Follow," she said as she turned to descend back into her tower. She gestured for them to sit in two bright white tall chairs, centered towards the edge of the room. "I know you have questions, but we have limited time before they are to return, for you are important pieces in this and need to be tested," she said in her own audible voice as she walked over to a taller throne like chair.

"I only have some of the answers you seek as for the rest you will need to travel north to the floating mountains of Azure," she began in a more comfortable tone.

Finn raised a finger in question, looking briefly to Nirayus with a confused look on his face. "If I may inquire? What is farther north that could be of any help to the humans who are suffering in the south?" he asked, wondering why they would need to travel in the opposite direction.

Lu-Sea shifted in her seat to glare at Finn. "That journey is not for you to take aquarian. Kaiden and Nirayus must go alone," she said, gesturing to the small elf in the oversized chair. "The rest of you will find out soon enough of your importance." she stated

Nirayus, excited for her confidence in Kaiden's return, perked up. "What is this test you spoke of?" she asked, unsure that she really wanted the answer.

Lu-Sea's being flickered again, and her face appeared inches before Nirayus's blank stare, her cold gaze entering into her soul. Nirayus could hear and feel something entering her mind, almost feeling like her identity was to be taken from her. Her body started to tremble in its place in the chair as she fearfully tried to move her unresponsive limbs.

"Yes, little one I am in your mind," Lu-sea's eerie voice announced in her head.

Nirayus's eyes glazed over a glossy black color as she was somehow in a dark echoing room standing alone with an elven woman she did not recognize. "Who are you?" she tried to say but was unable to move her mouth.

"First and foremost, I have arked myself into your spirit. You and I are locked away in a spiritual plane as our shells sit back in our physical reality awaiting our return."

Nirayus stopped struggling to break free and focused to calm her mind, starting to feel more comfortable with Lu-seas less ominous voice. She looked less taunting in this form, more beautiful than intimidating like the elves she was used to. Her skin was a pearly greyish blue color with vibrant blue hair like her own and something felt familiar about her that put her at a strange ease.

"You are questioning my appearance little one, although my origins are of no importance to you in this moment moon elf, you have only seen me inhabit the body of our enemy's queen to keep them at bay, her spirit locked away until I am ready to free her," Lu-Sea said cleverly. "What you see before you now, is merely a reflection of my true form, one which I must keep secret for your sake.

Nirayus was astonished by Lu-Sea's abilities, keeping an entire war at bay by holding their queen hostage without fear of attack while she resided in her body. It was both brilliant and devious, Nirayus was beginning to respect Lu-sea even though her motives were still a mystery.

"Why thank you young one, you hold much unlocked power yourself," Lu-Sea responded to Nirayus's thoughts, reminding her that her thoughts were not her own for the moment.

"Enough of this banter," Lu-Sea said with a wave of her hand, as her form floated closer to Nirayus in the empty room of darkness. "You are to play a big part in Kaiden's destiny and the events that are unfolding in front of us now," she said as she waved her hand to show a vision of the massacre at Solstice Gardens.

"But this is only the beginning, and you will need to be strong and support him, without you he will inevitably fail if you deceive him. You must check your commitment to the cause right here and now for he is not all that he seems, and you will have to accept him for who he truly is," she said in a stern voice of warning. "Search your heart now, I will destroy you here and now if I think you might fail him in any way, for the prophecy is of greater importance than even I can fathom."

Nirayus gulped but was unshaken in her resolve. "I have searched for him all my life and will never betray him no matter what the cost," she said firmly.

There was a long silence while Lu-Sea searched her heart and soul. Nirayus watched as the short, blue skinned elf examined things unseen, her long thin blue hair weightlessly floating into the shadowy ethereal behind her. She was older but how old Nirayus couldn't tell, her form dithered in and out, making it hard to focus on anything but her deep purple eyes.

"Yes, I see what he means to you is true and just and it will not fade or falter, when the time comes to learn his truths, your destinies will be fully intertwined, despite its tragic ending," Lu-Sea said, her mind feeling at ease and letting up on Nirayus's soul.

"Wait what?" Nirayus began, she had so many questions that she needed to have answered before feeling a jolt from within. Nirayus came to, as if being startled awake from a dream. Her heart raced as she looked around the room to see Lu-Sea still sitting in her chair with a smile on her face.

"What happened?" Nirayus asked in panic, feeling a deep discomfort but unable to remember why.

Finn gave her an odd look of confusion. "You were asking what the test was, which I myself am excited to take. It has been a long time since I have had something good to really ponder about," he said looking to Lu-Sea, waiting for her response.

Lu-Sea shifted herself to stare into Finns bulbous eyes. "Now for you, man of the sea," she said as Finn's body tensed up, and then relaxed as his already solid black eyes rolled back in his head.

Finn came to in a dark room; he watched as Lu-Sea approached in her true form. "You have done well guiding the young ones here Finn, I am pleased," she said with a nod of her head in appreciation as her smile quickly turned grim. "I fear the prophecy is ever changing and may have shifted out of control, my friend, as I have been watching as events have unfolded. We missed something and it is beyond my power to understand," she said with a wave of her hand as a vision of an ancient scroll materialized from the darkness. She waved her other hand as images of Solstice Gardens played before his eyes.

Finn let out a gasp at the sight of the massacre, he grasped at his chest to comfort his heart. He watched as thousands of people turned on each other, tearing one another to pieces, and turned into the horrific quillbacks within minutes with the last image settling on Martis.

"Kaiden is going to need you Finn, he will need your intelligence to help buy him the time he needs but most importantly your guidance in the things to come, more than he ever has before. The man before you, is his brother and his part in this prophecy is ever growing," she stated, her voice beginning to quiver. "He is always scheming and is twisting the fine fibers of fate, ever changing the prophecy and Kaiden cannot hesitate to destroy him when the time comes."

Finn nodded his head with a solemn look, unusually quiet. "Is this the prophecy?" Finn asked. "Is this to be the fall of man? With the arrival of the Salamanders? Have the creators plagued us?" he asked uneasily.

Lu-Sea's eyes lit up, the vibrant purple color, intense in the darkness.

"You are very perceptive Finn Worthington."

Finn cocked his head in confusion how his simple question could be perceptive, but his confidence started to rise that he may have figured something out.

"I know all your thoughts Finn and the true origins of your lines of questioning but the answers I promised you before must wait for now, your mind must be completely focused on matters at hand, the fate of your people will have to wait, for now," she said as she placed her finger on her temple for concentration.

She is visited by a hazy display as a massive beast stood atop the crumbling city of Sanctuary followed by an image of the lone survivor, Kaiden standing on a wall surrounded by a destroyed castle full of the dead as his companions lay at his feet.

Lu-Sea shared the images she had seen with Finn who began to shake uncontrollably in his catatonic state from fear. She moved her hands around to see the sky filled with terrifying beasts of flight, circling around the city as waves of brutish grey and green monsters heavily armed and armored flooded in like a wave of destruction against the toppled city. Lu-Sea stumbled, with a wince of pain.

"These are new visions I have not seen before nor do I know their meaning," Lu-Sea said in a worried tone. "I was wrong Finn, there is much more at play here, powerful beings that I had not seen before I met Kaiden in person. I fear you are right; the creator has abandoned us and been replaced with something much more sinister," she said as her knees trembled, grabbing on to Finn for support.

"I need time with my thoughts to find answers to these new events and I need you to guide the rest of them south. We need to get our pieces in place if we stand a chance to defeat these threats," she pleaded.

Finn nervously listened to her instructions, nodding his understanding. He was shocked by what he had seen and how it differed so drastically from what he had learned in the past. The creator had surely abandoned the humans and its effects would ripple destruction throughout the land. Time was dwindling faster than he had realized and knew that he could do his part, standing by his companions in their darkest moment. He had been taught the prophecy when he was younger and sought it out, eager to help where he could but it had turned to legend, a scary tale to tell children. He believed in his companions and would guide them, standing proud in his own mind.

Lu-Sea released Finn, he looked up to see Nirayus kneeling beside him for comfort.

"Are you alright?" she asked with a worried expression on her young face.

Finn nodded his head, his gaze never leaving Lu-Sea's as she stood up quickly, rushing to the Orb on the pedestal. "It is time," she announced.

CHAPTER 12

"OLD FRIENDS"

Kaiden and Gorman both landed hard against the sandy ground with a thud, the disorientation wearing off from being warped through the stones. Loud pounds, shouts, and screams filled their heads. Gorman reached out his big hand and grabbed on to Kaiden's shoulder to shake him coherent as he took a defensive stance, taking in the danger all around them. There was a big crashing sound as a body flew through the air, tumbling several times, and coming to a stop near their feet. They both looked at each other in shock to see the limbless body pour freely of its life blood.

"Kaiden, Kaiden!" Kaiden heard a voice call out.

"Is that really you?" a young man with long messy hair shouted out as he rode up on the back of a massive wolf, standing almost twice his height.

"Kaiden, how is this possible that you are here?" he called out again, his voice both frantic and surprised.

"Do I know you?" Kaiden asked confused, looking at the dirty leather clad rider and his cat like companion behind him.

"Move," Gorman shouted, pushing Kaiden to the side as another mangled body splattered near them.

"It's Arcus, remember? How are you here?" he pleaded, completely ignoring the danger around them.

Gorman's face contorted into a look of fear as his jaw slackened and dropped open. He looked around the massive wolf to see a beast he had never seen before less than one hundred yards away standing amongst a pile of fresh corpses. Its beady eyes turned and locked its predatory stare at them as it let out a deafening roar.

Shouts and screams bellowed out in excitement as Kaiden wheeled around realizing they were in the center of a giant ring filled will people. Thousands of cheering spectators sat atop overly massive walls lined with sharpened spiked logs aimed towards the center to keep whatever was trapped inside from getting out. He looked to his feet to see the hot burning orange sand stained with years and years of bloodshed.

Kaiden looked up to their enemy, a creature standing nearly thirty feet tall on two massively clawed arms with a body that tapered down to a long spiny tail. It lowered its head and prepared to attack, its big, curled horns spiraling to each of its scaled sides. Its eyes glowered at them as it let out a deep bellow of warning that shook even the armored scale plates that overlapped all the way down its spine from its head. Its jaws opened wide, exposing hundreds of long needle like teeth, snapping at the air. The beast whipped at the ground with its tail and with ground shaking force took off, lunging in their direction.

Arcus looked back to see the trampling terror as giant strands of roots and vines shot forth from the ground. He looked to see Taja's frantic face as she arked long tendrils of green light into the ground, puppeteering the roots into a defensive wall. The creature slammed through the wall, barely even slowed as it continued its charge at Gorman.

"Jump on," Arcus demanded, holding his hand out to Kaiden below. "Your spot's still open for ya," he said with an excited grin.

Kaiden briefly paused to glance at Gorman, standing his ground with his spear in hand. He looked up to Arcus. "Thank you but I must help my companion," he said as he sprinted over to Gorman, who was about to be mauled. Kaiden slammed into Gorman with all his might, pushing him to the side as the beast snapped its powerful jaws, its rows of needle like teeth dwarfing the size of the half ogre's spear. The creature's bite missed Gorman, but its jaw struck Kaiden, sending him high into the air as the creature's mouth wildly snapped at his body.

Arcus let out a wailing cry of fear as he saw his friend about to be eaten by the beast, his heart trembling hard in his chest.

The creature bit down around Kaiden's body when a thunderous sound of a sonic boom violently thrusted the creature's mouth agape. Kaiden's body was entangled in a vibrant golden light that wrapped around his limbs as he sailed through the air. His armor formed and hardened into place, righting itself midflight and landing firmly on the ground below, ready to fight. Clouds of the red dust billowed out of the torn-up terrain around him, raining down like a storm of hail. There was a sudden gasp heard through the entire crowd as thousands of Akarians were shocked by what they are seeing.

Kaiden sprinted towards the creature, his ornate silver blades firmly in his grasp as he leaped high into the air and slammed down onto the side of the disorientated creature. Slash after slash he fearlessly carved into the beast as it roared aloud, clawing with its arms, struggling to hit its armored attacker.

It made contact, flinging Kaiden off as his body tumbled along the ground and stopped at Saber's paws. Saber let out a sympathetic yelp, recognizing the man that was inside the mask.

"Kaiden?" Arcus shouted in panic, seeing his friend just mauled again for the second time, his face washing over with dread and confusion of what he was seeing.

Gorman rushed to his side and with a massive arm lifted Kaiden upright. "Here, try dees," he said, handing him two of his spears. Gorman turned and loaded another spear in his crossbow and readied his last in his other hand. "Let's take out dem arms," Gorman commanded as he raised his crossbow to fire the spear into its knee.

Kaiden whirled around and launched the spears with such force they went all the way through the creature's armored arm, tearing out bone and flesh alike. Gorman's spear sailed through the air and sunk itself in its claw as it tried to defend.

The creature let out a wild roar of rage as it struggled to stay standing and swung its tail around to thrash at its enemies. Saber wheeled around to encircle the creature as Taja barely dodged a swipe from its tail, rolling on the ground to come up by Gorman, steering clear of the walking armored suit.

The creature's tail whipped around trying to slam down onto the nimble wolf as Arcus rode him around, launching arrow after arrow into its thick scales, having little effect. He noticed Taja was back on the ground and brought Saber to a sprint through the creature's arms, causing its tail to swipe around, knocking itself off balance. He rode by, lowering his arms to pull Taja up on Saber's back, keeping the creature's attention affixed on him and the wolf as it struggled to stand back up.

"What is going on, hunter?" Taja called out as they rode around the perimeter of the great ring.

"Remember the friend I had told you about? That is him that somehow fell out of the sky," he replied, yanking Saber's hair and leaning to his side to get him to turn sharply, close by the creature's arms, hoping to keep it off balance.

"That is him?" she asked, confused. "What is that creature he turned into?" she added, looking back to see the armored figure leaping through the air, slashing at the beast's side.

"Not now," Arcus shouted back, "we need to somehow get close enough to strike a fatal blow."

Taja winced at the sound of killing the beast, for despite all the people it had murdered today it too was only trying to survive in the cruel savage's pit of entertainment. She watched as the spiny tail slammed down, narrowly missing the scared ogre and sending the armored figure crashing against the wooden wall.

"Taja, I need you to Ark us a barrier and tangle up one of his arms. Can you do that?" Arcus called back to her.

Taja felt a wave of panic wash over her already frightened thoughts, not wanting to be responsible if she failed her friend. "I don't know, it is too hard to control," she replied as her ears folded back in hesitation.

Saber turned again sharply, heading straight for the creature's legs. "Now, Taja!" Arcus shouted.

Taja flinched and looked deep within herself, pulling out every bit of power she could, visualizing and manipulating her ark within her. Suddenly an enormous bramble shield of thorns and thick vines erupted forth, twisting and turning around Saber like an exoskeleton, creating a protective cage where they sat. The vines tightened and hardened into rock hard strands of wood as Saber slowed from the extra weight but fearlessly charged headfirst into the creature's wounded leg. They crashed hard, the momentum almost tearing its limb from its socket as the creature crashed down to its side.

Taja opened her eyes wide, bright green flashes, flickering out like lightning from her eyes. She let out a cry as she raised her arms in the cage and another pair of vines exploded out of the sandy floor and entangled themselves around the creature's claws. They tightened and twisted themselves securely around its arms, restraining it firmly to the ground. A cloud of sand was thrown high into the air from the impact and as it rained down onto the onlookers above.

Saber wheeled around as Taja slumped over exhausted, the vines withering and breaking away slowly as he came to a stop. The beast's head flailed around with its horns as it roared and bit frantically at the vines around its arms.

Gorman planted his massive feet into the ground and pumped at the steam valve on his vambrace. It hissed, ready to fire the harpoon into the nose of the creature. The barbed bolt screamed through the air and sank deep into the flesh of its nostril.

Gorman let out a deep roar, pulling on the rope with all his might, forcing the creature's head down as it struggled to escape him. It yanked and pulled but Gorman's sturdy stature held firm like a brick wall tethering the creature down.

Kaiden didn't hesitate at the opening in the chaos, he ran and jumped up on the top of its head, stabbing into its thick skull repeatedly. Arcus, sitting atop Saber, watched as the armored being that used to be his best friend slashed viciously at the creature with little effect with his short weapons.

Arcus rode over to Gorman, who was holding the beast's head at bay. "Do you have any more spears? Kaiden can't puncture through its thick bone!" he shouted, barely audible over the roar of the beast as it started to wear out its captors.

Gorman struggled to keep hold, his legs starting to buckle under the constant pull from the creature's head. "No," he let out in a gasp, holding his breath to tighten his resolve. "Kaiden, kill da damn thing!" he shouted, not even knowing if his friend inside the suit could even hear him.

The crowd erupted into gasps as the beast broke free of the harpoon. Its head was now free as it snapped as Saber, causing Arcus to stumble off when the wolf quickly backpedaled. Taja lay slumped over the back of the wolf and crashed into the sandy floor, limp from exhausting all her energy.

Everyone in the crowd let out cries of excitement as the creature moved its head around, snapping its snout wildly trying to get at the unconscious tigress and staggered human.

Gorman recovered from the snap of the rope that sent him flying to the ground and spotted the helpless lioness, plotting a rescue. Kaiden's grip on the beast's head failed as a violent strike forward knocked him loose. His body was tossed high into the air as his suit began to glow.

From the main balcony around the arena wall where the Akarian leaders of Amid gathered to watch, a sword was pulled forth. Grizby, the general of the organized Akarian military, cursed his sword as it glowed a bright golden hue and rose out of reach.

Grizby was a large hulking man, decorated in fur and scaled pelts from the fallen creatures he had slain. He carried a large two-handed axe and sheathed an ancient sword he had taken from the body of an elven general. The fine sword's glow burned bright before sailing through the dust laden air and into Kaiden's open hand as he leapt through the air. He landed on the beast's head and plunged it deep into its wounded skull. Rays of golden light broke through the creature's flailing head, causing its eyes to rupture and mouth to pour forth a boiling golden light. Its head slowly lowered down to the arena floor in defeat as its last gasp of air wheezed from its lungs.

Kaiden pulled free the sword and raised it high into the air as the golden lights gleamed from the ornate blade. He reached back as the sword infused itself into his armored back, the handle sticking several inches behind his head.

The crowd stomped their feet cheering, cries of victory echoing through the arena and shaking the ground beneath them. The massive walls lined with spikes and pikes shook from the noise as impaled skulls and bony skeletons broke free and rained to the sand from the fervent stomping.

Arcus, Gorman, and Kaiden stood beside the humongous beast they had just slain, against all odds, looking out to the crowd and settling on the balcony of leaders in pride. Kaiden's armor retracted, bringing him down to a knee as his body adjusted to holding its own weight again.

Arcus shouted in joy and slammed into Kaiden, wrapping his arms around his lost friend in excitement. "We did it, Kaiden, we took it down!" He cried out, as he noticed Kaiden's empty expression.

"You ok, kid?" Gorman asked, coming to his side, keeping his eye on the unpredictable crowd. The constant eruptions of shouting and foot stomping seemed to only get louder, making it hard to hear.

"Did I do this?" Kaiden asked, tilting his head to the beast.

"Sure did," Gorman huffed with a proud smirk.

"Did I do that?" Kaiden asked in a worried tone, pointing to the trail of dead victims from the beast's rampage.

Arcus looked at his friend in confusion for his odd behavior. "No, that is from before you two fell from the sky," he said, walking over to help Taja.

Gorman let out a deep grunt of caution and pointed to three heavily armed men standing above them in the balcony staring at them. Two other men dressed in leather hides ran into the field, and to either side of the balcony pulled on large levers that began to spin large gears. A balcony type structure of animal bone resembling a beast's jaw opened at the bottom as a staircase began to unfold. The men at the cranks tirelessly turned their wheels as the wooden stair structure extended down to the bottom of the sandy ring.

The men approached, making their way down the long, steep staircase. The largest man in front was almost unnaturally large for a human, tall and wide, wearing heavy long-haired pelts with thick leather armor. Large beast skulls wrapped around his bulky shoulders for armor with matching rib bones attached to his chest. The second man was not as big and wore more sophisticated metal and leather mixed armor adorned with etchings and silhouettes of creatures doing battle across his breastplate. The dark polished grey metal was intricately lined with silver trim with a soft leather undershirt. Following behind was the man with the large axe, now missing his sword. His face looked older than the others but less wear from the scorching heat of the desert. He wore simple studded leather with a heavy fur cape and mantled hood.

"I am Radagar," the biggest of the men announced as he neared the group. "I am the leader and King of the Akarian tribe, followed by my brother Aldair," he said as he motioned to the smaller man in the metal armor. "Behind me is my General, Grizby, commander of the Savage Ravagers Army," he announced as the entire crowd of onlookers become deathly silent.

The men stood before Kaiden and Gorman, not even phased by the size of the towering half-ogre with Aldair never taking his angry scowl away from Arcus, clearly furious he was still breathing.

Radagar did not hesitate to pass on formalities and get straight to the point. "I demand to know what power you used to slay the Titanovore," he ordered, glaring at Kaiden, who compared to these men was considered scrawny and weak in stature.

Grizby eyed the half ogre with an almost familiar look, trying to place where he had seen him before and the only one of the three without a permanent scowl affixed to their face.

Kaiden looked up to the massive King standing brave. "I don't know what the armor is, it just is," he replied, not intimidated by the brute in front of him.

"Back off, he be under me's protection," Gorman huffed, stepping forward with his chest puffed in intimidation.

"An ogre without a club, how terrifying," Radagar mocked as Gorman reached to find he was indeed weaponless.

With a grunt of impatience Radagar pulled out a long two-handed sword with a sharp curved tip, its sheer size and weight far too much for a normal man to wield. He thrusted it forward towards Kaiden's face, stopping less than an inch away as his eyes focused inward on the blade's tip. Mumblings and gasps reverberated through the crowd above.

"I will not repeat myself, boy, hand over the armor," Radagar shouted, the impatient look on his face intensifying.

"Just give it to him or he will kill you, Kaiden," Arcus pleaded, holding onto Taja's limp torso across his lap as he tried to wake her.

Gorman stepped forward, ready to lunge if the King dared to swing again, his short tusks protruding out of his stern growl.

Kaiden's resolve was unshaken as his fists clenched harder, sending surges of adrenaline through his system. "It is not mine to give, it is me," he stated through clenched teeth.

Aldair's gaze left Arcus and rested on Kaiden, eying him, attempting to calculate his next move as their standoff intensified.

Radagar, who was never known for his patience, shoved his sword high into the air and turned to address the crowd. "This weakling who has defeated the Titanovore holds an item of great power. By rights he is free for defeating it, along with these cowards," he shouted, gesturing to Gorman, Arcus, and Taja. "But they defy your King's orders and must pay for their defiance, with this power we will defeat our enemies in the north and take back what is rightfully ours," He screamed, thrusting his arms in the air as the crowd erupted in excitement.

Grizby took a step back, meeting Kaiden's gaze with a look of apology in his eyes. Aldair reached for the short swords at his sides, ready to flick forward his blades in a moment's notice. Before Gorman or Kaiden could react, Radagar spun and cleaved his sword against Kaiden's side with enough force to tear him in two. The heavy sword stopped abruptly with a golden spark, stopping less than an inch from Kaiden's shoulder. Underneath lay a single patch of armored shell that had materialized to stop the blade.

Radagar frowned and shouted in rage, bringing his blade up to strike again. Within a flash Kaiden spun and pulled his sword free, the glow from the blade staining the air with a golden streak as it effortlessly passed through Radagar's thick body, followed by his arm's blade materializing in time to leave a second slash across his torso. Kaiden spun to a stop behind where the King had stood, facing down Grizby and Aldair, looking for any reason to continue his attack. Kaiden's eyes glowed a bright white as he peered into his enemy's soul as the armor slowly materialized around his body out of thin air. The dark grey and black plates glimmered in the bright sun of the Akarian desert.

Aldair glanced quickly at Grizby, unsheathing his swords halfway as he cautiously glared between Kaiden and the giant half ogre.

Grizby's look of sorrow was for what he thought would be another ruthless murder by his king, dissipated at the realization of what he had just seen. Kaiden stood tall, staring at him, sword in hand, and he knew this young man was special.

Aldair looked to Grizby for some sort of direction of how they were going to proceed with their attack but got nothing. Instead, Grizby let his giant axe fall to the ground with a loud "Pffft" in the sand that could almost be heard across the silent stadium. Onlookers continued their captivated stares from the show they had seen that day, the ruthless Radagar struck down within seconds, without a fight. Grizby went to his knee, kneeling before Kaiden and lowering his head.

Aldair's head glanced around in confusion. "You kneel to this? Old man!" he shouted, motioning to Kaiden, standing unflinching above Grizby. "He is not even Akarian!"

"You will bow down to him; you know that is our way!" Arcus shouted, rising to his feet. "He not only defeated the most powerful creature ever tamed by our tribe but also struck down Radagar in a single blow." His chest heaved as adrenaline and anger coursed through his veins.

Aldair aggressively approached Arcus, his hands hovering over the hilts of his blades. "But he is not one of us," he rebutted in Arcus's face.

Arcus focused all his anger towards Aldair for the pain and embarrassment he caused Taja. "He is one of us," he argued, taking a brave step closer to Aldair, "Five years ago he fled here from Sanctuary in a prisoner transfer. He lived with me and Saber, a nobody, just like me," he said with pride.

Gorman stepped beside Arcus for protection, for he knew when Kaiden snapped out of his trance he would want to hear more from this kid. He put his massive hand on Arcus's chest for protection, pulling him back as he leaned in close to Aldair, a warning scowl on his face to choose his next moves carefully.

Grizby continued to kneel, unmoved by Aldair's objection. Aldair took a step back from the heated Ogre and lowered his hands from his swords, scowling with frustration at how helpless he was. Aldair was always arrogant and was used to pushing people around, but without his brother he now had little power. He convinced himself there would be other ways to get back at the invincible man, he would just need to outwit him later.

Gorman looked to Kaiden, puzzled at what he could have done to be exiled from Sanctuary, a prisoner forced to flee. He realized he didn't truly know the kid he was traveling with and went off his honorable and companionate demeanor, never thinking he was possible of crime. Gorman shook his head slightly in thought; he was a different person and had started over, and it was his true self that shown through now.

Aldair's eyes scanned for the best way to flee as Grizby stood tall in front of him. "Will you follow our new King, Aldair, like you did your brother?" he asked proudly.

Aldair spit at the battle hardened veteran Grizby. "He is not my King, he is an arker. Inflicted should be treated like an animal," he sniveled.

Grizby stood unaffected and turned to Kaiden, who stared motionless at Radagar's body. "Shall I slay the traitor in your name, sire?" Grizby asked in a noble tone.

The glowing light from Kaiden's eyes went dim as the armor began to retract, rows of scales flipping and folding into thin air as if they never existed. Within seconds his armor was gone as he stood beside Grizby with a stern look on his face. "No, that is not the way these people will live anymore. Lock him up in a cage and we will deal with him later to determine his intensions," he said sternly.

Grizby nodded and turned to address the people. "From this day forth we follow the new King, Kaiden, man born of the sword," he shouted, looking proudly at the strong young man before him. "All Hail King Swordborn!" he shouted as the crowd exploded into praise.

"Swordborn, Swordborn!" they chanted, the echo vibrating the walls around them.

"What happened?" Taja asked in a weak voice, tilting her head up to the chanting crowd.

Arcus quickly went to his knee to the new King and then turned to help Taja regain her footing to stand. Grizby, Gorman, and the entire Akarian tribe all knelt before their King. A single tear welled up in Gorman's eye, knowing deep inside the great man Kaiden was to become and this was only the beginning. He turned to grunt at Finn and realized he wasn't there to taunt, not wanting him to see him express emotion or having to tell him to shut off his mouth.

As the crowd continued to shout its cheers for the new King, Kaiden turned to Arcus, who was standing beside the tigress. "We need to talk," he said in a level tone and motioned for Grizby to follow closely. "We need a place to talk in private. Do you have a Paladin's Hall or keep?" Kaiden asked.

Grizby nodded. "You now have the King's Barracks or the beast vault at your disposal. Which would you prefer?" he said, motioning for them to follow.

"Whichever is closer, we have a lot to discuss," Kaiden replied, looking over the carnage in the arena, putting a knot in his stomach.

Gorman reached his hand out to the overexerted Taja, offering her support, and got a nod followed by a weak smile. He lifted her tiny frame and cradled her against his big shoulder.

Arcus let go of her hand as she was lifted. "Thanks, Big Guy," he said to Gorman, who only gave him a grunt in response and began to follow after Grizby. Arcus whistled, calling on Saber as he climbed up to his back to follow behind. He had never been in the King's Barracks and had always wanted to see inside.

Kaiden was taken aback by the grand but primitive architecture of the city. Enormous ivory polished bones jutted out of the ground crossing here and there with tanned beast hides and canvas fastened to the bones, making massive structures of different shapes and sizes. Most of the buildings formed two semi circles facing each other with a large fire pit in the center for simple housing. Heavy braided rope and stakes fastened everything to the ground, holding it down against the unrelenting desert winds. Tables, training dummies, weapon racks, and all types of entertainment could be found littering the courtyard area around the burn pit. Women darted from tent to tent carrying drinks and food, wearing barely anything but bruises and dried blood.

Columns of torches lined a path leading into a structure built into a Titanovore's skull, which was raised up twenty feet in the air by pillars of wood and stone. Long sharpened spikes protruded out from the base of the structure like an impenetrable wall of long quills. The skull's jaw hung open, sunken into the ground with a pathway built through the shorter teeth, almost as tall as a man.

They followed Grizby's lead into the heavily fortified building with several leather and chain clad guards, all wearing a skull on their right shoulder and bone pieces resembling a claw fastened to their chest, the insignia of the Savage Ravagers. The giant skull was open and spacious on the inside, lined with torches and benches with large racks of weapons holding well-crafted axes, swords, and spears. They walked around a spiral stairway around a central column that overlooked everything below. Ornate wooden and bone chairs circled around a large table with a map of Allterra sitting in the center with a thin layer of dust and sand on top. Tables with cages sat along the edge of the platform with piles of chains at their bases to contain their slaves for entertainment or prisoners, for torture or a mix depending on the mood of the King's men.

"This is where the King meets with his generals to plan battle strategies, or get drunk," Grizby said, motioning his hand towards the table where intricately whittled figures were scattered over the map.

"It looks like more drinking than planning to me," Arcus said, disgusted to find out there really was nothing more to higher command than filth and drunken fighting.

Kaiden was still in awe at the sheer size of the structures. He absorbed all the details of everything in Amid, impressed by its grand size. "Why is everything so big? How many people live here?" Kaiden asked, looking up to the empty ceiling far above them.

"Well, you will be pleased, my King, to find that our tribe is at an all-time high in power. We currently have nearly ten thousand warriors in our ranks, five thousand slaves, and over a thousand gorillatites, trained and ready for battle," Grizby answered, looking around the room, never needing to explain its size before. "But of course, that is not counting our exotic beasts we have been training, sire, and as for the size, it is rare the King and his subjects are ever off their mounts. If you like we can visit the beast vault? You can take your pick and it would be smart to start imprinting on them now." he added.

Kaiden shook his head in thought, still trying to process everything that was happening and the fact he was somehow the King of an entire city when he needed to urgently leave. These people were clearly a ruthless and survivable people. He wondered how he had fit in to the story and how he met Arcus, the place was going to need to make a lot of changes. Nobody but Grizby showed any respect of authority and would need to be reformed; it both worried and bothered him, for their ruthless ways would be hard to control.

Two large, well dressed and armored men approached from the stairs, stopping on the last step before stepping foot on the massive central platform. "Sir, we give our swords to you and pledge our loyalty," one of them stated as they stood unflinching and proud to their king Kaiden Swordborn.

"I am Treylis, rider of a great Bastilia, and I have come to serve you," Treylis said proudly.

"I am Broma, the only rider in Amid to tame a Winged Wurm, and I too wish to serve you," Broma added.

The two men looked at each other, pleased with their resume of great accomplishments, while Kaiden furrowed his brow being caught off guard. "Arcus, do you know these men?" Kaiden asked, still wanting time to question the young man about his age claiming to be a friend from his past.

Arcus slid down Saber's side and stood next to Kaiden. "Both of those beasts would be hard to tame, although you and I had been close to taking down a Bastilia a few years ago," he said fondly.

Kaiden, confused by the answer, looked to Gorman shrugging his shoulders, then looked back to Arcus. "Do you know these men? Can you vouch for them? Are they trustworthy is what I'm looking for," he explained.

Arcus perked up, still confused why his friend was acting so strange. "Oh yes, there are far worse men to put your trust in. Broma, I have seen on the outskirts with Treylis, who is new, and I hear is an excellent tracker. They mostly keep to themselves, which for here basically means you're as trustworthy as it gets," he explained, giving a nod of acceptance to the men.

"If I may, these men are loyal to my Savages and battle tested, both ride the finest mounts, and have excelled at training," Grizby stated.

Kaiden looked at them and nodded, his eyes traveling back to Grizby. "I have all these people that I don't even know pledging their loyalty to me but all we did was come to retrieve part of the warping stone in the arena. I didn't ask for any of this. Why are you not next in line to lead since you were under Radagar?" he asked, hoping to offload this huge responsibility on top of his others.

Grizby looked shocked at the question but was quickly ready with an answer. "That is our way, the strongest leads the pack and from what I have seen, no man or beast could hope to best you. Sire. Although some will undoubtedly try."

Kaiden looked over the men again and around the room, settling his gaze back to Grizby. "You seem different from most of the men I have seen here, Grizby, more refined and professional," he said, looking over at Treylis and Broma, realizing they were listening. "Your men show a similar reform, too," he added, as to not offend his commanders-to-be and watching grins spread ear to ear at getting a compliment.

Grizby looked down at the table, his quiet gaze taking him far back through his memories as his stoic and proud stature faded to a hint of sorrow. "I was a general to Paladin Malik many years ago. I served him well and led men to many victories, along with Commander Darvish," he stated, looking up to Gorman.

Gorman's mouth fell open in realization of who he was standing in front of, aged and weathered by a difficult life in the desert. He stood beside one of his old generals.

"I watched as Malik's hatred for the inflicted fueled him with anger and hate, and I began to question the validity of his cause. On a mission we went to defend a small farming town that was under constant attack

ARKANGEL

from the ember elves, and I disobeyed an order. A family there had adopted a stray lionel cub and raised it as their own after the elves had murdered its parents. The cub was inflicted, and Malik ordered me to kill the child and the family, but I refused. Instead, I helped the family to escape and flee south but my plan was discovered by Malik and I was labeled a traitor." Grizby's tone was calm and collected, his face emotionless as he recounted his story. "As punishment he took my daughter from me, killed my wife, and banished me here. I was well trained and rose up in the ranks here, doing what I had to in order to survive. I had hoped that one day I may be able to organize enough men to strike at Malik and get my daughter back and was instantly promoted general by Radagar's lust for war," he said, motioning to all the battle plans laid out on the table.

"Then I heard that Darvish was killed on the battlefield and Malik's reign was overthrown, so I stalled the armies, not wanting to attack the innocents of Sanctuary. I feared after so long I wouldn't even be able to recognize my daughter, so I gave up. With the recent caiman outbreak up north, we haven't been getting many shipments of traitors or prisoners, so I wasn't sure how the city was doing and I was able to persuade Radagar to wait out the plague for our attack," Grizby explained solemnly, keeping his emotions in check as he spoke.

Gorman gently laid Taja into a massive chair and rested his hand on Grizby's shoulder in sympathy. "Mes be Gorman, son of Darvish an he still be livin," he said with an uplifting smile.

Grizby let a small smirk escape his stone complexion. "You are Darvish's son? I remember training you as a young lad. It's an honor to see you again, a fine warrior you have become. That is excellent news if my sources were wrong. I thought It would take more than a few elves to take that man down."

Kaiden watched the worn-out war vet Grizby as he told his story. "You are free now, I will hold no prisoners here, and when we get back to Sanctuary, we can help you reconnect with your daughter," he said, wanting to help. "If I am to lead these people there will be a lot of changes and most won't be easy."

ARKANGEL

Grizby snickered, his mind returning from long lost memories. "It has been far too many years, I wouldn't even know where to start looking," he said hopelessly before regaining his stoic posture. "I plan to stay here and serve you, sir, if you will have me. I will be of great use to you turning this place around into whatever you see fit. I believe it is a good time for change, but where would you like to start?" he asked, renewed with purpose and hope, placing his fist to his heart with a nod.

Arcus spoke up to the mention of change. "I will serve you too, Kaiden. It will be how we used to always talk about," he smiled, looking over to his exhausted friend Taja. "Someone special told me once that in order to make change we must be the change," he recited proudly, placing his fist to his chest, mimicking Grizby.

Kaiden gave him a brief nod of acceptance before addressing Broma, Grizby, and Treylis. "We came here on an important task and need to return soon. We are working on finding a way to stop the plague to the north before it can kill any more people. Our journey led us here, but it is important we move back through the crystal in hopes of obtaining what we need." Sanctuary is in a lot of danger and is under a menacing threat, which we have been tasked to help deal with. While I am gone it will be up to you three to reshape Amid until I can return. Do you accept?" Kaiden asked, glad to have found competent men so quickly.

Broma and Treylis nodded and brought their closed fists to their chest. Grizby also nodded, his fist still held proudly against his chest. "Is this the caiman curse people have talked about? Normal men transforming into hideous creatures?" he asked.

Kaiden looked up to Gorman momentarily and back to Grizby. "Originally it was thought to be a plague where people were turning to the quillback salamanders and rampaging the lands, but we believe we have found its source and are on the path to stop it."

Grizby nodded his understanding. "That is the one, we haven't seen much of it this far south and for us it is called the caiman curse. It sounds terrifying, watching as friends and families tear themselves apart to kill each other. I myself haven't had the misfortune of seeing it," he said, unsettled.

Kaiden agreed and stared off for several moments, recounting the horrors he had seen in his brief memories. He nodded his head in agreement. "We need to be on our way. Until I return, I want you three to work on ending the slavery and mistreatment of all the woman immediately and provide a safe place to live in the meantime with food and work to start building their lives as equals, not possessions. I want to see the needless killing and stealing stopped, especially in the arena, and use your soldiers to enforce the new rules and keep the peace. I will deal with those who refuse when I return," he said, turning to leave back to the arena. "As for the arena, suspend its use and construct a fortified tower to the crystal above and keep it heavily guarded at all times. I want that used as the King's chambers, and you three may construct safe lodging as well," he added, feeling accomplished and a little excited to have a place of his own. "I know this is no easy task, but I believe that you can accomplish these things before I return."

Broma, Grizby, and Treylis all voiced their acceptance and followed up with a tap of their fist to their chest. Kaiden gave them an appreciative smile and motioned for them to leave.

"Arcus, may I have a word with you?" Kaiden asked, motioning him over to the other side of the table. "I must apologize if things seem strange to you, but they are to me too. I have lost all memory of anything past a few weeks ago. You said we knew each other before then?"

Arcus nodded in excitement as if his brother had been returned from the grave. "Yes, you lived here for around five years or so before the accident," he said, his voice changing into awkward uncertainty.

Kaiden nodded, catching the tone. "I woke up at Gorman's feet in an attack by the quillbacks and he saved me. Shortly after I was attacked again and found out about this armor and have struggled to find out where it comes from or even how to control it. We found ourselves helping Sanctuary with the plague since I am the only one able to withstand their attacks," he said, overwhelmed but somewhat relieved to be speaking with someone he felt he had a connection with. Something about Arcus felt familiar, like they had known each other for years, and it helped him feel at ease. He could sense an aura of good about the man despite his appearance and felt he could be trusted.

Arcus's face lit up at the sound of adventure. "You didn't have that armor before when you lived here, and if you did, we wouldn't have been so hard up," he laughed. "Do you know where you got it?" he asked excited.

Kaiden smiled at his excitement and intrigue in his story, and he could see how they would have gotten along together in the past. They were about the same age, both around six feet tall but Arcus had scruffy hair that draped down to his shoulders. "I don't, I just know it is there whenever I get into danger. We have other companions too, waiting for us to come back so we can put an end to the plague," he said, feeling the sense of urgency to return as his thoughts drifted to Nirayus.

Arcus placed his hand on his friend's shoulder. "I will help you in any way I can, brother. What would you like me to do?"

Kaiden smiled and placed his hand on Arcus's shoulder in gratitude. "Thank you, I am relieved to finally find someone from my past. You will be invaluable to me, thank you."

Arcus smiled, relieved to have his best friend returned to him with the prospect of adventure and leaving Amid finally at hand. He paused, inspecting Kaiden's smile. "Where are all your scars?" he asked in confusion.

Kaiden briefly looked over his hands and arms, inspecting them like he had never noticed, but found nothing. "I don't know. Did I have scares before?" he asked with a furrow of a brow.

Arcus shrugged. "Head to toe, but no matter, I just can't give you a hard time anymore and will have a little more competition now with the ladies," he chuckled.

Kaiden's thoughts went straight to Nirayus and how much he missed her. "No competition here, my friend," he responded with a smile.

"Oh no way, did you find yourself a girl?" Arcus asked excitedly, batting his eyelashes to mock him.

The grin only grew on Kaiden's face. "Let's just say I have dibs on the cute elven princess."

Arcus threw his hands down as his eyes shot open. "What! A princess? You really have been gone a long time. I can't wait to meet her; does she have a sister? Or wait, even better a bunch of maidens?" he asked excitedly before looking to Taja as his eyes turned to worry for her.

Kaiden put his hand on Arcus's dirty shoulder with a squeeze. "You will, my friend. Soon," he chuckled. "As far as the maidens, we will just have to see after we save everyone."

Arcus shifted to give him another big smile. "I can't wait to catch you up on all our adventures again." His eyes quickly moved back to Taja.

Kaiden nodded in agreement, smiling at the prospect of unraveling the mysteries of his past, and walked back over to the group.

Arcus returned to Taja, who was starting to recover quickly and was now alert. "You saved us in the arena." he said with a pause. "Well, you saved me several times and I wanted to thank you."

Taja's heart warmed up as she gave him a gracious smile. "And you me, hunter. Are you leaving with your friend?" she asked, a hint of sorrow in her timid voice.

Arcus looked back at Kaiden, his new sense of purpose swelling inside him. "Yes, this is a chance to be the change." He paused, seeing the loneliness in her eyes. "I would like for you to come. Maybe you can help fix the curse with your arking abilities?" he said, trying his best to convince her.

Taja looked down at her wounds she had suffered in both the arena and her short time with Aldair. "You know that's not how it works, and I am a danger to myself and others, I couldn't risk it," she said, rising on her weak legs.

Arcus put his hand gently on her arm. "No, you saved us and were invaluable in the arena, and if you weren't there who knows what would have happened to me, or more importantly Saber," he argued with a wide grin. "I know you are afraid of your gift, but this may give you a good chance to be able to control it and travel across the land helping others. We can stop the curse, or the plague, before it spreads south," he said enthusiastically, supporting her weight to stay balanced.

Taja searched Arcus's eyes and face, for she could see how much he had wanted to change and sincerity in his eyes. For once she would like to be a part of something, a part of a family. She feared failure and hurting the ones she cared for and was afraid to lose control. After what Arcus had risked setting her free, she trusted him and hadn't found that in a long time and if he trusted this strange human Kaiden, so much that maybe she could too and find her purpose.

Her snout vibrated with a low purring sound, a happiness she hadn't dared to feel for some time. "I will travel with you, hunter," she said with a shy smile.

Arcus slammed his hand on the table in excitement and then realized his obnoxious gesture. "Or you could stay here and feed Aldair in his cell?" he chuckled. "And you will need to carry your own weight, no more dragging you around in a net," he added with a smirk.

Taja slowly shook her head, already questioning her choices. "You have a lot to learn, hunter," she whispered.

Grizby was found waiting on the outside of the King's Barracks and led them to a dock suspended by ropes in midair, several staircases twisted and turned, leading to different levels above and below. A wide variety of beasts sat tied to the dock with the raised platforms providing easy access to the top of their mounts. Grizby motioned for Treylis to lead them over to his Bastilia with a massive platform and saddled perched on its back with enough seats to sit several people safely inside its shielded blockade of wood, to shoot their bows from.

They got on the back of the beast, which slowly backed up from its dock, Treylis standing further up than the rest, guiding the massive creature with a series of ropes attached to its head and chest.

"To the arena, Treylis," Grizby commanded as they took off from the floating docks to arrive at the emptied arena only minutes later.

"Now this is how a King should travel," Grizby said proudly.

Gorman reached for his gut to comfort it with one hand. "Mes no like da sway like a tree," he said with a sour look on his face.

Arcus and Taja gave a chuckle and looked to the equally uncertain Saber, whose knees wobbled at the lumbering movements. Treylis brought his bastilia up to a halt alongside the stone sitting high up in the air.

Kaiden drew his sword, looking at Grizby. "I am sorry about your sword, my armor tends to grab things it needs sometimes," he said, offering him the handle.

Grizby waved his hand in dismissal. "It is for you, Sire. It is a fine blade, fit for a King such as yourself. The crazed ember elf I cut it from spouted off about its great history of power, which at the time I thought was just a bunch of gibberish, but now I see that it was only making its way to you," he said, placing his fist to his chest in honor.

Kaiden nodded and used it to chip several shards from the prismatic stone. He placed them in a pouch at his belt and reached his hand out to place on Grizby's shoulder. "Take care, friends and good luck. I know this will be a difficult task and I will return shortly to help, thank you," he said, feeling the compassion in the weathered man's eyes.

"I will not let you down, Sir," Grizby said with a nod.

One by one the companions reached for the stone and disappeared into thin air. Grizby turned to Treylis, still holding his reigns. "Come on, boys, we have work to do."

CHAPTER 13

"DARKNESS IS UPON US"

When Kaiden touched the warp stone he instantly found himself atop Lu-Sea's glass tower. He was standing on the platform that had risen through the obelisk with the ceiling from her diamond shaped chamber opened wide like a claw, grasping at the warp stone.

Gorman appeared out of thin air and looked around hastily to catch his bearings, his hand firmly supporting his unsettled stomach. He realized they were on the platform high in sky below the suspended crystal. "Get mes down," he shouted, the icy wind swirling around his body.

Moments later Saber appeared with a whimpering whine as he tried to back into a safer position without much room on the platform. "Where are we?" Arcus shouted against the wind, looking through the dark clouds passing around their bodies.

A beam of light tore through the clouds as they began to disperse around them, washing away in the strong wind. Arcus and Taja gasped with the beauty of the land laid out before them, able to see for miles over the rolling hills and mountains in the distance.

Taja grabbed tight to Saber's fur, looking down to see just how high up they are from the ground with not much room for the teetering Saber and the ogre to stand on.

ARKANGEL

Kaiden looked up to Arcus who was completely transfixed by the view of Allterra below, like a little boy taking in the prospect of a grand adventure. "We are on top of Lu-Sea's tower in Shiver Spire Coast, if you think this is crazy, just wait until you meet her yourself!" Kaiden shouted up with a chuckle as the platform began to slowly lower inside.

"It be freezin up here," Gorman shouted down, threatening for the lift to move faster.

They lowered down into the room as the glass above slowly closed together at the top, enclosing them all safely inside Lu-Sea's chamber. Kaiden grinned when he saw Nirayus stand up to greet him, throwing her arms around him. She pulled away to look at the giant wolf and its riders only a few feet away. "I am so glad you are back safe, who did you bring with you?" she asked uncomfortably, noticing Arcusbane staring at her.

Arcus slid down off Saber's saddle who kneeled to the ground, unsure of his surroundings. "I am Arcusbane, Kaiden's best friend," he stated, his eyes barely visible through his long messy hair.

Nirayus bowed her head slightly. "I am Nirayus," she offered reluctantly, feeling uneasy with the dirty human. She looked over the wolf to see Taja sitting in the saddle, intrigued, only briefly ever seeing a lionel before but had heard interesting stories about them.

Kaiden sensed Nirayus's discomfort and intervened between the manner-less Arcus. "Everyone, this is Arcusbane, Taja, and Saber who are from Amid," he said, gesturing to the wolf.

Finn's eyes went wide with interest, knowing the type of people who lived in Amid and very curious about the stone's ability to warp them so far away in so little time, He wondered where the stone might go that his people had locked away in Krustallos.

"Arcusbane knew me before my memory was taken from me and is now one of us, with his companion Taja," Kaiden announced.

Taja's ears pinned back with a hiss at the mention of her being Arcus's companion, still a little uneasy with the sudden attention. She snapped out of it and greeted everyone shyly, not used to meeting new people or being a part of a bigger group.

Gorman reached his hand up to the dainty Taja and helped her down from Saber's back. "Mes glad yous come with us," he said with an awkward smile.

Finn took note of the interaction between Gorman and Taja and moved in with haste to stand awkwardly close. "Your markings are simply exquisite; the patterns are almost perfectly symmetrical all the way down to the tail," he said, following the darker lines of fur along the visible parts of her body. "I have heard that is the sign of strong blood, is that true? And I can tell you are gifted as well, it's a soft, warm power, healing? Nature? Your kind is known all over Allterra for their healing abilities, very well renown," he stated as he held her tail, making her feel extremely uncomfortable.

Arcus turned to Finn, standing up as straight as he could to appear bigger to the towering Aquarian. "Get your hands off her, she doesn't belong to you," he warned.

Finn quickly retreated as Gorman's massive hand pulled him back. Taja hissed as her ears pinned, her eyes darting back and forth between Arcus and Finn.

Kaiden raised his hands up to break everything up. "OK, OK, Finn can get a little, curious at times, he doesn't mean any harm," he started to say before being interrupted.

"I belong to no one," Taja said with a scowl.

Lu-Sea, completely entertained by the argument and misunderstandings of lessors decided to intervene, her ominous voice filling everyone's mind. "You will all have plenty of time to know and trust one another in your journeys ahead but for now the time for petty arguments are over," She commanded.

Everyone stiffened at the feeling of their minds being entered by Lu-Sea, as Gorman let out a grunt of frustration. "Yous don't be talkin, yous sent us to almost death," he roared aloud in a threatening tone as he moved closer to Lu-Sea.

Lu-Sea stood still, unalarmed or unblinking from the ogre's approach. She let him feel like he had any power, letting him walk up, taunting her with his enormous size until she flicked her wrist and brought him swiftly to his knees. His body went completely numb and slammed flat against the floor as her hand grasped at the air in front of his face.

Kaiden's urge to move in to help his incapacitated friend was denied, he could feel his entire body restrained as well but it was different like when he was encased within his armor. Something wouldn't let him move or lash out at the woman, something inside him must had known her to be a truly unpredictable threat. He could feel her presence like a blanket wrapped tightly around him but as he focused, he could almost feel his will unraveling the blanket until his attention snapped back to Gorman.

Lu-Sea stood up from her crouch, grasping at nothing, pulling it up towards her as a shadowed version of Gorman is dragged out of his body. His lifeless body lay limp at the ghostly figure's feet, it stared at her in terror. The ghost trembled and writhed in pain from being torn from its own skin and choked by her immense power.

Her voice deepened to a terrifyingly ominous tone. "I command the spirits of the living and am charged with much more than your minds can fathom. Do not threaten me over petty little things for I have plotted your courses and it must be followed exactly for you to succeed. One wavering choice will send this land plunging into an endless war and your journey will all be for not so from this point forward you will do as you're commanded," the voice rang in their minds.

Her eyes shifted ever so slightly to meet Kaiden's stare. "You best remember that hero, before this is all over you will be met with many choices, but you must follow your heart in making them. Sometimes they won't be easy and will often appear to be the wrong choice but stay true to your heart, never forget that."

She threw her fist down at Gorman's body as it began to flail violently on the ground until he started gasping for air. He rolled over to his side, weakened and sore, fighting to regain the strength to move his cumbersome body. He looked up into Lu-Sea's eyes with both horror and respect nodding his head in a slight bow.

"Mes sorry," he said, panting, barely able to breath as the sweat on his brow began to roll down his scarred face.

Lu-Sea's cold dark eyes moved to the other companions, looking for disapproval and found none. "Excellent, now hand me your warp stone shards and that simple necklace around your neck, hero," she said to Kaiden, almost sweetly.

Nirayus wondered how she could possibly know about the necklace hidden beneath his tattered shirt and was sent into alarm. That was the necklace she had made for him when he was young and possibly the only link they still shared together, that he might remember. She felt the urge to protest but lowered her head in fear, not wanting her spirit to be torn from her body like Gorman.

Kaiden looked down, confused about how she knew he was wearing a small stone necklace. He still didn't know why he had it, but it was his only personal possession he still had and knew it was special to him for some reason. He placed his hand gently around its circular shape hesitantly and pulled it free over his head to hand over with the shards.

Lu-Sea's face lit up with a pleased grin "Thank you Kaiden," she said as she grasped them tightly in her hands. Her fist began to shake in place and a blackened glow emitted from within. She let out a long-held breath of air and opened her palm to reveal the shards were now fused together within the center of the stone ring.

"Wear this at all times, it will prove invaluable to you in many ways," she said in an almost ill-omened tone.

Kaiden hesitantly grabbed the necklace and looped it over his head, securely sliding it back under his shirt. "You said that you would help us after we found out where the stone went, and we did that. It goes to the arena in Amid, I am afraid all the warriors you sent were just used for entertainment and food for their beasts," he said with grief in his voice, remembering the piles of bodies stacked all over the ring. "But I put a stop to it and your people are safe to travel now," Kaiden said with hope.

Lu-Sea's eyes returned to their vibrant yellow color as she gazed back at Kaiden like she was judging him. She could tell if he were lying or telling the truth, no, she was doing something else. She was searching his soul to make sure he was ready for what he would have to do next.

Finn took the opportunity to pull out the golden locket he had from the fight with Lanthor. "We got this from High Paladin Lanthor after he had turned from the plague and it was of a curious design, it seemed to enhance his strength and healing and we were hoping you could tell us where it came from and if it is in somehow in relation with the plague?" he asked to interrupt the awkward silence.

Nirayus saw the necklace and was reminded. "I have also seen one similar on the human Arkhunter Vixis, it enhanced her abilities and made her immune to arked energy," she said with a hint of frustration.

Lu-Sea grabbed the amulet in her dark orange hands and closed her eyes, reading its power within. Her eyes flick open to Kaiden and decided its origins should not be revealed at this time to avoid adding to the ever-growing conflict she sensed building within him. If he knew that the amulet held the remnants of power once stolen from him, he could lose all focus when his ultimate trials lay just ahead.

"I can say it is a token of pure good, procured by evil and when in the wrong hands can give them powers, they should not be able to possess as it was meant for one person to hold and one person alone," she said coyly, looking over the group. I shall keep it here until it is needed for," She paused, searching carefully for the right words to use. "Let's say it is too important and will be needed one day, I shall keep it safe until that day comes," she said as she motioned for an Aquarian girl to come retrieve it.

The beautiful young girl's bright purple, blue, and pink hair shimmered in the light as she walked along, her crystalline glossy skin distracting Finn away from the topic.

"Take that to the vault," Lu-Sea said aloud with her natural deep voice, turning to the companions with a look of sincerity and intense worry. "The time has come for all of you to play your parts in this. The plague you face is in fact the product of an evil scheme for power, one that every minute is gaining more power and momentum before it floods over the land," she said, looking to Kaiden and Nirayus standing closely. "Kaiden, you will take Nirayus north to Azul, the ancient city of angels to uncover a weapon you will need to help with defeating the evil that has yet to make itself known." Her face twisted as if suddenly in sharp pain. "Even now I can feel it drawing closer and the two of you will need each other to retrieve the weapon.

Lu-Sea steadied herself, resting her weight against a nearby table like she was about to collapse. She eyed the other companions, not liking the importance of the responsibility she was about to place upon them. "The rest of you will make all haste back to Sanctuary and will be charged with keeping it safe until Kaiden's return," she warned in a serious and grave tone. "You will need to convince Sanctuary of the imminent threat and to prepare for the worst in very little time," she said as her already troubled expression worsened. "The four of you will be forced to make very tough decisions, ones I do not envy you for but keep in mind that the cause is above us all individually and that if Sanctuary falls before Kaiden's return then all is lost. Search deep within yourselves and find the strength you need to continue to fight, not only for man, but for all of Allterra," she finished, with a stone-cold voice.

"Say your goodbyes, I will meet the two of you up at the warping crystal," she said, looking to Kaiden and Nirayus who have an almost panicked look spread across their faces.

Gorman was the first to move, more than ready to leave the tower at the first chance he had. He stepped up to Kaiden and Nirayus and placed his hand on Kaiden's shoulder. "Be's careful kid and yous keep him out of trouble," he said solemnly, looking to Nirayus.

Nirayus nodded with a slight smile, relieved she was not being sent to Sanctuary. She would take a dangerous journey with Kaiden any day over being walled up in a castle full of humans.

Kaiden looked up to Gorman. "Thank you, my friend, I will do what I can to hurry back. Warn Scarlett and ready the troops, I don't like anything that worries even Lu-Sea, be alert and careful."

Gorman nodded his agreement, looking out the door where Lu-Sea had exited with a scowl. "Now get mes out a here," he grumbled, limping to the lift.

Nirayus and Kaiden moved off the platform as Finn approached, wrapping his long arms around them. "I will keep Gorman safe and stop him from doing anything stupid while you're gone but I fear a job that big will be difficult so hurry back, find this weapon and we will be standing guard waiting for you back home," Finn said with a hint of sorrow in his voice. "If you find a baby Angel looking for a home be sure to bring it back to me so I can add it to my collection of friends and raise it as my own," he added.

Gorman let out a pained grunt. "Dat be all we needin, flyin fish," he said with a halfcocked smirk.

Kaiden smiled, a tear welling up in his eye as he chuckled. "Finn, please be safe and watch over Arcus and Taja. They have been through a lot. Watch their backs, okay?"

Finn looked back in playful fear of the lioness. "Yes, I'll do what I can," he promised.

Nirayus reaffirmed her tight grip around Kaiden's waist as he called Arcus and Taja over. "I wish we would have had more time to." He paused momentarily. "Reminisce, when I get back, I want to hear all about life in Amid, okay? Taja and I look forward to getting to know you as well, please keep this ruffian in one piece," he asked with an uneasy laugh, not knowing how to warn them about what to expect, being such outcasts in the town of nobility and how they may be treated.

Arcus smiled a deep brotherly smile to his best friend Kaiden, eager to help in any way he could and held his arm up parallel to Kaiden's chest. "This was our oath to always watch each other's backs." Arcus said with a wide grin. "But it looks like you are in charge of watching a lot more than just mine," he added with a wink to Nirayus, peering at her between the gaps in his long hair.

Kaiden raised his arm up to meet Arcus's. "Thank you, my friend, we will celebrate when I return," he replied, giving a warm smile and nod to Taja, who timidly approached a bit closer.

"You risk your life to help others and stop this curse," she said shyly. "You must be as great as the stories I have been told and I will do what I can to aid in your name," she said with a slight bow and turned to leave back to the platform, her tail wrapped around her leg for comfort.

Arcus motioned towards Taja as she left. "She has been through a lot and some of it is because of me but she is strong, and her word is her bond and I have no doubt in time she will prove herself," Arcus said before turning to follow her to the platform.

Kaiden looked at his team of companions as the floor began to slowly lower below. "Take care of each other," he shouted, with a sad wave of goodbye.

Nirayus gave him a squeeze around his waist and turned to walk with him up the stairs to where Lu-Sea had gone outside to the crystal. She stood unmoved by the freezing cold, wind blowing hard against her long hair and skirt.

"Kaiden, remember that what you are about to learn may be unsettling but you need to take charge of your destiny, rely on friends and loved ones that will help support you. Nirayus here is strong and will help you through the darkness ahead." Lu-Sea echoed in his mind with a compassionate look of worry on her face.

"Remember Nirayus he will need you, keep him focused. Your destines are intertwined with one another and you will play just as an important role if not more. I see the strength in you moon child, it reminds me of me when I was young," Lu-Sea's voice whispered in her mind amongst the howling wind.

Kaiden and Nirayus shared a look in each other's eyes, reassuring each other and together, reached up to touch the stone, and in a blink of an eye were gone.

Gorman and Finn watched the floors go by as the lift lowered, both feeling a big loss with Kaiden gone. "We's got him dis far," Gorman said with a shrug of his shoulders and a hint of sorrow in his voice.

Finn placed his webbed fingers on Gorman's shoulder and for once wasn't immediately pushed away. "Lu-Sea is very wise and like she said, we all have our roles to play, and we got him safely here and I'm sure he couldn't have done it without you big guy plus it's been a while since you have killed something right? I'm sure there will be plenty of quillbacks for you to fight when we get back," Finn said with a reassuring smile.

Gorman cracked his knuckles and nodded his head in agreement. "Could be usin a bit o' fightin," he said with a wide grin as the ball of his fist firmly smacked the palm of his other hand.

Arcus turned back from atop Saber to check on Taja. "Are you ok?" he asked with concern.

A slight smile came to her face. "It's nothing but danger and adventure with you isn't it, hunter? I'll have you know I am no fighter," she stated, almost playfully.

Arcus grinned. "Oh, I have seen you fight."

Taja crossed her arms over her chest, still wearing the shabby torn shirt Aldair had dressed her in. "There are other ways to do things," she huffed.

Arcus swung his leg over Saber's side to better face her. "You said I needed to change and now we have a good cause to fight for. I think it's the most important thing we could be doing and for once I am on the right side of it," he protested only to see the smile growing on her face.

"Are you saying I can't give you a hard time anymore Hunter?" she asked playfully.

Arcus let out a chuckle. "See if I bring you along next time?" he said, moving back into the saddle. "At least I have you, boy." he said moving his fingers though the wolf's long fur to scratch on top of his head.

Saber dipped and wiggled his back legs, wagging his tail in content while he growled his agreement. Taja panicked, almost being thrown from his back when he squatted, she grasped desperately for his long hair. Arcus looked back with a smirk on his face to see the shocked look in Taja's eyes.

Taja let out a groan, "Dogs," she said, unable to hide her smile.

The lift touched silently onto the ground with several stairs leading down to the main floor. Gorman saw his mother Tomba standing there with a giant Ogre towering several feet above her. His tusks jutting out several inches from his mouth with long brown hair and light, clean tan skin. He wore furs and leathers that took well to his burly, muscular shape. Gorman shook off Finn's hand in embarrassment.

Tomba stood beside the ogre with a look of excitement spread across her face. "Oh Baby, look, it be you's papa." she said, close to tears.

Gorman stepped forward, down the short flight of stairs in shock, not knowing the ogre before him but somehow seeing a resemblance.

"Son, is that really you?" Darvish said, opening up his massive arms to Gorman, who in comparison still looked like a young boy.

Gorman's eye welled up in tears to hear his father speak to him again and embraced him in a big hung. Darvish pulled back slightly, "I have heard you are quite the Hero son, making your old man proud." he stated pridefully.

Gorman leaned back, his eye red and dripping with tears that he struggled to keep at bay. "Mes thought you be dead," Gorman cried, "Me's failed yous," he managed, holding back his tears between sniffling for air.

Arcus and Taja watched atop Saber. Taja, overwhelmed with compassion watching the heart tugging reunion of the grizzled ogre she had barely known. A sting of pain struck her heart in remembering her own family and that she would never be able to see again, the memory of seeing her mother's fur pelt draped over the human hunter taking the air from her lungs.

Finn kept his distance, knowing that they must be on the move quickly and he fought the urge to commiserate the special occasion. He eyed the selection of steeds, trying to find the best suited for the long and harsh journey south.

Darvish squeezed Gorman tight, fighting back tears of happiness and pride for his son. Tomba rubbed her hand on Gorman's back. "Sanctuary be needin yous, Baby," she said, giving him a big hug. "We be proud of yous boy," she said, letting go of her son reluctantly and taking her place next to her husband.

"Mes come back father," Gorman promised, regaining his composure.

Darvish gave him a nod. "I know you will son, go give those lizards hell," he said in pride and reaching behind him to reveal a gift. He held up a simple blue sheet draped over a long item in his hand. "This is for you, it's our family sword, do you remember its name?" he asked with a smile.

Gorman stood with his mouth agape at his father's gift. It was his Father's great sword that he took into battle. Ancient relics like these were sometimes bound to a person or a family that were woven together in love or destiny, making a name for themselves through time.

Gorman nodded. "Dis be Redemption," he said weakly, barely able to speak.

"It is yours now son, it is nothing but a toothpick in these hands, let her serve you well," Darvish said as a tear finally broke free to trickle down his stoic cheek.

Finn approached, dragging the horses along with him. "I hate to break up this reunion here big guy but by my calculations the sun will be up soon, and we have a lot of ground to cover." Finn said as a big smile spread to his thin lips looking at Tomba. "Hello Mama," he said, expecting a rise from Gorman but getting nothing as he continued to blink wide eyed at his new sword.

Gorman strapped the large weapon to his back along with his spears. It was considered a great sword for any human but for Gorman could easily be wielded in one hand. He climbed onto the sturdy war horse Finn had brought him and looked back to his happy parents.

ARKANGEL

"Love yous Baby," Tomba shouted, pulling herself closer to Darvish.

Gorman nodded with a big smile and turned his horse to follow Arcus and Finn as they raced out the tunnel to Sanctuary.

CHAPTER 14

"THE ARKANGEL"

Kaiden opened his eyes, the brisk wind swirling around his body as the first signs of daylight rose over the horizon.

Nirayus let out a gasp. "Kaiden, look!" she said, pointing down to the ground hundreds of feet below them.

Kaiden looked down and saw that they were near the edge of a cliff atop a small stone landing. A pedestal stood in the center of the ancient, ornately carved stone landing below their feet. "I have never imagined anything like this," he said, looking up from the rock to the ground below.

The Azure mountains rose up to tall, pointed peaks but were suspended in air with a dark smooth stone that tapered down to a point to create a diamond shape. The glossy smooth stone on the bottom portion sunk down into bottomless holes in the ground. The entire mountain slowly moved like a boat in water, rocking in a calm sea.

Kaiden gathered his courage to peer over the side of the stone platform they were on to see the dark hole below with nothing holding up the mountain. He looked across the vast beautiful landscape, seeing everything from forest to plains and sea.

Nirayus looked across to the other mountains nearby to marvel at their sharp glimmering black stone the mountains were resting on. She wondered what ancient power could possibly be powerful enough to accomplish this great feat.

Kaiden reached down and grabbed Nirayus by the hand. "Come on, let's go up this way," he said, pointing to a stone staircase carved into the mountainside. The intricate detail carved into each plate must have taken days to create each step, he thought.

"I wonder who took the time to carve all these," Nirayus wondered to herself aloud.

They climbed the steps that continued higher and higher up the mountain face, switch-backing as they ascended.

"I wonder where these lead?" Kaiden asked, out of breath.

Nirayus giggled. "Who knows. They look elven to me, possibly even older by their designs," she said without even a hint of exhaustion in her voice.

She helped push him up the stairs until they came to flat ground. Pillars stood in two rows, intricately carved with the same ancient looking engravings as the steps. Kaiden looked closer to notice the carvings were of large beasts wrapping themselves around the pillars with massive wings and tails, breathing jets of fire that wrapped its way up the pillar. The art was like nothing he had ever seen before.

"These are not elven, we have no history of beasts like these," Nirayus said, intrigued, running her fingers softly over the smooth stone. "I wonder how old these are?"

Kaiden didn't respond, transfixed by the markings that were somehow familiar to him. He looked to the far side that jutted out from the mountain face, suspended by pillars underneath. It had railings out to the sides but not at the far end towards the cliff. Long grooves in the stone towards the end made it look like something big was pushed off at one point, maybe many big creatures judging by the sheer number of grooves like something was clawing at the surface.

He turned to Nirayus's voice. "Look, that looks like a door of some type," she said, taking several steps back. From several feet away it looked like a big round slab of rock had been rolled into place. Pictures of the winged beasts swirling around the top of the door accompanied by winged humanoids all seeming to be facing a central groove in the center. At the bottom of the door stood stick figure beings in varieties of danger with skeletal beings and horned demons rising up against each other.

Kaiden walked over to inspect the center hole when he collapsed to his knees. He shook and writhed in pain, his head flew back, and his eyes turned a burning bright white. His body slowly lifted from the cold stone into the air as his body began to flicker a golden light followed by a sonic boom shaking the entire stone structure.

Nirayus flew through the dust filled air and tumbled down several stairs. "Kaiden!" she shouted in terror, ignoring the pain she felt in her beaten body.

As he hung suspended in air his armor whipped out and encased him in his suit of scales as she realized the resemblance to the creatures depicted in the carvings. He then lowered down to the ground and stood autonomous, his eyes glowing an intense white as streams of smoke billowed forth.

Nirayus got up from the stairs and limped over to him. "Kaiden, Kaiden, are you there?" she pleaded as his gaze went to the stairs and he began to walk, ignoring her presence.

A loud pounding sound filled the air as the bright morning sun became blocked. Nirayus looked up to see winged silhouettes coming down upon them. "Kaiden, I need you," she shouted and pounded her fist on his shoulder.

He quickly turned to face her reactively to the attack, his elbow raised with his blade inches from her face. His eyes met hers, the white piercing light from his, forcing her to look away. At the sight of her face the blade within his forearm retracted and the arm moved down to comfort her, to make sure she was ok.

"Kaiden is that you?" she pleaded, grabbing onto his shoulder in fear.

Once the armor judged her to be ok it let her go and continued its autonomous march up the path. She raised her hands defensively as the shadows descend upon them. They looked like older featureless humans with large glowing eyes and elongated faces. They were tall and very slender adorned with heavy golden armor and wielded long bladed pole arms and glaives. Their pale white coloring tinted tan from the shine of their golden armor. They all fell hard around them, crashing to the ground with a tremendous force.

Nirayus let out an ear-splitting cry, raising her arms high into the air. The air around her rippled with lightning. It arked from her hands and body like a static surge hitting multiple winged creatures' full force. The flash of light soon diminished to reveal no effect on the creatures as she stood in shock. The creatures just stood there; their weapons held at their sides untouched.

She knew she had to protect Kaiden since for whatever reason he wasn't moving to react, her anger and terror turned to blind rage as the arked lighting from her fingers swirled into orange and red. She erupted into a flurry of flames, releasing a relentless fury on the creature beside her. Blast after blast, she cried out as it slammed against it, enough power to level a small fortress. The creature just stood unblinking, waiting for the onslaught to end.

She keeled over in exhaustion, all her power spent. She gave out a heartbreaking sigh of failure and closed her eyes, expecting to meet her end. At least Kaiden should be safe inside his suit she thought, her final thoughts finding solace knowing he would be ok as she grasped her necklace.

"Stand up," a voice boomed, the sound so deep it caused the dirt around her to tremble. She looked up startled and saw the creature didn't even have a mouth, how was it able to talk?

The booming voice echoed again. "Move."

Her head rang, wondering if all the sound was in her head. Nirayus stood and walked in line behind Kaiden, her legs weak from unleashing so much power.

Most of the creatures flew away further up the mountain, leaving one to escort them up, not threatening in any way but constantly reminding her to keep moving if she fell behind. She wondered if this weakness is how humans always felt exercising and getting tired.

After several hours of ascending the mountain the natural rocks and foliage subsided to sparse trees and dirt. They entered under a large stone archway and followed down a long flat path lined with smooth stone. Intricately chiseled buildings were carved into the mountainside and large stones like a small village. Dawn started to take over as the leftover sunlight was blocked by the massive mountaintop they were climbing.

Nirayus briefly looked behind her off the mountain and could see far over the land down below, it was truly breathtaking she thought to herself, wishing she could share the moment with Kaiden. The path was lined with ancient pillars with the same ornate looking designs as they had seen before but these held up curved stone ceilings to protect from the elements. Ahead she saw a large temple like structure with grand arching doors, and balconies with bannisters lining the upper levels.

They were escorted through doors so big she wondered how they could possibly move so easily and quietly without the strength of giants. She watched as Kaiden entered the building that opened up to a massive round courtyard with several different rings of elevation. Flowers and plants of all different variety adorned intricate statues of different animals, beings, and creatures that she recognized and some she did not.

Kaiden walked down the path of the garden and stopped in front of three of the winged creatures. The middle one slightly larger and looking more decorated than the others stepped forward to meet him. The creature towered easily three feet taller with long elegant rings of golden plate armor protecting its slender body. Its skin was a light white and grey with a unique scale like pattern imprinted into its skin. It reached behind its long billowing blue and gold cape to retrieve a metallic box. Suddenly a reverberating voice echoed through the chamber as Nirayus looked up to notice the inner walls were lined with simple benches.

ARKANGEL

"All rise my angels," it echoed.

Nirayus wheeled around realizing they were surrounded by easily hundreds of these angels as they all stood up and stepped up onto the benches with their wings unfolding and lifting high into the air. She turned back to Kaiden as time seemed to slow to a shocking halt as the winged creature bowed to him, lifting the box up in an offering.

The box flipped open to reveal a bright golden light that poured out like a glimmering steam causing Kaiden's armor to respond with a glow of its own. His armor began to shine so bright that it was hard to look at. Nirayus moved her head slightly, but her eyes couldn't help but stay transfixed on what was happening. Metallic blue light erupted from his body like veins encircling his armored joints and limbs. It pulsated as the golden glow subsided and he began to slowly lift into the air. He leaned forward slightly as large wings unfolded from his back and stretched outwards to his sides.

Kaiden fell back down with a ground shaking crash, cracking the stone beneath his feet. The wings stretched again and then folded up behind his back as the intense blue light dimmed.

"All bow to the Savior, The First Arkangel," the echoing voice pounded through the air.

In one motion hundreds of the angels all took to their knee where they stood to face Kaiden. A rumbling humming sound filled the air, the vibration so intense it was like the air itself was replaced by a thick insatiable sound as they all began to chant.

"We bow to thee, first of your kind, united soul of being, creature, and creator. We pledge our souls to you and our service for eternity to come. We pledge our strength and loyalty to the divine among men. We bow before thee as The Arkangel, guardian of the land and thus brings us to an end of one sacred vow and into another."

Suddenly Kaiden's armor retracted as he stood there wide eyed, taking in the sights around him. A new blue and gold cloak draped from his shoulders with folded wings embroidered to the back. He looked in shock at the kneeling angel before him, looking straight into his large, globed eyes. Kaiden could somehow sense the creature's soul, one of purity and loyalty that lay within its timeless shell.

"Who are you?" Kaiden managed, feeling calmer from the creature's aura of purity.

"I am Azeal the eternal," came the thunderous sound as it moved its head slowly. "I know you seek answers, my friend, and they will come in short time. First you must pass through the eternal gate as has been foretold to face your final trial of ascension," it said standing to almost twice Kaiden's size.

Nirayus ran and threw her arms around him. "Kaiden," she cried out in relief. "I was worried about you; I thought I lost you in there." she said, looking distressed.

"I know, I couldn't, it was like I was trapped in a cage, and I couldn't move," he replied, surprised he could even remember.

"You remember what happened?" she asked.

Kaiden nodded his head slowly in thought, hopeful that he may be finally be gaining control. "I was conscious, just unable to move or help you when you flew down the stairs, it was like I was being pulled to do something else, to follow," he said apologetically.

The three angels in front of him moved to the back of the massive courtyard where a hidden passageway opened into the wall. Two of the angels moved to either side, gesturing for them to pass through. Azeal, Kaiden, and Nirayus followed through and out the back of the mountain onto a ledge overhanging a drop all the way down and off the mountain.

There was a staircase that swirled up the backside and up to the very peak of the mountain. The circular stone platform displayed the incredible detail of star constellations and orbs all revolving around the central stone globe. Symbols of an ancient language encircled the entire platform with a central pole stationed in the center of the globe. The elegant metallic pole split in two and reached up several more feet into a semi-circle.

Azeal approached the rod and touched his hand to it as it began to glow a bright pink and purple color. The tips of the rods connected with a beam of light that started to spin, collecting in mass. The mass turned into a spectacular weave of pink, purple, and blue clouds with small bolts of electricity wrapping its tendrils around the swirling mass.

Azeal motioned for Nirayus to step to his side. "You are the key to opening the gate," the deep voice echoed.

Nirayus glanced at Kaiden, a worried look plastered to her thin face. "What do you mean?" she responded, caught off guard.

Azeal bent down and took a knee beside the short elf. He glanced at her dress encircled with the constellations of stars on the blue and black faded material.

"You are an Arkmage, are you not? One of the few beings capable of harnessing different forms of energy? You displayed your superior abilities down on the mountainside when we found you," the voice announced as he reached up to take one of her hands in his.

Her hand was so small compared to his, she thought, and was startled when she realized he only had three fingers and a thumb on both sides of his hand. He cupped her hand in his and peered into her eyes, his globe like glossy stare, peered deep into her soul. His vision was completely different than that of a normal being, which allowed him to view her not only as a physical person but see exactly who she was on the inside and able to see what made her unique, all within a glance.

"Yes, you have power, great power, though most of it is still locked away and still unknown to you. It lay dormant, deep within you, blanketed by emotional barriers, waiting to be released," Azeal said calmly as he looked to Kaiden with his featureless stare. "There is more in here, something has been locked in your mind and hidden from you from long ago. I cannot unlock such a barrier and must be revealed for yourself in time," He warned as he stood back up in front of her, satisfied she could do what was needed.

Nirayus felt suddenly breathless and weak yet defensive and judged. There was more to her that she didn't know about? How was that even possible? Who could lock up parts of a person in their own mind? She felt overwhelmed but forced herself to focus on what she needed to do so that Kaiden could complete his trial. She filled herself with resolve to be strong and pushed aside her thoughts and feelings.

"The gateway before you is ancient and primal, the original creation of this land. It was created with the basic elements and can only be activated with them," Azeal's voice echoed.

Nirayus shook her head. "I can't Ark that many elements all at the same time, it isn't possible," she said, starting to tremble.

Kaiden stepped close to her and put his hand gently on her side, squeezing her tight. "Yes, you can, I have faith in you," he said confidently.

She turned and rested her head against his chest, hugging him close as her eyes began to well up in an old memory or her mother.

"I never mastered my gift," she said, looking up into his eyes while tears began to freely roll down her soft white cheeks. "I refused to learn more about it on that dreadful day so long ago," She cried, lacking the strength to hide from him any longer.

She looked into his eyes, scared, alone, overwhelmed, and terrified she would let him down. "I didn't know how to tell you before, Kaiden. I was going to, but you are so important to so many people I couldn't distract you away from them," she cried.

Kaiden gently lifted her chin up with his hand, looking into her eyes and for the first time looked straight through her, seeing into her being. A turbulent frenzy of power and fear encased within a shell of love and loyalty. He saw himself there at the center of her thoughts.

"It's ok, Nirayus, what are you not telling me?" he said, his feelings swirling inside himself like wildfire.

She gently reached and pulled on his necklace around his neck, pulling it free from his shirt to hold gently in her hand. "I gave this to you when you were young," she said, feeling relief for finally telling him the truth. "The day my mother was murdered, I was lost and dying of starvation, but a little boy found me in the woods and gave me food and this to help find my way home," she said softly, caressing her golden compass with her other hand. "It was you, you gave me this and in return I made you the smooth stone you wear around your neck," she said with a chuckle, thinking it adorable he would still be wearing a rock over fifteen years later.

Kaiden was taken aback by her words and confused. "You have known who I am this whole time?"

She smiled up at him, her legs feeling weak from her trembling as he held her close. "I had no idea who you were and returned to that same place every year, hoping to find you again. Then fate brought us together in the gardens, but I had no Idea it was you until I saw you at the lake getting dressed and noticed this," she explained, her face brightening with a smile.

Kaiden was shocked, thinking back to all their times together and having no idea of their connection. He was frustrated with himself for not remembering, he should have known somehow. He felt bad that she felt the need to keep this from him and now understood why they had such a strong connection. Lost for words he pulled her close and embraced her as the rest of his worry and stress momentarily drifted away.

Azeal embraced their shoulders with one of his massive hands. "Your souls have been destined from the beginning, this is all meant to be and everything that led you here no matter how tragic and difficult has all been to prepare you for your trials ahead. You are two halves of a sphere and together you are whole," he explained, lifting their spirits.

"We have waited here, protecting this gate for thousands of years, waiting for the two of you to find your way here. That was our part and although you are young you both hold great power within you," Azeal said, removing his hand and stepping back towards the gate where the swirling cloud of energy was spinning furiously in place.

Kaiden pulled back slightly to look into her big blue elven eyes and brushed a tear from her cheek with his finger. "We will do this together," he said with a loving smile.

They held their arms out towards the gate as Nirayus's hand began to pulsate into vibrant blues and reds. Kaiden's hand for the first time began to emit a soft golden light with mists of grey swirling around his fist.

"You can do this Nirayus, I believe in you."

Nirayus grit her teeth and squealed in effort, her hand now rapidly changing from oranges, blues, reds, purples, greens, and then white. Their hands erupted with raw power blasting a beam of energy forward and into the mass as it started to grow. Bolts of energy arked between them and lashed out as the beams furiously strengthened and grew. In a flash the mass exploded, knocking them back several steps as their arms cooled down into their normal skin tones. They peered into a swirling vortex of misting energies blending together and arking to the tip of the poles.

"Hurry Kaiden, you must go, there won't be much time but the answers you seek are through that gate," Azeal said in wonderment, holding up a hand to block Nirayus's advancement.

"You must go alone; she will die if she goes with you," Azeal warned.

Nirayus looked to Kaiden, her hair waving wildly in the storming winds from the gate. "But what will happen to him?" she asked nervously.

Azeal's booming tone did little to settle their nerves. "If he is not strong enough, he will perish, but his armor will delay it and will help protect him from the harsh environment," he explained, motioning for him to go through.

"Be careful Kaiden and hurry back to me," Nirayus begged, trying to stay as strong as she could for him. She believed in him and their future and knew with everything they had been through together and apart that they would find each other again.

Kaiden leaned in close and gave her a long kiss, his heart beating rapidly in his chest as he squeezed her tightly. "I will come back for you no matter what," he promised before taking a deep breath and turning to fly into the gate.

CHAPTER 15

"FORTIFY THE GATES"

Finn and Gorman rode hard and fast through the long day, their horses on the brink of collapsing from exhaustion. Saber, being far faster would ride several miles ahead to scout, then come back to report if anything were amiss. Gorman's horse slipped and tripped forward several feet, barely recovering before coming to a halt and refusing to move. It kicked and jerked its head, flaring its nostrils in protest as it went to drink from a small stream nearby. Finn stopped and let his horse follow, to quench its thirst.

"Wes stuck," Gorman shouted angrily, frustrated the horse's health was failing.

"Why Lu-Sea not send us in da stone?" Gorman shouted again, kicking at the dirt road in a fit.

Finn approached cautiously with a finger held up in interjection. "I do not believe there is a stone in Sanctuary and the desert sands surrounding Amid would have only hindered our progress further so I believe we are taking the best route possible unless you know of any others she spoke of and where they might go?" Finn explained, trying to help but only angering the ogre further.

Gorman gave Finn an angry glare as he shook his fist. He was so worried they wouldn't make it back in time that he lost sight of finding a solution instead of cursing at the problem. At this rate they were easily another day away if they didn't think of something. His mind raced from good to grim as he toyed with the thought of just taking Saber for himself and riding ahead.

Finn looked back to the mountains they had passed over, the dark clouds that had gathered on the far side. He was glad to be past the frigid cold at the very least and decided they would get there when they needed to and there wasn't anything they could do about it. He turned to look up the road when the sound of growling could be heard from the distance.

Saber came sprinting back from up ahead, his speed on the open road was truly something to be desired by any warrior.

Arcus called down to Finn. "We have company, there is a female hunter riding our way fast and will be here shortly, what should we do? She could have a fresh horse we could take?" he added looking to their horses laying down beside the stream. "Well at least it's alive," he added sarcastically.

Gorman shook his head in disapproval. "Mes be no raider," he huffed, torn on what was the greater good.

Arcus scowled, taking offense to how his idea was taken. "She could just give us the horse if we explain the urgency," he clarified.

Taja dismounted from Saber's back and went to tend to the horses, her heart ached for the strain they were putting on the animals. They were being pushed to the edge of life so they may make it back to Sanctuary as soon as possible while not really knowing the true urgency. She crouched in between them as a soft green light emanated from her hands and washed over their bodies like a refreshing spring.

Vixis's horse breathed heavily as it sprinted over the hill where it came to a sudden halt. She leaped from her horse in front of the companions, her sharp eyes surveying the placement of their weapons and readiness to attack.

She lifted her hands in plain sight to put them at ease. "Where is Kaiden?" she demanded, breathing like she was the one running the last few miles.

Gorman, Finn, and Arcus shared a look of puzzlement. "And who would be the one looking for him?" Finn asked hesitantly, noticing she resembled an Arkhunter with the golden amulet draped against her chest.

Gorman reached for his sword, releasing the massive blade from its sheath with one arm, "Mes seen dat neckless before Arkhunter," he warned in an alerted tone, whirling his sword around, ready to strike.

Vixis backed away slowly, not used to having to back down from a fight. She held her hands up to try and keep them at bay and calm. Though her heart pumped quickly within her breast with excitement, usually getting a rush for battle, especially when she sensed one with the gift nearby.

"I am Vixis," she shouted. "I have been sent by Paladin Rhyker and Scarlett who said he had traveled this direction with the half ogre and Aquarian," A smirk came to her face. "Just a guess but I would assume that would be the two of you. But you, are not Kaiden." she said, eying the scraggly haired Arcusbane.

Arcus playfully smiled as he pushed his long hair from his face, eying the beautiful warrior in front of him. "Who says I ain't?" Arcus responded.

Vixis couldn't help herself from flirting, always up for playful banter. "Come prove it honey, let's see what you're packin," she said coyly, lightly biting at her bottom lip, her gaze unmoved from his face.

Finn walked up curiously and reached for the amulet around her neck to inspect it closer, it was an exact duplicate of the one they had found around Lanthor.

"Oh sweetie, you'll need to buy me a few drinks first before I'll let you do that," she said with a grin, batting his hand away.

Finn looked at her confused by the meaning of her statement. "You are an Arkhunter correct? The one that attacked Kaiden and Nirayus in the gardens because if you are still looking for them you are in the wrong place, they are off to who knows where to retrieve a weapon to stop the

ARKANGEL

plague and I wouldn't mess with him, he won't take too kindly to you continuing your attack on his mate," Finn said with a small bounce of his mandibles.

Arcus wheeled Saber around, closer to Vixis. "What did you need with Kaiden? I am not him, but I will gladly help you out in any way I can," he asked with a big smile curling on his face.

Vixis shook her head at the band of misfits and sighed. "I have been sent to tell him that the city is about to be under siege, and he may be the only one that can help turn the tide of battle in our favor. Thousands of Sanctuary's soldiers have been turned into those salamanders along with an army of ember elves. They march towards Sanctuary as we speak." she said hastily with a sense of great urgency growing in her tone. "Rhyker and I barely escaped with Lanthor, but we made it to Sanctuary where they are safe, for the moment," she added.

Gorman's eye opened wide. "Army be marchin on Sanctuary? Embers? Lizards?" he asked, in fear, barely able to spit out the words.

Vixis nodded her head before returning to her horse, ready to continue searching, no matter where it took her. She knew she owed the people of Sanctuary a great deal after blindly following Martis. "Where did he go? I must reach him before it's too late," she pleaded.

The companions all shook their heads, Finn cocking his to the side in confusion. "Lanthor is dead, he was turned and attacked us and Kaiden had to put an end to him, but I helped, well we all helped, I just did the most I believe," he added excitedly.

Vixis nodded in understanding. "I was told by Scarlett what happened but that wasn't Lanthor, it was some kind of abomination of Martis's who has betrayed us all and is the cause of the plague and is the one leading the siege, but he fears his brother and that's why we need him," she said while going for her horse.

"He be gone," Gorman grunted. "We's all dat be left, he send us to protect da city," he said in pride, putting his sword firmly back into its sheath.

Finn motioned towards the horses and Taja. "We have been riding for almost two days to get to Sanctuary and need to get there as fast as we can to help prepare, we were sent by Lu-Sea and she sent Kaiden and Nirayus to get the weapon, but he will return," Finn explained with a twist of his head. "Will you come with us?" he asked, curious at the opportunity to further question an Arkhunter.

Vixis was surprised by their offer to join their party. Arkhunters were used to working alone or with mercenaries only in it for a few coins or drinks, never actually part of a party with purpose. "I suppose we will just have to make do for now, won't we?" she said slowly. "If we hurry, we may be able to slip past the army before they reach the north wall."

Taja perked up to the sound of the new voice, her trance of healing touch interrupted as she petted the exhausted horses. She looked to see the new human woman speaking to the group as Arcus gawked at her beauty, her ears unknowingly pinned behind her head.

"The horses will be fine in an hour or so. They will be good as new and should last through the night," she said gently, her glare intentionally ignoring Arcus.

Vixis lurched as Taja approached, every fiber in her being telling her to strike the arker down but forcing herself to resist. She knew Martis was corrupt and had lied to her of the evil deeds of the inflicted, so she steadied her sword arm, resisting the urge to attack. She had no idea the depths his mind-washing had affected her, but she prided herself on her own stubbornness.

"We don't have an hour to waste if we are to beat the army to Sanctuary," Vixis argued.

Arcus tripped over his own words in excitement. "You can ride with us, Vixis, and leave your horse for Gorman and then Finn can alternate between the two tired horses to ease their burden," he offered as Taja let out a hiss in protest.

Vixis chuckled at the tension and accepted the offer without a thought, leaping up onto Saber in a single jump and wrapping her arms around Arcus's waist. "Alright, show me what you've got, see if you can impress me," she whispered in his ear to toy with him. Taja reluctantly crawled up to the empty spot amongst the equipment attached to the back of Saber's saddle, a deathly scowl pressed to her face.

Finn and Gorman mounted their horses and took off down the road as fast as they could go with renewed energy and urgency spurring them forward.

Dark energy arose from Martis's hands, swirling up into the night sky. He had gone over what he was told to do over and over again, practicing in his mind until every detail was flawless. His time to prepare had been cut short and he had been so close to completing he would have to make do with a lack of power, but was confident his sheer determination and will would more than make up for it. He was short on the lifeblood needed to fuel his incantation, and despite the hundreds of barrels full, it wouldn't be enough, and the blood from the slaughter in the gardens was now wasted.

Black tendrils of lightning lashed out around him in rage as he steamed in anger. Why was he cursed with such incompetent followers? He knew his time to reign was drawing near and the thought of his power made him squirm and shiver. His eyes began to glow bright red and his face contorted, long sharp horns punctured through his skin as he screamed in pain, the same pain that brought him so much pleasure. He would no longer be the charming man he once was, he would be more of an icon of pure power and fear, he thought as streams of blood rushed down his cheeks from his eyes.

He lifted his arms up into the sky as the black tendrils continued to lash out around him. "I call to the creator himself. Our time is almost upon us, I will unleash you from your prison and we shall rule this land unchallenged together!" he shouted maniacally into a chuckle as the mists of chaos around him billowed through the lizard filled fields of Solstice Gardens.

He stood still amongst the storm and called out in a dark ominous voice that shook the ground like a quake. "Feora, Feirun, gather the troops, it is time we march to take what is ours," Martis shouted.

Feora found herself feeling uneasy with what she witnessed in Martis's transformation, causing her to shutter and fumble as she left the destroyed chapel. Her chest felt tight with panic, she hadn't realized the true darkness of his plan and suddenly wasn't comfortable with his sinister look. What had he done? She thought they would rule together but was only being treated like a pawn in his game. She shook away her thoughts, Martis was the strongest man she knew, and she was confident he knew exactly what he was doing. She would do anything in her power to help him succeed.

Feora drew out her sword and walked across a piece of fallen rooftop that lay across a wagon. She stood high into the air holding her sword towards the dark sky as she commanded her deadly army. "My precious Salamanders," she bellowed as her chest heaved with exhilaration and excitement. "Are you hungry? Hungry to take what is ours? To take what you want? Tomorrow the world will belong to us, and you shall hunger no more," she called out, thrusting her sword into the sky.

The creatures roared in rage, tearing and clawing at each other and the ground, rummaging for the pieces of torn flesh still scattered through the estate. They all looked up to Feora on the tower of wreckage and formed into rows, their warped bands of leather and plate mail clanging together as they moved. She looked to see Feirun commanding his troops of embers in the camp they had taken over from the humans and knew their time for battle drew near.

Feirun was in a complicated position, he needed a victory, needed to knock the humans down before completing his conquests elsewhere. He had loved his queen and would do anything to get her back from Lu-Sea, but first he needed the humans out of the way. He hated Martis and his selfishness but thought he was the only one powerful enough to destroy her. Since their defeat in the great war, he had been building and plotting his revenge and would stop at nothing to get his beloved queen back. He found it a twist of luck in his favor that his enemies were about to destroy themselves. The true might of the ember elves was in their relentless lust to conquer and the mighty Feirun would take over the weak any way he had to. He didn't believe in the human's devotion for higher powers and saw it as their delusional weakness, one he wouldn't hesitate to exploit. But for now, he would do as commanded, biding his time.

"My Embers!" Feirun shouted.

"Draw your swords, harden your grips, and let your hate burn deep within. We will destroy the humans hiding behind their walls and spark the beginning of a new era, the era of fire." he shouted recklessly as he raised his arm, wielding his king torch gauntlet and spraying a stream of intense fire over thirty feet into the air. Shouts of battle cries rang out over the fields as they bashed their weapons together, shouting praise to their king.

Martis's movement became labored and disjointed as he jerked his limbs around as if somehow trapped within his own body. He watched Feora command his troops into marching formation. He managed to move his hand as it trembled with uncontainable power as he gestured to the stack of barrels by his convoy of wagons.

"Stack the barrels precisely where I marked, not one shall be off, or I will tear you to pieces where you stand," he hissed as his heartbeat rapidly within his chest. His excitement heightened beyond anything he had felt before; it was his power growing. True power was finally his at last and Kaiden wouldn't stand a chance.

He counted the barrels that were stacked intricately on the wagons. The weight was too great for a horse to bear so he had several of his Lizard beasts chained together to pull the wagons. They were essential to his plan, the blood from his sacrifices so carefully drained into the barrels, almost enough to amplify his power beyond limits, enough to tear his creator free from his plane and into theirs. He let out a rumbling giggle as he watched the last of the barrels being strapped into place.

"Now move!" he shouted, his voice sounding like thunder in a storm, his dark mass of clouds following from above.

The companions rode hard, and their steads were on the brink of death. They came to a stop at the top of the last hill before entering the forest surrounding Sanctuary. From there they could see Solstice Gardens and a thick mass of black and orange figures seeping from its gates.

"Look over there," Vixis pointed to the swirling clouds flickering black lightning into the early morning sky like a tainted sickness spreading through the air.

They stood in shock, unable to count or fully fathom the sheer force marching towards Sanctuary. Thousands upon thousands of Lizardmen and Ember elves marching in line after line, clanging their weapons together and shouting to praise to the destruction to come.

Gorman clenched his fist and hit his knee in anger. How could the paladins fall so easily into this war, how could they have been so blind? For the first time in a long time, he felt the cold reality of defeat. He reached back and drew Redemption from its sheath, its bright blade still gleaming in the early darkness. He felt hope again and his mind went to wonder what Kaiden was having to face without him in order to get the weapon they needed. Kaiden entrusted this burden to him, and his resolve quickly strengthened as he shouted.

"To da city!" Gorman cried, focusing his mind on one thing alone, not letting his friends or his city down. He kicked at his tired horse, bringing it to a full run down towards the city. Finn mounted up onto his backup horse and released his other to be free, hoping it would stay far away from the castle. Saber took off after them, seemingly unhindered in his eagerness to run despite the extra passenger.

They arrived at the gates shortly after, frantic soldiers preparing for the worst as they brought bundles of arrows to the wall and lay logs down in an attempt to hinder enemy movement. A guard stepped up to question them, his eyes stuck on the massive wolf breathing heavily in front of his face.

Vixis jumped down, feeling comfortable to always take lead. "They are with me, Rhyker's orders," she stated, paying little attention as she pushed the guard to the side.

They opened the double doors of the side gate as Saber managed to squeeze himself through like a puppy excited to see inside a new room. The inner courtyard was teaming with soldiers doing everything they could to prepare with such little notice. Most had never seen war before with the last one coming to an end over a decade ago. Gorman eyed the recruits, watching them in their tasks, listening to them squabble. With an enemy like the plague, it was hard to judge the best way to deal with it when their walls had done little to protect them so far.

Scarlett and Rhyker entered the courtyard followed by the battalion of heavily trained and armored Paladin guard. Vixis spotted Rhyker's bright gold battered armor and sprinted to his side as Finn and Gorman followed closely behind. Arcus stayed close to the gate, watching as the torrents of black lightning tendrils approached, filling the sky with an eerie darkness and blotting out their much-needed light.

"Rhyker," Vixis cried, waving to catch his attention amongst the chaos. "I found Kaiden's companions, he had separated from his party already but is headed this way with some sort of weapon."

Scarlett motioned for her troops to continue as she stopped to join the conversation. Arcus tied a lead to Saber's saddle, motioning for Taja to stay put, a worried look of contention growing in his eyes, never envisioning the sheer size of the threat he had witnessed. Saber growled when his master left, unsettling the guards who passed by.

"We have little more than half their estimated numbers and that doesn't include ours that may turn during the battle," Rhyker admitted, his face washed over with the weight of stress.

Scarlett nodded in agreement, a small smile of relief showing at the sight of the companions return. "We have the walls, and we have the training, Rhyker, that's far more than the quillbacks have. Our archers will take them out with ease." she said, reassuring herself in wavering confidence.

Rhyker shook his head. "These things are armored now, Scarlett; our arrows will have little effect and the ones that do find their marks will only anger them further," he said as he embraced his chest in guilt of all his fallen men they were now plotting to shoot down.

Scarlett's eyebrows furrowed into a frown. "What do you suggest we do? They hold nothing back in melee, we cannot meet them in the field, and we do not have the time to rally the necessary horses to put together an effective cavalry attack, it would be suicide and only add to their numbers," she added in frustration.

Gorman looked around the inner courtyard where they were standing, the first line of defense against a siege. He saw all the long ballista bolts being hoisted up to the towers along with crates of ammo for their scatter cannons.

"We's has enough ammo for ballista's and da scatter cannons?" Gorman asked out loud in thought, looking to the other wall's defenses. "No catapults?" he added.

Rhyker briefly glanced to all the towers looming up above and then back to Scarlett for confirmation.

"We have a good number of bolts for the ballistae and the scatter cannons we have enough iron rounds for a few volleys but not enough to keep them at bay or significantly damage their numbers." Scarlett answered with a slight shake of her head. "The castle is poised for an attack from the east where the giants would attack us from, and we aren't as protected from the forest, so we have fewer anti siege weapons set up here. We need every person possible armed with a bow on the walls." she said, gesturing up to the multi-tiered walls.

Rhyker shook his head is dismay. "No, it won't be enough," he said trying to think of the best way to thin their numbers before being overrun. The Lizardmen were fast and strong but lacked real intelligence but what worried him even more were the waves of ember elves that would follow. They were devious, fast, smart, and one for one were far superior in combat than most humans.

"The castle does have some defense measures the dwarves built in, but I will need to meet with the engineers to get a better understanding of our options," Rhyker said, his hope rising in remembering the dwarven engineers that designed the place had specialized in the unconventional.

Finn listened quietly to the Paladin's reports on the prepared battlements. He was not a military tactician by any means but often thought about problems in a different angle then others. He watched all the men moving around and remembered their battle with the monster in the courtyard in the south end of the castle and had an idea. He held up his hand to get their attention.

"Well, I have quite the plan if you ask me," he blurted out in excitement.

Everyone looked at him like a child interrupting a serious adult conversation.

"No, I really do," Finn stated again, moving his hand around to point out his plan. "We open the portcullis just enough to let a few hundred of the quillbacks inside then drop it down, slowing their advancement. Then we line the inner walls and walkways with archers firing down from all sides making it easier to find the cracks in their armor. Then groups of soldiers on foot can stand firm in formation and cut down the stragglers that are able to cross the open courtyard." He explained as his words gained in momentum and eagerness. "Then if we could get one of the scatter canons to fire down on the inside here in the courtyard, we could take them down even faster and have better accuracy effectively needing less ammo," he said with his head slightly cocked to the side in thought.

Rhyker frowned at the thought of letting them through the gates. Scarlett started to slowly nod her head in agreement, working through the specifics in her mind. The plan was crazy, but it could help to control the flood of creatures and limit the number of infections.

Scarlett's expression turned hopeful. "I like it, it's a good plan," she agreed.

Gorman and Rhyker looked at Finn like he had lost his mind. "And what of the soldiers they take down? They will only rise up further increasing their numbers," Rhyker interjected.

Arcus hadn't ever been important enough to take part in a council meeting in Amid if they were even considered meetings. His heart felt heavy with fear at the sound of the very real danger they were in, enough to even consider letting them in the gates. He looked to Taja sitting atop Saber, looking scared to be in a place she didn't belong. He felt sorry for being the one to drag her into this and his eyes fell to Saber, his wolf that wouldn't hesitate to jump into the middle of the fight to protect his master. His racing anxiety filled him with panic, with the few he cared for now in great danger, he truly wanted to rise to the occasion but felt powerless against an enemy. He had taken down beasts many times his size before but the teaming mass of caiman outside filled him with sheer terror. His mind raced as he thought of what to do, not wanting to let Kaiden down. He was an excellent shot with a bow but from the sounds of the arguments he wouldn't be much help. As the panic began to overtake him, he found himself walking back towards Saber and Taja, thinking it best to live to fight another day.

"Hold that gate open," he shouted, frantically climbing onto Saber's back.

Gorman noticed the wolf squeezing through the gate. "Arcus, where yous be goin?" he shouted.

Arcus saw the look on the half ogre's face, his heart racing almost as fast as his mind. He would think of a plan and just hoped it wouldn't come too late. He gestured to Gorman to go back as he watched him approach. He gave Saber a good kick as he leaped off into a full sprint, passing by hundreds of soldiers setting up wooden pikes in the ground as the sounds of war drew closer. Within minutes Arcus and Taja were away from the castle walls getting further and further from harm's way.

The road north was pitch black with gleams of fresh blood splattered on the lizardmen's armor. Loud bellows and shrieks tarnished the air with the sound of dread, filling every man with terror. The Lizardmen vocalized their hunger and need to kill as they screeched aloud, dragging their claws on the steel they wore clad to their chests.

Gorman shook his fist in anger. "Scrawny weakling," he mumbled in a huff.

Finn eyed the gate in confusion of why they had left. Though he had not known them long he didn't see Arcus's passion for adventure turning into desertion, though he could understand since he wasn't from Sanctuary.

Martis looked on to the castle from atop the hill. He was surrounded by his drums of blood, the ultimate source of his power. He almost had enough and shortly it would be flowing across the field like a spring flood. He risked tainting another land with the neverborn like in the Wither but so be it. After he brought Baladar into the world they would change it to how he saw fit and for once in his life he would have everything and Kaiden would have nothing.

Feora brought her troops to a halt several hundred yards from the castle wall and turned back to look at Martis for orders. Feirun and his men, still tirelessly clanging their weapons together shouted a fearsome war cry, ever ready to start the fighting. Feirun looked to Martis for orders as well as he sat atop his wagon of command, safely in the back.

Martis stood tall on his wagon, not caring to be out maneuvered or for his troop's well-being, he only wanted bloodshed and it didn't matter to him which side it was spilled from, he only needed more. He raised his fist high into the air as black tendrils of lightning crackled down from the sky into the palm of his hand. He held it like a ball of pure energy that swirled in a vortex of destruction and threw it with pure demonic strength, sending it slamming into the great wall. The men on top of the wall scrambled to keep their footing as the entire section cracked and shuttered in place, stone cascading onto the creatures below.

Martis raised up his arms and called out in his demonic voice. "For the creator, make me proud and tear these humans from existence, attack!" he shouted, reverberating through the entire battlefield like thunder.

CHAPTER 16

"ANSWERS LEAD TO QUESTIONS"

Kaiden passed through a bright array of colors and lights bombarding his senses until he was on the verge of blackout. His familiar golden light wrapped around his body to blanket him from the strobing rays of energy as he traveled. His armor sealed tightly around his body making him feel more at ease. The fact that he had begun to start staying fully conscious inside his armor made him feel more welcomed and accepting of its presence like it was a part of him. The eye lenses from his helmet changed and adapted to the flickering lights allowing his head to stop spinning and filtering out its harsh glares.

    Everything around him came to a sudden halt as his body flew through the air weightlessly and crashed onto a slick porcelain looking surface. He stood up feeling nauseous, his head spinning in a thoughtless fog, unable to focus his attention. He knew he had to fight through but could feel the panic of himself dying and needed to react. He looked back where he had come from, the gate he had jumped through looked so far away and he could see Azeal and Nirayus peering through it but unable to see him. In the great spans of space between gates was nothing but solid black dotted with stars and vibrant clouds of colors. He could somehow see his world up close through the gate but also far off in the distance with other worlds suspended in space along with it. It was confusing and he had no idea what to make of it while realizing he never thought about what he had been living on his whole life. It was too difficult to comprehend in his sluggish state, so he turned away from the vortex of swirling colors.

He opened his eyes to see a horizon that seemed to be continuously approaching him at a startling rate, his vision continued to travel further and further everywhere he looked the longer he looked the more he could see. His head started to sting from the overload of information entering his brain as he witnessed a constant stream of input overloading his senses. Bright white pillars surrounded him on his porcelain terrace that was in the center of a grassy field. He was forced to look down in fear of the torturous pain his brain felt when looking off in the distance, the distance that never ended. This world was filled with sights, sounds and all matter of beings and creatures he couldn't even begin to fathom as he tried to recount in his mind what he had just seen. The longer he glanced in any direction the distance of his vision continued to endlessly grow like his sight itself were traveling farther away from him.

His helmet adjusted the best it could and created a blurry fog for him to look through. The dense white fog limited his sight to only a few yards away so he could focus. The pulsating pain behind his eyes subsided and he could feel the buildup of pressure slacken. He clenched his teeth, his mind still in a fog but he knew he was here for a reason, so he decided to try and walk. His movement felt like he was trudging through thick tar, slow and painstaking, every step a struggle. Although his mind was sluggish, he was conscious for a change and able to think for himself.

His battle to move was real as he fought against his armored shell to move but he feared getting too far from the gate back home. He searched through his mind trying to remember what he was there for, why was he here? His mind began to slowly spin like he was spinning around quickly in a circle until an image of Nirayus entered his mind. He looked longingly into her big beautiful blue eyes and felt his panicking heart begin to calm itself.

With his spirits lifted he forced his mind to focus, he was there for a weapon and knowledge. He had so many questions about who he was, where he was from, and why he was cursed with this armor. So many things he wanted answered but the growing discomfort in his body told him he didn't have long to live in this world.

He managed a few more steps, keeping track of the pillars he passed so he could find his way back. He looked back to see the gate itself from the side was paper thin, a tear in thin air that was suspended in place, but he feared how long it would remain open. Curious, he moved further and noticed the gate didn't exist at all from behind but then a step back and it was there again, its vibrant swirl of energy inviting him back home.

He turned back around to notice a shadow in the fog from behind the pillar. "There you are, my child," he heard a soft, elderly voice hum in his head.

He moved closer to see the silhouette of a monstrous figure lumbering his direction with multiple deformed appendages moving and swaying as it approached. He could hear its heavy footsteps against the hard, sleek flooring. As it drew nearer static arced throughout the grey fog with little snaps of electricity firing all around. The static pulsated into a golden rain of falling embers and the silhouette seemed to shrink down into a smaller form.

Kaiden winced in pain, he felt his breathing becoming more labored as if he were only breathing through a small tube. He tried to ready himself for whatever foe approached him but suddenly he was unable to move, his body trapped within an armored tomb. His heart and being felt warmth, calming his nerves and a feeling of great familiarity washed over him.

"Ah yes, there you are, my DeltaBlade, you have finally made your way home, have we?" the ancient sounding voice commented.

From the fog an old man approached, hobbling on a stick and clutching at his side. His body weight resting so heavily on the stick that it wobbled and bent as he moved. His old white skin hung from his bones, elongating his features, making them almost unrecognizable. There was a trail of blood following behind him that escaped from under the hand on his side. He had long ears covered with wispy white hairs the protruded out from his head to hold up a mass of long dirty peppered hair that draped down past his shoulders. His kind eyes looked over the steadfast Kaiden as he hobbled over towards him.

He tilted his head to the side and lifted a long bony finger towards Kaiden and tapped on the face of his helmet. "Are you in there Kaiden?" he asked as he rested against the pillar. "Yes, I know you are my son, and I see you have met DeltaBlade."

Kaiden's heart started to pound harder, his mind pulsating with pain, but he somehow felt a peaceful connection with the stranger like he had known him from before.

"I am sorry you can't come out to talk with me my dear friend, but I fear you wouldn't last long without air," he said with a wheezing cough.

A wave of panic swept through Kaiden as he realized he was suffocating, very slowly. He felt completely out of breath just standing there as he tried to take a deep breath and failed. He tried his best not to get hysterical, telling himself somehow his suit was trying its best to keep him alive.

The old man looked up to him as if being included in a two-way communication with look of empathy resting on his face. "It is ok, calm yourself, no need to panic now," he said in a reassuring voice.

The old man slumped over in front of him, resting against the pillar but his voice was crystal clear in his mind. "Aw, let's see now what do we have in here? Think freely son, nothing to hold back or fear from me." he said as Kaiden's mind felt like it was unraveling like a ball of string beginning to fall apart. "Oh yes, you have a lot of questions in here, understandably. Ask what you will, I can hear your thoughts."

Kaiden looked at the old man in front of him, wondering who he was and what was wrong with him, was he injured?

"How rude of me, I am Galigus, and I am the creator of your species, the humans, at your service. I must say, I have never been visited by one of my creations before and am not entirely sure what I should or should not say," he stated with a hint of clever charm and wit.

Kaiden battled with the thought of creation and how this one person was able to create all the humans, and why did he only mention humans?

"Now, don't get too far ahead of yourself, you are an observant one, but we need to focus on what's most important right now. You see my son I know your past and I see your imminent future. I know your thoughts, dreams, and wants. You have limited time here and the amount of information I hold for you will not even begin to make sense to who you are now. You are my greatest creation and I have a great plan for you indeed," Galigus said in a jolly and slurring tone as if he had one too many drinks before entering Kaiden's mind.

Kaiden couldn't help his mind from questioning the voice in his head while looking at the dying man on the floor at his feet, he found himself becoming even more confused and stressed. Suddenly the man was up again and looking in on him through the lenses of his helmet with a wide grin on his face.

"Yes, I know you have forgotten your past and it is important for you to accept who you are now before I unlock your past from you," Galigus said as the bags under his eyes drooped unbelievably low.

Kaiden felt overburdened by what was happening and unable to move, feeling trapped within his mind, how was this a weapon he needed or the answers to anything he sought after, his eyes closed in concentration to focus on what he wanted.

"Ah yes, that is a tricky question indeed my son for you are not you anymore." Galigus responded as his face contorted into a look of confusion on where to start.

Galigus's big round eyes began to drift apart from each other in thought until he shook his head a bit that jostled his thin arms and hands. His white robe moved loosely on his tiny old frame as Galigus moved around in thought before his eyes narrowed back onto Kaiden.

"I cannot tell you everything from your past right now, but I can slowly grant you your memories back, but first you must face the reality that you have died my son and that you are not all human after all. Which you may have already noticed?" Galigus said with a compassionate look of sorrow and understanding on his face. He looked down to see himself hunched over on the floor covered in blood.

Kaiden looked in shock to see the old man both alive and dead in front of him at his feet, he tried to take a step back but was locked in place. He looked at Galigus in disbelief and back down to the body not understanding what was happening before he processed what he had just heard.

"Wait, I died? What do you mean? Kaiden asked impatiently. He could feel his emotions getting the best of him under the constant strain of pain he felt in his head. He wanted so badly to grab at his chest, he felt his heart racing but was unable to move. Suddenly he remembered he couldn't breathe and started to hyperventilate into panic.

"Shhh, Shhh, Shhh, calm my boy," Galigus whispered. "It is okay, you are okay, we both are okay, child," he said over and over until Kaiden calmed.

"You're not answering me, what do you mean?" Kaiden shouted out within his helmet.

Galigus blinked and in an instant the scenery washed away with the pillars and the grass gone along with the body at his feet. Everything was just a white mist surrounding them. Kaiden snapped alert by the surprise and was more receptive.

"There, now listen to me. You were born with a very rare gift, the power to ark the essence of souls. No human or being has ever had such a unique and powerful gift before."

Kaiden found his mind unable to focus and went back to think about the dead Galigus on the floor and stating he too was also dead. He felt uneasy and desperately wanted answers.

"Patience young one, I will give you your memories back and you shall see but first I need to explain to you why you are here standing before me."

When he heard about his memories returning his mind went to Nirayus and what she had told him before he left. He wanted so badly to be able to share in the memory with her and found himself able to focus again. "I am sorry, please continue Galigus," he whispered.

A smile spread to Galigus's face. "Yes, the girl," he said with a chuckle. "Oh, what one will do for love," he said as if remembering it fondly before his cheerful expression turned to one of stern warning. "You must be certain you are ready my child, the rare power that dwells within the two of you, when intertwined could have the ability to change the world and alter the course of time. You will need to protect her at all costs for your fates rely on each other," he stated, shaking his finger in warning.

"I will love her until the day I die," Kaiden asserted in promise.

Galigus's right eyebrow lifted. "Interesting way to put it boy. But now you must know that it is my soul that keeps you alive now. I died shortly after you were killed, and I saw my opportunity to Ark our souls together. I had foreseen the events to come much too late I am afraid, so my last act as creator was to construct this suit of armor for you out of my own soul and infused it with your arking ability before your soul was tainted. So, you see, you live only because of DeltaBlade here and he lives because of you," Galigus explained as his expression turned to sadness and loss.

The mist around Galigus's feet vanished to reveal his dead corpse laying on the white stone covered in blood. "As you will find, we have both been betrayed by our family. I was killed by my," Galigus paused for a second in thought, his long finger pressed firmly into his chin. "Sibling would be the best fit in your language and as you will find it is your brother who has started the plague and allied himself with Baladar which ultimately led to your death in the first place. Funny how things seem to just work themselves out that way," he said cheerfully, trying to lift Kaiden's spirit.

Galigus moved uncomfortably around the corpse on the ground as he recounted his demise. "Baladar was jealous at the success of my creations and had puppeteered your brother Martis into doing his bidding in a lust for power. He seeks to end all of humanity and replace them with his hideous lizardmen bent on destroying all life in Allterra. Baladar killed me to get the orb of creation, the tool we use to shape your world and has used it to create his army of beasts and grant your brother with dark powers of hate and violence and they have come up with a plan to tear him from this reality into yours. Together they will reign down destruction throughout your land and eventually the others, no one will be safe from their wrath, except you," Galigus said ominously. "With your allies we may still stand a chance, but you will need to rise up and be the leader you were meant to be," he added in an uplifting and encouraging tone.

Kaiden shook his head in thought, taking everything in that he had been told like he was waking up for the first time, completely naive to the world around him. His mind was at ease with the knowledge his memories would soon be returned but was almost scared with what he would find.

"If you're dead here on the floor, then how can I see you here talking to me?" Kaiden asked aloud.

Galigus smiled sharply at him. "I know this is all so much information to take in and just wait for the zinger of a headache when you wake up," he chuckled to himself. "I am now DeltaBlade, or at least what is left of me. We needed to come to this plane of creation to communicate and allow your mind to comprehend my existence. You are only half human and that part of you was not strong enough to support our arked union causing you to blackout and your mind to resist. I would defend you when your mind shut down and did my best to guide you here. Your arking abilities have strengthened and you have been able to stay coherent and remember my presence, but I kept control of your motions. The rest has been up to you but no matter the odds you still found your way here," Galigus said pridefully, looking around through the grey mist as if looking at a beautiful painting for the last time.

"Someday you will be able to see as I see Kaiden. Your soul is now eternal, intertwined with mine so we will have quite the long journey together you and I," Galigus said with a loving smile.

A sharp pain reverberated through Kaiden's body, his limbs beginning to convulse uncontrollably, only held in place by his rigid suit of armor. A grimace of pain spread to Galigus's face.

"Our time here is coming to an end; we must leave quickly," he shrieked, fading away into the mist of golden light, left with only his voice within his head. "Hurry back to the gate, you have control now," he said with a hint of desperation.

His suit began to shake violently in place as Kaiden's mind fought to stay conscious. Everything he had learned played in a loop through his mind, but he still had so many questions. It hurt so much to think but he fought to take control back over his body. He closed his eyes and concentrated as an image of Nirayus came to his mind. He needed to get back to her, he had promised he would come back.

A vision from his dreams with the woman's silhouette that approached him, turned into Nirayus as a young girl, she was alone and scared and he felt guilty for leaving her alone, but someone called for him and had to leave. He felt guilty but hoped his compass would help the young elven girl find her way home. He snapped to, determined to get back to her, refusing to leave her again. His legs and arms came back under his control as he painfully began to move forward.

"You must hurry," came Galigus's voice in his mind. "He is coming, if he catches us here, we are done for," the voice said in panic. "We are no match for Baladar's strength in this plane."

Kaiden looked back as the ground began to tremble and he noticed a huge hulking shadow approaching through the mist. He couldn't make out the figure, but it was large, bigger than any giant or beast he had ever seen. He looked back and found the gate and with every ounce of strength he had, leapt through the swirling vortex.

As he descended through the gate in a sea of nothing, he heard the familiar voice deep within his mind. "Your love holds the key Kaiden, you must awaken your ancestors. They will answer your call when you need them most. Follow your heart and lead your people, I will be with you, my son," Galigus's voice reassured him as he flew through the prismatic light.

Kaiden's eyes squinted closed as he fought to stay alert and conscious. He was startled by a flash of vibrant light as he passed through the cloud of colors and star filled sky, quickly approaching the small gate he could see so far away. He wondered who his ancestors were and how they would be able to help from the heavens? His body tumbled and turned uncontrollably until DeltaBlade took over, extending his wings to steady their speed.

He could see their massive round planet filling the entirety of his vision in his arrival and noticed all the areas he hadn't been. He could pick out Sanctuary, a castle so large it could barely be made out from so far away. With his memories slowly returning he saw the widespread desert far ahead and remembered meeting Arcus, his family, and the traitorous actions of his brother.

He clenched his fists in anger, he remembered it was Martis who tore his family apart when they were young. He knew the chances of his companions stopping Martis were slim, but he would do everything in his power to stop his brother this time before he engulfed the land in utter chaos. The exact same land he flew towards at breakneck speeds. His eyes traced the waters around Allterra and could see other masses of land off in the distance. He had heard Finn talking about it, but he said there was nothing else beyond the great oceans and was looking forward to share with his pioneering friend.

Most importantly he knew he was getting closer to Nirayus, his love since he was young. He couldn't believe that against all odds they had somehow found each other again. He hoped that after the war was over, they could spend more time together. His joyous mood was quickly displaced by loss and sorrow, having no idea what had become of his parents. The last time he had seen them was when Martis had turned them over to Paladin Malik. He wondered now if anyone had recognized him in their stay at Sanctuary and had no clue the entire time the evil that corrupted some of the nobles.

Were his parents worried about him? Did they think he was dead or were they out looking for him? He got an unsettled feeling in his stomach after what Galigus had told him, he guessed they were right, he had died. He would make it a point to track them down after the war.

The bright lights from the gate grew ever so close, blurred as tears

ARKANGEL

streamed down his face. He could see Nirayus looking back at him through the gate, but he feared the force from how fast he was moving. He winced and braced for impact, but his wings stretched out and turned to soften his landing on the ancient marble floor. He stood face to face with Nirayus and without a thought his helmet retracted back as he looked into her beautiful eyes.

"You're back," she squealed in excitement as she grabbed his face and went to her tip toes to kiss him.

He kissed her back briefly and pulled away. "I remember everything, I remember you and I when we were young, and I remember my brother Martis. We need to do whatever it takes to stop him, or we will be too late to stop his plan," Kaiden said, taking her hand in his and turning to Azeal. "Galigus mentioned my ancestors and that I need to awaken them for their help. Does that make any sense to you? Or where I may find them?" he said with an overwhelmed expression of worry across his face.

Azeal nodded and his voice projected. "Follow me to the Hall of Dragons," he said with a wave of his arm as they were guided back down the path from the Angelic temple.

Nirayus looked at Kaiden who was for once walking in his armor with his helmet and gauntlet retracted so he could interact and hold her hand. He must have somehow learned the origin of his armor and how to control it. He seemed so different now, somehow all grown up and confident in only the few minutes he was gone.

"What was it like in there?" Nirayus asked.

Kaiden thought for a second, keeping pace with Azeal who had much longer legs then they did. "It was very overwhelming," he said, holding firmly to her arm as they descended down the ancient stone stairway.

He gestured off the side of the magnificent mountain they were on with the beautiful northern landscape outstretched hundreds of miles in front of them. "Take in all the splendor of what you see in front of us," Kaiden said, taking in a deep breath of fresh air.

ARKANGEL

Nirayus nodded. "It is beautiful; I have never seen anything like it before or been so high in the sky," she said looking all around them, her eyes even sharper than his, giving her a very vivid and breathtaking view.

"Now picture looking at every point of detail all at the same time, but the landscape doesn't fade in the distance, everything seems close enough to touch all at the same time and the longer you look in that direction your vision just continues to extend even further, to every detail. It all happened at once and was very overwhelming," Kaiden explained with a forced chuckle, also remembering how he felt like he was suffocating the whole time.

"You don't see every detail?" Nirayus inquired, with a slight smirk on her face.

Kaiden looked from the view then into her eyes and realized she may see differently with her elven eyes. He bumped into her with his arm with a playful scowl. "Better than you," he smiled.

Nirayus slapped his shoulder and pulled his arm closer to her, his armor retracting further to let him feel her embrace.

Kaiden's head sank some at the memories of what Galigus had told him, the fact that he had died and the only thing keeping him alive was the Creator's soul. It was frightening. He wanted to get away to think and reflect and share with Nirayus but was afraid of what she would think of him. He was worried she might think differently of him, but right now he needed to be strong and focused on stopping Martis. He struggled with exactly what to say and decided he would have to wait for another time.

"I learned that the armor was forged by the creator himself, constructed from his soul. He was guiding and controlling the armor until I learned to control it myself," he answered, hoping it would be enough of an explanation.

"Then I met Galigus, and he was the creator of humans until he was betrayed by Baladar, who has given Martis the power he needs to summon him to our world. He also gave me some one my memories back which are still surfacing slowly, but I remember the important things," he winked.

Nirayus smiled up to him. "Did he tell you of our future?" she asked shyly, hoping to hear they would make it through this together.

Kaiden thought for a second, trying to decipher her intent while trolling through the painful experience for any hints of the future. "No, nothing of the future and unfortunately I didn't even get to ask everything that I was hoping to, my mind was so blurry and foggy, I couldn't concentrate. He did warn me of our enemy, Baladar, who has stolen some sort of creation orb and plans to come to our world and recreate it, destroying everyone else in the process," he said, his grim tone wiping the smile from his face.

Azeal's deepened eyes winced at what Kaiden was explaining. He knew full well the power of the orb and what harm it could do in the wrong hands. If the angels weren't tethered to the mountain of Azure, he knew they could turn the tide in the war for survival.

Nirayus let out an overwhelmed sigh, for she hadn't realized how grand the threat really was and that it could affect the entire land. It was a lot of burden to be rested on their shoulders.

"What are we supposed to do?" she asked, feeling helpless.

Kaiden pulled her tighter as they walked together behind Azeal. "He said that I should follow my heart and that I needed to find my ancestors," He responded sounding unsure of its meaning.

Nirayus was also confused by it, she hadn't met his parents but didn't know how the dead could be of any use to them. "Did he tell you why he chose you to have the armor?" she asked, searching for clues that could tie it to his ancestors.

Kaiden lets out a startled gasp, not expecting to ask such a direct question. Especially the exact one he wasn't willing to share at the moment. "Well," he said, stuttering for a second as his mind raced on what to say.

Azeal's deep voice echoed through the air, cutting Kaiden off. "We have arrived," he proclaimed, pointing to the pillars they had found before with the giant round door. They were standing just above the door, twenty feet above the smooth stone flooring.

Nirayus looked down and around the sides. "Did they run out of stairs?" she asked with a smirk, looking up to see Kaiden smile.

Azeal spread his wings. "The inhabitants of old had no need for stairs," he said jumping off and gliding easily down to the ground.

Azeal looked up after landing, his voice echoing around them as if he was still standing right next to them. "The stairs were put in by my people ages ago for when the two of you would someday find your way here," he said while stepping up to inspect the door.

Kaiden reached his arm under Nirayus's legs and lifted her off the ground with ease while his wings extended from his back. He stepped off and felt Nirayus's grab at his shoulder instinctively and was surprised at how smoothly they glided down to the floor below. He set her down with a smile that changed to confusion as they looked at the circular door in front of them. With the wings Azeal had given him he looked almost identical to the winged creatures depicted in the etchings on the door.

Azeal took a step back, looking up to the old plaque fastened above the circular stone doorframe. "I don't know the language of your people, but the words above were passed down to the keepers for when you arrived," he said, looking over the unrecognizable characters.

Kaiden and Nirayus both stepped back with Azeal to look at the plaque. It matched the characters etched below the drawings of the winged creatures wrapped the columns and door.

Azeal pointed to the last line above. "To gain entrance, let your heart guide and show you the way."

Kaiden fell deep into thought trying to think of what was close to his heart, but his mind just kept wandering back to Nirayus, before a memory triggered. His hand gently gripped the pendant she had given him from when he had first met her, he had given her the compass, so she could find her way home. He looked over to see her looking up at him, her hand holding onto it tightly.

"That's the same compass I gave you," his voice trailed off in both in shock for remembering and endearment.

Nirayus lifted the compass pressed against her chest. "Could this be it?" she asked excitedly as a big smile spread from ear to ear.

"I kept it safe ever since," She answered confidently. She unclasped the golden braid of wire and handed it to him. "Promise you will give it back?" she added playfully.

Kaiden gave her a smile and took the small round compass, placing it within the center hole of the door as they took a step back, but nothing happened.

Azeal stepped up and tried to roll the door open but was unable to budge it, he looked back to Kaiden's blank stare. "Are you sure this is the very same compass it requires?"

Kaiden and Nirayus looked at each other questioning. "That is the same necklace he gave to me when we were younger," Nirayus said as she stepped up to the door, tracing the engraved lines in the door with her fingers. Some of the characters felt familiar by touch and she closed her eyes, tracing them back and forth.

"Where did you acquire such a compass, maybe that will hint at its uses?" Azeal asked.

Kaiden looked closely, trying to decipher the meaning of the images on the door, ignoring the words he couldn't read. He thought back to when he was younger and found something wrong in his memory. The figure that gave him the necklace was somehow hazy or missing. He remembered getting it and being excited to have such a precious gift, one that made Martis swell with anger. He had hoped to play hide and seek or hunt for treasure with him, but Martis would never play, was always too involved in himself.

Nirayus pulled the compass out, her eyes closed as she clenched it tightly like she had for so many years. She thought that the ring around the edge was just moveable by design, but she ran her fingers gently around its rim to feel the etchings. She opened the delicate compass and folded the lid back and under to the bottom with a small click. She moved the dial slowly, feeling the characters she recognized as shapes of a sphere and stars and smaller moons. Once she felt the symbols of the dial were lined up correctly, she placed it back into the stone wall with a loud snapping sound and the door began to glow.

Dust that had settled for thousands of years started to fall and float into the air as the carvings in the wall began to emanate an intense blue color. The blue radiated throughout, encircling the door in a beautiful pattern all leading to a circle indent to the top. There was a bright beam of light shining straight down the stone platform that led off the cliff of the mountain.

Nirayus's eyes went wide in a realization that made everything they had been looking for suddenly become so terrifying and real. She knew without a doubt that she loved him for her own free will but were they truly destined to be together? Did she really have no say? She reached for Kaiden's shoulder, his armor sliding into itself to expose the top of his shirt.

"What are you doing?" Kaiden asked, confused over what she was after and how she had controlled his armor.

"Just trust me," she replied, reaching around his neck and pulling the pendant she had made for him out of rock. It now held the chips of the warping stone infused inside the stone ring, but it didn't interfere with the shape, so she inserted it into the indent in the stone door atop where the compass was. It was a moon shaped drawing with the light beam shining from its center. Once inserted the beam of light refracted from the crystal and thin rays traveled down the runway, hitting all the pillars on either side. They all began to spin slowly in different directions and a rough sound of grinding stone filled the air as the door behind them rolled into the side of the mountain.

There was a smaller grinding sound that lingered, echoing sounds plinking and bouncing as their amulet and compass were ejected into the mountain and appeared into a small stone basin beside the doorframe.

Azeal looked captivated at the ingenuity of the door and all its pieces that needed to be just right for it to open. His expressionless face, lacking the mouth or nose of a human, still expressed wonderment in his large eyes alone. He bent over to peer into the dark cave ahead of them and looked over to Kaiden and Nirayus, both fastening their amulets around their necks.

Kaiden's armor reformed, all except the plates against his face. "Nirayus, what do you see inside?" He was unable to see anything in the blackness.

Nirayus crouched down as if stalking her prey and entered silently, taking several careful steps within. Her eyes began to glow a golden color as she peered down the long open hallway lined with pillars stretching up high into the ceiling. Kaiden took a few steps in and a plate on the floor lowered, Nirayus being too light to activate it.

Channels along the tops of the walls ignited as streams of fire lit the long passageway and into a massive open cavern deep within the mountain. Along the hallways stood large stone statues inserted between pillars like guards, standing ever vigilant and watching. The large stones in the floor of the cavern were intricately carved and fit together in unique patterns with short geysers of flame now raising up into the air along the walls to light the entire room.

There were several large doors that lead off into different directions from the main room. Kaiden looked up and around in awe at the number of statues that went several stories high. Balconies ran along the edge of the walls with hundreds of the statues all standing vigilant facing the center of the room. On the far end of the room sat a large stairway up to a throne with a seat to either side. Despite the age of the ancient cavern, it was surprisingly undisturbed, not even by the usual nocturnal creature or insect.

Kaiden walked up to one of the statues intrigued, as it was almost like looking into a mirror, they resembled his armor almost completely except for their reptilian facial features and protruding horns. They stood anywhere from seven to nine feet tall, all chiseled so intricately and life like.

"This is so beautiful, it's like the statue garden where we met in Market Town. It feels like so long ago." Nirayus stated, grasping hold of Kaiden's hand.

Azeal approached from behind them, scanning the room with his celestial eyes, taking in all the magnificent detail work of the room and its furnishings. Large stone tables sat in rows near to one of the doors while two statues acted as guards to another heavy looking door made almost of solid steel by the look of it.

Kaiden lead Nirayus up to the thrones atop the staircase. Giant wing-like decorations jutted out from the backs of the thrones and encircled the sides as if hugging the throne in a protective shield. Nirayus ran her smooth fingers against the chiseled steel chairs wrapped in carved decorations and symbols. She found a disc shaped hole in the arm of the middle chair and looked to see another in the other arm. She looked up to Kaiden and pointed out the indents in the solid arms.

"Do you think our amulets could go in these as well? she asked excitedly.

Kaiden reached to retrieve his, scales and bands of armor retracting back for retrieval. Nirayus spotted a third place where something could fit into as well, it was disc shaped too but with the same shape as the wings coming out from the chair wrapping around its sides. It sat dead center above where a head would rest while sitting in the throne.

"I wonder what would go in there?" she asked, pulling the compass from her chest.

Kaiden looked over the throne and its markings and saw the patterns traveling different directions linking pictures of the winged creature together and spreading down to the floor. "I am not sure of what this has to do with my ancestors Nirayus. I feel like we are making an amazing discovery here, don't get me wrong, but at the same time our friends are in danger. Should we come back later after we save Sanctuary?" Kaiden asked reluctantly, feeling an overwhelming stress, not able to appreciate the true meaning of the Dragon's Capsule.

Azeal's voice echoed through their minds. "If the creator told you to seek out your ancestors, then you must do so in order to succeed. Stray from his command is to promise defeat. Follow your heart young ones, let them guide you," he said, leaving their sides to inspect the other rooms.

"He is right, just a little longer and if we don't find anything then we can travel back, but there is a reason the two of us made it in here and I would like to find it," Nirayus stated, holding up the compass.

She inserted it into the arm snuggly and motioned for Kaiden to do the same. A familiar blue light began to glow in the etchings and the light traveled down the patterns along the floor like a glowing blue liquid. Nirayus's eyes light up with excitement at her find, though after several seconds of waiting nothing happened beyond the light. She attempted to remove the compass, to try twisting the dial but found it spun freely inside, making several clicks.

She beamed with pride and gestured to Kaiden. "You should be the one to twist it," she said, hopping up into the chair to the left. Kaiden followed suit and jumped into the central chair, resting his armored palm onto the top of the compass's back, giving it a slow twist. It clicked once and the light continued to glow and stream further down, moving into the central pattern on the stone floor. Seconds later a low rumble of stone sliding against stone echoed through the chamber.

Azeal was caught off guard and moved over to behind the third chair, transfixed by the bright blue lighting. He was overwhelmed by how glorious the creators design truly was. He watched as the floor stones began to twist in place and slide away from each other, sinking deeper into the floor and folding under. A large round stone platform raised out of the now open floor, stopping several feet into the air as more stones turned and unfolded into a staircase.

In the center of the platform was a raised console with similar etchings and designs drawn into its surface. A rough crystal sat atop the console with two indents to either side of it where their amulets could possibly fit along with the one with wings slightly above the crystal.

Nirayus's heartbeat quickly with intrigue, she had never seen or imagined anything like it before and the more they discovered the more excited she became. She wondered where the mystery disc could be and now the console had two additional slots for discs. Who had them? She wondered to herself but more importantly what did they do?

"Yet another mystery object," Kaiden said looking to his companions in uncertainty. "This one has places for five amulets, and we only have two, we should return later," he said looking back to Azeal, "After we find the others, I am sure we can find them."

Kaiden quickly became alert from the look he saw in Azeal's eyes. He stood hunched over defensively peering up into the open ceiling. His eyes darted side to side, his head cocked to its side listening.

"What is wrong, Azeal?" Kaiden asked, looking to Nirayus who was also alert and listening with her long ears raised up slightly higher than usual.

Azeal's voice went to a whisper in their minds. "We are not alone," he said ominously as the three gathered into the central platform. He drew his glaive from his back, holding it to his side to swing at a moment's notice. "I have never felt this form of life before, it has power, power greater than I have ever known before," he warned, his normally stoic eyes winced in fear.

Kaiden took a step forward instinctively to get in front of Nirayus. "Is this some sort of elaborate ambush? If so, why would Galigus lead us here?" he asked, his eyes strained to see anything in the dark shadows of the ceiling.

Nirayus nervously swayed back and forth, looking desperately for an attacker. She flicked her wrists, igniting her hands in flames as they waited for their stalkers approach. They stood in the center of the massive cavern atop the platform surrounded by row after row of balconies and statues.

With a loud crash a creature leaped down from the ledge behind the throne and landed several feet in front of them. As it stood up straight, rock debris fell from its heavily armored body. Its size easily rivaling Gorman's and its mass dwarfed Azeal's tall thin frame. Its bright green eyes gazed at them, looking them over one by one. Its head and face scaled like a lizard, but its forehead branched wide into carapace and scaly fins, matching the rest of its body, sharp bone jutting out in patterns running down the center of his forehead.

"You must be son of Drakken," he said deeply, looking at Kaiden, his long pointy teeth showing through his lips as he spoke. "And you, daughter of Moon," he added with a smile that looked more threatening than intended. "I am Takis, eternal watchmen over the Drakken tomb." he stated, stretching his limbs like he had just awoken from a long slumber. "You must be an Angel, watchers over our sacred mountain, thank you for your unwavering service," he said with a bow, eying the gold clad Azeal, with his wings folded neatly behind him.

"I am Kaiden, I was given this armor by Galigus and sent to seek your help in defeating the plague that has ravaged the lands," Kaiden said with pride. "But my father wasn't a dragon, he was a man."

Takis lets out a hearty chuckle, his thick metal plates of armor clanging against each other from his hearty laughter. "You look Drakken to me," he said, returning to his awkward smile.

Kaiden closed his eyes and concentrated, retracting his armor into itself before vanishing. "I am human," he repeated, reaching for Nirayus's hand.

Takis's laughter only deepened. "The creator's armor takes the form of your soul; it is a powerful relic foretold for many centuries and you are its wielder, and it is you," He explained, his tone becoming more serious. "You have the powerful soul of a Drakken," he said thumping his fist to his chest.

Takis's eyes traveled down to Nirayus, standing there holding Kaiden's hand with a confused look on her face. "And you are the royal daughter of the moon elves. Your arrival has been foretold, centuries before you were born, it is the prophecy of the hundred-year war to save man. If you are here, then it has already begun and our duty to serve will be fulfilled," he said, his hand gesturing to the other statues along the balconies.

"We have slept in stone awaiting your arrival," he said before the row of scales lifted above his eye in thought. "There was to be another, the youngest of our clan, our Sentry Barrick who was supposed to be guardian to you until it was time. Has he fallen?"

Kaiden and Nirayus shared a look of confusion. "I don't know a Barrick; he must have passed before I was born," Kaiden answered.

Takis's features expressed a great sorrow at the mention of Barrick's disappearance. Nirayus felt sorry for Takis's grief and nodded in understanding. Takis shook off his emotion, his face returning to its stoic expression.

Nirayus looked around to all the statues that she figured may come to life at any moment, "How did you know we would be here? Who told you to wait?"

A glimmer shined is Takis's eyes as he looked down to Nirayus. "There is a lot at play here and prophecy is complicated young moon princess. For now, we will take this one step at a time and rescue your humans, the answers you seek will reveal themselves eventually," he responded with a small smirk curling to one corner of his face.

Takis gave his body one last stretch as he flexed his scaled limbs, "Then let it be time for our awakening, Kaiden, son of the Drakken." Takis roared as he walked up the stairs to join them at the center console. "With this crystal, you alone have the power to awaken them from their petrification," he stated with pride, motioning for Kaiden to use the stone.

Kaiden reached out and instinctively spread the three shards outwards as light began to reflect out into the statues. He could feel a warm golden light somehow emitting from his hand and into the stone and felt in control, felt that he was reaching through time and reaching out towards these beings surrounding him. He concentrated, following his heart to pull the veil of stone from their slumbering souls.

Takis's deep voice echoed through the massive open cavern as the sound of stone rained down from the balconies. "Let us fly towards our enemies and make our creator proud," he commanded.

CHAPTER 17

"THE SIEGE OF SANTUARY"

Gorman stood tall against the back gate leading into the inner paladin district of Sanctuary. To his sides were a hundred of the best, most heavily armored and trained Knights Sanctuary had, the Paladin Guard. Across the expansive courtyard, the portcullis opened as a flood of quillbacks began to spill through like a wave of black ichor. Claws slashing through the air and jaws cracking shut as they eyed their prey across the yard, eagerly sprinting with terrifying speed.

"Fire," Scarlett shouted with a wave of her sword as thousands of archers let loose their flame coated arrows into the wave of creatures below.

"Knock, Draw, Fire," Scarlett commanded again as the sound of arrows clanging into steel echoed through the courtyard. Shrill shrieks filled the air as some of the arrows sank deep into their scales and set them ablaze.

"Knock, Draw, Fire," she shouted again as another volley whizzed past the soldiers.

The portcullis slammed shut, trapping the creatures inside and pinning others to the ground as they squirmed to free their crushed bodies. Finn stood atop the inner wall with a crew manning a scatter cannon. He pointed out the center of the mass of heavily armored creatures, the ones protected from arrows and had them fire. The crew manning the cannon finished winding the crank, filling the dwarven made siege weapon with pressure and with a flick of a switch a ram shot forward launching thirty iron balls out into the yard that tore through both steel and scales alike. Bodies slammed so hard into the ground that they violently tore apart, throwing shrapnel and ripping into other nearby quillbacks. Finn watched in awe at the weapons effectiveness and pulled hard at the crank raising another stack of iron ammo up to the cannon for reloading.

Scarlett gestured over to Gorman to prepare as he raised Redemption high into the air, the mass of surviving quillbacks closing in.

"Fire!" Scarlet shouted again, the arrows raining down hard into the crowd as she thrust her sword towards Gorman, signaling his attack.

Gorman let out a commanding war cry and charged forward. He rammed his massive crossbow into the chest of one of the creatures and pulled the trigger as the spear shot straight through its head and punctured deep into the one behind it. He followed through with Redemption, cleaving clear through its armor.

The paladin guard closed in behind with their glaives whirling up and into the chests of the creatures, their sharp curved blades sinking deep into their blood-stained breastplates. Gorman shouted a command, and the men retreated several paces back dropping their long pole arms to hinder their enemies from advancing. They raised their heavy tower shields up with one arm and drew free their broad swords.

The front line of Lizardmen clawed and swung towards the men mindlessly impaling themselves deeper. With the weight of the next line of savage creatures trying to fight their way through the ones in front and were slowly killed, creating a wall of corpses.

Gorman shouted, "Charge!" as the men sprinted forth, shields held firmly in place, swinging their swords with precision and speed. The towering Gorman strapped his crossbow to his back and grasped Redemption in two hands. His heart ached as he saw the carnage unfold, knowing this would only be the beginning and that these monsters in front of them were their friends and loved ones twisted to do Martis's bidding. He looked through the gates behind him at the last line of defense in the paladin district, thousands of men and women about to lay down their lives for their city.

His strength and composure renewed at the thought of their bravery and vowed to himself he would lead them to victory. His hands clenched tightly around the handle of Redemption as he let out a roar, running into the dwindling mass of quillbacks. He cleaved his sword down into their helmeted heads bending the steel to collapse their skulls inside. Kicking hard onto their chests as his blade cut through the air, sinking deep into their chests, removing any claws or arms that raised to defend.

Rhyker stood atop the front wall beside a row of several hundred archers filling the dark skies with arrows. Amidst the black lighting their arrows were the rain sailing down into the heads and helmets of the creatures below. Since the enemy didn't have any ranged or siege weapons, being on the walls was relatively safe and Rhyker's confidence began to rise. Why would Martis think only soldiers could breach the walls designed to keep out giants he wondered, getting an uneasy feeling within his old soul.

"Load, aim, fire," Rhyker shouted at a ballista crew, hurling twelve-foot bolts through the air with such force it punctured through several of the creatures with ease. He commanded the scatter cannons to fire as far and high as the crew could manage to take out the back of the enemy lines, hoping to diminish the ember elves first. He looked behind and down inside the courtyard with a slight smile to see Finn's plan working as Gorman and his men mopped up another couple hundred of the trapped lizards. Rhyker could see the ground inside becoming hard to traverse with the pile of dead corpses forming trenches between the growing piles.

Rhyker was startled by a shrill hiss as one of the quillbacks lunged at him, knocking him onto his back. It snapped and raked with its claws, trying to break through his thick paladin armor. He kicked hard at the creature sending it flailing into the air. Recovering quickly, he swung his sword, sending it sailing back into the wall. He looked down to see the quillbacks had begun to scale the walls with their sharp claws, puncturing into the stone.

Soldiers filled the staircases circling up the high towers, he signaled for them to defend the archers. "They are breaching the walls, climbing up, unseen by the archers under the ledges." Rhyker shouted, hearing panic begin to ramble through the lines.

Rhyker hit one of the petrified soldiers square on his breast plate. "Do not allow them to come over the walls, do you hear me?" he shouted at the top of his lungs. The men all nodded hesitantly and stepped up beside the rows of archers, firing frantically into the air.

Rhyker grabbed one of the men and pointed to Paladin Scarlett, "Tell Paladin Scarlett that the creatures can climb the wall and to watch for any that may make it over," he commanded as he saw another reach over the wall and wildly stab its claws into an unsuspecting archer.

Rhyker let out a cry, the trauma of seeing his first man fall before his eyes jolting him into action. He roared, charging into the creature as it climbed over, the soldiers stabbing at it with their swords, doing little to slow it down. He plunged his sword into the side of the creature and received a slash across his face, a line of blood dripping down his cheek. The men halted, looking to their captain for what to do as he yanked his sword free, kicking the creature off the wall.

The archer flailed on the ground in pain and screamed, pleading for help, then went suddenly silent as a pool of blood spilled out of his mouth. Shiny black scaled appendages tore their way free, the muffled shrieking of the creature inside the man's mouth struck the soldiers with terror. Then the long snout protruded out, shattering through his jaw and skull. His arms fell free as the loose sleeves of flesh ruptured apart to expose the scaly arms from inside.

Rhyker shouted in horror, not wanting it to spread to any more of his men and plunged his sword several times into the dead man's chest, killing the creature inside before it could fully emerge. He looked up to see the soldiers all standing in shock, drawing their swords on Rhyker.

"You're going to change, aren't you?" one of them asked with a quivering voice.

Rhyker reached for his face, his wound had already sealed shut but the blood still remained on his cheek. He wasn't quite sure if he could be turned but didn't have the time to wait as the quillbacks started to breach their defenses.

The portcullis to the inner courtyard reeled up as another flood of the lizards sailed through the air. Piles of bodies created pathways that split them up to run down. Scarlett had her men focus fire down the paths creating denser concentrations of flaming arrows to hit their marks. They made their way down the passages, climbing and leaping over their fallen companions recklessly. They found their way through the walls of bodies and ran for the inner gate but were met with a surprise attack from Gorman and his men. Glaives and swords slashed out from the sides, dismembering the unsuspecting pack of Lizardmen.

Finn saw that the horde of creatures were now mixed with the more cunning ember elves who had climbed up on top of the piles of corpses. He shouted for Gorman who was caught up in a fight, unable to hear his warning.

"Gorman!" Finn called out, bouncing up and down waving his arms in the air, continuing to go unheard.

Scarlett, surveying the fighting saw the elves and Finn, commanding her archers to focus on the burly orange elves. The blazing arrows sank deep into their skin, cauterizing almost instantly in the already hot skin of the elves. They merely broke the shafts of the arrows, almost unhindered and began to wail in rage. A well-aimed arrow sank deep into the skull of the elf, killing it instantly as is tumbled down the pile of bodies, landing at Gorman's feet.

Gorman took a step back, looking up the tower of bodies and saw his old enemies emerging, striking fear into his heart. His Paladin guard moved in to defend the half ogre who had frozen in terror, their large tower shields only slowing them down against the vicious, unrelenting strikes of the elves. The elves slammed their twin cleavers repeatedly against the guard's shields, breaking through with overwhelming force.

Gorman fell to his back, backpedaling on all fours frantically as the elves slowly approached, toying with their prey.

"I'll be placing your ash right here, little ogre," an Ember threatened while pointing to a clear patch on his chest.

Finn looked to his crew, who were standing paralyzed, watching Gorman about to be cut down. The plan had worked almost flawlessly. They had been fighting through most of the day with very few casualties and everything was on the brink of falling apart. Finn made a split-second decision and pulled hard on the positioning lever to the wood crane he had been using to hoist up the scatter cannon ammo. The long wooden arm swung around, still attached to the platform holding racks of ammo fastened to it, he leaped onto it. The arm swung outward wildly into the courtyard as it slowly lowered down inside the city. Finn held the rope tightly as it crashed into the side wall and swung back violently to the other side, slamming hard into the other side of the wall each time. Finn let out a long-excited cry, his face spreading into a wide grin as he twisted to swing towards the enemy.

With a bone shattering sound, the crate and Finn smashed into the pack of elves, throwing them hard against the wall with a dead thud. The impact against the high wall sent their crushed bodies sliding to the ground trailing streaks of blood along the courtyard. The crate hit hard against the wall again, sending the scatter cannon ammo flying in every direction as the crate flung back to the other side. Finn held tight with his long-webbed fingers, spinning out of control, kicking at any unprepared elves, sending them hurtling to the ground. Gorman watched the commotion in awe as he saw Finn swinging through the air above him, kicking his enemies in joyful glee.

Scarlett let out a celebratory cry, leaping into the air and shouting praise for Finn's valiant effort. She failed to notice the pile of quillbacks that had made it over the wall and had started to pile up on the upper level. She cried out as the Lizardmen raked their claws through her ranks of unsuspecting archers. The messenger Rhyker had sent had been cut down before he was able to warn her of the imminent danger. His lacerated body tumbled down the stairs towards her feet and off the ledge to land with a thud in the grassy courtyard. Only moments to be split open by the ravenous creature that began to emerge from within him.

Scarlett lowered her faceplate and drew out her glaive, slashing and stabbing at the creatures that landed on the inner ledge. Rhyker charged at the breach, kicking and stabbing at the lizardmen coming up over the sides. Soldiers' bodies rained down into the courtyard only to turn moments later and add to the enemy's ranks. The lizardmen began to breach up and over the walls all over the northern wall, slashing and clawing their way through the soldiers and infecting them with their contagions. As their bodies contorted and ripped apart, new sleek, black scaled creatures spawned forth.

The few soldiers that were left alive hit the long lever lowering the courtyard portcullis down to stop the swarm of enemies pouring into the courtyard, but were caught by the burly ember elf, Feirun. He let out a roar, firing forth a stream of liquid fire that melted through the steel reinforced gate in mere seconds before tearing it free. Floods of lizardmen and elves stormed the courtyard, gaze fixated on the only thing keeping them from the heart of the castle, a large steel gate across the pile of corpses.

Scarlett cut and cleaved at the creatures as her transformed archers began to rise up against her. She turned and retreated through the hallways built into the wall that led down into the courtyard so she could meet up with Finn and Gorman.

Rhyker hit one of the creatures so hard, it slammed into one of the towers before spinning uncontrollably back over the wall. His last remaining soldiers fought to defend the entrance up to the tower with the ballista and several archers, trapped at the top. Rhyker cried out furiously, swinging and shattering the chests of several creatures with the back end of his glaive. He reached down, retrieving a shield and locked it to his pauldron to hold into place. He picked up speed into a sprint and rammed several of the enemy off the wall, scrambling to claw and slash at him as they fell.

Rhyker made his way past the handful of soldiers protecting the tower, running up the stairs to the top. He had been informed by the castle engineers that the release lever he had heard about would be located there. The shaken soldiers were relieved to see Rhyker join them, letting out renewed cheers of hope. He nodded, following their cheer as he went for a metallic device attached to the side of the tower's inner rim. It had valves, giant gears, and a gauge that would rise when the lever was pumped. None of which he recognized or knew how it worked since after the castle was constructed the giants stopped their constant sieging. He didn't know what to expect but thought before they lost the wall for good it should be used.

The night stretched on, unable to tell the time of day as the light remained the same under Martis's electrical storm. The light from the buildings being caught on fire outside the walls along with burning piles of corpses filled the night air with flickering light and an unsettling stench.

Rhyker looked to see if he could find Scarlett anywhere, not wanting her to be killed by what he was about to do. He scanned the inner courtyard to see Finn, Gorman, and thankfully Scarlett with a big group of soldiers standing their ground against the endless horde of creatures. He knew this was his time to act.

He pulled on the lever several times, over and over, watching a black needle rise and fall on the gauge until it rose to a part painted with a faint red. It made a loud clank sound and started to hiss loudly with steam spraying out of the valves. The grinding sound of large gears echoed up through the tower, distracting the soldiers who were fighting for their lives. The entire wall began to shake with a loud popping and cracking sound that snapped through the air like a whip, followed by a high pitch hissing sound.

Rhyker stood in place, his chest heaving under his heavy armor as he waited for some sign of what the lever had done or if he even worked it correctly. He checked over the edge of the tower and watched as lizardmen completely overran the first wall and flooded over the thirty-foot barrier like it didn't exist. He winced as he heard the cries of his swordsmen at the base of the tower get torn to pieces.

With a loud thunderous crack, the stone wall shattered throwing huge chunks of stone and bodies through the air, sending them raining down on the enemy below. All the rocks that were thrown, crashed hard into the swarm of creatures, crushing their bodies into the ground and rolling onwards over many more. Underneath where the stone had been was a thick, solid frame with tubes running every few feet horizontally across the wall. The hissing sound returned as a thin green liquid began to spray out of the long venting tubes. The green liquid sprayed and splattered several yards away from the wall, covering the entire area. Within seconds shrill shrieks of pain erupted from the front of the wall as the green acid melted through their glistening black scales and bone.

Rhyker let out a relieved sigh of triumph at the devastation the fallen wall and acid had caused to the enemy, halting their progress over the wall. Thousands of melting bodies pooled up into a thick black and green sludge that crashed up against the base of the wall like a great wave. The inside of the wall suffered very little structural damage and was still teaming with the lizardmen that had made it over. Rhyker descended the tower with renewed hope as he cut down the few stragglers remaining on top. He made it down to the lower, inner ledge, running around the perimeter of the courtyard to meet up with Scarlett, Finn, and Gorman.

Gorman growled in pain as a pair of long claws raked down his back with Finn immediately pulling the creature off, taking some flesh along with it. Scarlett swung her glaive in an upward cleave, sinking it deep into the belly of the lizard Finn had restrained. They heard Rhyker's voice call out to them as he pointed to the rope and crate Finn had swung on before. With a few gestures the men atop the inner wall pulled the levers and it began to rise up.

The remaining force of the human army manned the top of the inner ring wall, sending volley after volley of arrows down into the courtyard below. Feirun and a few of his elves worked at dismantling the gate to get into the inner wall as the elves stabbed their swords inward to taunt the soldiers guarding the other side.

The companions reached the top of the wall and stood there, inspecting the battle to determine their next move. Within an hour the dire situation had turned in their favor as the Lizardmen worked to get past the giant pool of acid slowly spewing from the wall. Martis watched the devastation that had been done to his army, filling his heart with a crazed lust. He could feel it was time, his blood felt as if it boiled within him, his power rising to his meet his greatness. He stood on top of his cart of blood, raising his arms into the air as the black lightning lashed out violently around him.

"It is time for our creator to return my fellow believers," he shouted, his voice echoing through the dark night sky like thunder. "We have done his work and my reward will be granted this very night. Our enemies' blood will be sacrificed, and we shall show no mercy in their slaughter."

His tone became so sunken and vile it was even hard for Feora to hear as she stood beside him, seeing nothing but eminent defeat at hand. The tendrils of lightning reaching down and wrapped around the drums of offered blood and lifted high into the air. Martis stood with his arms stretched out as if to give an embracing hug as he laughed uncontrollably, his eyes glowing a menacing red. The blood-soaked ground began boiling, bursting into the air like geysers all around them, sailing into the night sky. The lightning cracked and struck repeatedly as the drums exploded into a dense mist of blood. Martis's evil laugh boomed with incredible force projecting out into the mist as the lightning began to wrap and twist around into a massive solid form.

The crackling pulses of lightning and thick bloody mists swirled into a violent tornado. Lights of deep red begin to shine briefly from within as the storm strengthened with strands of lightning reaching out, whipping wildly into the night sky. Feora took several steps back in disbelief that Martis had accomplished what he had set out to do, he was summoning the creator. The effort and strain had been too much for Martis's body and he fainted, a strain that would have destroyed a normal man. Feora picked up his limp body and retreated away from the storm, not waiting to be caught up in its destruction.

Vixis grew tired of waiting within the paladin's tower. Rhyker had told her the importance of defending Lanthor, Trinity and the other Nobles but it wasn't any fun watching the battle from afar. She struggled to take orders and was now growing more impatient, hearing all the sounds of battle raging on down below.

She was to stay inside with a group of paladin guard to defend against anything that managed to make its way into the suspended building. She watched outside the window in hopes of a messenger coming to bring her to the front lines but still saw none. What she did see was a spout of flame coming through the gates and igniting groups of soldiers on fire. A small force of a few hundred men huddled on the inside of the wall as the last defense if the walls were breached.

She suddenly got excited to see Rhyker atop the main wall followed by Finn, Gorman, and Scarlett though she figured that meant they had lost the front wall. Her anxiety and thirst for battle got the best of her like always as she sprang into action.

"Stay here and watch the door sweetheart, I'll be back in no time," she said with a wink to the stone-faced paladin guard, eying the door like an unflinching hawk.

Vixis didn't even bother to raise the giant platform and jumped off, all the way down to the ground with a hard thud, her leather boots sinking inches into the soil. She sprinted towards the gate watching as the stream of flame ignited another unlucky soldier. She tackled the soldier to the ground, the force of the roll immediately extinguishing the flames. She looked up to see a large ash-stained ember elf with some sort of relic attached to his arm, blasting fire in on the soldiers as his men pried at the gate.

Feirun let out a hearty laugh at the sight of the woman glaring at him as if she were any threat to the King of the embers. Vixis briefly heard screams paired with what sounded like lightning strikes before it all went silent, followed by a loud crashing sound from the gate in front of her. She drew her crossbow and shot three bolts into the chest of an elf attempting to lift the damaged portcullis, failing to slow him down.

Vixis drew her sword and ran in to stab at the elves hoisting up the gate, the fatal wounds doing nothing but slowing them down as another elf would come in to take its place. Feirun's sinister laugh could be heard from behind as he narrowed in on his next prey. Her heartbeat rapidly in her chest with adrenaline, she loved a challenge, loved a good fight and these elves were about to taste the steel of her blade.

As the gate reached a foot into the air Vixis hacked at their legs, chopping one clean off as the elf fell to the ground. She pulled him under and chopped his head right off as she smirked tauntingly at Feirun. Feirun roared in rage, he gestured from behind as several of the lizardmen slithered under the gate after her. She chopped and sliced at their heads as they came through, easily keeping them at bay. She glanced at the other soldiers around her who were shaking so badly, one would think they were fresh out of an icy lake.

Feirun grunted and threatened her from the other side of the portcullis in frustration. "I will slaughter you human, burn your body and delight in adding your ash to mine," he cackled.

Vixis only returned with a wink. "Oh, I've got something special for you dear," she replied with a halfcocked smile.

Feirun rushed the gate and rolled under, taking out the legs of his own men. The heavy gate crashed back down behind him, shattering several skulls under its weight.

"Come on, little girl, show me what you're made of," Feirun taunted, rolling up to his feet and swinging with both of his cleavers towards her head.

Vixis ducked and dodged to the side as fluently as a mastered dance, swinging her sword into the back of his to put them further away while then coming back with a slice on his shoulder. He winced, surprised by her speed, lunged back at her, independently slashing meticulously with his right and left arms. Ember elves were unmatched masters of two weapon fighting which they used to overwhelm most combatants, except Vixis.

She laughed at him, rolling to the side to duck a blade and coming up behind him, landing the point of her sword into his back and quickly rolling away to dodge his next swing.

"Do you need me to move slower for you, handsome?" Vixis teased as Feirun's fuming face ignited in anger.

Feirun changed tactics, swinging his swords and surprising her with a kick to the stomach. His leg buckled, sending him down onto his back as she leaped away with a huff.

"Oh, I like a man who really knows how to treat a lady," she said playfully out of breath as her medallion radiated a bright golden color.

The soldiers behind her stood in fear, not knowing what to do if she fell in battle, leaving the King for them to deal with.

"Finish him," one shouted desperately. "Quit toying with him," came another.

Vixis loved the attention and didn't want to end her fun just yet. Feirun sprang to his feet and swung his sword high, waiting for her to duck as he brought his knee up into her face, sending her flying and landing flat on her back.

Vixis coughed as blood splattered down her throat and nose. The soldiers behind gasped in panic, several going to the gate and helping to keep it closed the best they could, so she wasn't overwhelmed by more embers. Feirun didn't hesitate, leaping into the air he slammed his sword down hard, narrowly missing her as she rolled out of the way. Dirt sprayed into the air, coating the nearby soldiers with a thin layer of soil. Vixis rolled up to her feet, realizing her sword wasn't in her hand. A dark smile came to Feirun's lips as he aimed his fist at her, triggering a jet of flame to burst forth, burning and tearing her leather armor, singeing some of her long brown hair with it.

Vixis let out a cry, rolling back to avoid the flame, coming to her feet safely out of range. Her skin was charred black on her exposed arm and shoulder as her eyes welled up with tears from the searing pain.

Feirun rushed in swinging his cleavers and slammed her hard in the back with one and the other slicing a big gash along the side of her face. She let out a cry that turned into a fiery rage as she rolled out of the way, coming back up to her feet.

ARKANGEL

Feirun lunged into the air towards her, swinging down with both his swords with a savage grin, lusting for another kill. Vixis slid under and pulled him down mid jump, holding onto his arm and braid of long black hair as she repeatedly kneed and kicked at his body wherever she could connect. She lifted the huge elf up over her head and slammed him hard into the ground like he was nothing but a sack of grain. She tightened her grip, dragging his body through the rough dirt and slammed him face first into the side of the castle wall. Both the on looking elves and solders stood speechless as the slender woman beat the king down. Feirun squirmed and shook, feeling his body being struck against the hard, stone wall as he cried out from the pain. He reached back frantically and grabbed hold of Vixis's head and used his legs to kick off the wall pulling her down to the ground with him. He put her in a hold, so she was unable to move and ran face first back into the wall, crushing her beneath his hulking body.

The companions atop the wall watched in horror as the violent storm of blood transformed and began to take shape. The floating pool of blood thickened into a solid freakish form of nightmares. Bright red eyes emerged from the liquid with long sharp black teeth jutting out from its long snout.

The demon mimicked Martis's hysterical laugh as the blood hardened into a monstrously tall red scaled creature. Black horns curled around from the side of its head out towards its face. Long muscular arms, with black shards of bone, protruded from its elbows and forearms accompanied by patterns of long sharp quills along its body. On its back was a set of folded and tattered wings that draped on each side of its long whip like tail. It stretched its legs up and out, its knees bending backwards like a beast with long scaly shins adorned with matching black spines. It let out a horrific roar that shook the very ground like a terrifying wind that lashed across the land, uprooting trees and leveling small farm buildings nearby.

Its eyes narrowed in on Rhyker across the outer wall as it began to charge. Its shoulder curled up into a wall of black bone and quills, ramming into the acid drenched steel wall, bending the entire structure inward. The tower with the archers shattered from the impact, crashing down atop the mass of lizardmen and elves below. The demon grabbed onto the steel wall, its long nails tearing into it with ease, lifting and tearing the entire section of wall straight off the ground and hurled it back into the forest.

"I am Baladar," it roared, people and elves alike covering their ears in pain to dampen the sound. "Where is your savior?" Baladar shouted in a ground shattering rage.

All the men standing on top of the inner wall were at the same level of the demon's glare as they instantly collapsed to the ground from fear, trembling and grasping for one another in panic. At Baladar's feet, hordes of lizardmen rushed past, unhindered by the wreckage of the wall, climbing over one another to cross the courtyard, below the companions.

Finn and Gorman sunk to their knees, trembling in fear with overwhelming sense of despair filling their hearts and locking them stiffly in place.

Baladar's eyes smoldered as he walked up to Rhyker, who was now the only one left standing atop the wall. "Where is your savior?" he repeated.

The scratching sound of the lizardmen climbing up the wall rang loudly in Rhyker's ears. He had failed, failed to keep the land safe, failed to protect the savior, and failed the ones he loved. His heart felt heavy, reflecting on all the time he had to prepare and somehow was caught by surprise. He was surrounded by darkness and defeat with nothing left to do but rise to the occasion and die fighting. He clenched his fist as his tear-soaked eyes began to emit a soft golden glow, he would not fail again he reassured himself as he stood tall with pride, eying the monstrous demon in front of him.

A loud roar bellowed from behind Rhyker, startling him into turning around. The thunderous roar was soon followed by hundreds of loud growls and eager cries. The companions pulled from their trances, standing to look over the backside of the castle toward the ever-growing rumble of sounds.

With a triumphant call Grizby's gorillatites climbed up the back of the wall and leaped up into view. His beast was adorned in polished steel and chain armor, its long arms and massive fists pounding the stone below it. Grizby swung his axe into the air with a cry for battle as his army of savages ascended the wall behind him. They all chanted and cried out wildly, shaking their swords in the air.

The loud roar echoed across the battlefield as Treylis approached beside the castle, his mighty beast almost as tall as the wall. Saber launched from the massive creature's back with Arcus and Taja surveying the battle taking place all around them. Arcus lets loose a steady volley of arrows with frightening speed at the lizardmen breaching over the wall. Taja spun her arms in the air directing long twirling strands of sharp, thorny ivy out from the ground below that reached up and entangled the steady stream of lizardmen on the face of the wall. The long thorns tore and punctured right through their thick black scaly bodies and held them in place. Saber bounded over to Gorman and Finn, with a happy snarl on his face as he chewed on the bones of a fallen elf. Scarlett smiled up at Arcus and Taja, relieved to see backup.

Grizby shouted to his men. "Tear them down, crush their bones, and let's send these demons back to hell," he shouted as the wall quaked from the huge gorillatites storming across it.

The gorillatites snatched up lizardmen as they ran, tossing and slamming their bodies against the walls as they passed. The wave of savage riders leapt from the high walls and landed onto the piles of bodies below, crushing the frantic lizards under their feet. Their long, massive arms grabbed at anything that moved and crushed them into the ground, shattering their bodies with ease.

Grizby sat atop the wall next to the companions with his gorillatite standing up on its short hind legs to beat triumphantly on its chest. "Looks like we almost missed the party," he said, looking down to the slaughter below.

Baladar glared at the small beasts and laughed. "You will never stop me, you fools, just more flesh for the eating!" He bellowed as he swung his arms down with frightening speed to swat at one of the gorillatites, hurling it across the courtyard and leaving a big splatter of blood on the white stone wall. He let out a maniacal laugh and began stomping around attempting to squish the gorillatites and their riders under his massive weight.

Gorman's nerves were reassured to see the Akarian army come to their aid, he had misjudged Arcus's loyalty but despite their newfound allies he still feared an imminent defeat. Finn frantically hoisted up the last few crates of scatter cannon balls in an effort to wound the demon.

"Welcome back," Rhyker shouted to Arcus, his faith restored in the outcome of the siege. He had heard the call and knew what he must do.

"You're a fool to think I'd miss out on this," Arcus snickered, glancing to Gorman and Finn.

Scarlett pulled herself back to her feet, still shaken from the spell of despair Baladar had caused with his presence. Her strength returned as she tightened her grip on her glaive, her resolve hardening with the hope of their new ally. She charged towards the edge of the wall, chopping away at the lizards trapped within the vines.

Arcus turned Saber to notice a group of ember elves who had gotten into the inner part of the city and began firing a barrage of arrows down upon them. He saw Vixis brawling with King Feirun, taking turns getting the upper hand as one slammed the other around like a ragdoll. Several ember elves cut down human soldiers like paper targets, swinging and chopping their swords onto them with such force that their thick armor did little to protect them. He saw Vixis slam the weary king into the ground triumphantly before jabbing her foot down onto his back, making sure he stayed down.

Arcus's arrows rained down, puncturing deep into the elves' flesh as Vixis looked up to see Arcus's wide grin as he rode the length of the wall. A smile came to her battered face to see him return as several Gorillatite riders landed beside her. She stood tall, looking at the horde of lizards clawing at the weakened gate, its hinges beginning to tear away from the wall. She pursed her lips and blew the long wavy hair from her face and gripped her sword tightly.

"Alright, boys, let's get this party started, huh?" Vixis cried out, running towards the few men still standing by the opening gate.

Vixis charged the gate, sword held high in the air as she let out an enraged war cry. The gorillatites passed by, smashing right through what was left of the gate, sending shards of steel and wood shooting into the dense pack of lizardmen. The gorillatites's massive fists beat down onto the scaly creatures, crushing their bones, breaking limbs, and tossing them high into the air. Vixis swept in behind, striking a finishing blow where she could as they charged into the packed courtyard.

Treylis charged in from the far side of the castle where the gorillatites had scaled the walls to engage Baladar. His great bastilia, almost as tall as Baladar, rammed him with its long horns. The horns sank deep into Baladar's red scales as it reared up on its hind legs and clawed at his chest with its long talons.

Baladar roared in pain and anger, swatting at the pesky gorillatites that were leaping up onto him and beating against his scales. Baladar's tail whipped with its long barbs, impaling several of the smaller gorillatites and sending their riders soaring to their deaths. He grabbed at the bastilia's horns, pulling them from his chest and pushing it back. He held firmly onto its horns, taking control of its head and pushing it down as he struck his knee up into its jaws. His tail flung around for another strike and impaled the armor plated bastilia in its side multiple times as blood began to rain down onto the crushed lizardmen below.

Grizby shivered in fear after seeing the bastilia so easily outmatched. He watched as the barbed tail stabbed at the creature's side, whipping against its massive saddle where Treylis sat. Treylis pulled hard on the side of his reigns and ordered his mount to seek shelter within its protective shell as it curled into a ball. When the bastilia's limbs recoiled safely into the spiked shell it became unstable and Baladar didn't hesitate to flip it over, picking it up off the ground and throwing it hard into the castle wall. The beast's heavily armored body crashed through a large section of inner wall as the bastilia's body relaxed. Grizby watched in horror to see Treylis's beaten and battered body separate into pieces and scatter lifelessly all over the ground.

Baladar let out a deafening roar of victory and made his way into the courtyard, headed straight for the defenseless companions. The archers along the upper wall fired their last volleys of arrows at the demon and watched as they shattered ineffectively against his thick scales. The archers dropped their bows and fled, running any direction they could go to get off the battered wall and into the inner city. Baladar let out a hearty laugh as his feet sloshed through the corpses below.

"I am your new creator and each of you will take to your knees or be destroyed, I care not which," he commanded.

Rhyker stepped up to the edge of the wall, his eyes glowing a deep golden color. He could feel their presence, feel his people getting closer and knew he must finally cast aside his disguise. He unclipped his armor, the heavy steel breastplate and pauldrons clanging loudly against the stone.

Confused, Scarlett ran to his side. "We must fight to the end, don't give in," she pleaded to him, trying to quickly piece back together his armor.

He turned to peer into her strong beautiful eyes and gave her a warm smile and kiss, a kiss that lasted eternity in her mind. He wished he would have been able to tell her everything that he wanted years ago without breaking his vows. But how could she love him knowing what he truly was. Scarlett's heart sank when she looked into his golden eyes, feeling an overwhelming loss from his goodbye.

A symphony of loud screams filled the air, and the sun broke through the dark clouds. Baladar turned around startled as massive jets of fire, acid, lightning, and ice struck against his unprepared body. The concussive force slammed him down against the ground, crashing against the massive Sanctuary wall.

The companions looked to the breaking clouds to see several winged beasts swoop down, blasting repeatedly at the fallen demon. Kaiden and Nirayus were on the back of a mighty black and green dragon launching blast after blast of bright green acid down atop Baladar.

Kaiden stretched his wings and lifted Nirayus up into his arms before leaping off, soaring and gliding down to the wall alongside their companions.

"Betta late den neva, kid," Gorman said with a wide grin.

Nirayus jumped from Kaiden's grasp and looked around the battlefield, taking in the mass amount of damage and death that had transpired. Bodies strewn about and piled high with the giant gorillatites jumping around bashing and beating quillbacks, tossing them into the air as they went.

"I can't believe this," Nirayus said breathlessly with a heavy heart.

Finn came to her side, his tone defeated. "Many good, brave, honorable soldiers have lost their lives today," he said somberly.

Saber took a nervous step back, getting overwhelmed with the battle raging around them. Arcus shouted down. "The battles not won yet, get on with fighting, we can all chat later," he yelled releasing another arrow into the fray.

Rhyker approached Kaiden with a friendly nod. "You must be the one everyone has been talking about. I see you have awoken the Drakkens and come to save us from this false creator, it's an honor to meet you," he said pridefully.

Kaiden nodded, his helmet retracting as he surveyed the battlefield, his gaze falling onto Rhyker and noticing his presence felt somehow familiar. Even with most his memories back nothing came to the surface about this man, but he couldn't help but notice a resemblance of some kind. Kaiden felt an overwhelming sense of good emanating from him, and he reached out to shake his hand.

"Paladin, it's an honor to meet you as well," Kaiden said, beginning to feel a wave of power washing over them.

Rhyker bowed slightly, eyeing the demon who was recovering from its fight with the Bastilia and dragons. "I believe it's going to take the two of us to end this, hero, now let's get on with it."

Rhyker gave him another smile and looked over to Scarlett, the sound of dragons screeching and filling the air around them with fire and lightning.

"It is my time," Rhyker said to Scarlett, who was already unsettled and exhausted.

She reached for his shoulder to hold onto him, but he lunged from the wall, plummeting down towards the ground. Scarlett peered over the wall in shock as a burst of golden light exploded all around and massive golden wings unfolded as Rhyker's body transformed into a massive golden dragon. Scarlett gasped in shock as the golden winged Rhyker attacked the demon, pummeling him into the ground.

A terrible cry of rage shook the walls as Baladar fought back up to his feet despite the constant blasting of elemental rays tearing into his scales. His body wreathed in the blood that had created him as he lashed out. He grabbed a hold of an orange and red dragon as it swooped down low to rain down fire. Baladar turned and swung the dragon, shattering its neck and spine as he used its body like a weapon, swatting away at the gorillatites.

Kaiden saw Baladar kill the ancient dragon, his heart feeling the pain of loss deep within as the ancient beast's limp body repeatedly slammed down against his allies.

"We all need to focus everything we have on the demon," Kaiden shouted, pointing to it as it stepped on the body of the fallen dragon and with a wild roar, tore it's wings off.

Rhyker, bigger than most of the other dragons, flew around and latched onto Baladar's back, wrapping his long golden arms around to pin Baladar's arms in a hold. He snapped and bit at Baladar's neck, trying to critically injure him as his long spear like tail whipped around and punctured the side of his body. The other dragons saw their opening and dared to fly down low enough to deliver blast after blast of elemental energy against the demon, tearing off flecks of scales with each hit.

Rhyker flapped his wings and pulled on the massive demon, pulling him off balance and stumbling closer to the city wall. Nirayus's eyes radiated a bright blue cackle of light that flicked out into the air with pure energy as her irises turned a vibrant blue. She moved her arms in a circular motion and lifted them up as two massive orbs of electrical energy blasted from her hands. She directed the floating orbs towards the restrained demon and held them steady with long strands of lightning radiating from her outstretched hands. She began gesturing and slashing with her arms, striking towards Baladar with the balls of electricity mimicking her moves with sharp arcs of lightning lashing out into his exposed chest, piercing through his weakened scales and tearing at his flesh. Arc after arc of lighting blasted towards Baladar as he cried out in unfathomable pain.

Kaiden gestured orders for his team and jumped off the wall and into a glide, sailing towards Baladar. Baladar thrashed violently with each jolt, unable to move as Nirayus continued to strike at him with her whips of energy. Arcus, Gorman, and Taja made their way out onto the far-left side of the outer wall to the edge of the destroyed tower. Finn and Scarlett headed down the stairs to support the remaining troops below still fighting at the portcullis. Kaiden circled around Baladar, drawing his sword and flying past leaving slice after slice into the demon's body with his sword.

Vixis leaped up the stairs to report to Rhyker, her mind blown by all the dragons circling around, majestically powerful creatures flying around with ease, helping them with their battle. She ran along the wall in search for Rhyker or Scarlett and was surprised to come face to face with Nirayus.

Nirayus gasped, her power dissipating as she backed away from Vixis in fear. She frantically looked for Kaiden, hoping he would see that she needed help, but he was stuck in his own battle with the demon. She knew her arking abilities didn't work against the Arkhunter with that golden locket around her neck, her heart began to pound in her throat. Nirayus was fast and nimble, but Vixis could easily overpower her in a struggle, her eyes darted around for anyone to help.

"I'm not here to hurt you sweet thing," Vixis stated, reluctantly sheathing her sword to put the tiny elf at ease.

Nirayus took several steps back to put distance between them, drawing her draggers to defend herself.

Vixis put her hands up towards her in sign of submission, "I'm here to help, I promise, hun," she said with a smile.

Without the constant barrages of electricity, Baladar's strength returned, regaining control of his limbs and breaking free of Rhyker's hold. He grabbed at Rhyker's wing and swung him around to slam against the castle wall and then back around to tumble through the air where he crashed down into the forest. His evil gaze flicked instantly towards his biggest threat, the small moon elf who had almost cost him everything. He roared out in a fit of rage, ignoring all other attacks as he set his focus on her atop the wall. He charged in; claws held high to strike down atop the blue haired elf.

Vixis saw the attacks incoming and sprinted forward, catching the massive fist across her back as she pushed Nirayus out of the way, sending her tumbling several yards along the top of the wall. Vixis's bones shattered to pieces inside her, crushing her almost flat into the crumbling stone wall. Baladar raised his hand to see her limp body fall free, crumpling down the side of the thorn covered wall.

Nirayus's eyes went wide in shock of what she had just witnessed and barely noticed in time to see Baladar's fist coming back down towards her. As it swung down a sharp spear impaled through its wrist as a heavy rope pulled taut, causing his fist to miss its target. Nirayus looked to see Gorman pulling on the rope wrapped around one of the cranes and tied to Saber who clawed his way across the wall, pulling with all their strength. Baladar's eyes narrowed in rage as his gaze fell to Gorman.

Nirayus didn't hesitate, her hands igniting into a fiery blaze. The dragons continued their onslaught of deadly projectiles that tore into Baladar's back to distract him. Nirayus whipped out long strands of flame that lashed out, searing gouges into Baladar's face as he shouted protests to his captors, pulling on his impaled arm.

"I am God to you!" Baladar quaked in rage, swinging his arm to the side, attempting to break free.

ARKANGEL

Taja reached towards the ground and pulled, as swirling vines emerged to encircle around the demon's feet, growing and tightening up around his legs. She struggled to keep the bonds together as she commanded the long thorns to stab themselves deep into his flesh. She fell to the side exhausted, whimpering from the strain.

"I don't think I can hold this long, hunter," Taja gasped with a cry.

Arcus fired his arrows at Baladar with little effect, only shattering on impact against his torn body. He felt powerless to help her as he looked to see Kaiden swinging back around to strike another blow. He stood up in his saddle, shouting inspiration to his friend.

Kaiden looked to see Nirayus was out of immediate danger and watched as she whipped at the demon with long strands of liquid flame that tore into him with ease. He flew down, sword tight in his hand as he plunged it deep into Baladar's chest.

Baladar cried out, the walls of the castle shaking from the impact of his screams. Kaiden's sword erupted in a golden blast as he plunged it deep inside. Baladar swatted with his free hand but Kaiden being so small in comparison was able to dodge around his strikes. Baladar's body shuddered as beams of golden light began to break free from within his body as the sword's power surged on, destroying the very soul of the demon.

Kaiden pulled his sword free and flew up to look the defeated Baladar in the face. "You have been beaten betrayer," he shouted.

Baladar's face winced in pain as his eyes went wide in recognition. "It is you," he shouted. "I killed you Galigus," he said, continuing his struggle against his restraints.

"I am DeltaBlade, the First Arkangel," he shouted in a loud steady tone.

Kaiden raised his sword high, preparing for a final strike. "It will be you that dies this day demon," he whispered to himself, lunging forward as the blade erupted into golden flame.

Kaiden flew straight for his face, its long-horned head twisting and contorting, attempting to move out of the way. Kaiden's sword struck true, sinking into its forehead, golden light pulsating over and over, the light emanating out from his ears, nose, and mouth. With a loud popping sound, streams of blood poured from his face as his eyes burst open from the burning golden light.

Baladar flew into a berserker's rage, slashing blindly into the air, breaking free from the companion's restraints. Kaiden felt the solid strike against his back, his entire being trembling in pain as his body went numb. Baladar's fingers wrapped around him tightly, the strength of the demon's crushing grip stinging through his body.

"How could this be?" Kaiden's mind raced. "He should be dead; how does he still have so much strength?"

Kaiden's mind went dim from the pain, the chaos from the battle below drifted from his thoughts. He began to lose consciousness, his vision becoming blurry, his mind spinning in a confused haze with nothing but an intense pain. He watched himself narrowly miss the demon's teeth as he slid down its throat.

He couldn't see much, his helmet adjusted to the lack of light only blocked by the steam and mist from his armor reacting to the acid within its stomach. He could feel the searing burn and the panic from Galigus's soul in the armor crying out, not wanting to die. Kaiden's mind scrambled, struggling to move his arms and legs, pinned by countless soldiers and beasts the demon had swallowed. He thought of Nirayus, the pull on his heart to see her again. She had become the light in his darkness, and he refused to fail her now or everything they had done would be for nothing. He had failed to save everyone, failed to stop his brother, failed to stop the demon and the prophecy had all been wrong.

His mind slowed but even a dying ember can flicker one last time before it expires as an idea struck and his armor retracted, releasing his body into the vat of bile and acid, his hand went to his amulet.

The companions all watched in horror as their friend and leader was devoured. To them the battle was instantly lost as the humans began to crowd around and shout out victory at slaying all the lizardmen. By now the gorillatites were exhausted having massacred the last of the ember elves and lizardmen. Grizby lead the charge after the last few elves who had fled into forest were hunted down and killed.

Rhyker, severely injured with his arms barely attached to his human form of a body limped his way back to Scarlett and Finn. Feirun awoke to a raging headache as he pulled his head out from under a pile of stone and snuck his way out the back of the castle. His near fatal injuries slowing him down as he splattered a trail of blood behind him.

Arcus dismounted Saber and embraced Taja who weakly put her arm around him for support as he lifted her down to lay on the stone wall. Nirayus struggled to breathe as her life crashed down around her from the inside and landed a final blow against her heart.

Suddenly Baladar disappeared, completely vanished from sight without a trace. The companions shared a look of confusion. Nirayus almost collapsed flat against the blood-stained stone in tears, lifting her head as her ears raised slightly for any sound of answers.

The dragons were circling around in the sky, hunting down any of the enemies that tried to desert at the last minute and slayed any of the humans that had yet to turn. Several of the dragons swooped down and landed atop the wall near Nirayus who lay weeping on the ground. The dragons shifted, their bodies shrinking down and contouring into their Drakken forms. Takis walked up to the defeated Nirayus, his face full of sorrow for everyone's loss as he bent down to comfort her.

A big sturdy arm raised out, pointing to the sky as the Drakkens began to debate amongst themselves. Their eyes being far keener than a human, spotted a figure falling from the sky towards them. Nirayus looked to see it too and noticed that it was free falling at incredible speed. The figure burst into flames as it plummeted, a tiny glint of golden light slightly above it caught her eye.

She raised to her knees in hope as the figures plummeted towards the ground looking to impact farther up the road towards the forest. Everyone stared in awe as the demon flailed its arms, desperately grasping at air as if it could latch onto something with its torn wings, doing nothing to slow its rapid decent. An instant before impact Nirayus saw Kaiden's limp body trailing above as the familiar sonic boom erupted into a golden explosion, slamming the demon into the ground. Trees, rock, and dirt were thrown high into the air, raining down in the distance. Nirayus's heart lurched in her chest as the fear of her love's death echoed within her soul.

CHAPTER 18

"VICTORY IN DEFEAT"

Martis awoke, gasping for air. He struggled to draw in breath without choking on the thick stench of rot and death all around him. His pristine white robes were torn and stained with soot, dirt, and blood. He let out a cry of anger and confusion, feeling powerless like part of himself was missing, his creator was no longer there, no longer a part of him. The empty feeling was like a hollowed punch in the gut, he found it hard to breathe and even harder to want to live.

Feora kicked the trunk of a tree off herself; it had pinned her to the ground, shattering her body from the impact. Her head spun and she shuddered in pain. She had no idea how long they had been there for, trapped under the pile of displaced trees at the edge of Baladar's crater. She stood up, the rank smell in the air making her feel ill and her body ached from her healing ability working to repair her body. Her amulet continued to pulsate a bright golden glow atop her torn red leather armor, which was barely being held together but by a few strands of fabric.

"Martis," she called out, looking around in the debris.

All she remembered was carrying him from the battle, walking towards Solstice Gardens when the ground quaked and a rain of dirt and trees fell upon them. She could hear someone coughing not far away as she moved towards the sound.

"Martis, are you ok?" she cried, scrambling to get to him.

"Do I look ok?" he shouted. "My robe is dirty and torn," he spat, brushing repeatedly at the stains.

Feora made her way over the mound of twisted branches and tree trunks to where she could see him lying in the dirt. She shook her head in wonder how someone so intelligent could act like a baby when not in control and when things had not gone their way.

"But you're alive, I see," Feora mocked.

Martis's eyebrows furrowed. "Am I, Feora? Am I truly alive? My power is gone, and I have nothing, NOTHING!" he shouted, smashing his fists into the ground.

"We can rebuild it darling; we can start over," she tried to say as empathetically as she could with how pathetic he looked.

Martis glared at her, his normal charming and sophisticated gaze twisted into an evil, reckless glare that almost frightened her. She was afraid he had completely lost his mind. She knew he struggled with power but found it endearing at times, his quest to better himself and those around him, though in the end only turned to reckless villainy. She cared little for anyone but Martis and herself and the world he promised her sounded wonderful, but at what cost? She went to kneel beside him, trying to reassure him by putting her hands on his shoulders but was only met with agitation as he jerked away.

Martis stood up, his body also sore and the condition of his now tattered robes had taken quite the beating as well. He looked around, trying to remember what had happened before he lost consciousness.

"What happened? How could a god be defeated by the weakness of humans?" he growled in frustration.

Feora leaped up to a pile of tree limbs and onto the edge of the new crater, spotting a battalion of knights carrying a body wrapped up in a bloody canvas.

"The last thing I saw was a sky full of winged creatures, beasts like nothing I had seen before. A human flew alongside them wearing some sort of armor that was detailed after the creatures," she said, wondering what it would be like to be able to fly.

Martis went into an instant rage, punching the trunk of a fallen tree as it shattered into splinters. "Aghhhh!" he cried out at the top of his lungs. "It was Kaiden!"

"How is he even still alive? I stole all his power, broke his weak little body and no matter what I do he always returns," Martis roared desperately, pulling at his hair as he collapsed down to his knees in tears. "I just for once wanted to be better than him. I am superior to him in every way, he was so weak and sickly, yet mother gave him everything when they should have just let him die and let his sickness end his miserable life," he sobbed.

Feora had seen Martis throw fits before but never seen him break, his confident and commanding personality torn down at the thought of his brother. She went to comfort him again, her arms wrapping around his shoulder.

"We will rebuild everything, and we can make our own place where you are in charge, you can be king," she said hopefully. "You would be a great and powerful king, Martis," she added in reassurance.

Martis shook in anger, his bloodshot eyes glazed over and streaming with tears of hatred. It wasn't enough and now Kaiden had even more power and it tore him apart inside with jealousy. He ignored Feora and pulled away from her loving embrace. He looked at the fallen Baladar, his massive body sunken into the crater's soil, contorted and broken. His anger flared again at the sight of the god that had failed him and left him powerless.

With a burst of rage, he ran over and struck the demon's horn, causing it to break away and stab into its arm, broken behind his back. Martis stood there with his chest heaving as his mind began to calculate and scheme on what he should do next. What were his best chances of starting over? Should he seek his own place and start a new home with Feora? Should he return to Sanctuary and confront his brother once and for all, all or nothing?

"Help me," a muffled old voice pleaded.

Martis turned to ignore the cry and passed Feora as she walked over to see who was in need and if it was even worth her time to help them. On the back of the demon's skull near the base of its neck, long black and slender, blade like arms had bored out of the skull. The razor-sharp serrated limbs had torn their way through the demon's thick scaly skin.

Feora's eyebrows contorted in confusion at what she was seeing as the voice returned.

"Help me," it called out in the direction of the strange moving spikes.

She cautiously approached, her hand moving to her side to find an empty scabbard, resorting to tightly balling her fists. As she got closer, she could hear something moving, sloshing in what sounded like a deep pool of thick liquid. A strange cackling sound came from within the back of the skull and the serrated blades quickly folded back and subsided as if startled.

Right as she peered over in the wound, for a split second she saw some sort of parasitic creature, with long tentacles and disfigured appendages lurking within the skull. Red gas started to steam out of the wound with the sound of a loud hiss. Feora leaned back to avoid the foul stench of rot to take a deep breath before peering back over. Through the haze she could see an old man trapped waist deep in fluid, desperately reaching for a glowing orb that was just out of reach.

Feora turned to get Martis just as he approached from behind her, a frown of displeasure smeared across his filthy face.

"My son," the old man pleaded at the sight of Martis. "Oh, praise be to you my ever-faithful child, you did it, you have summoned me from that prison and brought me back to your world. Come and let us get me out of here," he said in urgency as he struggled to reach for the orb. "Come and help me get out so I can retrieve my orb," he said as his voice became more desperate with his continued struggle.

ARKANGEL

"What is that?" Martis asked in a level and curious tone as he analyzed the old man's desperation in reaching it. He was fearful of something; could it be he feared for his life without it? Feared that Martis could retrieve it first? A grin spread to Martis's lips as he jumped down into the bloody ooze and picked up the glowing orb. It was a bright deep purple but somehow appeared to be all colors at once depending on how you looked at it, inviting the eyes into a trance. The entire orb was wrapped in a braided steel like material and etched with patterns Martis didn't recognize. Light began to glow through the different symbols and illuminated the text which he was unable to read.

Baladar instantly became aggressive, urgently reaching and stretching towards the orb. "That is mine Martis, give it to me, I am the only one who can use it. Give it to me and we will rule over this world together," he commanded, seething at the mouth.

Martis's eyes lit up, he knew what this must be, it was the orb of creation, and it was his, he had finally been granted the ultimate power. His body convulsed with uncontrolled excitement as his mind began to race with schemes.

"What is that Martis?" Feora called down, still eying the old man wearily as he frantically clawed towards Martis.

Martis's eyes took a very serious and commanding stare as he gazed at Baladar stuck in his own demonic fluids. "I have what I need from you, old man, and from now on I will be the ultimate creator in Allterra," he said in a serious tone, his voice sending chills down Feora's spine.

"This is what I have been looking for, dear," Martis called up in a monotone voice, spreading a look of fear over Baladar's face.

Martis reached down and with one hand grasped onto the old man's neck. He stared into his eyes as they returned to a sickly red glow. "You have served me well, but I have no more use for you," he stated calmly as he slowly squeezed, crushing his windpipe and with a flick of his wrist shattering his neck.

Baladar slumped down, his head twisted, and neck torn open from his protruding spine as his body slowly sunk into the pool of blood.

Martis climbed out, holding his prize proudly in front of himself with pride.

"Now to figure out how this thing works," he said softly, staring into its bright colors as he tore off a strip of his robes to wrap the orb into.

"Where are we going to go?" Feora asked, picking up pace to keep up with Martis who was now so full of purpose and drive.

He paused briefly to look back at her. "I would say the forbidden crypt would be a nice place to start," he responded with a wide grin as he turned to lead her into the forest.

CHAPTER 19

"1ST PALADIN"

"Wake up, are you okay in there?" he heard a female voice repeat to him in a worried tone. Kaiden's eyes opened at the realization that it was Nirayus, she was ok and after a few seconds realized he too was alive. He willed his armor to retract and within seconds could feel Nirayus's cool skin against his. His eyes went wide, where were his clothes? Luckily, he had a blanket close by to pull over himself.

"Don't do that to me," Nirayus whined, hitting his shoulder with her fist.

Kaiden's cheeks turned red. "I don't know where my clothes went," he answered as he searched for the memories of what had happened and how he ended up in the bed.

"No not that, I never know if you are alive or dead in there. You have been laying there still for two days." she said sitting up to look at him.

She had laid next to him the entire time he was unconscious, not knowing if he would ever wake up or not. Even though the damage his suit had sustained repaired quickly she still worried how he was doing inside. Taja and Finn took turns spending time with her, keeping her company through her distress.

Kaiden gave her a smile, thinking her worried expression looked cute on her face. "I had no idea it was that long, last thing I remember was an intense burning sensation all over and then a long falling feeling until I blacked out. Did we stop Martis and the Demon?" he asked as his eyes went alert from the memory.

Nirayus laid back down and curled up to him, resting her head next to his and on his shoulder, her long, silky blue hair strung over his chest.

"Maybe," she huffed, betraying her feeling of relief that he was ok.

Kaiden put his arm around her, squeezed her tight and rolled over to face her. He was startled by Finn's eyes gazing at him unblinking with a huge smile spread across his face.

"Don't mind me," Finn said, gesturing to Kaiden to ignore he was there.

Kaiden's face went red with embarrassment. "Can someone just get me some clothes?"

"It must have been quite the party in the belly of the beast my friend," Arcus said as he walked into the medical chamber with Taja in tow.

Taja moved quickly to Nirayus and gave her a hug. "Good, he has awoken like I had told you he would," she said softly to her elven friend.

Arcus approached Kaiden's bed and gave him an approving nod. "You gotta stop trying to kill yourself, every time I turn around your throwing yourself into danger, yet it just keeps spitting you back out somehow," he said with a chuckle.

Finn walked around and pointed to his grey and blue scaled body. "Who really needs clothes anyways if you think about it? I will never understand your human traditions of always needing clothes, I don't wear them, and nobody thinks twice but every single one of you has to wear several items all at once which seems ineffective if you need to bathe, defecate, or mate," he stated reaching down to pinch Arcus's shoulder. "I could see its benefits in harsh weather environments but…"

ARKANGEL

Gorman walked into the room interrupting all conversation with his deep voice. "Here you be kid," he said gruffly, moving Finn to the side of the room with his arm and the other full of clothes.

Arcus raised his forearm up to Kaiden while he responded with the same in their old gesture of friendship. "Glad you're still with us my friend," he said before motioning to Taja for them to leave.

Taja looked at Kaiden and then to Nirayus with a wink, making a slight purring sound and putting an embarrassing smile on Nirayus's face. She gently got up and left with Arcus, her tail waving happily behind her.

Nirayus looked over to Kaiden and their eyes met, she could feel the heat of her embarrassed pink cheeks and turned with a wide grin. "Oh, get dressed already, Rhyker and Scarlett keep coming down to check on you, we should go see them."

Kaiden grabbed at the brown and tan colored leather outfit Gorman had placed on the bed. It was a lot nicer than the worn old rags he had been wearing, for as long as he could remember. He peered up to see Nirayus turning her back to stand up off the bed, teasing him with a sense of privacy. Kaiden threw his pants on before Nirayus turned to give him a warm smile. He pulled his shirt on and fastened his sword and cape around his shoulders before taking her hand to lead her out of the room. They walked out to the crowd of companions staring at them holding hands.

"Yous be spendin a lot of time in dat room, kid," Gorman commented, referring to the other time he had to recover weeks ago.

Arcus let out a hearty laugh. "I was thinking that was awfully quick," he said with a wide smirk.

Gorman realized the joke and shared in on the laugh, Nirayus blushing, only ending up joining in with a giggle of her own. Finn looked to everyone's faces, lost and hoping to figure out some sort of detail as to why it was so humorous. Kaiden looked at Nirayus's flush face and gave her a squeeze, taking the opportunity to laugh with all of his friends in their victory together, even if it was at his own expense.

Exiting the medical hallway and out into the central section of Sanctuary they were greeted by warm sunlight. Kaiden looked around to see engineers and laborers hustling around, repairing the damaged buildings and walls. Horses pulled carts filled with stone as masons chiseled and chipped bricks. As people saw them approach, everyone stopped to meet the companions face to face and share their gratitude. Men, women, and children all started raising their voices to praise as they shouted out their names. People lined up behind to bring them fruit, flowers, and other presents praising the heroes of Sanctuary. Many were overjoyed to see Kaiden awake after being injured in battle and wanted to meet the man who could fly.

They made their way through the growing crowds and onto the lift to the Paladin's keep, high into the air. Shouts of praise and song echoed through the walls as they lifted into the sky waving and shouting to the people. Finn broke out in an awkward dance trying to impress their onlookers and nearly tumbled off the raising dais.

Kaiden's heart sank as he looked out of the windows of Paladin's Hall across the castle. He could see over the main wall all the devastation that lay on the other side with piles of dead bodies waiting to be tossed on a pyre. It had felt like a victory but seeing all the people who had died for that victory weighed heavily on his heart. He wished he had been able to get to the city sooner; he may have been able to save more lives.

"It is done, the survivors are safe, and the plague is over." Nirayus's voice interrupted his thoughts. She squeezed his hand and gently rubbed his forearm with her other hand as she pulled him from the window.

"No, get your hand off me," came a strong female voice from behind the solid hallway doors. "Why didn't you tell me?" The voice continued.

"I wanted to, but it was against my vows I was bound by and couldn't break it," a man answered, his tone giving away to desperate frustration. "Please try and see it from my point of view, I am still the same person Scarlett."

The companions looked at one another, unsure if they should

proceed into the main hall from the lift room as two guards stood to either side looking just as uncomfortable. Arcus let out a fake cough and pushed one of the doors open with his foot to give the hesitant Gorman a peek inside. Finn coaxed him to go inside to find Scarlett and Rhyker on the other side.

"We's interuptin sumptin?" Gorman asked uncomfortably as he looked at them one at a time.

"No, our conversation is over," Scarlett stated firmly with a frown towards Rhyker as she walked over to address Kaiden and Nirayus.

"Good to see you up, Soldier," Scarlett said with a warm smile towards Kaiden. "I'm beginning to think nothing can keep you down for long," she said inquisitively. "I guess everyone is just full of surprises lately," she added as her eyes jabbed towards Rhyker.

Kaiden, feeling awkward for interfering in their argument tried to change the subject. "It looks like the repairs are coming along nicely," he said, hoping to shift the topic in the room.

Rhyker stepped up closer and reached his hand out to shake Kaiden's. "I too am glad you are awake; we have a lot to discuss you and I, along with matters of the city," he said looking to the other companions. "Lanthor is getting weaker despite our best attempts at healing, so we need to speak with him right away," he stated with an emotionless face, attempting to conceal his argument with Scarlett.

Rhyker gestured for them to follow as he walked them past the main foyer and around to the back of the structure where the high paladin's chamber was located. As they reached the door, a beautiful young woman with black hair walked through the doors.

"Rhyker, Scarlett," she addressed with a slight bow. "I just brought Lanthor and Trinity their meal, I am glad you are here, Trinity has been asking for you."

Rhyker nodded. "Thank you, Raven," he said as he led them inside.

The high paladin's chamber was long with the front room being almost completely glass overlooking the garden district and barracks below. The sun was high in the sky and the entire room was warm and well lit. Kaiden blinked, his mind racing and flooding with more of his old memories that he had pushed aside to focus on the battle.

They made their way into the bedchamber, a second bed squeezed in by the window so Trinity and Lanthor could spend time together. The moment Kaiden stepped foot through the door, his legs went weak and Nirayus had to quickly grab his arm and shoulder to keep him steady.

"What's wrong?" Nirayus asked softly.

Kaiden just stood there in shock, overburdened with his thoughts and memories. "Mama?" he managed with a blank stare on his face.

The weakened Trinity's face contorted in terror as she let out a wailing cry for help. She kicked and flailed, trying to backpedal further on the bed, falling off the back against the wall, her sobs and pleas getting louder and more distressing.

Tension filled the room as everyone looked to Kaiden in confusion as he furrowed his brows, trying to piece together what was happening.

"Leave me be, Martis, please, you monster, please stop, please no more," Trinity sobbed from under the bed. "Please leave me alone," she cried.

Kaiden took a slight step forward looking at Rhyker, who was the tensest, his blank stare looking at Kaiden as if seeing him for the first time. Kaiden knelt to the marble floor to look under the bed. "It's Kaiden, Mama, Martis is gone now," he said in a soft voice, his heart aching with sorrow to see her in such a frail condition, mixed with excitement for finding his mother.

Lanthor let out a deep, sickly cough that ravaged his body, leaving him breathless. "You are the boy everyone is talking about. Come here, son," he asked between gasps for air.

Kaiden's gaze reluctantly left his mother who he had not seen or remembered for so long, never knowing what had happened to his parents or if they were even alive.

ARKANGEL

"Come, Kaiden," Lanthor's weak voice repeated.

Nirayus helped to shuffle Kaiden towards Lanthor and stayed close, being sensitive to matters dealing with mothers and knowing how he must be feeling. Lanthor tried to sit up as best as he could, pushing his pillows behind him, barely able to bend around to lift the pillow. Taja gently went to his side to help him find comfort, bowing slightly with a friendly purr.

"I have been told you are to thank young man for saving the city and stopping the plague," Lanthor managed before erupting back into a wheezing cough, reaching for a blood-stained handkerchief to wipe his mouth.

"I don't have long in this world," Lanthor said in a raspy voice as he managed a bleak smile, looking to Trinity over the side of the bed. Her thin hair over her face, covering her bony appearance with her tear-filled eyes.

"Give her time, my boy; she had to endure more than any of us ever could," Lanthor pleaded as he pulled at the handkerchief again to clear his throat.

Scarlett's devastated expression could bring tears to the bravest of soldiers; she wasn't taking Lanthor's condition very well. To her he had been like a father and a teacher, and she felt very alone, more than ever before.

Kaiden glanced at his petrified mother, bringing severe sadness to his heart as he looked back uneasily to Lanthor. "I had…" He paused to look at Nirayus for support. "I had lost my memories for some time and was lucky enough to find these friends and companions," he said, gesturing to the group around him. "Each one of them has helped me with everything I have been through, each in their own way and have kept me going. I couldn't have done anything if it weren't for each of them sir. They deserve the credit," Kaiden admitted.

Lanthor's face brightened as his eyes lifted in pride. "You're turning out to be more like your grandfather than you realize, young man," he said glancing over to Trinity. "She is my daughter, and that I suppose would make you my grandson," he stated with a smile, breathing slowly to try to control his coughing.

Kaiden looked in shock, making the connection.

"We have never met, young Trinity here left with you before you were even born," he said in a tone of sadness. "I was a different man then and tried to marry her to this great man here."

Rhyker's heart sunk, he had very much loved Trinity and saw the arrangement a lot differently than she had.

"But she was headstrong and in love with another, I don't blame her, I wish I had had the intuition to be a better father and listened to what she wanted. I was too caught up in my duties to the city I suppose," Lanthor said, looking back to Trinity with a warm smile, hoping it would ease her fear. His weak arm was barely able to move out towards her before collapsing down onto the bed to rest, looking down in disappointment.

"Kaiden," Lanthor said, trailing off into a deep breath as he pulled the handkerchief back to his mouth. "Kaiden, I want you to take my place son, I am proud of the man you have become and would leave Sanctuary to you if you would have it?" he said solemnly, looking peacefully into his eyes.

Kaiden's head spun, he felt honored and overburdened with everything that had happened, his armor, his memories, his feelings for Nirayus, and on top of that was somehow King of Amid as well. His thoughts drifted to Takis who said he was from Drakken ancestry, not even human, and now was to be responsible for Sanctuary. It was becoming too much for him to handle as he froze in place.

He felt Nirayus's hands reach around his arm in support. "It's okay, follow your heart," she whispered. Her soft fingers slowly running up and down his arm for comfort. Kaiden turned to his companions in hope of finding answers but was somehow still at a loss for words.

Gorman was always the first to vouch for him and in some ways felt very protective, almost like a son he had never had. "I's will follow you Commander," he stated proudly, sinking down to one knee.

ARKANGEL

Kaiden was caught off guard and touched at the same time to have such a loyal veteran of war bend a knee to him.

Arcus followed only moments later, going to his knee. "As your best friend I know you best of all and believe in what you stand for, I have never met a more worthy person," he said as Taja nodded her agreement and went to their knees.

Finn made a gurgling sound, watching the odd display in front of him and put his hand on Gorman's shoulder as he went to his knee, shuffling to lift the other to mimic his brutish friend. "This reminds me of a story of one of the great kings of the sea. His name escapes my thoughts at this very moment, but he had rose up from nothing and saved the entire reef from…"

"Wrap it up, fish," Gorman interrupted gruffly with an elbow to his side.

Finn looked to everyone's blank stare, blinking. "He does die shortly after, but it was what he stood for that mattered. Kaiden I will follow and honor your leadership, my friend," he said, eying Gorman's elbow, not wanting to be prodded again.

Scarlett knelt unquestioning for he had proven himself more than enough for her and his commitment in saving their people. "I will serve you proudly," she stated as she lowered her head to him in service.

Rhyker knelt too, a beaming sense of pride echoing within his soul. Something about the man before him was special and the word of the prophecy had proven to be true with the legendary hero, he had waited for standing in front of him now. He had stood guard, sentry over man, protecting them, which he had almost failed to do but now found honor in his chance to serve him. For two thousand years, he had waited, nominated by the Drakken order to stay awake and watch for the savior. Now that the prophecy had been fulfilled and the horrible war it spoke of avoided, his duty was done and a new one was about to begin.

"I will serve you with honor," Rhyker said as his eyes emanated a soft golden color, sealing his life and fate to Kaiden.

Kaiden looked around to all his friends supporting him, with all the struggle they had gone through he had failed to realize what he had meant to them and the hope he had stood for. He looked down to Nirayus, a soft smile on his face as she sunk down with his hands in hers. She lightly kissed the back of his hand and looked up into his eyes.

"I too believe in you and will stand by your side no matter what life throws our way," she said genuinely, squeezing his fingers in-between hers.

Lanthor let out a gasping chuckle. "That is it then, the people have spoken," he managed before erupting into a coughing fit.

Everyone arose back to their feet and praised him; even Trinity got a slight smile on her face as Kaiden looked at her in the corner.

"I will make the announcement and prepare a celebration," Scarlett said, giving a bow and leaving the room.

She was in such a whirlwind of emotion, being pulled in so many directions her stomach ached, and she wanted to be by herself. Rhyker watched her go with a worried expression on his face as she left.

Amongst the cheering Trinity rose up timidly, momentarily lucid to what was happening before her. "Kaiden, is that really you? Are you really my little boy?" she asked, shaken as if in disbelief.

The room became silent as she offered her hand up to him. Kaiden moved a little closer, not wanting to scare her away. "It is me, Mama," he said with a tear rolling down his face. "I never thought I would see you again."

Trinity's hand recoiled, bringing it to cover her mouth as she sobbed in disbelief. "I knew that monster was lying to me. All he knew was lies, lies, hate and deceit. Hate for you, hate for me, and hate for your father," she said between the tears as she lost her strength and started to collapse.

Kaiden put his arm around her and steadied her, helping her get back into the bed. The frail woman looked nothing more than a skeleton covered in a thin sheet of skin, her will and determination to her boy again being the only thing to give her strength.

"Rest now, Mama," Kaiden said, laying her head back gently on the pillow.

Trinity lifted her hand up to his cheek. "You are my little boy, aren't you?" she asked, reassuring herself mentally after the eternity of loneliness and abuse. "You are all grown up now, Mama is proud of you," she managed, her eyes squinting from the tears as she drifted off to sleep.

Kaiden stroked her forehead with his thumb, supporting her head with his hand, thankful that he had been reunited with her. He could barely feel her inside his soul even though she was so near, but he could feel hers uplifted with joy. He had a gift with sensing people, looking into their soul to see whom they truly were deep within, but her soul had become so weak and faint he couldn't sense her. His father's though, somehow shined bright like a star. Kaiden had been told that Martis had their father Glover killed for some reason but somewhere inside his father was alive and he could feel it.

Rhyker put his hand on Kaiden's shoulder. "Congratulations, High Paladin, you are the first of the three and we will work together to restore our great city. There will be a celebration tonight in your name and for the people to accept you as their leader. As it turns out you are royalty as well, it must be a lot to take in I am sure and I am here to help you in any way I can," he said with a golden gleam in his eye. "By the way, your friend Grizby is staying with his men in the barracks along the inner wall just past the market. He was waiting for you to wake. Takis would also like to talk with you, as would I sometime before he heads back north to join the others. He is staying at the Silver Shilling, in the noble district."

The smile on Rhyker's face gave Kaiden a sense of relief, as if he was someone he could trust in getting the help he would undoubtedly need in running the city. He hoped he may also have the answers he wanted about the hall of dragons and how they could possibly be his ancestors. So much had happened so fast, he just needed time to sort through all his thoughts.

Rhyker turned to leave and paused momentarily by the door to look back. "I heard rumors Vixis had been found as well, buried under some of the stone that fell in the attack. They said somehow, she survived but was barely holding onto life. I believe she was being taken to the medical hall but with the overcrowding who knows where she ended up."

Nirayus looked up to Kaiden. "We should go see her," she said with a hint of guilt in her tone.

"Why? She tried to kill you last time she saw you," Kaiden questioned with a frown.

"Well, I can't imagine she is much of a threat now, but she saved me on top of the wall. When the demon's fist came down it was aimed at me, I may not have been able to dodge out of the way in time if it weren't for her pushing me away. She was so focused on me and I on her, neither one of us saw it coming," Nirayus explained. "I owe it to her to at least say thank you before she passes," she said looking into Kaiden's overburdened eyes.

Kaiden expressed a scowl of frustration, remembering her attack on them when they had first met and the bolt she had shot into his shoulder. "Alright, it's by the barracks so we can stop by on our way," he answered as Nirayus squeezed his arm when they turned to leave.

Lanthor let out a cough that refused to stop for several seconds. "Thank you, my boy, I will get some rest before the ceremony, I wouldn't miss it for the world," he stated, laying back in his bed, his body relaxing as his breathing slowed to a quiet wheezing sound.

Kaiden gave him a smile as Lanthor quickly drifted to sleep, as if finally having the weight of the world lifted from his shoulders. Outside the room, Gorman stopped them.

"I's go wit da men to help Scarlett ready da celebration," Gorman huffed in his gruff voice. "Later, kid," he added with a smirk.

Kaiden nodded and looked over to Finn who was vying for his attention.

"Where will you all be staying, I assume we may be here for some time," Finn asked, looking to Nirayus for objection, his mandibles bouncing with excitement for the question.

"Well I would say that since Lanthor is in the Paladin's suit for now it would be wise if we stayed at the Paladin's Citadel in the center of the noble district, plenty of room for all of us and if I remember right I heard it has been unused for quite some time and we should be able to make it work as a good base of operations," he explained with great enthusiasm as he looked for approval.

Kaiden chuckled at his friend's enthusiasm and motioned for Arcus and Taja to go with Finn. "That will work just fine. Why don't you go along too and make sure Saber is comfortable if there are any stables nearby and find a place inside that fits your needs?"

Arcus's eyes lit up at the thought of living in a fancy citadel, even though he wasn't quite sure what it was, but it sounded grand. It would be the first time he had ever lived in anything other than a shabby shack or canvas tent.

"You are too generous," Taja said appreciatively with a slight bow as a low purr rumbled in her throat.

Nirayus hugged onto Kaiden. "I've got you to myself finally, though with you being first paladin now your attention will be needed elsewhere I fear, what ever will I do?" she teased.

"Well, I haven't officially said yes, Nirayus; we can still leave here if you want? But we still have a few things to check in on first," Kaiden stated, still feeling overwhelmed by the responsibility.

Nirayus chuckled and shook her head. "No, no, your people need you and you belong here. I know you will be a wonderful leader to these people; you can bring them so much change for the better. I couldn't take you away, that would be selfish of me," she said with a playful smile and slipped away from his grasp.

"You know all I want is you, Nirayus," Kaiden responded, moving closer to her.

Nirayus quickly dashed ahead, far faster than he was and looked back with a smirk. "Oh yeah? And who says you can have me? Prove it and catch me," She teased as she took off running.

Kaiden laughed and sprinted off after her, barely able to keep up with her nimbleness. "Wait up," he called out in playful laughter. She continued to toy with him, staying just out of arms reach as she effortlessly dodged and weaved around to flirt with him. He took a deep breath and charged after her, down to one of the supporting towers.

"Oh, you can surely do better than this savior?" she mocked.

Kaiden slowed for a second, until her guard was let down, then with a burst of air giant wings unfolded from his back and propelled him forward. He latched onto her, scooping her tightly into his arms as they laughed together.

"You caught me," she said with a playful slap to his chest.

Kaiden's dragon like wings flapped downward, lifting them high into the air as they watched the beautiful gardens pass by below. Their moment of time together lasted forever in each other's arms but was over all too quickly as they glided down towards the medical hall. People called out in praise and awe, pointing up to the infamous Kaiden as they soared across the sky.

They landed gently in front of the entrance to the medical hall. The sight of all the wounded lying about tore them from their moment of happiness as their hearts broke for all the injured. They walked amongst all the wounded inside to find someone who could help them find Vixis.

Kaiden gestured to a nurse carrying blood-soaked blankets outside to be washed. "Have you seen a woman by the name of Vixis?" he asked. "She is about this tall, brown leather armor."

The nurse's eyes brightened at the description. "Yes of course, everyone knows her, she is back through there and should be able to leave soon," she said with a smile before continuing to her duties.

Kaiden and Nirayus looked at each other in confusion. "Ready to leave?" they said together as they followed down to where the girl had pointed.

"Aren't you such a sweet thing? Cute, too," they heard amongst the low ambiance of painful moaning. "Oh, come on hun, can't you find me a stronger drink?" The familiar voice said again around the corner.

They rounded to see Vixis standing in front of a mirror half dressed as the injured men in their beds did little to hide their stares. Vixis bent down to pull her dark brown leather pants on under her short, tattered medical rags. She fought with the skintight pants, giving the other patients quite the show as she slowly pulled them up.

Nirayus's eyes widened with embarrassment as she watched Vixis's shirt come flying off, her arms doing little to cover up her chest as she pulled her new leather corset and bronze breastplate on, flipping her long brown wavy hair out from under her armor.

Kaiden cleared his throat, trying to get her attention as she spun around and locked eyes with him. Vixis was incredibly beautiful he thought and even though his heart belonged to Nirayus, it was hard not to be transfixed by her and her unpredictability made his heart pound.

"Oh, it's you two, aww it's so sweet of you to have come to see me Kaiden," she said fluttering her eyelashes at him.

Nirayus perked up. "It was my idea, I wanted to thank you for saving my life on the wall," she said, gesturing at her lack of injuries. "That is incredible, your healing ability, I saw you crushed and covered in tons of stone," she added, thinking it may not have been quite the sacrifice she had thought but she was still grateful to be alive. Who knew what she would try to do with Kaiden if she wasn't around, she thought?

"Would you mind lacing this up for me?" Vixis asked with a sly smile to Kaiden and pushed up hard on her low-cut chest armor, spinning to him while holding her hair up with the other hand. Kaiden gulped uneasily and fumbled to tie the lace down her back to fit tightly around her thin waist.

Nirayus smacked his shoulder with a scowl as protests came from some of the injured men more than willing to help her. "Thanks, love I owe you one," she said with a wink. "So, what's next, fearless leader?" she asked, attaching her sword to her side as she collapsed her small crossbows to attach to her back. "I'm looking for a new master after finding out Martis was corrupt in his ways and I think I could please you in many ways," She played with a slight purse in her lips.

Nirayus interrupted, regretting her decision for the visit. "We are going to thank the Akarians for their aid in the siege and get ready for Kaiden's Paladin ceremony," she said with a smile while attempting to turn Kaiden around to leave.

"Oh congratulations, love," Vixis said earnestly. "You know I love a man in uniform, and you are a man of many," she flirted, bending down to lace up her tall boots.

Kaiden managed a smile and turned to leave with Nirayus. "We are glad you are alive and well, Vixis. We have a lot to do before tonight," he said as they rounded the corner to leave.

Moments later Vixis appeared behind them. "That's awfully sweet of you, Kaiden, I'll tag along until something else grabs my attention," she giggled, matching his speed to stay right beside him.

Nirayus let out a breath of frustration. "Humans," she said under her breath.

The trio made their way down to the nearby guard barracks by the main inner gate. They could hear the few horses left inside the stable complain about being tethered next to the rowdy gorillatites. Their deep snorting breaths were enough to cause alarm to the casual person walking past.

They entered the main chamber to see Grizby standing by a hearth, his elbow and forearm resting on the mantle as he stared into the flame.

"Long time no see," Kaiden stated as he walked in and clasped his arm to his chest.

Grizby was pulled from his thoughts and turned to greet his king and returned his gesture of loyalty. His mouth dropped in shock as his tired old eyes fall upon Vixis in disbelief. "Leslie?" he muttered wide eyed. "Leslie is that you?" his voice trembled.

Vixis looked to Kaiden in confusion and then back to the big, bearded man. "No," she said in hesitation. "I am Vixis but how do you know of that name?" She commanded, losing her usual flirtatious demeanor with a startled expression on her face.

Grizby left the mantle and pulled off the thick furs draped across his shoulders and tossed them aside. "My wife, you have her face. Do you know who she is? Is she alive?" He questioned humbly.

Vixis lost her cool, drawing her sword and in the blink of an eye had it pointed at Grizby's throat. He quickly raised his hands up in surrender, still caught off guard of the woman's likeness and her temper.

"You are no father of mine," she scowled. "How dare you make accusations like that in front of me and expect me not to end your life. What you claim is not possible," she shouted, her voice so sharp and cold it would strike fear in any soul.

"Vixis," Kaiden interjected. "This is a good man, drop your sword now," he demanded as he stepped up next to Grizby.

Vixis scowled at Kaiden, enraged. She wasn't used to people telling her what she could and could not do but she knew he may be the only person capable of stopping her if he wanted to. She let out a frustrated huff, blowing a long curly strand of hair from her face as she threw her sword back into its scabbard.

"My father was an evil man and I saw his body burst to a pile of ash when Paladin Malik saw to end his treason," she shouted. "He murdered my mother, betrayed our high paladin's orders on the battlefield and would have done worse to me if he hadn't been found and cut down. You are not my father or the traitorous husband to my mother," she seethed as her fists clenched so tightly, they began to tremble.

Grizby's head lowered in sorrow, his sturdy face showing his age and lifetime of grief. "Is that what they told you? he asked while fighting against his emotions, years of hurt not knowing what had ever happened to his family.

"That is not the truth of what happened," He muttered painfully.

"That is exactly what happened, I saw it," she yelled before exiting the room and slamming the heavy door behind her.

Nirayus scowled, she couldn't decide if she liked or loathed that woman. For someone so impervious to harm she was undeniably damaged on the inside and it intrigued her, wondering what led her to become the person she was.

Kaiden put a supporting hand on Grizby's shoulder. "There will be time to work that out later, thanks to you and your men Grizby, this castle wouldn't be standing is it weren't for you," he said in hopes of lifting his spirits.

"Nirayus this is Grizby, the general I told you about in Amid," Kaiden offered, realizing they hadn't met before and trying to move on with the conversation.

Nirayus gave him a warm smile, feeling sorry for his emotional distress stained in his saddened eyes. Grizby lowered his head in deep thought and looked back up to the door as if expecting Vixis to return and run into his arms.

"How are things in Amid?" Kaiden asked curiously, pulling his thoughts off Vixis.

Grizby drew in a long deep breath, his composure returning to his serious face. "Not well I am afraid, Sire. We have unrest that needs to be dealt with and I am afraid my absence will only make it worse. Amid needs you to return as soon as possible," he said as he leaned down to wrap his mantle back around his shoulders.

Grizby slapped one of the solder's feet that laid passed out on one of the barracks beds. "Get up and get the men ready for the return home," he commanded, the authority and grit coming back into his tone.

Kaiden looked down to Nirayus; he knew he needed to return. It was important to him and he wanted to further explore his memories and time with Arcus. The thrills of life without rules were intoxicating for the people but it needed to be put to an end and they needed someone to enforce it. He looked into her eyes, he wanted time to spend with her and explore what they had started. His memories had reminded him of all the awful things that happened to the women and their unwanted children.

ARKANGEL

Kaiden shook the memory from his mind. "You're right, Grizby, we will be behind you by a day or two and come establish some rules for the people to live by and a way to enforce them. What is this unrest you speak of?"

Grizby nodded his approval. "Thank you, sire. There is a group forming against the legitimacy of your rule. They call themselves The Desert Sun and they are plotting to rise up against you. I think it wise we put an end to it before it gains too much momentum, but I am sure it is nothing you can't handle," he stated.

Kaiden shook his head; if it wasn't one thing there was always another to deal with. "I agree, we need to ease into the transition for these people. Living a life of crime without consequence is hard to give up on top of following a new ruler. For now, we will establish a new enforcement team to help uphold the new laws and when I get down there, I will deal with the opposition," Kaiden replied with a frustrated sigh.

Grizby nodded his approval. "Yes, sire, I will set up a team right away," he said as a smile spread across his face. "I know just the group," he said as he turned to retrieve his weapons.

Kaiden put his arm around Nirayus as they moved towards the door. "Take care, Grizby, we are on the edge of change, and it will be for the better," he promised before shutting the door.

Grizby stood tall, his back towards the closed door, looking down to the fireplace as a tear rolled down his cheek.

"I can't believe how rude Vixis was to him; he looked to be an honorable man considering all the horrible things you have said about that place," Nirayus said as they left the barracks, on their way to Sanctuary Hall.

Nirayus was finally at ease in the human city despite being the only elf she had seen. She had friends here and needed to get used to spending time here if she wanted to be with Kaiden. She began to think of the celebration and remembered she was wearing the same hunting outfit from weeks before. She stopped and lifted to the tips of her toes to sneak a quick kiss from Kaiden.

He gave her a surprised smile. "What was that for?" he asked, pulling his thoughts from Amid.

She returned his warm smile. "I need to get ready for your big night, you can't expect a girl to wear this old thing, can you?" Nirayus said with a sly smile as she pulled on a tear in the fabric.

Kaiden pulled her close and gave her another kiss. "Alright, I should go speak to Rhyker and Takis and will catch up to you at the celebration," he said, reluctant to let her hand go.

She looked at him from the corner of her eye as she parted ways with a grin. "See you tonight."

Kaiden looked back to the beautiful moon elf as she walked away; she had a way of making his heartbeat faster and his head spin. He turned and headed towards the inn where Rhyker said he would find Takis. He passed the front gate and could hear a commotion as the guards lined up at the sight of him, chattering excitedly amongst themselves.

"Kaiden," he heard a deep, gruff voice call out as he looked to see the Drakken walk out of the door to the inn, barely fitting his wide body and wings through the doorway.

His dark green and black skin glinted off the lowering sun as paladin Rhyker came up behind him. Takis walked to meet up with him, a fresh scar across his shoulder from the battle with Baladar. Kaiden noticed the scar and remembered all the Drakken in their dragon forms who had given their lives for the humans. Such ancient souls had been stolen from this world by Martis and Baladar. Even though only a few had fallen, it still somehow seemed like such a huge loss compared to their few and finite numbers.

"I'm glad you have come, Kaiden, we have an urgent matter to discuss," Takis implored, looking to Rhyker with a grim expression on his face.

Kaiden watched as people walked by with both looks of intrigue and fear on their faces as they saw the Drakken born up close. His interest in the townspeople vanished as his heartbeat nervously from the dire expressions they wore.

Rhyker stepped closer. "I am sorry I have not been honest with everyone and wanted to be upfront with you," he admitted, looking around at the humans walking by. "I am what is called the Sentry. When the other Drakken went into hibernation, I was elected to stay awake and watch for the signs and warnings of the prophecy. I got distracted in my role as a human and failed you," he said in regret. "I was supposed to protect and prepare you and I failed to recognize the signs and am sorry for that, Sir," Rhyker said, lowering himself down to a knee.

Kaiden looked to Takis and then down to Rhyker. He had only just learned about everything that had been happening in Sanctuary and didn't feel betrayed or let down by this man by any means. He placed his hand on Rhyker's massive, armored pauldron. "My mother's choice to leave the city with my brother and I was out of your control, Rhyker and I do not blame you for anything that happened here," Kaiden stated in hope of putting his mind at ease with anything he was feeling guilty for.

Rhyker stood at the relief of not being to blame but he still didn't believe it fully himself. His look of wounded pride subsided as he looked to his friend Takis standing next to him, someone he hadn't seen in so long and was excited to catch up on everything that he had witnessed over the long years. He noticed Takis had a different display of emotion on his face and from the looks of him, it seemed important.

"Kaiden, as I had promised, we have aided your people and helped stop Baladar in his destruction of Sanctuary, but I fear there is much more that needs to be done and we need to leave right away," Takis stated outright without wasting time on celebrating their victory.

Kaiden's head cocked in confusion, then eyed Rhyker to see the same look of confusion spreading on his face.

"What more is there to do other than rebuild the city? We defeated the threat and with it the plague," Kaiden responded defensively.

Takis's wings tightened up behind his back as his posture straightened, as if uneasy. "We only defeated one threat, but I fear your brother is still out there and could somehow come into possession of an orb. It is all but certain his creator was carrying one, the very one that allowed him to enter this plane. If he has found the orb and learned to use its power, we are in a lot greater danger than we ever were with Baladar," Takis explained uneasily as if treading around a truth and not sharing the whole story.

Kaiden gazed off towards the castle gate, watching his people enter in excitement to see his ceremony, their joy and happiness of victory. He had wanted it to be over so badly he had not stopped to think about if Martis was still alive. His anger for the carnage his brother had caused enraged him and his hands clenched firmly into fists.

"We need to find and stop him before he can hurt anyone else and we need to find the orb," he commanded, instinctively moving to action towards the gate.

Takis swiftly moved to his side as one of his wings outstretched to block his path. "We will survive the night young hero, go and enjoy your party, give the people a night to celebrate and rejoice and we will leave north first thing in the morning."

Kaiden looked up into the sky, where had the day gone, he thought to himself. His mind drifted to the people's Sentry, Rhyker. "Was this part of the prophecy as well?" he asked in a tone of defeat.

Rhyker and Takis shared a look to each other as Rhyker stepped closer to respond. "Think of the prophecy as an ever-growing tree. As we travel up the path, it splits causing unforeseen forks and branches into pathways only forged from our actions and decisions. The prophecy is complicated and speaks of many alternate realities that may or may not come to pass but it is important we start your training right away and follow the correct path," he explained carefully as to not overwhelm him.

Kaiden only shook his head slowly, continuing to feel pressured and overwhelmed by his growing number of responsibilities. His mind went to his friends who he would have to call on again to help him to respond to the growing threats, but he decided to take Takis's advice and give them the night. He would let them share in their victory and prepare them in the morning.

"Ok, Takis, I understand the importance of retrieving the orb and we will leave with you in the morning," Kaiden promised, looking to the entrance of the Silver Shilling Inn and the reactions on the patron's faces as they walked into the room filled with Drakkens for the first time, giving him a laugh.

Takis looked back to see his friends awkwardly sitting inside at human tables and let out a hearty grunt of laughter. "Now to enjoy some human drink," he said joyfully as he walked back inside.

"Kaiden," came a familiar female voice.

He turned to see Scarlett walking towards them, the normally very serious and soldierly woman was out of her paladin armor and dawning a beautiful dark red dress. Kaiden was taken aback by how beautiful she was and never would be able to guess the woman in front of him was the deadly soldier he had witnessed on the battlefield.

She gave him a warm smile as her gaze dropped momentarily as if embarrassed to be outside of her armor. "It is time, Sir, everyone is ready for the ceremony, along with all the people flooding in to see you take your Oath," she stated, trying to ignore Rhyker's gaze.

Scarlett wrapped her arm around his to escort him towards the grand hall. Her eyes darted over to take notice of Rhyker staring at her in her form fitting dress and smirked. "Now let me escort you there, Sir," she said as she pulled him along in excitement.

Kaiden gave her a forced chuckle but was honored to walk alongside the tall, beautiful woman. He considered himself lucky to have such trustworthy Paladins at his disposal and looked forward to getting to know them better outside of battle. He had seen them act so strong and selflessly and he was finding it difficult on how best to warn them of the possibility of more danger.

They made their way from the inner gate by the inn and through one of the noble markets. People were waving and praising them as they passed which they kindly returned. Rhyker followed closely behind, still fully decked out in his armor, as it was almost an ornamental piece itself, representing their culture and city's stature.

"Is it really you?" came a child's voice in awe, running up to meet Kaiden.

"Come back right now, Maius," shouted the young man's mother.

The boy stood in admiration of the city's hero, the man who could fly and soon to be first paladin. It was like a dream come true for the boy. "I want to be just like you when I grow up." he said cheerfully. "Mother says that I am the new man of the house since father got the plague and I told her I was going to be just like you," he said with a hint of sorrow.

Kaiden knelt to meet the boy's eyes. "It's a big job to be the man of the house, think you're up to it?" he asked upliftingly.

Maius looked to the ground and kicked at a small rock stuck in the soil. "Yeah, I'm brave but I wish Father could come back," he said as his voice trailed off.

Maius's mother caught up. "I am sorry, Sir, if he was a bother," she said with a nervous bow while scooping her son up to leave.

Kaiden smiled at her and Maius and shook his head. "No bother at all, you have a brave little man there, worthy of being one of my paladins one day," he chuckled.

Maius's eyes lit up. "Really? Mama did you hear that?" he asked excitedly while kicking his feet and chopping with his hands at invisible enemies as he was carried away.

"You are playing your role well," Scarlett stated with a grin of approval.

Kaiden was silent for several seconds before giving his response. "A lot of lives have been needlessly lost and it's important we spread hope if the city is to pull itself back together," he responded.

Rhyker piped up from behind. "Spoken like a true paladin, one would say you were born for this," he added.

ARKANGEL

They arrived at the entrance to the grand hall and Kaiden suddenly realized he hadn't had time to prepare and was only wearing a long sleeved deep blue tunic and brown pants. He wished he would have been able to change as he noticed everyone else was in fine clothes and dresses. As he entered the tall building with vaulted ceilings, he could hear joyous music being played while the people laughed and danced.

The walls were lined with mosaic windows and decorative banners with great statues of Paladins and heroes throughout history. The city's insignia of the Paladin's high shoulder pauldrons with a sword going down through the middle was embroidered in the center of the deep blue banner trimmed with gold and black borders.

Kaiden stood proud to see all the people singing and dancing to celebrate, putting the plague and attack in the past. Table after table sat on the sides with decorative plates holding a wide assortment of fresh fruit, meats, and pastries. The smell of cake made his stomach growl; he hadn't stopped to eat and would be sure to take advantage of all the finely prepared food.

People bowed and thanked him as he walked around the lower story of the great hall. To either side of the long open room were stairs that went to more rooms on one end and then up to a grand balcony at the other end with thrones that sat high above the open room, accompanied by seats for guests to sit. He was happy to see everyone mingling and dancing and gave a wide grin to see the finely dressed Arcus and the exotic Taja in a dark green dress approach him.

"Nice party," Arcus stated, looking to all the food along the wall while holding as much as his fingers could carry with him.

"You know, I had no idea there were this many people in the city," Kaiden said with a chuckle, watching all the guests pass by.

Arcus slapped the side of Kaiden's shoulder with his fist playfully. "We did it, Kaiden, we have finally made names for ourselves. Just wait until you see the Paladin's citadel, it's a little big but I'm sure we will manage," he joked, trying to talk through all the food in his mouth.

Kaiden laughed, remembering the old shed they had lived in before for so many years in Amid. "Who says you made a name for yourself?" Kaiden asked with a serious smirk.

Arcus was startled still, with a confused look on his face as Kaiden burst into laughter. "I am messing with you, Arcus, none of this would be here right now if it weren't for you, brother. We couldn't have won without you. You turned the tide in battle and took charge long enough for my return, I can't thank you enough," Kaiden added proudly.

Arcus's grin returned as he lifted his forearm and elbow up to meet Kaiden's in their usual greeting, trying to hide how touched he was from his best friend's compliment. Arcus continued to chew on his food and started to dance on his feet playfully with Taja who tried her best to join in with him.

Finn walked up, still not wearing any clothes but a big white ruffled jabot that went down his chest. Arcus and Kaiden burst into laughter. "Finn where is the rest of the suit that goes with?" Kaiden asked through his laughter as Finn looked around to see he was indeed missing the rest of the outfit.

Finn joined in on the laugh at his own expense and twirled around in a silly saunter, dancing around with everyone as he disappeared into the crowd.

Gorman snuck in, hunched over as if it helped him not tower over the crowd. "Good, he be gone," he said in an attempt to whisper. "Dat crazy fish be tryin to dance wit me," he added with a worried expression on his face.

Arcus immediately burst into laughter at the thought of what that would have looked like with the two of them parading around with all the fancy nobles. Kaiden looked the ogre up and down, shocked how noble he looked in fancy clothes instead of being strapped head to toe with weapons and armor.

"You look good, my friend," Kaiden complimented.

"You toos, kid," Gorman responded, his attention still focused on where the seven-foot fish was lurking.

Kaiden hadn't had the opportunity to listen to much music in his life or dance but found the beat of it uplifting and made him wish he could find Nirayus. His search soon came to an end as the party seemed to slow to a silent halt. The music paused and everyone in the room turned towards the stairs. Jaws dropped and whispers could be heard all over in the silent room as Nirayus began to walk down the balcony stairs. She searched the room as her eyes quickly settled on Kaiden's gaze. She wore a golden dress that hugged her petite curves that flowed down like a cascade of sparkling gold waterfalls. She grasped the dress tightly in one hand and almost floated down the stairs as her hips swayed to the music that began to play again.

Kaiden suddenly remembered to breathe as reality caught back up with him and he stood in awe. She approached him and intertwined her fingers into his as they looked at each other and the world around them drowned out of existence.

"Are you going to say anything?" Nirayus asked with a sly smirk on her face as she fluttered her long-painted lashes.

Her normally straight, silky blue hair bounced in curls against her shoulders as she swayed left and right. Kaiden put his arm gently around her waist and pulled her tightly against him as they swayed back and forth with the music.

"I am speechless; there are no words to describe how beautiful you look," he stuttered, looking down into her vibrant, icy blue eyes.

She let out a giggle and punched his shoulder playfully. "You better think of something before I go dance with your open-mouthed friend Arcus over there," she teased.

He pushed her away, holding tightly to her hand, spinning her around weightlessly on the dancefloor, and pulled her back to him with a deep bow, embracing her back tenderly and staring into her eyes. He had never danced before but just let his heart guide him as he fell for the beauty in front of him.

"You are breathtaking," he whispered.

Her long, thin ears lowered in embarrassment as her white cheeks tinted pink. She could feel his heart pounding in his chest as they pressed firmly against each other, and they spent an eternity in each other's eyes. She had never known love before or flattery and usually resorted to being playful.

"I see you dressed for the occasion, I feel a bit under dressed," she said with a mocking chuckle.

Kaiden let out an embarrassed laugh, being reminded of his simple clothes that must look like a poor beggar compared to her elegant beauty.

"I was delayed by Takis," he said slowly in thought, feeling the weight of reality sitting heavily on his shoulders.

She pushed him back to look at him in seriousness. "Is everything ok?" she asked.

Kaiden got lost in her smile again and felt his heart weaken in wanting for her to be close again, she had become a pillar of strength for him and needed for her to be close, needed her strength to keep him focused.

He dismissed her worried expression with a shake of his head. "Everything will be fine," he said hastily to reassure her. "Let us enjoy this special night together without worry," he added with a big smile as he swooped her off her feet and high into the air.

She let out a giggle and gasped, clutching onto his arms tightly as he spun her high into the air.

Clapping erupted from all around them as the music slowed to a stop and they noticed everyone had moved to the sides, so they could dance together. They looked up to see Rhyker and Scarlett standing beside the upper thrones along with Lanthor, sitting nearby with Trinity. Everyone was staring up at them in silence as Rhyker spoke to the crowd.

"I am pleased to say that despite our hardships, we have pulled through. Together as a people our strength bonded together was enough to put an end to the attack and we have prevailed," he shouted holding up a glass in cheers to everyone.

The crowd began to clap and gave praise up to Rhyker, expressing their gratitude.

"We suffered a great loss, and many great men and women lost their lives to keep us safe and our beloved First Paladin Lanthor suffered greatly at the hands of our enemies," Rhyker continued as the people sighed and expressed their sorrow.

"But with tragedy comes triumph and a new hero has arisen, one that has led us to victory and one who will lead us into the future with peace and prosperity," he shouted as the crowd erupted again into praise as the people moved to usher Kaiden and Nirayus to the stairs.

Rhyker gestured for them to proceed as he began to clap along with Scarlett. The crowd started to chant his name in praise of saving them from Martis and the demons. As they reached the top of the stairs, Trinity stood up and wrapped her arms around her son with tears of joy streaming freely down her face.

"I am so proud of you, my little boy," she said lovingly as he bent down to help her sit comfortably back in her chair.

Kaiden took to his knee in front of Lanthor who beamed with pride at his grandson. Lanthor struggled to pull his sword from his side and set the point into the stone floor at his feet, moving closer to embrace him. After several seconds of Lanthor's weak voice whispering into his ear, Kaiden came to his feet with a white mantle of fur that Lanthor had placed around his broad shoulders. Kaiden took his family's sword and raised it up to the crowd. He pulled Nirayus close to his side and looked upon his people who called out praise of congratulations.

Like a rumbling thunderstorm the clapping echoed throughout the stone walls and came to a sudden halt. Panicked voices started to spread as the tall doors burst open to the great hall and two guards dragged a bloody body into the center of the room. They shouted out for aid and called up to the paladins in urgency.

Scarlett, Rhyker, Kaiden, and Nirayus all rushed down the stairs to meet with the concerned Gorman, Arcus and Taja who circled around the badly wounded man. He lay upon the ground coughing and grabbing at his chest, trying to catch his breath as blood splattered from his mouth.

"A Fleet... A Fleet," he tried to call out in warning.

Taja bent down as a green light swirled forth from her palms and blanketed the man in a soft glow to ease his suffering. Kaiden knelt beside him to try and make out what the man was trying to say.

"A war fleet!" he cried out as a stream of tears started to wash away his blood-soaked face. He coughed relentlessly; his eyes stared unblinking into Kaiden's as they comforted his head. The sheer look of terror on everyone's faces only escalated, seeing the man's thick metal armor mangled and torn. Jagged shards of steel bent and jabbed both in and away from his bleeding body.

Kaiden looked back at the streak of blood leading from the entrance of the door from where they dragged him in. "It's okay, take your time," he said, trying to comfort the man.

The wounded man gasped out for breath, choking on the blood streaming from all his wounds as his body started to convulse uncontrollably. He grasped onto Kaiden's tunic, pulling him close. "The monsters from across the sea will kill us all," he managed with his dying breath before slipping away into the cold veil of darkness.

.

ABOUT THE AUTHOR

Brandon has always made creativity the basis of who he is. Artist turned writer; his stories are a culmination of ideas dating all the way back from childhood. He was inspired to put those ideas on the page with the aid of his daughter who helped shape the characters and world. He has always been a fan of epic fantasy and games such as Dungeon & Dragons role playing, also influencing his love of the genre. To find out more or see where the adventure tales us from here, please visit DeltaBladeBooks.com.

Made in the USA
Middletown, DE
16 October 2024